CW01080665

Black Friday 13 is the fifth book from the talented pen of award-winning Irish writer John Mulligan. His previous works include *Dancing on the Waves*, *Following in the Footsteps of the Four Famous Flannerys*, *No Place in the Sun*, and *The Book* (written under the pen-name A. Watcher). John won the prestigious international 'Fish Award' for short fiction in 2012, and has been a runner-up in the same competition on a number of occasions. He is a two-time winner of the Roscommon Writing Award, and his expertise is often sought as a judge in literary competitions. In addition to his books, his short stories and features have been published in numerous publications in Ireland and the UK. He contributes a popular and sometimes controversial weekly column to the Roscommon Herald newspaper in Ireland.

Black Friday 13

A novel by
JOHN MULLIGAN

Monument Media
Dublin, Ireland

Black Friday 13
Copyright © 2022 John Mulligan.

ISBN: 978-1-9162531-6-2 (Paperback)
ISBN: 978-1-9162531-7-9 (eBook)
2 4 6 8 10 9 7 5 3 1

Cover design by David Diebold
Typesetting by Monument Media Ltd.

Printed by Mullen Print, Dublin, Republic of Ireland.

This book has been typeset in Adobe Garamond, a digital interpretation of the roman types of Claude Garamond (1480-1561) and the italic faces of Robert Granjon (1513-1589). Since its release in 1989, Adobe Garamond has become a typographic staple throughout the world.

First printing edition 2022.

Monument Media (Publishers) Ltd
1 Ardgillan View,
Skerries, Co Dublin
K34 W593

www.monumentmediapress.com

www.johnmulligan.net
www.johnmulligan.eu

For Una

'I have seen the future and it doesn't work'
— Robert Fulford

Author's Note

The events and characters portrayed in this book are entirely fictitious and bear no resemblance to any person, living or dead.

Should anybody find that any similar event or events did happen elsewhere, that is simply coincidence and nothing should be inferred from it.

Chapter One

Miriam O'Hagan high-heeled her way rapidly down the corridor, carrying her laptop and a bundle of files under one arm and a steaming mug of scented coffee in her free hand. She pushed the conference room door open with her shoulder, reversing into the room and swivelling around to unload her various papers and her drink on to the end of the long, oval table. Ignoring the various members of her staff who sat expectantly in the other chairs, she rummaged through a couple of files and extracted some sheets of paper. Opening her laptop, she reached for the biscuits that filled a bowl in front of her place, munching a thick chocolate confection with obvious satisfaction. Sipping her coffee, she sat back and surveyed the room. Some of the younger members of the team appeared to shrink into their chairs as she ran her gaze around the table.

'Right,' she said, 'anyone hazard a guess as to why I called this meeting?'

There was silence, with some shaking of heads.

'I wouldn't have guessed myself, to be fair,' she said. 'In short, it's back. Another variant of our friend the Corona Virus, but a very different animal altogether. This time, it looks like it will really wreak havoc with normal life,

1

not to mention what it will do to people who catch it. Yes, Billy?'

Billy Robinson lowered his raised finger and straightened himself in his chair.

'When did this news break?'

'It hasn't, yet, but it will be out there by tomorrow. I got it from our usual source in the US government lab in Palo Alto.'

'A new strain of Covid, or a new virus?'

'Not a new strain, as far as they can judge, but a very substantial variant.'

Karen Doyle raised a hand, hesitantly.

'Yes, Karen?'

'So, do any of the existing vaccine types match it?'

Miriam sat back and smiled broadly.

'No, it will take a completely new vaccine, so we know what that means.'

Billy Robinson's face broke into a smile.

'Plenty of government money for research, I guess. Will we be getting a slice of it? The Covid-19 debacle paid off my mortgage, we could do with another one like that.'

Miriam rubbed her hands together and smiled broadly.

'Yes, boys and girls, we're in the money, I would say. If we play this right, there can be big bonuses for everybody, and a slice of the action if we beat the big boys to the solution. I could be looking at six millionaires around this table if you guys work your butts off and find a vaccine that gets past the American FDA.'

'Even if we find part of the solution, like in 2020.' Billy Robinson sat forward eagerly. 'We didn't even get the formula, but our prep work helped some of the big boys to design it, and we all made a killing.'

Miriam stood up and began to walk around the room.

'We need to remember one thing about that, Team. Okay, we made a fair bit of money last time around, but we were so close to cracking it. Sooo close. We could have actually done it, we just didn't have the imagination to make that final leap.'

Karen Doyle stood up excitedly, then seemed to remember herself and sat down again.

'I wasn't working at Boyle Labs then, I was just starting college, but I remember the excitement around here when we heard that a little lab in a small town in the west of Ireland was part of the Covid-19 solution. It was the talk of the place for weeks.'

Billy Robinson nodded in her direction.

'We might have been small, but we were industry leaders in our own way. And as Miriam said, we almost hit the jackpot. Still, we did okay. It set me up for life anyway.'

Miriam stood behind him and put her hands on the back of his chair, swivelling him slightly from side to side.

'No, Billy. You see, you're happy enough if you have the bills paid and you have time to go fishing on Lough Key every evening, or go out for a nice dinner once a week in Clarke's, but some of us want more than that. We didn't do okay, we did well, but we should have been first past the post in twenty-twenty. We just didn't have enough belief in ourselves, we didn't think that a little town in the west of Ireland could be the epicentre of world-class scientific research. We knew we were good, but we didn't have that faith in how good we were.'

She resumed her walking around the room.

'Yes, we made some money, and the reputation we gained has kept us all in jobs and ensured we were able to attract the kind of funding that has allowed us to build to the size we are today, but we weren't risk-takers. We couldn't jump across the chasm, because we were afraid we mightn't make it, afraid of the fall.

Well, this time, we won't hold back. If we see a result on the far side of that canyon, we'll jump and try to get to it. I don't want us to be the second person who landed on the moon. I want us to be the guy that said the bit about the giant steps.'

Kevin Kelly raised a hand.

'Yes, Kevin?'

'It was a giant leap, I think. Small steps, and a giant leap.'

'Yes, whatever. It's just a figure of speech.'

'But I think it's important to be accurate in these things.'

'Kevin, that's precisely the problem. Nearly a decade ago, back in twenty-twenty, you were a young scientist in your first real job here, with just myself and Billy and with Caroline doing the paperwork.'

'Caroline wasn't here then.'

'Not Caroline the lab technician, I was talking about original Caroline, Caroline-in-the-cabin, the guinea pig minder, the brilliant woman who recruits our testing volunteers and gets them their food and shit. Anyway, back in the day you stumbled on the answer to the problem, as much by accident as anything, although to be fair you knew what you were looking for. And you proposed the answer, which was in fact correct, but it was just a hunch and you weren't able to bridge the gap between your results and your solution. And we know the rest.'

'I wasn't here at the time.'

'Yes, Karen, I know that. You were still asking your mummy for permission to go out at night.'

'I mean, so what happened?'

'We sold our package of research to the big boys, and they arrived at a conclusion that was pretty much what Kevin had guessed at, but the only difference was that they made about ten trillion dollars out if it, and we made, well, considerably less.'

'To be fair, we did okay.'

'We'll have to agree to disagree on that, Billy. We made a decent bit of money, but I can never stop thinking about the one that got away, to use your fishing terminology. We had the equivalent of a fifty pound, whatever that big fish is that you catch in Lough Key, and we let if off the hook.'

'Pike.'

'What?'

'Pike. It's a big fish, a predator. Some of the biggest ones in Ireland are to be found in Lough Key. I caught a thirty-five pounder once.'

'There must have been a lot of bachelor dinners in that one!'

'I didn't eat it, Miriam, I threw it back. Or gently placed it back in the water, to be precise.'

'That sums up the difference between you and me, Billy. You're happy to take what you get, I don't throw anything back. I want it all, and I want this one. So let me tell you this, Team. From today, all holidays are cancelled, all Saturdays and Sundays with your families are on hold. We are going to find a vaccine for this new Covid strain, and we are going to hold the rights to every needle that stabs some old lady in a nursing home, or makes every schoolchild on the planet cry. And we are going to get rich. I will divide a decent slice of the royalties for this among the six of you, I want to make us all richer than Croesus. But if anyone wants out, isn't prepared to work around the clock for the next couple of months, raise your hand now and go back to your bench, where you can enjoy testing water samples for the County Council.'

She looked around the room, slowly, her gaze halting on each member of staff.

'So, are we all in? Is everybody going to give this their best shot?'

Billy Robinson banged his fist on the table.

'Yes, by God we are. Let's do this thing!'

Miriam stood up and gathered her papers and laptop.

'Right, what the hell are we waiting for? Billy, you go after the data from Sean in Palo Alto, see what we're dealing with here, get everything they know about it. Get the best deal you can from him too, he's a greedy bastard. And Kevin, start proposing some theoretical solutions, see if we can do a bit of lateral thinking that gets us there first. Join forces with Karen, use her analytical skills to challenge your postulations, to weed out the non-runners. I want to see the two of you joined at the hip from now on; sleep together if you have to. The rest of you, double up on what you're doing, take all the work away from these three so they have a bit of time and space. I may deploy some of you to work with Billy or Kevin and Karen as we find out more. And we'll all meet back here same time tomorrow for an update.'

She turned at the doorway before she left the room, looking back to where her scientists were chattering excitedly.

'Time is something that's not on our side, ladies and gentlemen. This is a race, not a stroll in the park. Get your butts out of those chairs and get us to the winners' enclosure this time.'

Chapter Two

President Donald Daniels paced around and around the Oval Office, his aides waiting silently for him to speak. The President was clearly in a bad mood, and nobody wanted to trigger one of his outbursts by speaking out of turn. Eventually he seemed to realise that he was expected to say something. He sat heavily into the big leather chair behind the Resolute Desk, before directing a question to the big man who sat in one of the two wicker-seated walnut chairs on either side of him.

'Well, Vladimir, what does this mean, exactly? A new strain, I thought we'd had loads of new strains of this damned bug, why the big panic with another one?'

The doctor cleared his throat before he spoke.

'Mister President, it appears that this is a mutant, a variant that has strayed outside the parameters of the expected, so to speak.'

'Vladimir, can you cut the damned fancy talk and tell it to me in ordinary language, the kind I have to use to speak to the morons out there? What does this mean, exactly? Keep it simple, Okay?'

The older man stammered as he responded.

'It, it is the same virus, okay? But it has mutated, it

has changed in a way that the current vaccines can't recognise it and therefore can't deal with it. So we have no way of slowing it down across society, no way to block its spread.'

'Mutated, you mean like the zombies? Why would it do that, did the damned Chinese do something to it?'

'No, Sir. It just changed, same as the other variants, but this time it changed by quite a bit. The other changes were incremental?'

'Instrumental?'

'Incremental. Small, I guess.'

The President banged his fist on the desk.

'Then why didn't you say 'small' for God's sake? Can you guys not keep with normal words, and cut out that Harvard crap?'

'Sorry, Sir. What I meant to say was that it used to change in small ways from time to time, but now it has changed in quite a big way very quickly and the vaccine doesn't recognise it as being the same virus. That's where the problem lies.'

'So, small changes are okay, but big changes not so good?'

'Yes, Sir.'

'So, how big a problem is this new thing, this changed virus?'

'It's big, Sir. Really big. We have what is effectively a new pandemic, and no weapons in our armoury to deal with it.'

'As big as 2025, or 2020?'

'Bigger than 2025, I'd say, Sir. Probably as big as 2020 and the Covid-19, but worse in some ways.'

'Worse? Why?'

'Because of the big anti-vaxxer movement now, Sir.

Even if we manage to find a vaccine for this, only half the population will take it.'

'Hard to blame them, Valdimir, after the side-effects back in 2025.'

'Side effects, Sir?'

'Yes, you know, the importancy problem in men, the hair falling out, turning black men into paedophiles; all that stuff.'

'Impotency? Those things didn't actually happen, Sir. That was all propaganda, put out by the white supremacist groups like the Klan as part of their attempt to increase the spread in big cities, to kill off as many Liberals and low-income blacks as possible.'

'Are you sure of that, Vladimir? I read all about it on the internet, seemed legit.'

'No, Sir. That was all made up. But it makes for a problem now with stopping this new variant. Even if we come up with a vaccine, how do we get people to take it?'

The President resumed his pacing in silence for a while, before stopping again to speak.

'There are some good people in the Klan, I just wanted to say that. They gave me a medal last year for my services to nationhood. A real good dinner, too, if I remember rightly. So let's not blame those good people for what is basically a problem the Chinese dumped on us a decade ago.'

'Yes, Sir. But like I said, we are going to have problems with the uptake of the vaccine.'

The president turned and pointed a finger in the direction of his Chief of Staff.

'Major Callaghan, you got any views on this? If we get a vaccine, and I'm sure our fine scientists here or in Russia will crack that one, is there any way to deliver it to the entire population, to get them to want it?'

The Major stood and looked around the room.

'Sir, I have some views on this issue, but I would ask all present to leave the room, with the exception of yourself and Doctor Belyaev. There are matters of security involved and not everybody here is cleared to that level. Sir.'

The President pointed towards the other staffers who were seated on the two couches that faced each other on the other side of the large, oval rug, and waved them towards the door.

'You heard the guy, everybody get the hell outa here, we got important things to discuss.'

The Attorney General paused before leaving.

'Do you need me here for any legal stuff, Sir?'

'No, thank you, Lucy. I'll call you back later if anything comes up and you can advise me then.'

When the last of the departing staffers had left the room the Major sat and pulled his chair closer to the desk, and spoke quietly.

'Mr. President, there is a way we might be able to handle this problem, but I guess it depends on what Doctor Belyaev thinks about it.'

'Well, shoot, Major. Tell us what's on your mind.'

'You remember Operation Reduce, last year?'

'Yes, I remember. Is it working?'

'Yes, Sir. Did you not read the report?'

'No, I don't have time to read all the shit that lands on this here desk; what happened with it?'

'Well, Sir, you will recall that you wanted a project to inject an anaphrodisiac into the water supply in cities where we were experiencing large growth in black populations.'

'Yeah, we called it the 'ghetto blaster,' if I remember rightly.'

The officer allowed himself a slight smile at the reference.

'Yes, Sir, I do believe that you yourself coined that phrase; it was funny, to be fair. Pity we couldn't have used it, but there would have been riots in the streets if people knew what we were doing.'

'We were doing a good thing for America, gentlemen. It's something I feel very proud of, but you're right, we can never tell anybody about it. How did we explain what we were doing though, and did it have any results?'

Doctor Belyaev stood and began to pace up and down between the two couches.

'The short answer, Sir, is that the project appears to be bearing fruit, or not bearing fruit to be more precise. Birth rates in the ghettos in major cities, mostly in darker-skinned areas, are dropping. The South Side of Chicago, for instance, has seen a five percent drop compared to the previous year, and it's early days.'

'Five percent? That don't seem like a whole lot?'

'On the contrary, Sir. When you factor in the fact that birth rates were rising at three percent a year in that area alone, you have an effective drop of more than eight percent against the graph.'

'Eight percent? But I thought you said five?'

'Eight in total, Sir; five plus three. And in fact it's slightly more, but I won't go into that.'

'Okay, whatever, I was never great at math. But what about how your guys did the job, how did they actually do it? '

'With the help of Major Callaghan's team, we installed a specialised piece of kit in the local water-pumping stations, Sir. It was stamped 'Fluoridation monitor,' and it was locked and sealed with a Federal seal, with access allowed to just two of the Major's most trusted agents, although even they didn't know what the chemical was. They have spent all their time visiting the waterworks in all these cities, making sure the tanks are full of the anaphrodisiac chemical. It only needs tiny trace amounts of the drug to put guys off their nookie.'

'You gotta remind me of the cities, so I don't drink the water when I'm there. Mrs Daniels would be mighty disappointed if I came home on a weekend and couldn't ....'

'Don't worry, Sir. The project specifically targets a couple of hundred pumping stations across the country, but none of them are in middle class areas. It works extra well in summertime too, when guys drink a lot more water, and when you'd normally expect extra sexual activity.'

'Okay, Vladimir, so it works, great! So, Major, how does this affect this virus thing?'

'Well, Sir, I figured that if the boffins can come up with an oral vaccine, one that can be added to the water supply in crowded cities, or in Klan and far-right supremacist areas, we could inoculate the most critical segments of the population, where most of the anti-vaxxers find fertile soil for their nonsense. The rest could take the vaccine as an injection, same as before.'

'Is that possible, Vladimir? Does the Major's theory stand up?'

'In theory, Sir, Yes. It would depend on whether we can come up with a vaccine that doesn't damage populations if overdosed, obviously, or doesn't have side effects in larger than recommended doses.'

'And is that possible, do you think?'

'I guess so, Sir. Particularly if the vaccine doesn't generally have side effects of any kind, or has side effects for just a tiny number of people.'

'Like the Covid-25 one?'

'Yes, Sir. Except that was never given by mouth, it was always either injectable or as a nasal spray. But I guess it is worth a shot, what's the worst that can happen?'

'Damned if I know, Vladimir, you're the expert on these things.'

'Sorry, Sir, I was just thinking aloud. I guess we might lose a few civilians, but we'd save more lives than the handful we might kill off. So, yeah, on balance I'd say it's worth a shot.'

'Anything about this strain that we need to know, Vladimir? Like, does it kill kids or just old people?'

'All we have so far, Sir, is that it has just emerged and is quite aggressive. But there is one thing, early data seems to suggest that it doesn't attack black populations in the same numbers as the rest of us.'

The President jumped to his feet.

'Shit! Are you saying this is a white man's disease? Holy guacamole!'

'No, Sir. And it's early days. But the data does show a tendency towards a higher numbers of white-skinned types in terms of being targeted by the virus.'

How much higher?'

'Well, actually we have no cases in black populations so far, Sir.'

'Then we have no time to lose, gentlemen. We must find a vaccine quickly, and get it into people quickly.'

'I'd imagine that would mean spending a lot of money, Sir.'

'Major, if we need to spend money to fix this problem, then we'll spend money. Even if it means rolling them old presses and printing some more.'

He stroked his chin and put a finger in the air.

'Just a minute, surely we can't use this plan to vaccinate Blacks, you say they don't catch this damned bug?'

The Doctor leaned forward, eagerly.

'We will have to do it everywhere, sir. Black folks don't seem to catch it, but they can be very strong vectors.'

'Victors? What the hell are 'victors', Vladimir?'

'Vectors. Carriers, Sir. They can be used by the virus to jump from one white person to another, while not affecting the vector, the carrier, in any way.'

'So why the Harvard words, Vladimir? Keep this crap simple, so I don't need a dictionary to figure it out.'

'Sorry, Sir. Anyhow, we'd need to broaden the reach of our secret mass-vaccination strategy, over and above the areas we hit with Operation Reduce. We'd have to cover all the Klan and white supremacist areas, all the white ghettos where the anti-vaxxer nut-jobs have influence. But we have that data from before when we planned the other operation.'

'And you have the kit, the pumps and shit?'

'Yes, or we can get them. We used existing equipment from the water treatment industry, we just calibrate it to suit. This stuff is plentiful, and cheap.'

'Okay, start planning this now, from this minute. And find out everything there is to know about this new bug, and about the companies that are likely to develop a vaccine for it. Make sure the specification for the vaccine means it will work equally well by adding it to the water.'

'As well as being injectable, of course. Yes, Sir.'

The President sat back in his chair and pushed it away from his desk to indicate that the meeting was over. He focused on his two aides with a stern look.

'Very good, gentlemen. Let's do this, and quickly. And remember that our conversation doesn't go beyond this room, let's not start a public panic either. Okay, get out there, and make this happen.'

Chapter Three

Lucky Oyeleye nervously approached the passport control desk in Dublin Airport. It was a lot colder in Dublin than in Lagos, but the place was clean and looked very prosperous. If he could get past this final barrier, he would be in Europe and on the way to a better life. He adjusted his tie and tugged down the sleeves of his new shirt so that the gold-plated cufflinks showed below the cuffs of his suit jacket, and he smiled broadly as he placed his passport on the desk. The policewoman looked at him sternly, unsmiling and with a searching gaze that unnerved him slightly.

'So, Mister Oyeleye, what is the purpose of your visit to Europe?'

'A holiday, Madam, to see your beautiful green land.'

'And how long do you intend to grace us with your presence, Mister Oyeleye?'

'Three weeks, Madam. Unfortunately I have limited vacation time available to me, I would like to stay longer but my work awaits back home.'

'And what kind of work would that be, Mister Oyeleye?'

'I am a teacher in a school, Saint Patrick's College in Lagos, I teach religion and politics, you see. Our school was established by Father Ignatius Mulcahy back in the middle of the last century, he was an Irishman of some note.'

Lucky hoped she wouldn't pry too much further. Although he wasn't exactly a teacher in St. Patrick's, he did have some part time work there as a janitor, and had gone to school there for a year before being kicked out as a result of a slight misunderstanding. In truth, Lucky hadn't been the one who instigated the intimate activity with Father Mulcahy, that had been entirely the doing of the elderly priest, but who would believe a poor boy from the shanty town on the edge of the city dump?

'Indeed, Mister Oyeleye, there were a lot of our missionaries who established schools in Africa, so I suppose this is a kind of a homecoming for you?'

'Yes, indeed, Madam. I look forward to seeing The Cliffs of Moher, the Book of Kells and of course the seminary at Maynooth where Father Mulcahy nurtured his vocation from God.' He hoped that list would be enough, he had learned the names of several other places in Ireland but found his mind a blank now that he faced the officer's desk.

The officer stamped the passport and passed it under the glass screen with an attempt at a smile.

'Enjoy your vacation, Mister Oyeleye. But remember that this entry visa is for an absolute maximum of three months, plus a day's leeway in case of flight cancellations or delays; you must leave by the date on the stamp.'

'Thank you, Madam. Don't worry, I will be gone long before then.'

Lucky tried to stay calm as he walked through the baggage hall. He collected his small suitcase from the carousel and walked through the customs area unchallenged, exiting to the cold air outside the terminal. He switched on his mobile phone and called his wife.

'I made it, honey. Got through everything.'

'That's fantastic, Lucky, now let's hope the job and the place to stay works out, and I'll come over and look after my husband. What is the country like?'

'It is cold, and not too friendly, although some of them seem okay, and there aren't many black people here. But there is no drought I think, the rains seem to have come early. There is certainly plenty of blessed rain today, I am sure they will be glad of it.'

'It is probable that they are not friendly at the airport, there will be people there from everywhere. I'm sure you will blend in better when you get to Belgard and meet Samuel.'

'Okay, Honey, I have to find a bus to Bolgard, I need to get there before dark so I can find your brother and sort out my bed and my job. I will call you in a few days.'

'You do that, Lucky my love, and don't forget to send back the suit back to Akpan, he will need it to get into Scotland next month.'

'I don't forget, honey. Bye!'

Lucky walked up and down the pavement in front of the airport, looking at signs but unable to find one that said 'Bolgard.' He approached a uniformed man wearing an official-looking peaked cap.

'Excuse me, Sir, where can I find the bus to Bolgard?'

The man looked him up and down.

'Howya, son. Sure I'm not a Guard, I'm a bus inspector. Boyle, yeah? You need the Sligo bus, I reckon, that passes through the place. You'll get it in the surface carpark, through there.' He pointed towards an area beyond the multi-story carpark.

The Sligo bus was starting to move when Lucky tapped anxiously on the door. The driver opened it and gave him a friendly greeting.

'Ye nearly missed me, lad, but jump in. Where are ye headed for?'

'Bolgard, I believe it's on the way to Sliggoe.'

'That'll be twenty euro for a one-way, or ten euro return, it's a special offer this week. And I'm not a guard; guards don't drive buses in Ireland.'

'But I don't want a return.'

'Then you'll have to pay the twenty. Although if I was you I'd take the return, I'm just saying.'

'Okay, I take the return. Thank you. And can you let me know when I get to the correct stop?'

'Sure, no bother. We'll probably stop there for ten minutes anyway, if we make good time.'

Lucky handed over the money and took a seat near the back of the bus. He felt sleepy after the long flight, but he was afraid to doze in case he missed his destination. Samuel had said that it wasn't far, no more than an hour, so he resolved to stay awake, but the thrumming of the hydrogen engine and the gentle bouncing of the bus soon lulled him into a deep slumber.

He awoke with a start, for a moment unsure of where he was. It was dark outside, and from a quick check of his phone he figured he had been on the bus for two hours. He panicked slightly, then wondered whether the phone might have changed to suit local time, he had a vague idea that there were a couple of hours of time difference between Dublin and Lagos. Holding on to the seats as he walked, he made his way towards the front of the bus and spoke to the driver.

'Excuse me, Sir, have we passed Bolgard yet?'

'Boyle, yeah? No, it's another twenty minutes, it's the next town after Carrick. Don't worry, I'll give you a shout. And I'm only a bus driver, different uniform altogether.'

Lucky resumed his seat in the back of the bus, staring at his reflection in the window beside him. Rain streaked the outside of the steamed-up glass, and the tyres made a swishing sound on the wet road. He felt lonesome for home, and he was tired and hungry.

The bus slowed, and swung off to the left down a narrow road, past houses that glowed warmly from the lights within. A few minutes later it pulled to a halt beside a dimly-lit bus shelter where a number of passengers waited, bundled up against the squally rain. The driver switched off the engine and stood up, turning to call back towards the rear of the bus.

'Here ye are, son, welcome to Beautiful Boyle. This is far as I can get you.'

Lucky picked up his small suitcase and got off, turning his suit collar up against the weather. He wished he had brought a warm coat, Samuel had said nothing about the terrible climate, but maybe it was just a bad day. A number of people stared at him as he alighted, he felt conscious that he was the only black man at the bus stop. One woman shied back from him slightly, a fearful look on her face. He smiled at her in an effort to allay her fears, and spoke quietly to her.

'Hello, Madam, do you know where is the centre of the town?'

She pointed down the street, to her left.

'Along there, just a hundred yards or so, that's the middle of the town. Although there's not a lot there, are you looking for somewhere in particular?'

'I am looking for my friend, Samuel Okanwe. Do you know him?'

'I don't know, I never heard the name, is he.....?'

'Black? Yes.'

'No, I was going to say 'curly-haired.' Is he the same as yourself anyway?'

'Yes, like me, not as tall, but same skin and everything.' She pondered for a minute.

'No, I don't think there's any black man in Boyle, at all. There was a priest, he was curly-haired all right, but I think he's gone back to Africa or wherever it was. No, I'm sorry.'

She climbed slowly up the steps to the bus. Lucky turned away and walked towards the town centre. He debated whether to spend some of his scarce money on a bed for the night, and wondered whether it might be expensive. He might have to make his limited funds last until he got paid, but he was tired and cold, and needed food.

He saw a building called the Royal Hotel as he crossed the bridge. Although it appeared locked he rang the bell several times, but nobody answered. He retraced his steps slightly and paused by the stone railing on the bridge and took out his phone to call Samuel. Under the light of the ornate lamp at the centre of the span he extracted the sim card from the phone and fished in his wallet for the Irish one Samuel had sent him, laying both sim cards on top of his wallet on the stone parapet.

He didn't see the youth approach, but caught a sudden glimpse of a hand that moved swiftly to grab the wallet. He reacted quickly, grabbing the young man's wrist and twisting it downwards to break his grip. In the struggle to save his money, the two sim cards spun beyond his reach and disappeared into the racing river below.

The youth wriggled out of his grip and ran away, crossing the bridge and disappearing down a side alleyway. Lucky pocketed the wallet and phone and sighed deeply. Without the sim card, he would just have to keep asking people until he found Samuel.

The smell of food drew his attention, and he followed his nose around the corner to where a small take-away pizzeria was doing a good business, with people stopping in cars and collecting their meals in flat boxes. He pushed through the door and approached the counter.

The man behind the counter was friendly and welcoming. Lucky spoke hesitantly.

'How much is the food, Sir?'

The man pointed to a menu board above the counter, close to the ceiling.

'Starts at ten euros for the basic Margherita, goes up to fifteen for the fully loaded ones. You want to try a sample?'

'Yes, please!'

The man used a cutting wheel to carve a generous slice away from a pizza on the table beside the oven and passed it to Lucky on a paper plate.

'Here you go, try that. Best Pizza in Boyle.'

Lucky wolfed down the food quickly. The man smiled.

'Man, you look like you needed that. Are you hungry?'

'Yes, Sir, I didn't eat all day.'

The man leaned forward and spoke quietly.

'You just arrived in Boyle?'

'Yes, actually I just arrived in Ireland but I'm not sure where to go next, is the hotel closed, do you know?'

The man laughed.

'That's not really a hotel, it's a place where they give money to lazy guys who pretend to be starting a business. You know, government money?'

Lucky laughed at the thought.

'In my country they just take money from you all the time, and if you start a business they take more money. That's why I left and came here.'

21

'You want another slice?'

'Yes, please, if you can spare it.'

He passed over another slice and Lucky chewed it hungrily. The man seemed very friendly, but his accent was different from the ones he had heard all day.

'Are you from Ireland, Sir?'

'No, Man. I came here from Moldova two years ago, and I got a job here. Then the owner won a share in the lottery and decided to retire so I took over, now I have my own business.'

'Wow! In two years after you come, you got your own pizza shop! This would be my dream, to do something like that. Do you have any jobs?'

'Sorry, it's just a job for me, the town is not large and I can make a living for just me. Sorry.'

'Is there a place I can stay, not expensive? I have to find my brother-in-law, his name is Samuel Okanwe. Do you know him? He is like me, same build but not so tall, same colour too.'

The man shook his head.

'I don't know him, and he certainly doesn't come into the shop. I don't think there is any black man in Boyle though, or if there is he doesn't eat pizza. But maybe he is not here very long.'

'No, he has been here a couple of years, he says there are plenty of jobs too.'

Sorry, I don't know him, but is he sure about the jobs? There aren't a lot of jobs here, unless you do the drug testing in Boyle Labs.'

'I do not know this work, I don't have a scientific education I am afraid.'

'No, it's not like that, they test drugs on people, to make sure they are safe I think. You have to stay there for maybe a month, but they look after you and give you all your food. Actually they send a van here for pizzas one, two times a week; they are good customers.'

'And they pay you, to eat these drugs? Is it dangerous?'

'No, it is safe I think, it is before they start to sell them to everybody, a kind of final check after the monkeys or whatever they do first. They pay a lot of money, I think, I was going to do it but I found this job.'

Lucky felt a glimmer of hope. If he got a bed, and some money for a month, it would get him started.

'How much do they pay you for this work?'

'I'm not sure, it depends on how long the experiment is to last, but many thousands I believe.'

'Thousands? Wow, I never saw so much money. I could live like a king in my country if I had such money. Where is this place?'

'You go up the hill just there and you will come to a railway bridge. After you cross it, Boyle Labs is there, you can see the big building with the high fence and gates.'

'Thank you, my friend, I will go there immediately. I appreciate your assistance. My name is Lucky, by the way, Lucky Oyeleye.'

'And I am Marius Albescu, I am glad to meet you. Do you want the rest of the pizza, it is on the house.'

'Thank you indeed, my friend, you are a good man. I will return when I am rich and buy your biggest pizza.'

Carrying the food and his bag, Lucky hurried out into the rain and turned the corner towards the railway bridge.

Chapter Four

Homer Kendall Junior mopped his brow with a handkerchief and drank deeply from the glass of water on the table in front of him. He refilled the glass from the pitcher and looked around the room. The place was about half full but that was as much as you could expect; people cared less about the Klan than they used to, despite the threat from the way the black population was slowly advancing in numbers and influence. He banged his gavel on the table and called the meeting to order.

'Brothers in arms, please pay attention and let us get through the business of the evening as quickly as possible. It's damned hot tonight and I want to get home to my family, as I'm sure you all do too.'

The chatter stopped and the room fell silent. Homer spoke again.

'As Grand Dragon of this branch, I want to welcome you all here. As is traditional, I must ask, is everybody here a native-born, white, Gentile American citizen?'

There was a chorus of yesses, and a shuffling of feet and chairs. The Grand Dragon spoke again, hands clasped in prayer.

'Then let us start with our prayer. We avow the

distinction between the races of mankind as same has been decreed by the Creator, and we shall ever be true in the faithful maintenance of White Supremacy and will strenuously oppose any compromise thereof in any and all things. Amen.'

'I call this meeting to order, gentlemen. As you all know, and as it says in our good book, we have held the line since eighteen sixty-five against the heathens, unbelievers and every kind of racial contamination since our forefathers stood aghast and pale, wondering at the meaning and purpose of the gathering gloom after the South's defeat by the Union of evil.'

'In the last couple of hours I have spoken to the Imperial Wizard, who is known to you all, and to the Klud who looks after the spiritual needs of this Klavern, and I have something of great importance to impart. We have a major problem, gentlemen.'

The serious tone of the Grand Dragon's voice made the assembled crowd sit up. It was clear that this wasn't Homer's usual preaching about having to deal with uppity Blacks giving him a hard time when he stopped them at police checkpoints. The members tended to ignore these rants, glad that Sheriff Kendall's obsession with stopping black-skinned drivers meant they could get away with things that they might not get away with in towns other than Corner Creek. They listened intently to his words.

'Brothers in arms, two things have become known to us today, and they are extremely worrying. First, the black population in America is growing faster than the pure American race, and in another couple of years they will control us all. If the Blacks all go to vote in this district in ten years' time for instance, we could have a black Police Chief, a black Mayor, and the state of Tennessee would be sending a black senator to Washington. I don't have to tell you, we have a problem, gentlemen.'

William McCauley, the owner of the gas station at the corner of Pond Street and Main, raised a hand.

'So, Sherriff Kendall, what's the second problem?'

'I was coming to that, Bill. But I want you all to swear that anything I say here won't go beyond this room. Not to a neighbour, not to your friends or families, and not to your wives. In fact, especially not to your wives.'

There was a chorus of swearing and general assent.

'The Imperial Wizard told me something he heard from some of his kinfolk in California, apparently he has a relative who works in a big government laboratory in Palo Alto. It appears that this Chinese disease that has hit this country several times in the last ten years has come back, a new design by the goddamn Chinese it would appear.'

Suddenly everybody in the room was paying attention. Randy Corless, the Corless twin who was widely reckoned to have inherited less brains than his sibling, jumped to his feet.

'Them Chinese ain't no better than them coloured boys, we oughta run 'em all outa town.'

Homer Kendall's large belly shook as he laughed heartily.

'Where the hell was you when we did just that, back in twenty-five? You was drunk on that moonshine of yourn. That Chinaman that had the store on Main, we lit up the sky for that fella, we sure did. Ain't a Chinaman between here and four counties away now.'

He drank deeply from the glass and refilled it from the pitcher.

'Anyhow, the problem ain't Chinamen, right now. Problem is, them Chinese communists over in China

26

made this new virus so it don't touch the Blacks, just decent Christian folk, and they sent it here. Now what the hell we goin' to do about that?'

William McCauley cleared his throat and spoke again.

'Mebbe the Blacks got one o' them vaccines for this, mebbe they're giving it to all their kinfolk? Mebbe that's why it ain't affectin them?'

'We'll have no talk of goddamned vaccines here, I don't want to hear none of that shit here.'

'I was just sayin', Sherriff, mebbe the Chinese is givin' a vaccine to the black folks.'

'Are you suggestin, Bill, that we let the government inject a vaccine in us, mebbe take over our minds? Is that what you're sayin?'

'No, Sherriff, but mebbe we oughta look at the possibility, I'm just sayin.'

A chorus of shouts from the room seemed to suggest that the government should stick any vaccine up their asses, along with their federal tax bills. Homer Kendall Junior banged on the table to restore order.

'Brothers in arms, let there be no more talk of vaccines. Praise the Lord, we didn't use them before now, and with his help we ain't gonna pollute our blood with shit made from dead black babies and chemicals from Asia. But we gotta stay away from black folks, that's for sure. Mebbe they can't catch this new disease, but they sure as hell can spread it around. Now if their numbers is increasin, and they bring this plague and pestilence into our homes, then it is clear that the real problem ain't the goddamn Chinese, it's the same problem we always had, it's the goddamn Blacks.'

'So here's what we gonna do. From this day forth we gonna have no interaction of any kind with black folks.

If they works in your business, fire them and clean the place real good. If they works in your house, cleanin and cookin, send them away and get your wives to do that work, for now anyways. If they comes in your store, turn 'em out right away. And no whorin with black broads if you go to the city or anyplace where they hangs out. And I'll make sure that no black man can drive through our town without being stopped and hunted out by the law. Yes Jacob?'

A well-dressed man at the back of the room had raised a hand.

'Is Mexicans black folks, for the purposes of this exercise? You see, I got me a couple of Mexicans that work on my ranch, real good workers too, and I'd hate to send them away. Can't get Christian folk to do farm work no more.'

The Sherriff pondered before he spoke.

'I don't believe they is black, Brother Moore, they is all Christian people I believe. But I'll ask the Imperial Wizard to check it out, just in case. So don't fire them just yet, but don't let them in the house in case they is carrying disease.'

He banged the table again and stood up.

'I hereby call this meetin' to a end. Remember what I said, don't speak to nobody about it, and be careful out there. Now, let us end as we begun, with our prayer.'

Chapter Five

Miriam O'Hagan looked around the table at her assembled team. They looked weary, and all were drinking strong coffees to keep tiredness at bay. She waited until silence had descended before speaking.

'Right, folks, I won't keep you long, we've all got work to do. Firstly, well done to everybody for really notching things up several gears over the last twenty-four hours. What have you got for us, Billy?'

Billy Robinson placed a couple of memory sticks on the table.

'I got it, the data on the genome sequencing for the new variant, our guy came good.'

'Excellent, how much is it costing us?'

'Ten grand, but it seems fair. We're probably the only ones in the world outside of the US government that have this information.'

His boss laughed and shook her head.

'Don't be daft, Billy. Do you think that cheating, lying Sean Moriarity is loyal to us? He'll already have sold this information to half a dozen labs, plus President Daniels will have already given it to the Russians. But at least the Russians have the expertise to do something with it.'

'I suppose you're right, Miriam. Anyway, I agreed ten grand. But I negotiated some additional information out of him.'

'Such as?'

'He sent me the points of difference between this strain and the base strain, specifically the bits that appear to be bypassing the existing vaccine.'

'That gives us a bit of a head start anyway. Anything else, any other little nuggets of information that might give us clues towards finding a solution?'

'There was one other thing, right enough. He said the new strain is having no effect on black-skinned people, they appear to have immunity to it already.'

Karen raised a hand tentatively.

'That seems to suggest they have had exposure to it before.'

Billy shook his head.

'No, that's the whole point, they haven't. There seems to be something in the biology of black-skinned people that protects them from the infection.'

Kevin Kelly had been doodling on his pad, appearing to be in deep thought.

'Maybe there's another angle altogether, we might be missing a trick here.'

Miriam sat forward eagerly.

'In what way, Kevin? What are you thinking?'

'We're assuming that black-skinned people have immunity, but maybe there's something in their DNA that means that the virus doesn't recognise them as a host?'

'You're losing me now, Kevin.'

'It's simple, really, I mean the virus doesn't see fish or lots of animals as potential hosts, or it doesn't find a home in plants for instance. So maybe there's some detail in the DNA of black people that causes the virus to say, 'nothing to see here, keep moving.' Do you understand my thinking?'

Karen Doyle stood up excitedly and began to pace up and down.

'So that thing, that little bit of host DNA that tells the virus that this particular door is locked, that has to be in the part of the helix that defines skin colour. After all, all human DNA is identical except for the minor differences of appearance, height, eye colour, hair colour, etcetera.'

'And skin colour.'

'Yes, Kevin, of course, and skin colour. So the first thing we need to do is build the virus in the lab, that's just a matter of taking some of the Covid-25 we have in storage and using the lasers to bend it into the shape of the new variant. After that we can attempt to infect a black person with it. If she or he shows the presence of antibodies, then it's a natural immunity. But if they don't ....'

'That's it, Karen. We need to look at their DNA, and find a way of inoculating white people with the little bit that is naturally present in persons of colour. Or is that what you call black people now, I'm never sure what might cause offence?'

His boss laughed.

'Call them black people, Kevin, among ourselves anyway. I'll check out the most politically correct term before we go public, assuming we crack this nut. And I believe you guys are the ones to do it.'

Kevin raised a hand.

'Just one problem, where do we find a black person, a person of colour, in Boyle? If we need to experiment on a volunteer, we're going to need the real thing, not just some local lad whose parentage is a bit vague, or some slightly tanned lad from Dublin with a curly head on him. We need the real McCoy, ace of spades black, the kind of a lad you'd have trouble spotting at night unless he smiled at you.'

Billy Robinson nodded vigourously.

'No problem, I'd say. Caroline often has black guys in the guinea-pig building, I'm sure she'll be able to get us one pretty quick. She gets them through an agency from England, they're glad of the few euro, given the jobs situation back home. I'll go over to her now and ask her to order one, the blacker the better.'

Miriam gathered her papers and stood up.

'All good so far, folks. Can you go through the genome sequence between now and tomorrow, and pay particular attention to the bits that differ from Covid-25? And see if you can manipulate an existing viral sample to replicate the new variant. Then dig into what actually makes black people black, see where it fits into this jigsaw. I'll see you all here for a working lunch at one tomorrow, can somebody call Marius in the pizza place and order us the usual?'

Chapter Six

The President paced nervously around the Oval Office, making his habitual peculiar, slow tapping sound as he walked with one foot on the big oval rug and the other on the polished wooden floor. The Doctor and the Major shuffled their feet on the rug as they rotated slowly in their swivel chairs, each man keeping his gaze fixed on the moving figure. Neither dared speak until their boss had spoken first. Finally, he stopped his shuffling and looked at the two men.

'So, what the hell am I going to tell these news-hounds? That the country is sailing across shit creek in a boat with no pedals?'

He stopped behind the desk and sat heavily into the worn leather chair. Doctor Belyaev placed a single page document on the desk in front of him.

'This is all they need to know, Sir. There's little point in causing alarm, just tell them that the Covid has started to spread locally again, but that we are working on it. That sort of thing.'

'I hope that paper don't got too many of them Harvard words in it, Vladimir. I find it hard to pronounce them words sometimes, I get tongue-twisted and I forget what I has to say.'

'This is all in simple language, Sir.'

'Then read it out, Vladimir, let me hear how it sounds.'

The doctor retrieved the paper from the desk and held it at arm's length. He cleared his throat and began to read.

'Ladies and Gentlemen, blah blah blah etcetera, I have called this briefing to let you know of a threat to our nation that has emerged in recent days, albeit one we can manage.'

'All beet? What does that mean, exactly? I told you before, Vladimir, easy with the Harvard shit.'

'Sorry, Mr President. It means 'although.' You know, it's like, no big deal, folks; we got this.'

'Now you're talking normal, Vladimir. That's how you need to write this shit. You wanna start again?'

The doctor made some notes on the page and again held it at arm's length before speaking

'Okay. Ladies and gentlemen blah blah etcetera, I called you guys here to tell you there's some bad news about public health, but it's nothing we can't handle. Your government and your President, we got this. That old Communist disease the Chinese sent us before, well, they made some changes in it to try to get around the vaccine we give to anyone who wants it, and now we gotta make a small change to the vaccine and give you some more of it over the next few months to fix the problem. So a few people will catch a kinda flu, right? But it's no biggie, and going by our past successes in dealing with these things, we'll sort this all out in time for Thanksgiving.'

'That's better, Vladimir. What do you think, Major?'

'Yes, Sir. That's real good. Ain't nobody could be confused by that.'

'Yeah, I like the way it reads easy. Carry on, Vladimir.'

'Well, Sir, at this point Gerry Garcia from the Courier

will ask a question we wrote for him, so be sure to go to him when he puts up his hand.'

'Okay, the usual drill, I got it.'

'Yes, Sir. Gerry will ask you if this is a new virus or just a variant, he'll make it sound like a variant is no big deal but a new virus might be a worry. Then you say 'Thank you for the question, Gerry, that's a good question, I'm real glad you asked that because I was coming to that. This is not a new virus, it's still the old one but it has been altered just a little bit so not everyone who is vaccinated is a hundred percent safe from it, so that's why we need to update the vaccine. But it's definitely not some new virus; that would be a worry. No, this is the same old Chinese disease that they send us from time to time because they envy our freedom and our way of life, and we can fix it in the same old way. I'd like to reassure the American public that our great scientists and medical people are working late nights for us all to fix this problem as quick as possible.'

'And then you ask for questions, Sir. If you get stuck on anything, just say 'I think I'll pass that question to Doctor Belyaev,' and I'll deal with it.'

'Okay, Vladimir, that's good, I like that. So, Major, you happy with that?'

'Yes, Sir, that's all good.'

'Okay, that's all that sorted. Now, Major, how goes the preparations for the vaccination in the water supplies?'

'That's all in hand, Sir. We already got all the necessary pumps in storage in our military base in Memphis, as well as all the fittings, the guys are already out there fitting them. They don't know shit, they just think it's to do with fluorine in the water.'

'Good, good. You confident we can get a vaccine that

can go in the water supply, Vladimir? One that won't wipe out half a city?'

'We're drawing up a specification for the vaccine right now, Sir, it will be going out to any of the labs who worked with us before.'

'These are all American labs, right?'

'Not really, Sir, our labs are pretty good, but they aren't necessarily at the leading edge of this technology anymore. So we will go to a few selected contractors across the world, in Russia of course but also in Europe.'

'And in England? I like England. I really want to go there, to meet the King and Big Ben and see Bucking Tom Palace and all that stuff.'

'I'm afraid not, Sir. Since they left Europe ten years ago they've really gone backwards in the sciences, they don't get involved in knowledge sharing and all that. So they aren't really at the races. I'm sorry.'

'And in Ireland? The Irish vote is important to us, don't they make a lot of medicines and shit?'

'Yes, Sir, they sure do. We will be sending the spec to one small Irish lab, they have a track record in vaccine development. But we won't do that straight away, we'll let our guys and our Russian allies have a head start. We'll share it with the Irish and Germans a couple of weeks later.'

'I like it, I like it. Okay, guys, let's go and meet the press.'

Chapter Seven

Lucky Oyeleye stepped into a doorway as a sudden squall of rain threatened to soak him to the skin. He finished the remainder of the pizza and waited for a few minutes for the rain to ease before continuing his journey. The ground rose to cross the railway and dipped down again and his heart lifted as he saw the big bulk of an industrial building through the gloom. Its high, windowless walls gave no indication of what purpose the edifice might serve, and only a small sign that said 'Boyle Labs Ltd.' indicated what lay within. A high, green steel security fence ringed the site, and he approached the gates with trepidation.

The main gate was closed and there appeared to be no sign of life, but another small gate a little further along had a small portable office building just inside it, and a light glowed from the windows. As he approached he could see a middle-aged, red-haired woman with her head bent over a computer. He looked for a doorbell or an intercom to try to attract her attention but there was none.

Lucky shouted in the direction of the office, politely at first, but increasing in volume in an effort to attract the woman's attention. When that failed, he rattled the gate hard, but she still didn't look up from her desk. Frustrated and cold, he picked up a handful of pebbles and began to lob them at the windows of the office.

That gave him a result. The woman jumped up and rushed to the office door, triggering the sensor on a large floodlight as she stepped outside. She was tall and well-built, and she was angry. Lucky put his hands to his eyes against the glare as she shouted in his direction.

'Bloody bastard kids, fuck off and go home before your mother comes looking for you! I'll kick yer arses from here to Cootehall if I get my hands on ye!'

Lucky raised his hands in a placatory manner.

'I'm sorry, madam, I was just trying to attract your attention.'

'Sorry, mister, I thought it was them bloody kids again. We're closed, what do you want?'

'I'm looking for a job, a testing job. You have such a situation for me?'

She walked closer to the fence and looked him up and down.

'Did you come from the agency? Well about time, I had given up on you. Are you the guy who was supposed to arrive last night? Your friend is in here already, why couldn't you get here in time? Why do some lads never read the instructions we send them? Why do I bother my arse with giving information to people?'

Lucky was stuck for words for a moment. He wondered whether this was the place Samuel had spoken of. Maybe Samuel was working there and they were actually waiting for him to arrive, like she said.

'Well,' she said, 'have you no tongue in your head? Are you the person for the testing? What kept you? Why didn't you call and let me know you'd been delayed?'

'Yes, I believe I am. Somebody tried to steal my wallet

on the bridge, back there, and I lost my phone card.'

She laughed.

'Yes, Mickey Small, he tries to mug anybody who as much as stops on the bridge. I don't know why they don't just lock him up. I'm just waiting for him to try it on me, I'll throw the fucker into the river.'

She pushed the fire-exit bar to unlock the small pedestrian entrance, and snapped it closed again once Lucky had come through. She directed him towards the cabin and its welcoming warmth.

'Come in here until I get your details, and I'll show you to your room. How was the journey? Do you want tea? Did you eat anything? Jesus, you're soaked, I'll have to get you dry clothes. Did you come far? Never mind, sit down there and I'll get you sorted.'

She tapped on her keyboard and Lucky surveyed the office. The large desk was stacked with paperwork, and the end wall was lined with large metal filing cabinets. The other end of the office had a small kitchen area, and she pointed towards it with her pen.

'Put that kettle on there, good lad. Make us both a cup of tea. There's biscuits in the tin there, help yourself.'

Lucky did as he was told, rummaging around to find two mugs and a couple of tea bags. As he made the tea, she called out various questions to him.

'So, you're Eddie Elliot, and your date of birth is September nine, two thousand and six?'

'No, madam, I am Lucky Oyeleye and my date of birth is August twelve, two thousand and four.'

She swore as she scrolled through details on the computer.

'Bloody agency, they never seem to get it right. Never mind, you're here now. And your address is four Kilden

Street, Gorton, Manchester?'

'No, it is not correct. I am from Lagos, in Nigeria.'

'So you live in England then?'

'No, I come from Nigeria. Samuel told me there was work here.'

'Samuel? Who is Samuel?'

'He is my brother-in-law, he works here, you said. Do you want sugar?'

'Yes, one spoonful. But don't stir it, I don't like it too sweet. Okay, let's start again. Name?'

'Lucky Oleleye.'

She spelled out the letters as she typed. 'L-U-C-K-Y, O-L-E, O-L-E, O-L-E?'

'No, it is O-Y-E-L-E-Y-E.'

'Okay, Lucky Oyeleye. That's a fucking funny name, are you lucky by nature?'

'I do not think so, but maybe now I am here my luck will change.'

'That's the spirit. I just need you to read this contract and sign it, and tell me that you understand it.'

She handed Lucky some pages that spat from the printer, pointing out the places on each page where he needed to sign. He took a pen from the desk and signed everything, just giving a cursory glance to the words on the pages. She looked at him with raised eyebrows.

'Aren't you going to read that in more detail?'

'To tell you the truth, madam, my reading is not as good as I would like it to be. I can read simple things, but such an amount of writing on a page I find difficult. But I understand what it says, I must accept that if something bad happens, I am basically…'

'Fucked. That's the word you're looking for. Yes, this contract covers Boyle Labs against any claim arising out of any side-effects or long lasting damage to any of your organs for an indeterminate length of time that is only ended by your death, even if that death is caused by any mistake or negligence on our part or on the part of the companies for whom we test the products. But that will never happen, these things are safe as houses, they test them on monkeys and pigs before they get near a human. Although there is a lot of pressure on drug companies now to skip the pigs and go straight to humans, the animal rights crowd say that pigs can't give informed consent.'

'I never thought of that, to be honest. But they do not give informed consent before they are made into bacon either. But maybe it is a higher type of pig we are talking about.'

'A pig is a pig, Mr... Do you mind if I call you Lucky?'

'Yes, no problem; that is my name.'

'And you can call me Caroline, I'm the manager of this side of the business, and I will look after you well, don't worry. Nothing is too good for our testers, we bring in good meals from local restaurants, the very best, and pizza once a week if you like it. There's a great pizzeria here.'

'Yes, I know, I met the guy. It is really good. So have I got the job?'

'Yes, of course, welcome to the team. Let me tell you first of all what the living arrangements are. You'll be sharing a room with another, ah, foreign guy, same skin tone as yourself. You'll have a lot in common, I'm sure.'

'A black guy, is he from Nigeria also?'

'No, he's from Manchester. His name is Awe.'

'Awe? That is a strange name.'

'It's his initials, He is called 'Apple Wedgewood Enright,' apparently his mother gave him famous names so he would have a good start in life. A bit like your mother did, maybe?'

'Yes, although mine is a common name in Nigeria, many parents give the name to their children so that they may be lucky in life.'

'Well, let's hope it works out for you. Anyway, yes, where was I?'

'You were telling me about living arrangements, do you provide the accommodation also?'

'Of course, it could never work otherwise. Two of you will share a room, en-suite, nice and warm but no windows I'm afraid. Sometimes we have to keep people unaware of what time of day it is, or to simulate shorter or longer days.'

'Like the chickens in a chicken farm?'

'Yes, I suppose so. But the food is better, and you don't have to shit on the floor.'

'Yes, quite. So, do we get a radio, or a TV?'

'No, I'm afraid not. Not a TV as such, but we have a database of music and movies and TV shows and you have a screen to watch what you like. And you can take exercise in the gym at certain times. You won't find the week passing, it just flies by, I promise. Mostly we don't mix people from different rooms, in case of any cross-infections, so it can be hard to keep your head right, but if it was easy we wouldn't be paying people this kind of money to do it. And of course you can leave at any time, but you get no money if you don't complete the trial, and you will owe us for the food and accommodation.'

'I am okay with that, how much will I get for the week altogether?'

'Three thousand euros, did the agency not tell you?'

Lucky figured he had better say nothing in case this

woman figured out he was an imposter.

'Sorry, I forgot. Yes, I remember now. Three thousand euro. And what do I have to do, for this money?'

'Did you not read the leaflet? Or maybe they didn't give it to you, that agency just want their fees and they want me to do all the work for them. This is a trial for a new kind of sticking plaster for small wounds, to see how quickly your skin heals from a small cut. That's why we specified two, two people like yourself and Awe.'

'Black people?'

'Yes, you don't mind if I call you black?'

'Of course not, I am black.'

'I'm never quite sure, what to call, ah, black people. Anyway as I was saying, you will be testing this new plaster, the nurse makes two small cuts, scratches really, on your arm and she puts the new plaster on one and a normal plaster on the other. Then she checks every day and records the image until both cuts are healed. That's it.'

'And this will take one week?'

'Yes, but if you like, I can sign you up for more trials in the future.'

'When would that be? I need the work, to be honest.'

She gestured towards the big building behind her.

'I never know until they tell me, it might be the week you finish this one, or it might be a month, I honestly have no idea. But I'll let you know anyway. Now, grab your bag and follow me, and I'll show you to your room. Just give me your phone, please, I'll return it when you leave.'

Chapter Eight

Special agent Mike Connors flicked the drive motor of the Tesla up to maximum as he joined US 75 out of Knoxville. Agent Gary Hillman pushed his seat back and settled down for a short nap. The driver looked across at him and laughed.

'You're turning into an old man, partner; this habit of nappin' after you've had a good lunch.'

'I don't call a hamburger and fries a good lunch, but when it comes to takin' naps, I like to bank some rest when I can.'

'So how do you manage when you're flying solo? You don't always got the luxury of a chauffeur.'

'I make out okay, If it's a mapped road I just put the car in auto-drive mode, or I just pull over at a truck stop and shut my eyes for a half hour. Like I'd do now if you stopped with the talk.'

'Okay, I read you. Anyhow, we'll be at the next site in an hour or so.'

'That's the pumping station at Corner Creek?'

'Yeah. Hillbilly Heaven, that's what that place is. No law and order around there, the Police Chief is a Klan bigwig, and the moonshiners can run riot all they want, as long as they're white.'

'Thankfully, there ain't many places like that, it's a waste of time having both of us tied up on jobs when we could be covering twice the ground.'

'Too risky going in there on your own, and without pretty heavy firepower. Flashing a Secret Service badge wouldn't cut no ice if you ran into a couple of them moonshiners.'

'Goodnight!'

Mike Connors kept his thoughts to himself for the next hour, watching for highway signs and taking sips from a water bottle. As he prepared to turn on to the country road that led to Corner Creek he nudged his partner awake.

'Almost there, look lively.'

Gary sat up and adjusted the seat back. He rubbed his eyes and looked around him.

'We're in the Boonies now, for sure. Reminds me of a place I used to work when I started out, up near Clarkesville. I was a young agent on illegal alcohol duty, we used to raid stills and dump the liquor, and try to arrest the perps.'

'Try?'

'Yeah, it was never easy to prove that a guy who was nearby was actually involved, and they always denied it. They'd say they were huntin' or something, so even if we arrested them we almost never could make it stick.'

'Hard to operate in this terrain, I'd imagine. A lot of woods and a lot of hills, they could probably see you comin' long before you'd find a still.'

'Yeah, and they near always had the benefit of advance warnin', I reckon that local LE was up to their necks in it. If you had the local sheriff along you could sense their reluctance, and they often blasted off their sirens way before we got to the target area. Naturally the place would be deserted when we'd arrive.'

The driver pointed to the sign that said 'Corner Creek.'

'Call the water board guy and tell him to meet us at the pump station, usual story.'

Gary punched numbers into his phone, and the call was immediately answered.

'Hank Krutski. How can I help you today?'

'Mister Krutski, this is Gary from the FDA, we're just looking at pumping stations on the public water systems, we have to do an audit of best practice across the State. I guess you got the email from our boss.'

'Yeah, I got it. You want to look at my station?'

'Yes, Sir. Take us no more than an hour, you can just let us in and then we'll call you back when we're done.'

'Okay, you know the way?'

'Yup, we got the co-ordinates. Ten minutes, I reckon.'

When the agents reached the gate they saw a large truck with the 'Tennessee Water' logo on the side, and a small, skinny man who was opening the locks. He looked at them in an unfriendly manner as they got out of the car.

'Damned if I know what the hell the Federal agencies want with my station. I run a good ship here, I don't need no city boys tellin' me how to do my job.'

Mike raised his hands in a placatory gesture.

'Damned if I know either, Mister Krutski, but it pays the rent, so I ain't arguin' with them. As long as we're doin' this job, we ain't never found a problem with a station in any of these country towns, they're always run by guys that have been in the job a long time and know what they're at. I'll be more than surprised if it's any different here, but we gotta give them clerks a full list with all them little boxes ticked.'

The man relaxed and smiled slightly.

'No offence, mister, it's just that I see these city boys come

46

through here every so often, all of them with some hornet in their pants about some new regulation or some way them Feds figured to make life difficult for normal folks. But you guys is just doin' your jobs, makin' a buck like the rest of us, so I ain't gonna make life no more difficult for you than it is already. I'll just open her up and let you boys do what you have to do. We got nothin' to hide here.'

He unlocked the door of the big, steel-clad building and switched on the lights, stepping back to speak, away from the thrumming of the pumps. He pointed inside at the line of big, blue-painted pumps that fed from a huge steel pipe that ran the length of the building.

'That's her, guys. Twenty-two pumps, there's a sign on the wall opposite each one that tells us where it's sending water to. Eleven destinations altogether, one pump in service and one on standby, with automatic changeover controls and valves on each one. So if pump number one goes out of action, that's one of the ones serving the town of Corner Creek, then number two cuts in and the telemetry tells us back in the depot that number one is in fail mode. Same story down the line, but you guys know all that anyhow. And I guess you also know not to touch anything with a Federal seal on it, there's a lot of monitoring stuff here to do with national emergencies and shit, but that won't bother you, you just need to be sure the water supply is safe, right?'

Gary nodded his thanks.

'Yeah, this station type is pretty common, we've seen dozens of them, no problem. We should be done here in a couple of hours at most, so we'll call you when we're about ready so you can lock her up.'

The Water Company man climbed stiffly back in his truck and drove down the road. The two agents quickly went to the trunk and pulled out a small stroke-pump and a stainless steel tank with an electronic control box attached to it. They worked fast, unscrewing a blank bung from the supply side of the line and screwing in the adaptor to fit the pump. In a matter of minutes they had attached all the mechanical hardware, and Gary quickly fitted the electronics and wired them back to the power supply. They unscrewed the filler cap on the tank and added some water to test the pump, then closed it and sealed it with a Federal seal. The marker plates on the tank and on the control box said 'fluoridation sampling meter, property of FDA. Do not tamper.' They stepped back and Mike Connors checked his watch.

'Pretty fast, my friend. Fourteen minutes, start to finish. It's all ready for whatever the FDA wants to add to it.'

Gary agreed.

'When you get used to fitting these kits, they take no time at all. This one was real easy, whoever built this station left plenty of draw-off points for sampling and stuff. So what do we do now, call the guy and tell him we're done?'

'I reckon we might just do that. We could push on over to the other side of the State, the next place is on tomorrow's schedule, but if we got it done this evening, and make an early start tomorrow, we can be back home a day early for a change.'

'Let's do that, you call him and I'll clean up and put the garbage and the tools in the trunk.'

Chapter Nine

Lucky Oyeleye blinked in the glare as the woman led him through a heavy steel door set into the side of the grey-painted building. Inside, the brightly-lit corridor was a surprise after the nondescript stony yard outside. The polished floor gleamed like a hospital corridor, with the same faint smell of disinfectant he would have expected in a medical centre. A number of heavy, fireproof doors led off the corridor, and she led the way through one of these into an equally brightly-lit reception area. A stout woman in a nurse's uniform sat behind a semi-circular desk, and she looked up as they approached.

'This is Nurse Mary Cohen, she is in charge of your medical care while you are here. You must follow her instructions at all times. Nurse Cohen, this is Mister Lucky Oyeleye, he is our late arrival on the Kissitbetter trial. He'll be sharing with Mister Awe in room six.'

The nurse looked Lucky up and down, grunting an unsmiling welcome.

'Funny fuckin' names some of you lads have, but maybe that's normal in Manchester.'

'I am not from Manchester, Madam, I am from Lagos.'

'Lagos? Is that in the North of England?'

'No, it is in Nigeria.'

'I thought you were supposed to be from Manchester. Anyway, England, Nigeria, they all seem to have funny names. I need you to change out of those clothes, we'll give them back to you when you leave. We'll have them cleaned for you, don't worry.'

She looked him up and down again, measuring him with her eyes. She went to a cupboard behind her and pulled out some clothing in cellophane packets.

'Shoe size? I reckon about forty-four?'

'Yes, forty-four exactly.'

She picked a pair of slippers from another cupboard and added them to the pile. She pointed to a doorway on the other side of the room.

'Take a shower in that room there, put all your clothes, everything including jocks and socks, in the basket and leave them there. Change into these scrubs and the slippers and come back here to me when you're done. But don't take all bloody day about it. And leave your bag here, we'll take care of it as well.'

Lucky picked up the pile of clothing and made his way to the shower room. It was warm and windowless, but the water was hot and the shower took away the chill he felt in his bones and made him feel better. He dried himself and pulled on the unfamiliar clothing, a blue and yellow surgical scrubs with a 'Boyle Labs' logo embroidered on the chest. He slipped his feet into the slippers and returned to the reception area. The nurse looked at him and nodded.

'Right, well done. Now sit there and I'll start the trial immediately, you were late starting so we have to try to get you into the process quickly. Roll your right sleeve all the way up and I'll do the business. Has he signed all the necessary, Caroline?'

The other woman nodded.

'Yes, all done and dusted.'

The nurse pulled on a mask and a pair of blue surgical gloves, and placed a small tray on the table beside where Lucky was seated. She peeled the protective film off the tray and picked out a paper ruler and a short pen. She cleaned Lucky's upper arm with a surgical wipe and measured and marked two lines on the skin.

'Did Caroline explain what this trial entails?'

'Yes, I think so.'

'You think so? Well, you have to know so. I've just drawn two lines on your arm with a sterile pen, and they are exactly two-point five centimetres apart. They're for my guidance, I'm going to make two small cuts between those lines, more scratches really, and so each cut will be exactly two point five centimetres long. You with me so far?'

Lucky nodded.

'You have to say 'yes' or 'no,' nodding isn't consent, okay? So, are you with me so far, do you understand what I've told you?'

'Yes, madam, I understand.'

'And are you okay with that, with my making these slight incisions?'

'Yes, madam.'

'Okay, then after I've made the incisions, I will put a normal sticking plaster on the upper one, and a sticking plaster from the Kissitbetter trial on the lower one. Then I will cover both plasters with a large, waterproof covering that will protect both wounds. You are not permitted to remove either the outer covering or the inner plasters, even if they are causing discomfort. If any of the dressings are causing a problem, you press the bell and I will come and change them for you. Do you understand all that?'

Yes, madam. I understand.'

'And do you consent to this procedure?'

'Yes, madam, I do.'

'Good lad, you catch on fast. I think we're going to get on. Now, brace yourself, Bridget, as the Bishop said to the Reverend Mother.'

Lucky flinched slightly as the scalpel bit into his skin, but he hardly noticed the second cut. The nurse expertly cleaned off the slight ooze of blood and applied the plasters and covered both with a large, square patch. She gathered the wrappings and the tray and put them into one large bin, and dropped the scalpel through a slot in the lid of a yellow 'sharps' bucket. She gave Lucky a half smile.

'That's it, you're done. I'll see you at the same time tomorrow. I'll come and visit you though; you don't have to do anything. Caroline will show you to your quarters now and take your order for dinner.'

Lucky followed Caroline through a door into another corridor, this one controlled by a key fob and what looked to him like a camera that studied her face for a few seconds before an electronic voice said 'pass.' She led him down the corridor and used her fob to unlock a door with a number six on it, tapping on the door quickly before entering.

'Awe, this is Lucky. Lucky, Awe.'

Lucky stared at the young man who lay on one of the beds. He had a high afro hairstyle, and was dressed in the same blue and yellow scrubs and slippers. He pulled the earbuds from his ear and sat up quickly.

'Man, I is glad to see you. Where yo been, Bruvver?'

'It is a long story, sir, but I am glad to be here.'

'I is so glad to see you, man, I getting tired talking to them walls.'

Caroline explained the features of the unit to Lucky, pointing out the bathroom and the small kitchenette with its table and two chairs and its tea and coffee-making facilities. She opened a small cupboard built into the wall.

'This is where your meals are delivered. It has two doors, one that opens in here and one that opens to the service corridor. Your door has to be closed before the other one can be opened, and vice versa. So if you forget to keep it closed, you can't get a food delivery. When you finish eating, you put all the plates and cutlery into the cupboard and lock the door, and our service team will take them away when they are delivering the food.'

She pointed to the fridge with its selection of snacks and soft drinks.

'Because this is a skin trial, it doesn't matter what you eat, within reason. So help yourself to whatever you want from here, and let us know when you're out of anything. Food is from the Open Table Restaurant tonight, so it's all really good, their menu is on the screen there. I'd recommend the fish and chips, but whatever you want, really.'

Lucky was anxious to please, this place seemed too good to be true.

'Fish and Chips sounds good to me, madam. That would be very fine indeed.'

And you, Awe, you sticking with the vegan special?'

'Yeah.'

'How do you eat that shit day after day? Okay, I'll order those now. Lucky, you also have your own screen there, with earbuds in a sealed packet on your pillow along with the remote control, so you can each watch whatever you want. If you both want to watch the same thing, you can put the sound into the speakers, I showed Awe how to do it earlier.'

'And one other thing, you're locked in here, but in an emergency the doors will automatically unlock, and the signs will light up and show you the way out. You can also break the glass on the button beside the door, in case all else fails, but remember that if you do it in a non-emergency situation you will be considered off the programme and you will not get paid. You will also owe us for the accommodation and the cost of replacing the break-glass unit. Clear on all that?'

They nodded assent.

'When I ask a question about consent, I need an actual answer. We don't do nods in here. So, are you clear on that? Lucky?'

'Yes, madam.'

'And you, Awe?'

'Yeah, whatever. I told you already.'

'Okay, gentlemen, food will be delivered through the hatch in the kitchen about half an hour. Have a nice evening.'

She closed and locked the door behind her and Lucky walked around the room, examining all the features that had been pointed out earlier. He opened the packages that contained the earbuds and the remote, and the one that held the razor, soap and toothbrush. His room-mate looked at him without speaking. Lucky spoke first, to break the awkward silence.

'So, you come from Manchester England, is that a big city?'

'Yeah, I guess. Dunno, really, big compared to what? Big compared to Boyle anyhow.'

'How do you pronounce the name of this place, is it Bolgard or Boll?'

'Bolgard? I never hear it say that way, Man. It's Boyle,

same like boil the kettle, you know?'

'Oh dear. Maybe this is where I make the mistake. My brother in law lives in Bolgard, in Dublin. This place, it is not in Dublin?'

The other man laughed.

'No, Man. Dublin is like, the city. This is, like, nowhere, basically.'

Lucky put his head in his hands and moaned.

'My brother in law, he will think something has happened to me, he was finding me a job and someplace to sleep.'

'But you got a job, here, and there be nothing wrong with the beds and shit.'

'True, yes you are right.'

'And the money, Man! They giving us three thousand of them euros, that be like four thousand pounds, Man! That's a shit-load of money, Man!'

Lucky cheered at the thought.

'Yes, I suppose so. It is certainly a lot of money, and only for this little cut on my arm. Or is there more cutting they will do?'

'No, Man. That's it, they be just going come around and change the patches every day, and see how good it fixed. All we gotta do is lie here and listen to music, and eat what we want. If we had some weed it would be heaven, I be never goin' home then.'

Lucky shook his head.

'I can't believe this is so easy, are you sure they will pay us, maybe it is just a trick to get us to do the thing, they will say at the end that it is a mistake.'

'No, Man. I was here before, two year ago, they have me here for two week swallowin' pills, give me eight thousand pound. I mean, I lays at home swallowin' pills and I has to pay the man for they. I don't care what they asks me to do, I stayin' here any time they lets me.'

'But if it paid that well, why did you wait for two years, why did you not come back sooner?'

'Shit, Man, story my life. I went crazy with the money, party much, lotta pills and shit, they lock me up for sumfing, can't remember. Eighteen month minus two good-boy month. Soon as I get out I ask the agent find me more job here.'

'So, this time, do you think you will have a better outcome?'

'Yeah, sure, this time I goin' take it easy, maybe some weed and a little party, but nuffing crazy, you know? I got a kid now, I think. Mebbe I go live with the girl.'

A bell pinged from the kitchen area. The man on the bed jumped up excitedly.

'This here the food, Man! Let's eat, Bruvver.'

Chapter Ten

Randy Corless steered the pickup carefully along Main Street, one eye closed to try to clear the double vision that had stayed with him all morning since he woke up to a poke in the ribs from his brother Buddy as he slept beside the still. He vaguely recalled Buddy telling him to get up and bring a case of number one brew into town to William McCauley's gas station, and to collect a hundred dollars for the last lot. Now, he felt hungry, the effects of his tasting session of the previous night beginning to wear off.

He swore as he spotted the Police car pulled half way across the street, creating a roadblock to slow traffic to one lane at a time. He thought about making a U-turn, but the eagle eye of Homer Kendall Junior had already focused on the battered truck and its unkempt driver. He pulled up beside the Policeman and looked straight ahead. A tap on the window forced him to turn and look at the Sherriff, and he gave a toothy grin and wound the window down.

'Morning, Sherriff!'

'Morning, Randy, you been deliverin' to your wholesaler again?'

'No, Sir, I been getting gas, she was damn near empty.'

'Kiss my ass, Randy, I knows where you been. You been at the sauce early too, reckon I could light them fumes from here.'

'That just some burp I got that's left over from last night, Chief, I'm all good to drive.'

'You about as good to drive as I good to fly an aeroplane. You about as good to drive as my grandma is fit to get up and dress herself this morning.'

Randy grinned.

'Yore Granma, she dead twenty yearn, Chief, reckon her clothes don't fit her none, nowadays.'

The police chief threw back his head and laughed.

'Get yer ass outa here, Randy Corless, and mind you don't hit no Christian folk on the road. And you owe me a bottle for this, drop it off next time you in town.'

Randy put the truck in 'drive' and pulled away in a cloud of blue smoke. The Chief waved the next car forward, and spoke through the open window to the worried-looking black driver.

'Howdy.'

'Good morning, officer.'

'Good morning, my ass, why it took you so long to stop? You been drinking?'

Randy grinned as he looked in the mirror; that driver was going to get a lesson about driving through Corner Creek; for sure the guy would pay the toll next time and stick to the Interstate. He flogged the truck up the hill and on to the gravel road that led to the small farm in the woods, pulling up in front of the cabin. He tripped and almost fell as he got out of the truck. His brother shouted angrily at him from his chair on the porch.

'Keep yore feet under ya, ya gonna wreck that damn truck one a these days. Where you think money come from? We gotta make every buck on them bottles, damn welfare checks don't buy too much.'

Randy laughed.

'Don't get yore ass in a heap, Buddy, I ain't never wrecked no truck, I can drive good if I's careful. But man, this here brew is real good, best we ever made, I reckon. I still see two of everythin, an it gotta be eight or nine hour since I drunk it.'

'Lucky yo didn't kill yoself, I test that stuff when you went to town and it ninety-five percent. That shit can kill a damn horse.'

'Mebbe we oughta put some water in it, we don't want ourn customers to all die, kill off the business.'

'We can't use water from the well, for sure.'

'No, we can't put well water in it, it too dirty from the runoff from the Moore ranch. I can smell the cattle shit every time I draw water from that well. Y'all can't smell it in the coffee, but it sure as hell would make the whisky taste real bad. We mebbe gotta buy them gallons o' water in the store, use 'em to water it down.'

Buddy shook his head.

'Costs too damned much, and you never know if them Feds is watchin' what yo buy in the store. They got all kinds ways of knowin' where you spend yore buck, I hear.'

'Then how we gonna water the whisky?'

'I been thinkin', we could bring in our own water from the town supply.'

Randy shook his head vehemently.

'That shit is expensive, Buddy, y'all gotta pay 'em every month for every gallon you draw. And I hear that iffen you got a leak, y'all gotta pay 'em for the water that spills out too. Anyhow, the Feds would know we was usin' a lotta water, y'all think about that?'

'I weren't thinkin' of letting 'em know, ain't none a they goddamned business. The big water main for the town runs along the road down the hill thar, ain't no more than a couple hundred yards away through the wood, we can tap into her and nobody be no wiser. I already got the spigot, jest need me some pipe.'

Randy shook his head in wonder.

'You surely got the brains in this family, Buddy, Ma allus said it.'

Chapter Eleven

Miriam O'Hagan tapped her pen against her coffee mug to get the attention of the team.

'Good Morning, ladies and gentlemen. I won't keep you long, we've all got work to do, but I want to brief you on a number of issues.'

'First of all, well done again for your efforts over the last few days, you're an impressive bunch of boffins by any standards. You are all giving this a lot of attention, and every day I look at you I am more and more convinced that we can do this. There isn't a lab in Russia or Germany or anywhere else that can match you guys in terms of productivity, or in an ability to think outside not only the box but outside the room. So although things may get heated over the next month, and angry words may be exchanged, we all need to get over that and keep focussed on the prize. I'm going to go around the table to a couple of you who are involved in key parts of this project; that's no reflection on the people whose extraordinary efforts are keeping the rest of the ship afloat, but all this effort is in all our interests, long term. I'll start with Kevin. Kevin?'

Kevin Kelly stood up and cleared his throat, speaking

hesitantly at first but with his voice growing in strength as he began to speak about the things he was comfortable with.

'Thank you, Miriam, I appreciate your kind words. I'll bring you up to speed briefly, the detail is for another day. Suffice to say that we have synthesised the new variant in the lab; we have a real live virus variant right here in Boyle, safely locked away in a safe in the secure area. We could, if we wanted to, get involved in chemical warfare against England this minute. That was a joke, by the way, they're doing a good job of running themselves into the ground as it is.'

'Anyway, it wasn't difficult to synthesise it, the data we got from our former colleague in California was very detailed, and so I'm quite confident that what we have is the exact variant that is starting to affect some American cities. You will have heard the American President on TV yesterday talking down the threat, so it looks like they haven't a clue, and that they have no idea where to start. Normally if they had a handle on the way to deal with this, it would be buried in the speech somewhere, but there was nothing.'

'Our next step is to attempt to infect a, erm, black person with the virus, and to check for antibodies before and after, and compare. We also need to infect a white person, and to look at the antibody response. I understand that Caroline has not one but two, erm, black persons of colour in the GP wing, they're just finishing a trial for that Kissitbetter patch. Once she has had them checked out lung-wise etcetera, we can spray a suspension of the virus up their noses and then see what happens. We will have to ensure very tight controls on isolation of course, even more strict protocols than usual. Full spacesuits for anyone handling it, airlock protocol, deep clean of all areas where testers have been, etcetera. We don't want to infect half the town with this damned variant.'

'That's it from me for now, I'll hand over to Karen and she will tell you what she's found out since Monday. Karen?'

Karen Doyle got to her feet and looked around the room nervously.

'Ladies and gentlemen, thanks for your attention. Just one update in particular that I only found out an hour ago. It appears that the specification for the new vaccine will be much broader than a mere injectable immuniser. Our former colleague Sean has again come good, in fairness, they got a secret briefing from the US department of Health that the new product must not only be injectable, but must also work as a nasal spray, and also, get this, as an oral suspension. They want to be able to give it in a glass of water, in dilutions as high as one in ten million!'

Billy Robinson raised a hand.

'Are you sure about the last bit, Karen? That seems very strange indeed, I've never heard of a spec like that.'

Karen reddened slightly, annoyed at the inference that she had made a mistake.

'I'm absolutely sure, Billy. I made him go over it twice just to be certain. They want to be able to give it as a drink, like by adding just one drop to a glass of water, or to a barrel of water, more exactly.'

'So it will have to be very stable, at all temperatures?'

'Not just that, it will be crucial that an overdose will just be dealt with by the kidneys, without harming the patient. If they want to add drops to water, it will be difficult to control the dosage. And they appear to want to be able to give it out randomly without controls, so it must be safe if people come back and take several doses, or if somebody gets the dosage wildly wrong and gives somebody the whole vial instead of just a drop.'

Miriam directed her question directly to Karen.

'What do you think? What are they up to? Are they thinking of bypassing the medical system altogether and getting untrained people to dispense it?'

'I honestly don't know, Miriam, although it looks as though that could be a possible answer. Sean had no idea either, and he wasn't too concerned in any case. He said that somebody above his pay grade will figure it all out. But is certainly throws away the rule book when it comes to pandemic vaccinations. If a safe vaccine is manufactured, with effectively no need for any kind of controls in terms of dosage, it will rewrite the entire narrative in this field.'

'And can we do it, do you think? Can we be the ones to break the mould and be first to the post with this kind of technology?'

'I believe so, Miriam. Look at it this way, we are ahead of the American labs at least, and maybe ahead of the others too. The spec hasn't even been released and we already have a synthesised virus sample, and we have our couple of potential test people locked away in the GP unit. We also have some of the best minds in the scientific world right here, in Boyle, so I don't see why not.'

'Have you any thoughts, Karen? On the science? This could be your day in the sun.'

Karen blushed again, looking down at her notes before giving an answer.

'I have a theory, I've discussed it with Kevin and I'm sure he doesn't mind me laying it out before the rest of you guys. I've looked at the genome of this virus in detail, it's icosahedral in form, or isometric if you prefer the term.

The viral genome is made up of double stranded RNA. This kind of virus, as you know, normally interacts with proteins functioning in a narrow band of cellular processes as well as in intracellular transport and localisation within the cell.'

Miriam held up her hand to interrupt.

'Karen, can you keep it simple, maybe circulate the others on the pure science later on the secure internal mail. You need to remember that my training was in mathematics and physics, I rely on you guys to run the ship while I hustle for business and make it all pay. So, can you give me the kindergarten version?'

'Sorry, Miriam, I tend to forget that not everybody is a bio. Okay, in short, I think I can see the area where the bit of protein lies in the DNA of a person of black colour. I think I know what it is in other words that causes the virus to turn away and say, I don't like this pub, I'm going down the street to somewhere brighter, where I feel safer maybe, or where I'm not barred.'

Billy Robinson clapped his hands.

'Good analogy, Karen. You'd make a fine teacher. Go ahead, sorry I interrupted.'

'Okay, as I was saying, I think I have figured this out, not the detail, but I have the right area, I'm sure of it. I think we're very close to designing a protein that can be given to a white person to make their DNA appear black to an intruder virus.'

Miriam sat forward excitedly.

'Close? How close?'

'I don't know, but I really do think I've almost got it. I pretty much have the detail, I just need to be sure that the body will start to manufacture it once it has been shown what it looks like, if you understand my over-

JOHN MULLIGAN

simplification. But I can almost say that I know what it will look like.'

'And assuming you are on the right track, would the product be both injectable and capable of being administered orally?'

'Yes, that's the whole point, once it's ingested in any way. Of course injection is still going to be the surest way of delivering it to the blood and other interstitial fluids.'

'The what?'

'Sorry, the blood, lymph and cellular fluids. Injection into the blood and/or muscle is always going to be the best delivery method, but in theory it should be possible to use broader strokes, like orally in suspension.'

'With no risks from overdosing?'

'Not if it's given orally. The body is designed to deal with a lot of foreign matter taken by mouth, the kidneys and bowels are more than capable of getting rid of any surplus. I mean, we all take stuff into our bodies that maybe would be better off going straight to the toilet, to give our kidneys a break.'

Miriam gathered her papers and indicated that the briefing was over.

'You guys keep on this, keep talking it over among yourselves as much as you need to. Many hands, and all that. This is all looking good, so keep the pressure on. And remember, we're a team, so no secrets, no trying to be a hero. Share, share, share with the information, like we always do. Now get back to work, and we'll meet again tomorrow, same time.'

'And just one more thing. Or two more things, to be precise. First, they're black people, not people of colour or anything else. I asked Caroline to ask the two black guys in the GP unit what they liked to be called. So it's

66

definitely not Blacks, or Negroes or any variant thereof; it's black people. And secondly, myself included, we should really stop calling them 'guinea pigs' and stop referring to the drug assessment and testing unit as 'the GP unit'. One of these days one of us will use the 'GP' term in the wrong place, like at a press conference when we claim our rightful place among the nations of the world, so to speak, and we'll look bad. Now, get to it, time is money.'

Chapter Twelve

Major Mike Callaghan had a spring in his step as he marched smartly along the corridor that led to the Oval Office. He saluted the aide at the desk in the outer lobby and stood to attention while she picked up a handset and called through to the President.

'It's Major Callaghan, Sir. Okay, I'll send him in.'

The Major strode towards the door and tapped lightly before entering. President Daniels sat behind his desk, idly doodling on a blotter.

'Come in, Mike. You wanted to see me?'

'Yes, Sir. I wanted to report on progress with the water injection systems.'

'Good, I hope you have good news for me on that front?'

'Yes, Sir. As of this morning, all the existing pumping stations on the Project Reduce programme have had the additional stroke pumps and reservoirs fitted, so we're ready to add the vaccine whenever it is ready to go.'

'And the new ones that we identified, the Klan areas, anti-vax hotspots etcetera?'

'All complete as of yesterday, Sir. It all went very smoothly.'

'Good work, Major. Any problems, any issues? Did

anybody question your guys about what they were doing?'

'No, Sir. All installations are complete and tested, and no reports of any of the installers being questioned about purpose by existing plant operatives. It appears that local managers and staff in water companies are so used to Federal health and safety control and monitoring systems being installed, they don't consider this as anything out of the ordinary, Sir.'

'Excellent, Major. So what happens next?'

'Well, Sir, we are retrofitting telemetry on all the installations nationwide while we are waiting on the vaccine, just adding a piece of kit to every stroke pump control panel to let us know when it is running, how much product it is delivering, and when the reservoirs are running low. We've filled the tanks with water for testing purposes, and so far it looks like the systems will last for about five to six weeks before refilling. That is about half as long as the anaphrodisiac systems; we'll be using about twice the volume of the vaccine compared to the anaphrodisiac in order to get faster immunity in populations, Sir.'

'Any provisiac? What does that mean, exactly? I didn't want to ask the Doctor the other day in case he thinks I'm not up to speed. I never really trust our Russian comrades, even though they are our closest allies nowadays.'

The Major shuffled his feet uncomfortably.

'I, ah, I'm not a hundred percent sure of the exact science in any of this stuff, Sir, I'm just a military man, they didn't teach us science at West Point, just tactics. But as I understand it, it's the equivalent of throwing a bucket of cold water over every horny dog in the state, puts the young males off chasing poontang all the time, they lose interest I guess.'

'So what we've done is make these folks lazy when it comes to chasing tail?'

'Yes, Sir, I believe that sums it up pretty good. But like I say, I'm not too sure how that all works, except that it does, so that's good enough for me.'

'Spoken like a true soldier, Major Callaghan. Just shoot when you get the order, don't ask too many questions?'

'You got it, Sir. Kill them all and let God sort them out, as we used to say about the Arabs.'

The President laughed.

'Yes, we shoulda done a lot more of that, not listened to every bleeding-heart liberal telling us we needed to see the world from the point of view of the so-called 'third world.' I reckon we need to remember that this is America, the leader of the free world, and we need to look after America first. Let the Arabs and the goddamned Chinese look after themselves. We need more men like you in charge of our military, Major Callaghan.'

'Thank you, Sir. That's mighty kind of you to say so, Sir. Do you mind if I ask a question of my own?'

'Sure, fire ahead.'

'I just wondered about two things, Sir. First, when do you expect the vaccine to be delivered to my team, and how long do we got to install it in the tanks?

'Well, Major, I don't have an exact answer for you to either of those questions. Doctor Belyaev tells me that the specification for the vaccine has already gone out to the American and Russian labs, and will be going out to labs in Europe in another week. So your guess is as good as mine, they might crack this in three months, maybe, which would take us up to Labor Day or a week or so after it, and I guess you would have another couple of months to put the shit in the pumping stations. But those are just guesses, I leave that kind of stuff to the experts.'

'And how about FDA approval, Sir?'

'Don't worry about that, Major. Once we have a vaccine we'll organise the manufacture and you can start putting it in the tanks while we wait for the FDA, so the minute they green-light us we can just turn the taps on. So you should target Labor Day, is what I'm saying.'

'That's good, I just needed an estimate, Sir. Thank you.'

'So is that workable for your guys, Major? How long will it take for you to place this stuff in the water places?'

'We can do most all of them in three to four weeks, Sir, including the ones on Operation Reduce. But if I have to ramp that up, we can do that too. I just have two agents cleared for this work, and they are on a need-to-know basis with what we are putting in the tanks, but if necessary I could draft in a couple of more guys with a high security clearance level.'

'Hold off on doing that just yet, Major. At the end of the day, we gotta cater for the worst case scenario.'

'Such as, Sir?'

'Well, if this all blows up in our faces, we just got two guys to silence. Last thing we want is a whistle-blower explaining how a whole bunch of Blacks or Klansmen just had their balls fall off or some such shit. I like to keep these things tight, so far only me and you and Vladimir know about this, and the two agents know just enough and no more. Let's keep it that way, I want to be back in this chair in thirty-three, and I guess you will be due a promotion at that point too. If a bucket of shit hits the fan, I'll be back selling trucks and you'll be whitewashing the kerbs in some army base in Arkansas.'

'Understood, Sir. And Doctor Belyaev, Sir?'

'Vladimir? Nah, Vlad will be getting that big prize the Swedes give out, he'll get the credit for this vaccination strategy and I'll be having a word with their ambassador, the guy we got the dirt on from that seminar weekend last year.'

'Drugs and hookers, Sir?'

'That's it, Major. Don't get me wrong, I ain't no spoilsport, but there's a time and a place for everything.'

'I agree, Sir. Will that be all, Sir?'

'Yes, Major, keep up the good work. Off you go.'

Chapter Thirteen

Lucky woke from a doze as he heard the tap on the door. It opened sharply and Nurse Cohen entered, dragging a surgical trolley. She shook his room-mate's foot and roused him from his sleep.

'Wakey, wakey, boys. Time for the body-work.'

Awe sat up sleepily and swore.

'Man, I was dreamin' I was in Gorton, that some chick was shakin' my leg.'

'Well, try not to sound so disappointed. Sit up there and roll up your sleeve.'

Awe yelped as she ripped off the patch, followed by the two sticking plasters. She took an electronic tablet from her trolley and photographed both scars, before wiping the skin with an alcohol wipe and sticking two new plasters in place. She followed by placing a large patch over both dressings.

'Any soreness, itching, anything like that.'

He grinned at the older woman, grabbing at her leg.

'Yeah lady, I got an itch right enough, but it ain't on my arm. How about you fix that for me?'

She slapped his hand away and laughed scornfully.

'I'd say you're the world's leading expert on scratching

that particular itch. Careful now, or I'll throw you off the programme, send you off to your precious Gorton without any money in your pocket.'

'You can't do that, we almost done.'

'You didn't read the small print, Sonny; I can do pretty much anything I like. Now behave yourself, I'm old enough to be your mother.'

She turned to Lucky and pointed to his sleeve.

'Roll up, roll up! Let's see how that arm is doing.'

Lucky pushed the sleeve up to his shoulder and the nurse pulled the patch from his arm, more gently than she had with his room-mate. She peeled off the two sticking-plasters and looked closely at the wounds.

'You surely heal well, Mister Oyeleye. That scar is almost gone on the normal plaster, and completely gone on the Kissitbetter one. Excellent, that's remarkable. You have great recovery powers, you surely do.'

She used the small tablet to photograph the wounds and then put everything back on the trolley.

'That's you done, Mister Oyeleye. Finished, apart from a check-up by Doctor Mannion in the morning, you've completed the programme.'

'But it's not a full week yet?'

'Doesn't matter with a trial like this, we can't get a better result than a one hundred percent restoration of tissue like we got with you. So you can collect your money in the morning and head for Lagos.'

Lucky was suddenly worried.

'I don't want to go back to Lagos, there is nothing there for me. Do you have any more work for me, here?'

The nurse unlocked the wheels on the trolley with her toe and moved towards the door.

'That's not my side of the business, I just look after

patient welfare, stick the needles in the arms and make sure the pills go down the throats. Or just stick on a few plasters, as in this case. But I don't do the recruiting, that's Caroline's department.'

'Will you speak with her? I would very much like to do some more of this work, please.'

She opened the door and pulled the trolley into the corridor.

'Leave it with me, I'll talk to her before she goes home.'

The door slammed and the lock clicked shut. Awe lay back on the bed and looked in some amazement at his room-mate.

'Man, why you want do another trial straight off? I'm goin' crazy in here, I gotta get out for a few weeks. I'm goin' back to Gorton. Party party, you know?'

Lucky sat on the edge of his bed, shoulders slumped.

'I do not wish to leave, if at all possible. I need to earn some more money.'

'But you got money now, Man. You got four thousand pound, man. Come to Gorton, you like it, lots of black bruvvers there, and plenty chicks and weed and shit, you know?'

'No, thank you, Mister Awe. I am married already, I have a good wife. Also, I need to earn some money to pay for my airline ticket.'

'Ticket? Where you goin'?'

'Nowhere. I have to send money home to the people that paid for my ticket to come here, it is two thousand euros. And I have to send my suit back to my wife, she can give it to another relative so he can get into Europe.'

'Man! That sound complicated. Why he need the suit, this other Nigga?'

75

'So he looks respectable. The people that pay for the ticket, they also give lessons on how to speak to the police in Europe, what things to say, you know?'

'So this guy coming to Ireland too?'

'No, he intends to go to Scotland.'

'Yeah, I hear a lot about Scotland, some bruvvers from Gorton, they go to the border sometime, try to cross over to Scotland. But it not easy, too many polices and armies guys.'

'Yes, we hear about this way to access the European Union, to cross the border from England, but I hear it is almost impossible. It is better I think to fly there, wear a nice suit and talk about the places you want to visit. You have to be polite, rudeness will get you back on the next flight, if you are lucky. Or maybe in jail for a few days, I hear all the stories from people that tried.'

'Man, everybody want to be someplace else. I just want be back on my manor, money in my pocket.'

The dinner orders were delivered at six thirty, the pinging of the cupboard door alerting them to the arrival of the food. Awe tucked into his bowl of lentil stew, and Lucky half-heartedly ate his steak and chips. They opened two cans of soft drinks from the fridge and lay on their beds. Lucky was downcast, reluctantly engaging in the usual banter with his room-mate. Awe looked at him sympathetically.

'Hey, Man! Lose the long face, Man! She say she talk to the lady, so maybe you ain't goin' nowhere. Mebbe you gonna have a long stretch in this here jail? That make you happy, Man?'

Lucky shook his head.

'I don't see it like jail, Apple. I have never slept in a bed this good, never had a shower in my house, especially not in my own private bathroom. And I never got such food in my life, delivered to the kitchen. We don't even have to wash the dishes! And in one week they pay me more money that a policeman makes in two months, even the most crooked one. I honestly feel that I can stay here forever, if they will have me.'

Awe laughed in amazement.

'Man, yo never done no time in prison. You spend a month in HMP Manchester and yo change that rap. I go crazy in solitary, like here. I just stay for short time they allow me, then take the money and live for a while.'

'I think maybe we have different aims in life, Mister Apple.'

'It look that way. What aim yo got?'

'To have a good job and a nice house, and to have children who go to a good school and get good jobs. And maybe a car, but not necessarily. The bus is fine.'

'That crazy. Man! Yo can get house anyhow in Gorton, DSS give it you. You break it, they give you other one. Also money, not much, but you can make extra, you know. And if you want car, you take one, no problem.'

'But do you not have any ambition?'

'Yeah, course! I want to be the boss pill-man, drive big car and got nice suits, chicks come runnin' an all that. But that for later; for now, I like party.'

They lapsed into silence for a while. Awe picked up his remote control and flicked through the choices on the screen.

'You want watch sumpin? Or you want watch by yourself?'

'I do not mind, much. What do you have in mind?'

'This here called 'Moone Boy,' it made right here, in Boyle, many year ago. Big nigga from this town here, he

77

the star, guy that wins all the statue, you know?'

'Statue?'

'Yeah, gold statue they gets for best movie guys. He wins lotta dem. You think they is real gold? That nigga gotta be rich, man!'

'Okay, switch it on, we'll watch that one.'

Chapter Fourteen

Randy Corless sweated in the heat as he dug the loose soil around the big water main. His brother Buddy kept watch for any traffic on the dirt road. Buddy looked down into the hole and pointed to the pipe.

'Dig around her, y'all need ter git the clamp around her.'

His brother chopped under the exposed main with the spade until he could get his hands right around the pipe. Buddy handed him a bottle and a rag.

'Wipe her off with the whisky, get her clean so she don't leak when she clamped up.'

Randy uncorked the bottle with his teeth and spilled some of the contents on to the rag. He wiped the dirt off the blue plastic pipe until it was clean, then took a swig from the bottle before corking it again.

'Gimme that doohickey thar, get her done while she clean.'

Buddy separated the two halves of the clamp and passed them down to his brother.

'You know how to fix that thang?'

'Shore I does, jest put the two bits around the pipe and bolt 'em together, right?'

'You got it. You ain't so dumb.'

Randy bolted the two halves of the circular collar in place around the water main, tightening the nuts with an open-ended spanner. His brother started to unroll the coil of piping that he had hidden under the trees, feeding the free end of the pipe to Randy.

'Jest fit her in the spigot thar, tighten her up, and we suckin' gas.'

Randy did as instructed, pushing the end of the small pipe into the spigot that protruded from the newly-fitted collar, and tightening up the connecting nut. He screwed the valve down and heard the rasping sound as the inbuilt cutter opened a hole in the side of the heavy plastic water main. The coil of small piping jerked as the water started to flow. Buddy whooped as he saw it come alive.

'We got her! We got ourselves some water company juice. Get outa thar and fill in that hole afore someone sees us.'

Randy frantically filled in the hole, and Buddy started to roll out the big coil of pipe that was by now spraying water from its free end, dragging it up the hill in the direction of the cabin. Randy used the mattock to dig a shallow trench to hide the slim, black pipe, covering it over with earth as he went. In half an hour they had laid the pipe all the way to the house. Buddy folded over the end of the plastic pipe to stop the flow, tying it in place with a loop of baling wire.

'Reckon we put a faucet on her tomorrow, but we done good today.'

'We don't need no faucet, we can bend her over any time we wants to stop her.'

'We oughta done that years ago, we been drinkin' that well water all our lives, carryin' it in buckets. We coulda had it come here by isself, no hardship.'

'Waal, we got her now. We got runnin' water in the house.'

'Not in the house, asactly, but it shore is damn near it. Fill up that coffee pot thar and make us a brew.'

Randy unfolded the end of the pipe and drank from the flow of water before washing out the coffee pot and refilling it.'

'That damn good water. No more cow-shit flavor.'

Buddy sat back in the chair on the porch and watched as his brother put the pot on the stove. He rocked forward and back for a while, saying nothing. Randy looked at him quizzically.

'Y'all thinkin' about some thang, what ya got?'

Buddy slowed his rocking, putting his feet on the wooden floor.

'You remember that ole ice machine we picked up at the town dump?'

'Yeah, it still in the barn. What you thinkin?'

'Waal, now we got water, and we got a little tap into the power company line too, we got us the makins.'

'Makins of what?'

'Ice. We can make ice. That machine she fine, she jest need some oil in the compressor. We got free water, free 'lectric, we can make us some ice.'

'We don't need no ice. I told ya, shoulda left that damn machine right there, in the dump. Near broke ma back puttin' her on the truck, she weigh about half ton, I reckon.'

'We don't need no ice, but Bill McCauley, he sell a lotta ice every day. Five dollars a bag, folks jest linin' up to buy it.'

'Why don't they make they own ice, they all got fancy houses and refrigerators?'

'They too lazy, ain't nobody want to bother fillin' little

trays of water and waitin' for 'em to freeze up. They wants to go to the icebox and tek out all the ice they need.'

Randy pondered this information for a minute. He added coffee grounds to the pot and put two mugs on the plank that sat across the corner of the porch railing.

'So how we gonna get the bags?'

'Ain't no problem gettin' bags, you can telephone the place that we gets the bottles from, and they send them in the truck.'

'How much you think Bill McCauley pay us fer the bags of ice?'

'Danged iffen I knows, but it all profit, 'cept fer them bags. I reckon he pay us three dollars, easy.'

'Damn, you shore is one smart dude, Buddy. Ma always said so.'

Chapter Fifteen

Lucky sat up as he heard the tap on the door. He paused the episode of the Moone Boy show and took out his earbuds. In the other bed, Apple Wedgewood Enright snored loudly. Caroline poked her head around the door.

'Lucky, can you come with me, please?'

Lucky got hesitantly to his feet, nervous about the possible reasons for being summoned from his cosy cocoon. Despite the boredom of the project, he was feeling very comfortable and well looked after in the small space he shared with the half-crazy Englishman. The woman looked him in the eye as she closed the door behind them, smiling in a friendly manner.'

'Why the serious face? Don't look so worried, the boss just wants to talk to you.'

She led him back to the reception area, and through another door that was guarded by a keypad and a face-recognition camera. Lucky followed and found himself in the softly-lit corridor of a wood-floored office-building. She opened a door and waved him into a boardroom with a long, oval table surrounded by comfortable office chairs.

'Take a seat there, Lucky. I'll be back in a minute with Miriam.'

Lucky sat nervously into one of the chairs and waited. In a few minutes Caroline returned with a slightly plump, blonde woman who was heavily made up and smartly dressed in a blue skirt and matching jacket. He stood up as she entered, and she extended a hand in greeting.

'How are you, Mister Ole Ole? I'm Miriam O'Hagan, I'm CEO of Boyle Labs. Thank you for coming to this meeting at such short notice. Please, sit down, make yourself comfortable. Would you like tea, or coffee?'

'It is Oyeleye, Madam, Lucky Oyeleye. But you should just call me 'Lucky.' And thank you Madam, I had some of your excellent coffee just a short time ago, I am fine.'

She laughed and pointed to the bottles of water and glasses that lay in front of each place on the table.

"Lucky' it is, so. Help yourself to water if you feel like it. Now, you must be wondering why I wanted to see you?'

'I hope it is because you have more work for me, Madam. I appreciate the employment you have given me this week, but quite honestly I am a little short of money and I would appreciate the opportunity of being of further service to your fine organisation.'

'Well, now, Lucky, I suppose that's the nub of what I wanted to say to you, with certain conditions attached, you might say. In short, we were very happy with your assistance this week, you're a good, healthy specimen of a man, and you have a physique that can withstand a bit of prodding and poking, so to speak.'

'I hope I am in good health, Madam, certainly. I do not smoke or imbibe alcohol, or take drugs of any kind.'

She laughed loudly and flapped a hand at Lucky.

'Less of the formalities, Lucky, and call me Miriam. And as for the smoking and drinking and taking party pills, I'd say that makes you unique among all the candidates that come through that door there.'

'Yes, Madam, Miriam. Thank you.'

'Now, let me tell you why we asked you to join us. I'll get right to the point, you have done very well this week on the wound-dressing trial, your case has given us some really good data, the kind that clients want. I'd say a lot of that is down to your underlying good health and healing abilities. Now, we are embarking on another project that requires some volunteers whose overall health is good, and whose bodies are able to fight off minor infections etcetera. Are you interested?'

Lucky brightened at the news.

'Yes, Madam. Miriam, sorry. Yes, it would be my wish to stay here as long as possible, assisting you with your scientific endeavours.'

The CEO screeched with laughter.

'My word, Lucky, you have a way with words, you surely do. Well, we can certainly do business if you're up for it. We are looking for a few fit and healthy individuals, one of whom at least is of African origin.'

'Black, you mean, or South African?'

'Yes, black, exactly. We need to firstly take some small blood and tissue samples from you, nothing too intrusive of course. Then we want to expose you to a mild form of a virus, won't kill you or anything, but you might get a bit of a cold. However it is our view that it will not affect you at all, and that is actually the result we are looking for. Measuring that will involve swabbing your nostrils and throat, as well as a small blood sample, a momentary discomfort but nothing to worry about. How does all that sound to you?'

'It sounds very good, Miriam. I would be delighted to do this work for another week.'

'A week? We're probably looking at up to two months, do you think you could handle the boredom? It would involve living on your own in a room like the one you're sharing with that other young man from England, and possibly also sharing with people from time to time to see whether you are carrying a virus that might infect them, even if you are showing no sign of symptoms.'

'And there is no danger in this for me?'

'No, of course not. Just that you might catch a cold or a flu in the worst case scenario, but we would make sure that it didn't impact on your health.'

'Then I am happy to accept, where do I sign the paper?'

'Caroline has a contract prepared, have you got it there, Caroline?'

The other woman produced a printed contract from her folder and put it in front of Lucky. He signed all the pages where she indicated, and placed the pen back on the table before excusing himself.

'Please, is there a bathroom nearby? I have drunk too much of your excellent coffee and tea.'

The CEO pointed to the door at the other end of the room.

'Through there, Lucky. We'll go through any questions you might have when you get back.

As the door closed behind him, the two women high-fived each other in delight. The CEO was the first to speak.

'What a frigging capture! Totally compliant, black as a ton of coal on a November night, and healthy as a trout as well. We need to treat him well, okay? Last thing we want is him deciding to walk away, a good healthy black man is a rare fish around here.'

The administrator smiled wryly.

'Lucky won't be going anywhere, the poor devil hasn't two cents to his name I'd say. He asked me to get his suit cleaned, he has to send it back to the next family member for when they want to make a break for the border. I find the whole thing really sad.'

'Did you get it cleaned?'

'Yes, of course, but there's bugger all in his bag, just a few threadbare clothes, a cheap tracksuit and runners and a picture of a young lady, might be his wife by the look of it.'

'Ah, the poor lad. That reminds me of the stories my grandfather used to tell me, about emigrating to England back in the last century, after the war. They used to send back the suit and a few bob for the next guy to buy a ticket.'

'England? Who would want to go there for any kind of a better life?'

'We tend to forget it wasn't always like it is now, it's not that long ago since it was okay, before they left Europe and went their own way. It's only since Scotland left them that they really started to slide. Anyway, we'd better show a bit of support for our newest recruit, can you take him down town and buy him a few decent clothes? I wouldn't want him leaving here looking like a tramp when the trial is over. Put it on the account in Boles.'

'I'll do that now if you like, they don't close for another hour and a half.'

'And do you know what we should do? We should book him into Frybrook House for a night, we get a good corporate rate there. It would be nice to let him have a taste of luxury away from that cell he's in.'

'I can do that, no problem. I'll look after his borrowed

suit as well, parcel it up and post it for him. I'll get him to just give me the address.'

'Anything else he might need? It might be the last night he spends outside of here for a month, or maybe more, we don't want him cracking up on us.'

'I'll see if he needs anything, but he's not the kind to be too demanding, from what I've seen of him. He's a nice lad anyway, and it won't kill us to be nice to him. He's a key part of this project, and if it all comes together well, a few euro won't be here or there.'

'I agree, but don't go mad with my money either!'

Lucky re-entered the room and sat down again. The CEO smiled.

'Well, Lucky, we're delighted to have you on the team. I was just saying to Caroline that she must take you down town and buy you some decent clothes, and see whatever else you might need before you lock in here for a few weeks. Anything come to mind?'

'Thank you for your generosity, Miriam, but really there's no need for you to be any more generous than you have been already. But there is one thing.'

'Just ask, the worst we can say is no.'

'I wanted to go to the post office, to send my suit back to my friend in Lagos.'

'Consider it done, Lucky. Just write out the address and Caroline will take care of it. Anything else?'

'Please, I would like to call my wife back home, she will be worried that I haven't called her.'

'Of course, you can go to Caroline's office when you come back from town, and call her from there. Just one thing, you cannot discuss the detail of the trial you have been on, or the one you are embarking on. The confidentiality clause in the contract strictly applies.'

'Of course, but what should I tell her?'

'Just that you are working in a laboratory, as an assistant to my team. Tell her you just do the work, filing paperwork and that kind of thing, and that you don't really understand what it entails. Are you okay with that?'

'Yes, I don't like to be untruthful to her, but I suppose in this instance it is justifiable.'

'Good man. Okay, I'll leave you in Caroline's capable hands, and we'll talk some more during the week.'

Chapter Sixteen

Mickey Small stood in the shadows beside the bridge, waiting. A man stopped under the light at the centre of the span and peered at his phone, removing a glove to answer a message. Mickey saw his chance and darted quickly from his hiding place, grabbing at the phone and hitting out at his victim.

Dazed and sore, he looked up at the street light from where he lay on his back on the wet street.

'Why did you hit me? You didn't have to do that, I'm calling the Guards.'

The older man laughed uncontrollably.

'Ye should do that all right, Mickey. And tell them you met a lad that was more than a match for ye. Now, do ye want to get up and have another go at me, or do ye want to crawl off to whatever hole you came out of? Face it Mickey, as a mugger, you're a failure.'

Mickey got unsteadily to his feet and ran away, ducking down the lane behind Boles shop and on to Saint Patrick's Street He ran towards home, but had second thoughts and doubled back and ran into Clarke's Gastropub and took a seat at the counter.

'A pint of Smithwicks, Miss.'

'The young woman behind the bar smiled.

'I thought you were barred, Mickey?'

'No, I'm not, Alison unbarred me again, I promised I wouldn't do any mugging in here anymore.'

'You mean attempted mugging? I thought that woman gave you a good few slaps and took her handbag back?'

Mickey straightened his shoulders indignantly.

'I gave it back to her, there's no way she'd have took it back off me only I let her. Mickey Small doesn't surrender, I'm tellin' ye.'

'I'll give ye half a pint, if ye have money.'

Mickey went through his pockets and dug out some coins.

'Is that enough?'

The barmaid laughed and drew a half pint of beer from the tap. She scooped up his money and added some coins from her tip jar before ringing the total up on the till. Mickey took a sip and wiped his mouth with the back of his hand.

'That's the finest. Man, when I get a few quid I'll come in here and have ten pints, so I will, and some o' that nice food.'

'Are you coming into money, Mickey?'

'I am, surely. I had an interview for a job.'

'A job? Who would be thinking of giving you a job?'

'Boyle Labs, I had an interview with them a couple of months ago, so I'm sure they'll be calling on me soon.'

The barmaid turned her head away and smiled.

'Oh, any day now, Mickey. Any day. They'll probably send a taxi for you.'

'And I answered an advertisement for a job as an aeroplane engineer, I told them I do watch every episode of Air Crash Investigations, I know them off by heart.'

'One of them will surely be looking for you one of these days so. You'll be in the money, no more mugging.'

'They will, and when I get my wages I'll come in and buy ten pints, so I will.'

'The taxi might even be at home now, Mickey, waiting for you. You'd better check, maybe?'

He looked anxiously at her face, looking for any sign she might be joking, but her expression was impassive.

'Maybe I'd better go home, in case they call.'

He drank up the remainder of his beer and banged the glass on the counter.

'I'm off, so, see you soon.'

He pushed open the door and ran away towards the outskirts of town. Outside the small cottage he retrieved the key from under the stone and went inside and closed the door, settling himself into the solitary armchair. The remains of the meals-on-wheels dinner were still in their foil dish, so he took a fork from the sink and began to eat the cold food, anxiously keeping an eye on the street in case of visitors.

Half an hour later, he began to think that there was nobody coming, so he decided to try another mugging. He put on his black coat and black balaclava and ran back down the street, swinging right into the lane behind Boles. He ran up and down the lane a few times, looking out for any possible victims. One man looked promising as he staggered out of the pub by the bridge, but he was big and Mickey wasn't sure whether he could take him on. His back was still sore from having hit the roadway hard earlier, and he didn't want a repeat of the incident.

The man took a packet from his pocket and extracted a cigarette, clicking his lighter several times until it flared. He put the lighter back in his pocket as he drew deeply on the smoke, exhaling a long cloud that mixed with the steady drizzle. Mickey decided to try his trick.

'You dropped your wallet, mister.'

'Did I?'

He reached into his inside pocket and took out a wallet, and Mickey darted forward and tried to grab it. The man roared at him, causing him to stop in his tracks.'

'If ye do, Mickey Small, I'll throw you over that wall into the river, I swear to God. Go away and mug someone else.'

Mickey turned sharply and ran back down the lane. He didn't see the big black man emerge from the back door of the clothing store, or the woman who followed close behind him. He cannoned into the man who looked at him in surprise before dropping the bags he was carrying and grabbing him by the arm in a strong grip.

'You! You're the man who tried to mug me last week. You made me lose my sim card, you knocked it into the river.'

'Never saw you before, it must have been someone else, I'm not the only mugger in Boyle, you know.'

The woman picked up the bags and laughed.

'Oh yes, you are, Mickey Small. Our own Boyle mugger, but to be honest we're all getting a bit tired of it by now. Would you not try another career, like robbing banks or something?'

Mickey dropped his gaze and looked at the ground

'I'm sorry, Mister, I thought you wouldn't miss a few quid, you looked rich.'

Lucky laughed sadly.

'I'm certainly not rich, Sir. But please, you should remember that all crimes have victims, you hurt people when you try to steal from them.'

'Sorry, I won't do it again. Will you let me go now?'

Lucky relaxed his grip on the man's arm. He was about to run away when he recognised Caroline.

'You're the woman from Boyle Labs. Any word of my interview? When am I getting the job?'

'Don't call us, Mister Small, we'll call you.'

Mickey ran off down the lane.

'Okay, I'll wait at home so, you can send a taxi.'

Chapter Seventeen

Miriam breezed into the boardroom, her mood more cheerful than usual. She closed the door and sat heavily into her chair at the end of the table.

'Right, guys, sorry I'm a bit late. I know you're all busy, so we'll crack on with all possible speed. I've asked Caroline and Nurse Cohen from our secure unit to join us in these senior team meetings as well, they're trusted members of the squad who are key players in all of this, and they may need to input into some of what we are discussing today. So, without further ado, Billy, can you start off?'

Billy got to his feet and pointed to his colleagues who were seated to his left.

'Great progress by the team, Miriam. Essentially, Karen has cracked the puzzle, although Kevin has some reservations, but we'll come to those in a minute. From a pure science point of view, I'm nailing my colours to the mast, so to speak, I don't think those reservations are anything we should worry about. Of course I respect Kevin's scientific analysis, but I think the risks are way off the spectrum and the likelihood of any problem occurring is so small as to be incalculable. Anyway, having said all that, I'll hand over to Karen first.'

Karen Doyle got to her feet and used her small remote control to switch on the projector. The first image appeared on the screen, an electron micrograph image of a strand of human DNA. She used the laser on the end of the remote control to point out a number of sites on the complex image.

'If you look here, and here, you'll see the areas where the differences between a black-skinned and a white-skinned person occur. This strand is from my own DNA, and this one…'

She clicked the pointer and a second slide appeared, this time with sections of two DNA strands in the image.

'…this second one is from our associate, Mister Oyeleye. You will see here that this tiny site, just here, is where the differences occur. The variance between my DNA and that of Mister Oyeleye, apart from the chromosomal gender variance of course, is a tiny fraction, thousandths of a percentile and almost immeasurable. But that's it, just there.'

She circled the red light from the pointer around a small area on each image.

'So, Mister Oyeleye is definitely black-skinned, and I am definitely white-skinned. But why does the new variant of the virus happily attach itself to me and turn up its microscopic nose at my black friend? Well, I finally figured it out.'

Kevin Kelly interjected.

'Or you are almost sure you figured it out, you mean?'

'No, Kevin, with respect, I have figured it out. I know that you disagree with the risk end of things, but there's no denying the core science.'

She clicked the pointer again and a smaller image, one of an organic molecule, appeared.

'This is the difference. This tiny molecular entity, effectively an enzyme, is the signal to external forces that the DNA belongs to a person of colour, a black man or woman.'

Miriam interrupted briefly.

'Does it differentiate, between men and women? In other words, is the virus know or care whether the host is male or female?'

She clicked the pointer again.

'No, it doesn't. If we go back to the previous slide, we can see that the gender bit is way down here, and the bit where colour is stored is up here.'

'Okay, that's good anyway. Carry on, sorry.'

Karen clicked forward to where her molecular diagram filled the screen.

'As I said, this is the bit, this is the chalk-mark on the door, the red traffic light that tells the virus to keep going, nothing to see here. And we've isolated it, and synthesised it. We have a vaccine, guys, subject to some testing of course.'

Miriam put her hands up.

'That's fantastic, Karen, but do we have a vaccine or don't we?'

'We have a theoretical vaccine, Miriam, but we've actually made it, it exists, back there in lab number three. We have synthesised the marker for black skin in a format that can be administered to a person, and we can in theory use it to convince the virus that anyone carrying the marker is black, regardless of their actual skin colour. And we know that putting it into the body will, in theory at least, start the synthesis of the marker within the body's own DNA structure, changing its appearance to an intruder virus to that of a black person.'

Miriam stood up and reached over to shake the scientist's hand.

'Jesus, Karen, that's bloody genius. So how far are we from actually being able to say that we have a product?'

'We have to do some more testing, to make sure that the body of an inoculated person not only manufactures the marker but also retains it in their system. We want to be sure that the vaccination actually gives long-term immunity, by which I mean a year or more.'

Billy nodded agreement.

'Yes, the last thing the manufacturers want is a vaccine that lasts forever. In an ideal world, it needs to be renewed every year, that's what keeps the shareholders happy.'

Karen picked up the remote control and idly turned it over and over in her hands.

'The biggest challenge is the short term though, there's no point in administering a vaccine that works well for a week and then fades away as the body absorbs what's there and stops replicating it. We have to trick the body into believing that the enzyme we introduce into the body's cells actually belongs there, but I think I have found the pathway for that. Anyway, our next step is testing on a small number of volunteers. I'm happy to be one of those, for what it's worth.'

Billy Robinson stood up as his colleague resumed her seat.

'Thank you for that, Karen, but I just want to say two things. Firstly, I don't believe any of the core team should take the vaccine just yet. If there are unknown side-effects, we don't want our key people out of action for even a day at this point.'

Miriam nodded.

'I agree, Billy. We can't take chances in case somebody

98

goes down with a fever or something for a week, we need all hands on deck right now. So, what was your second point?'

'It was just a word of caution before we get too much ahead of ourselves. I'm not taking away from the extraordinary piece of work that has been delivered by Karen, but Kevin has raised a matter of concern that we need to at least consider more fully. As I said earlier, I'm backing Karen's judgement and expertise, but as a scientist I know that we ignore the sceptics, the challenging view, at our peril. So I'll hand over to Kevin and he can explain more fully.'

Kevin Kelly got to his feet and spoke, hesitantly at first.

'Thank you Billy, and Karen too. If I'm honest, as a research scientist I'm just a little bit jealous that our most junior researcher has beaten us all to the draw with her genius, she's delivered an extraordinary piece of work these last weeks. In another time, we'd all be getting behind her bid for the Nobel Prize. But I wouldn't be a scientist if I didn't hypothesise the dissenting view, to challenge the research and so make it stronger. I think it behoves all of us as scientists to always do that, so that our thesis doesn't fall when it gets outside these walls.'

Miriam shook her head.

'We're in the commercial field now, Kevin, not behind the subsidised walls of the University, so while a certain amount of challenging is, as you said, a healthy thing, we have to be careful not to swing too far the other way. If I recall, without pointing any fingers, it was this over-cautious approach that lost us the big game in twenty-twenty, and I had to sell on your own brilliant piece of research to a company that became globally mega-rich on the back of it while we all got a few thousand quid on top of our wages.'

'It's not all about money, Miriam. And I resent the

implication that I screwed up the last time we were in the middle of a major pandemic research programme. I was the one who actually produced the goods, at the end of the day, and you were the one that decided to cut your losses and sell the research on.'

Billy moved to cool tempers and bring the meeting back to normal.

'Boys and girls, let's stop with the throwing punches and start pulling together like we always do. Don't be so touchy, Kevin, none of this is personal. And Miriam, I know you're the boss, but stop poking the crocodile with a stick. You need to get over what happened years ago, it adds nothing to the debate. Carry on, Kevin, you were saying?'

Kevin took a deep breath before commencing.

'Sorry, I shouldn't lose the plot. But look, I have a concern, and I need to lay it before you all. Most of you are scientists, and you're all smart people, so you need all the facts before making decisions. It's just that I see a risk in the strategy. It's a small risk, I'll grant you that, but always remember that a ten cent O-ring brought down the NASA space programme.

So here's how I see it. Karen's research and postulation is very sound, and it is, as I said, a piece of genius. But the risk is there and I can't get it out of my mind, to be honest, small and all as it is.'

'So, spit it out, Kevin, you've got our attention now.'

'It's like this, Miriam, there is a tiny possibility that the enzyme won't just mask the actual skin colour of the vaccine recipient, it could in theory, and I know it's a long shot, but it could in theory move along the strand to where the chromosomal race differences occur.'

'I don't get it, Kevin. Like I said, I'm a physicist. Spell it out for me.'

'In short, Miriam, it could persuade the body that its natural skin colour is actually black.'

'So you mean, it could cause black patches on the skin or something?'

'More than that, I think it could, in an extreme scenario, it could turn the person's skin black.'

'Temporarily, you mean?'

'Maybe, but once that trigger had been pulled, it could also be permanent. I don't know, is the honest answer; we're in completely uncharted waters here, and there's obviously no research on it.'

'Jesus! We'd be ruined if that happened.'

'Us, Miriam? Ruined? I'm thinking about all the people whose lives would be turned upside down. I'm not all that worried about us.'

'Well I am, I have to worry about us, while of course being responsible too. I have no desire to turn all the white people in South Africa black, although a part of me is tickled pink by the idea, but I also detect a slight vibe here, guys. Are you sure this is not a boys versus girls thing? Billy and Kevin, noses out of joint because our junior biochemist who also happens to be a woman has cracked a problem that I gave to you all to solve? Are you sure it's not a macho thing, a bit of professional jealousy?'

Billy laughed.

'Don't be daft, Miriam. Like I said, I support the science behind what Karen has done, but as a scientist I have to hear the alternate view and challenge it too. I have looked at Kevin's postulation, but I believe that it is so far off the scale that it is damn near impossible.'

'But not impossible, is that what you're saying?'

'Everything is possible, a bit like the monkey typing the bible if you gave him long enough, but this risk is more diluted than a Homeopath's aspirin. So while I can't rule it out, I wouldn't rule it in.'

'Okay, so where do we go from here, Karen?'

'We need to test it on a white person, somebody with no black heritage whatsoever if we can find such, and we need to try to give him or her immunity with the vaccine, Then we need to attempt to give Mister Oyeleye the virus to see whether he carries it, even though we know already that he probably won't catch it, but we're still not a hundred percent certain that he can't pass it on. Ideally, we should get the new volunteer to share the room with Mister Oyeleye for a few days at some point and see whether he can generate antibodies in the other volunteer that way. If not, we can try the nasal spray and try to infect him that way.'

'That all makes sense. Caroline, can you get us a white volunteer at short notice?'

'I can, Miriam, but it takes a couple of weeks for visas and all that.'

'Can't you get somebody locally?'

'Not a hope, they all believe that we do experiments on the people here, you know the rumours that go around. Although there is one guy who keeps pestering us for a job, maybe he'd do it?'

'Can you check, time is not on our side here.'

'Okay, I'll get right on it. I'll let you know in half an hour.'

'Can you not call him?'

'He doesn't have a phone, but I know where he lives. I'll send a taxi for him right now.'

Chapter Eighteen

Major Callaghan and Doctor Belyaev sat side by side on one of the couches in the Oval Office. The President sprawled on the other, drinking from an aluminium water bottle. He looked across at his two aides and spoke testily.

'This had better be good, gentlemen. I got me one hell of a hangover, that Ambassador Kuznetsov sure knows how to throw a party. I can't even remember getting home. Well, in fact I didn't actually get home, they gave me a bed in a guest room at the embassy. I don't even remember taking my clothes off, not to mention folding and hanging up my suit, but I guess I must have done; it's funny how you shift to automatic when you've had a few too many. So, spit it out, guys, what was more important than my nap, this morning?'

The Major spoke first, hesitantly.

'We wouldn't have called if it wasn't urgent, Sir. We have some news on the pandemic front.'

'I sure hope so, that damned Chinese disease is starting to creep east, it's all over California and coming this direction in a big way. I heard they shut the cat-houses in Nevada yesterday, our funding friends in Vegas won't be happy if businesses are affected like that.'

'We are aware of all that, Sir, but we maybe have some hope on the horizon. I'll let Doctor Belyaev explain.'

The Doctor got to his feet and started to pace around. The President bellowed at him angrily.

'Sit the hell down, Vladimir. You're making me look up at them lights, and my eyes hurt. Sit the hell down and talk from there. This ain't Harvard, I don't need a damned lecture. Just tell me what you got.'

Doctor Belyaev sat down heavily on the couch.

'Sorry, Mister President. In short, Sir…'

'Yeah, short would be good.'

'In short, Sir, one laboratory appears to have developed a vaccine for the new variant.'

'Damn! I knew those guys would do it. Our labs, or yours?'

'Neither, Sir. A small lab in Ireland, the one that came good before. Looks like they've done it again.'

'Son of a bitch! Do we own them?'

'No, Sir. But Major Callaghan has made some enquiries.'

The Major opened a brown paper folder on the coffee table in front of him and took out a number of sheets of paper.

'Yes, Sir. Vladimir is right, we got this information from a usually reliable source this morning. It appears this lab has synthesised a vaccine that can handle this new variant.'

'Holy guacamole! They sure work fast over there in Ireland. What do you have on them, Major?'

'Not a lot, Sir. Mostly information from the last time they hit the vaccine jackpot. That time around, they were a small operation with serious cash-flow issues, and we managed to buy their research off them for a jar of beads, more or less. A couple of million bucks if I remember rightly, they didn't exactly jump at it but we had been digging and we knew they couldn't afford to go into production themselves.'

'Could they not have made some kinda deal with big pharma?'

'It appears we had that avenue closed off, Sir. Our administration at the time told all the likely partners to hold back, told them that we weren't going to approve an Irish vaccine unless a US company owned the patent.'

'So they surrendered?'

'Case of having to, they were afraid to gamble on the approvals side of things.'

'And you think they'll be a pushover this time? Who's the guy that makes that decision for them?'

'I don't think they'll bend too easily this time, Sir. And it's not a guy, it's a dame. A lady called Miriam O'Hagan, a tough cookie from what I'm told.'

He pulled a photo from the folder and pushed it towards the President.

'That's her, a scientist but in the math and physics side of things, sole owner of the business but apparently her most senior guy, an old-school biochemist called Billy Robinson, may own part of the action, like maybe a five percent slice. Looks like he was maybe brought on board in the early days when she had no money, and he got a wedge of the pie instead of wages for a while. It's all hidden in a fog of private company structures in the Isle of Man.'

'Good looking broad, I like them with a bit of meat on them. But where the hell is the Isle of Man? Is that in the Caribbean someplace?'

'No, Sir, it's part of England, although not really part of England.'

'Couldn't be clearer, Major. I was never good at geography in school, so can you explain?'

'It's an island near England, Sir. A bit like the Bahamas as far as tax goes, a popular place for English and Irish companies to hide their money.'

'They got an Isle of Woman too?'

'No Sir, I don't believe they do.'

'Dang. I thought them Europeans always had to have one of each, a woman for every man. But like you said, it ain't in Europe.'

'It's in Europe all right, Sir, but not in the European Union, and it's not in England or Ireland.'

'Okay, I learn something new every day in this job, although I'm not sure what I've learned today, so far. So, you got any more on this lab?'

'It's called 'Boyle Labs,' Sir. It's in a small town called Boyle, tiny place with about three thousand people. The town that is, the lab only employs a couple of dozen. They got three streams of work, they do a lot of research and development work for pharma companies, they do all the water and sewage testing for all the county governments in the country, and they have a high-security bio-testing facility on site too.'

'What do they test?'

'They do final pre-approval tests on medicines, Sir, they test stuff on volunteers before it can be approved for general human use.'

'A guinea-pig farm? Like a Chinese prison, interesting. This place, what's it called again?'

'Boyle, Sir.'

The President waved the photograph about.

'Boyle. Never heard of the place, it must be a real backwater. What about the lady, our blonde broad here?'

'We don't have much on her, Sir. It's mostly information we dug up last time around.'

'We gotta buy this formula off her, we gotta make sure that a US company comes out with this vaccine first. Imagine what the damned Chinese would say if the USA had to be pailed out by some broad in a little town in Europe? Nah, we gotta get our hands on this formula. Will she take money, what's her price?'

'Bailed out? I don't know, Sir. I can start to make discrete enquiries, but I would need some kind of approval before making even an indirect approach. This lady has been around this track before, and she knows the kind of money she can make if she develops this vaccine fully and brings it to market. We're talking astronomical sums of money, Sir. Billions of dollars.'

'But what would her price be, Major? Fifty million? A hundred million? We could pay fifty million right off the bat, I can tell you that right now. Or maybe more if we have to, but I'd have to take it to Congress and they might just delay it to make us look bad.'

Doctor Belyaev leaned forward, lips pursed as though lost in thought.

'If I may, gentlemen. As a scientist and a doctor I don't think money will be the entire driver of this woman's thought process. She will also have other considerations.'

'Such as, Vladimir?'

'Well, this vaccine has been developed in the shortest time ever. They only got the brief a couple of weeks back, after all.'

The Major smiled wryly.

'As far as we know, Doctor. But our guys, and the Russians, they had it a couple of weeks before that. Are we going to naively assume that there were no leaks?'

107

'It's a possibility, from the US side, but hardly from the Russians. The country of my birth doesn't do leaks.'

'Don't be so damned naïve, Vladimir. Everyplace leaks.'

The President raised his hands in exasperation.

'Gentlemen, please, can we leave the fighting for the school playground? The fact is, they got the brief and they worked on it, and now they got a result and we don't. So, how do we get that formula from them? You were about to say, Doctor, before we went off track?'

'I was saying that money may not be the sole driver, that she may have other considerations.'

The Major laughed out loud.

'Like the common good, or wanting to save the planet? Not from what I see in the file, this is one hard-nosed operator, there's no other way to say it.'

'No, I don't mean altruism.'

'Vladimir, what did I tell you about Harvard words? Not in my office, Okay?'

'Sorry, Sir. I don't mean that she is motivated by love of the human race, I think money is the goal.'

'But I thought you said…?'

'Yes, Sir, I said money may not be the total picture. Look at it this way. She's the sole owner, or almost sole owner of a biochemistry facility that stands to make a lot of money out of this, either way. Like you said, we will have to pay her fifty million at least, with maybe some royalties for a year or so, I think we're all agreed it will be of that level anyway. So, what would you do, Mister President, if you were in her shoes?'

The president looked at the picture on the table.

'I'd probably fall over; them heels sure is high!'

The others laughed politely at the joke for a minute before

the conversation became serious again. The President was the first to speak.

'Sorry, guys, I couldn't resist that one. But to answer your question, Vladimir, I don't know what I'd do. Try to raise the stakes a bit, and take the money and run, I reckon.'

'But if you'd been there before, and you'd been stiffed the last time?'

'Maybe that would cloud my thinking, but I don't think I'd take on the United States Government. I still think I'd take the money. What do you think, Vladimir?'

'I'm trying to look at this from a woman's point of view, Sir, as well as from the point of view of somebody who, A, knows we need them, and, B, who got the crappy end of the stick last time they dealt with us. Against that, I'd be looking at the future of my company, which would suddenly be very saleable, particularly if it came with a downstream comet-trail of royalties and a track record of major scientific discoveries. I wouldn't want to jeopardise the value of the company in my rush to grab the cash.'

'So, you're the broad, this Miriam O'Hagan, and I've just offered you fifty million. What's your next move?'

'I'd look for more, but not cash. I'd look for a five percent royalty on sales of the product for a year, probably accept somewhere around two to three. And I'd look for indemnity against all claims in the event that somebody suffers adverse effects from the vaccine?'

'You think it might not be safe?'

'Highly unlikely, modern vaccines are made in a different way than they used to be, if the body doesn't like the product it just passes it right out and gets rid of any harmful bits.'

'So why raise it here?'

'Because it's a risk, Sir, however small. And anyone buying the company will factor in that risk and put a huge premium on it. It's called 'contingent liability,' the kind of thing that due diligence lawyers home in on straight away. However if the liability has been taken over by another party, such as the US government, it disappears off the balance sheet.'

'Like when you wind back the mileage on a used truck? Exact same truck, but it looks a helluva lot better when you park it out on the front lot. I get it, Major. So if you were to negotiate with this woman, could you do a deal on that basis, do you think?'

The Major flipped open a leather-bound notebook and made some notes.

'I believe so, Sir. So, Fifty million, tops, plus a licensing deal of two percent to start, maximum five at a stretch. Plus we take on board all the potential liabilities in the event that a few people suffer side effects? Does that sum it up, Sir?'

'Yes, can you start to kick things off on that front? Do we have anybody living there, anyone in the local Town Hall on our payroll, anything like that?'

'We found one interesting snippet when we started looking. Would you believe we have a major Hollywood superstar who comes from there, Sir? A guy called Chris O'Dowd.'

'The non-stop Oscar winner? Holy guacamole! Can we call him in, tell him it's time for him to do his patriotic duty?

'I don't think so, Sir. He's not a registered member of the party, for a start, and he's a known liberal who believes black folks are absolutely equal to the rest of us. Doesn't even own a gun. His wife is the same, apparently, all human rights shit and stuff. Quite a few of their friends are black or Hispanic, apparently.'

'Damn! We can write him off. Anybody else, surely we got somebody within a hundred miles of there?'

'We've obviously got a 'cultural' guy in the Embassy, his actual job is checking for communists in government and around the country. His cover is he likes to fish, that gets him 'access all areas' in Ireland.'

'They got good fishing in Ireland? Holy guacamole! I gotta go to Ireland, Major, the Irish vote is important to us, and you know I love to fish, we should make a trip. But for the moment, get that guy back here, or go and see him, and tell him more or less what we need to find out. The usual, who's sleeping with who, who's got a drug problem or big gambling debts, I don't have to tell you the drill.'

'Yes, Sir, we're on it, I assure you. We also have one other possibility that might be worth following up. A year or so back we had a job application from a guy who lives right in that town, just half a mile from the plant, he wanted to join our Secret Service. It might be worth looking him up, we could give him a short-term contract just for this job, once he checks out as clean.'

'So have you done any background on him?'

'Yes, of course, Sir, no record of anything, not as much as a traffic stop, the original Mister Clean. His CV says he's an air accident investigator, so he's probably a pretty smart cookie. He's Irish too, a guy called Mickey Small.'

'We need guys like that, Major. Tell your embassy officer to make discrete contact, see if this Mister Small can be our eyes and ears in this place, what's it called again?

'Boyle, Sir.'

'Boyle it is. I must try to remember that. Okay, thank you gentlemen, now get outa here.'

The Major and the Doctor got up and left the room, chatting as they passed through the outer reception area before parting company on the main corridor. Major Callaghan left the White House and walked around the building to make an unannounced inspection of all the guard posts. Doctor Belyaev left a few minutes later by the main gate and walked briskly to his apartment building on Nineteenth Street. He let himself in to his top floor apartment and locked the door, taking a small, nondescript phone out of a locked drawer and fitting it with a simcard from his wallet before dialing a number. He waited for the phone to be answered and spoke quietly.

'Comrade, things are moving fast here now, we need to start taking certain actions very quickly. I will go to the yellow building this evening and we can have a conference call with the team to discuss everything. You will need to notify Comrade 'Z' and respectfully request him to join us by video link on the secure line. This is very urgent, Comrade; there is no time to lose.'

Chapter Nineteen

Homer Kendall Junior raised a hand to flag down the old pickup as it drove slowly down Main Street. The driver slowed to a halt and leaned out the open window.

'Mornin,' Sherriff!'

'Howdy, Randy. Whar yo goin' this time a day? Yo ain't usually up yet.'

'Jest goin' ter the gas station.'

'Yo deliverin' moonshine, Randy?'

'Moonshine? No, Sir. Jest ice.'

'Ice? Ice, my goddamn ass. Lemme see what ya got in the back.'

Randy got out and walked to the back of the truck, dropping the tailgate and pulling out a thick sheet of industrial insulating board.

'Thar ya go, it all jest bags a ice, Sherriff.'

'Damn my hide, if it ain't. What yo game?'

'Ain't no game, jest some ice fer Bill. Ken I put back the inserlation? Ah don't want her ter melt.'

'Yeah, put her back. Damned iffen I know what you boys get up to half the time, 'cept I know it ain't legal, fer shore. Y'all got my whisky?'

Randy fished a bottle from under the seat and handed

113

it to the policeman, who quickly secreted it in the trunk of the cruiser.

'That strong stuff, Sherriff. Take it easy with her, y'all be seeing two a everythin'.'

'I ain't stupid, Randy. I takes her with water and ice. And speakin' about ice, can you deliver one a them bags a ice to ma house when yo done at the store?'

'Sure will, Sherriff. That be five bucks.'

The policeman laughed.

'That funny, Randy. Real funny. Now off yer go afore I find sumpin wrong wit that thar truck. I reckon it won't be hard.'

Randy pulled away in a cloud of blue smoke and drove to the parking lot behind the gas station. William McCauley shuffled out and peered into the makeshift coolbox on the bed of the pickup.

'Looks good, Randy, put them bags in the freezer thar quick afore they turns back ter water. How many yer got?'

'Fifty bag, Bill, cept one less, forty-nine. Sherriff Kendall, he tol' me ter drop one off in his house.'

'And I guess he pay same as he pay for his coffee here?'

'Guess he don' pay fer nothin', but I guess that part a the job.'

'Yeah, it's jest what it is. At least he don't give me no gyp about bathrooms and stuff, all them ordnances would cost a damn sight more than a few cups a coffee.'

'Kin I get a few bucks, Bill?'

'Shore, Randy, Come in the store and I'll fix yer up.'

Randy folded the bills into the pocket of his overalls and got back in the truck. He reversed on to Main Street, turning right and heading towards the smart end of town. He followed the street to the light at the end, turning off uphill to the Mountain View neighbourhood. He parked outside a huge house with a broad lawn to the front and crossed the grass to ring the bell. A tall, blonde woman opened the door and gave him a puzzled look.

'Yes?'

Randy stepped back a little.

'Beg yo pardon, Ma'am, I got yer ice.'

'Ice?'

'Sherriff tell me bring yer some ice. I got her in the truck.'

'Okay, bring it here.'

Randy collected the last remaining bag from the truck and carried it to the door.

'Here ya go, ma'am, one bag ice.'

She looked at him angrily.

'Y'all don' expect me to carry it in to the icebox? Bring it inside!'

She turned and walked unsteadily through the marble-floored hallway towards the kitchen. Randy picked up the bag and followed to where she pointed out a large freezer.

He put the bag inside and stepped back, surprised at the mess that was the kitchen, with dirty plates everywhere and a general air of untidiness. The woman noticed his surprised gaze and responded defensively.

'Y'all pardon the condition of the house. The damned maid is gone, she musta jest run off, ain't nobody to do nothin' around here no more. I don' know how my husband expect me to run this house with no maid, but he say we ain't getting another one.'

Randy shuffled his feet and looked at the floor.

'Guess it ain't easy, Ma'am, shore is a big place.'

The woman seemed to slump, she reached for an almost-empty glass and refilled it from a gin bottle on the counter.

'You want a drink? I got gin, vodka, whisky. Or I got some moonshine?'

'No, thank you ma'am. It too early fer me, I best be on my way.'

The woman opened the refrigerator and reached inside; Randy heard the clink of ice as she added several lumps to her glass.

'Please yourself. How much I owe you, for the ice?'

Randy was tempted, but thought better of it.

'That be okay, ma'am. Guess it on the house.'

'Everything is on the house, with my damned husband. Pity he can't get a maid on the house, or in the house more like.'

Randy shuffled his feet nervously and began to move towards the door.

'Guess I'd better be goin, Ma'am, got thangs ter do.'

Chapter Twenty

Vladimir Belyaev pulled down on his trilby hat and turned up his overcoat collar as he stepped out of the apartment building, walking two blocks to where he waited with a small group of people at the N6 bus stop. The bus pulled in by the curb and he stepped on to it just as the doors were about to close, prompting a man who had been leaning against the wall of the nearby store to jump on board too. Vladimir kept his hat pulled down and his gaze towards the floor as the bus moved away, sensing the young man pass him by and take a seat two rows back. He smiled to himself at the crude tailing skills of the agent, this guy would never get a job in the Kremlin, for sure.

At the Fulton Street stop he made to stand up, smiling as he glimpsed a reflection in a chrome bar of a following movement from the man behind him. He sat down again, sure now that he was being tailed. At Edmund Street he exited swiftly, and was pleased to note that the young agent did likewise. He paused for a minute and looked around, noting that the other man melted into the shadows at the street corner.

He strolled up the steps to Saint Nicholas Orthodox Cathedral, pushing through the glass swing doors. Inside

the door he stepped sideways quickly, hurriedly exchanging his coat and hat for his brother's navy coloured bomber jacket and baseball cap. Igor Belyaev stepped back into the main body of the church and walked slowly towards the main altar, head bowed and hands clasped as if in prayer. Vladimir saw the agent slowly and silently enter the church, taking up a position in a corner where he could watch the back of Igor at prayer.

Vladimir slipped quietly out the side door, attracting barely a second glance from the agent. He strode swiftly down the path and walked down Edmunds Street towards the Consulate. At Wisconsin Avenue he nodded in response to a discrete hand sign from the KGB officer who ran past in his exercise gear, and he hurried across the street and turned into Turnlaw Road, where a small pedestrian gate yielded to his touch and he stepped into the shadows inside. A plain door opened and Ambassador Kuznetsov clapped him on the back as he entered the darkened hallway in the building.

'Well done, Comrade Belyaev, our training never fails. These Americans, they are idiots, they don't know how to follow a target.'

'I don't dismiss them so easily, Comrade Kuznetsov. Even a fool only has to be lucky once. Still, they should hopefully follow Igor back to my apartment soon, and report that I was just going for prayers, as I always do. They don't have reason to suspect anything, after all I am their government's chief medical adviser.'

'Yes, and a Harvard scholar too! It was a long process, gaining their trust, so we need to be careful always. Your presence at the highest level in government is very important to Comrade Z. This meeting won't take long, and we can drive you back to the carpark under your building and pick up Igor at the same time, nobody will see us.'

'Will the President be joining us at our video chat?'

'Yes, he is very interested in this matter, as you know. He sees an opportunity to show the world once again that Russian scientists are superior to those in the United States of America. Let us go to the secure room.'

The Ambassador led the way down a corridor and into a lift that took them down to a basement level. The meeting room was warm and comfortable, furnished with large, soft chairs around a circular table. A large screen on the end wall showed traffic moving slowly by the end of Red Square, near the cathedral of Saint Basil. Both men took their seats and an army officer made adjustments to the microphones and cameras at each man's place at the table. A subaltern brought a silver tray with a bottle of iced water and some black caviar in glass bowls with small silver spoons. The two soldiers withdrew and the Ambassador pressed his on-button, motioning to the Doctor to do the same. Their faces appeared in small squares at the top of the screen on the wall.

A moment later, the Moscow traffic scene faded out and the screen as filled with a view of a sumptuous room in the Kremlin, with the President seated in a leather armchair and flanked by two senior army officers. The Ambassador raised his glass in a greeting.

'Good evening, Comrade President. I trust that life is good with you.'

'Comrade Kuznetsov, and Comrade Belyaev, I am glad to see you. How is your life in the land of the free?'

Both men laughed loudly at the President's question.

'Nothing is free here, Comrade. In fact, everything is very expensive.'

'Good joke, Comrade Kuznetsov, good joke. And how

are you, Comrade Belyaev? I hope you are keeping safe the health of your adopted country, and of course the President, my friend Donald Daniels. We need him to stay alive at all costs.'

'He is alive, for sure, Comrade President. Or he was, about eight hours ago when I last met him.'

'You need to tell him to take better care of himself, I saw already some footage of him from last night at the party, he is not very particular about what he drinks. And I noticed when Comrade Vanda put him to bed, he is very flabby and unfit. He didn't even try to make love with her, can you believe? What a pussy he is! I am thirty years older than him and I believe I could wrestle him easily. Americans are not real men, I am sure of that.'

'I will advise him to take better care of himself, but I fear the habits of a lifetime have left him like that. I am glad to see that your own health is good, as always, Comrade President.'

'Yes, thanks God, I live a healthy life and it has served me well. I have been in this job, one way or another, for thirty years and I feel as good as the day I traded our uniform for this suit. President Daniels needs to be careful or he will not even survive to take the job next time. Narkotiki and prostitutki are all very well for young men, but not as you get older, particularly the narkotiki.'

'I fully agree, Comrade President.'

The Ambassador raised a glass to the President and then to his colleague.

'I want to propose a toast, Comrades. To President Zhadnyy, and to all our comrades in the KGB. Za zdorov'ye!'

They all raised their glasses to the health of the President.

'Za zdorov'ye!'

The President put down his empty water glass and sat forward in his chair, his clear blue eyes holding his officers in a steely gaze.

'So, Comrades, let us get down to business. You have information, Comrade Belyaev?'

'Yes, Comrade President. In short, a laboratory in Ireland appears to have synthesised a vaccine for the new variant. President Daniels wants his people to tie down the formula in a contract with them immediately, to make it appear that an American research company made the discovery. They are sending their 'cultural attaché' to the place to try to make some local contact.'

'Damn them! Do you have all the information, where is this laboratory, who is the director, and what people does the USA have on the ground there, the names of their spies?'

'Yes, Comrade President, it is an institute called 'Boyle Labs,' and the director is a woman called Miriam O'Hagan. It is located in a small derevnya, a village-town not far from the Capital City, Dublin.'

'I understand that nowhere in Ireland is far from the Capital, Comrade. How far, exactly?'

The doctor laughed nervously.

'Quite so, Comrade President, the entire country is very small, for sure. This village is approximately two hundred Kilometres away from the main city. It is a settlement of not more than three thousand persons, and the institute employs between fifteen and thirty persons, depending on the work at any time.'

'Why the variance?'

'They employ sometimes some persons on whom they test medicines, before they make them available to the general population.'

'They don't have any prisons?'

'I believe they are not allowed to test medicines on prisoners, Comrade President.'

'I don't understand this attitude, it is no wonder the West grows weaker each year. Who will find out in any case? If a prisoner disappears, who gives a shit?'

'Exactly my sentiment, Comrade President, but such are their ways, strange as they seem.'

'Very well, so this laboratory institute, it has the formula for the new vaccine. The question is, how do we get it? Do we buy it or do we steal it, which is the best way?'

'It is not as simple as stealing it, Comrade President. A discovery like this will be stored as data somewhere, and if we come up with the exact same formula, it will be seen that we copied it. Also, and more importantly, that wouldn't stop them giving it to the Americans, so we would have wasted the effort.'

'So, we must buy it, or nothing?'

'Exactly, Comrade President.'

'And have the Americans made an estimate of the price?'

'Yes, Comrade President, at least fifty million US Dollars, they believe.'

'That amount will not be a problem. The money is not actually what is most important, it is a matter of National prestige. In any case, if we get this formula we will make a hundred times that amount. Do we have a supply of cash in Dublin?'

Yes, Comrade President. As you know, Dublin is our European intelligence headquarters, so we have two pallets of cash, up to a hundred million euros, stored there at any time.'

'Yes, I knew we had substantial resources there, we had to pay a lot of money to that party when we had them in the government there a few years back. Too late we found out they were not real communists, it was just a convenient label, but at least we got a lot of information from them. In any case, we have the funds there if we need them urgently. Do the Americans have anybody else in those parts, near that village, apart from their 'cultural attaché?"

'Not exactly, Comrade President, but they are trying to recruit an aeronautical engineer who lives there, as we speak. He has approached them for employment as a spy, and they are now going to try to check out his trustworthiness and offer him a payment to find information for them.'

'The usual, who sleeps with who, who is under the power of the Mafia because of drugs or gambling?'

'Exactly, Comrade President.'

'You have a name for this potential spy? If he wants to do some spying work, he may find us a better employer than the Americans. One night with Comrade Vanda and he will work for us for nothing!'

'Indeed Comrade President. He is called Mickey Small.'

'Then let us hope he does not have a small brain, and that he will understand that his best interests lie with us. Very good, you have noted these details already, comrade Kuznetsov?'

'Yes, Comrade President. I have already spoken to our Comrade Ambassador Turgenev in Dublin, and instructed him to make enquiries about Boyle Labs, that is the name of the institute that Comrade Belyaev spoke about. I will also instruct them to find this man who wants to be a spy, and to give him that opportunity.'

'Good work, Comrade Kuznetsov, but we must inject some urgency into this matter, if you will excuse my joke.'

The others laughed politely.

'Comrades, I want you to give this matter the highest priority. Send Vanda Jakovf to Ireland tonight, if possible, or tomorrow morning at the latest. Tell Comrade Ivan Turgenev to give her a cover story and some money, and see if she can obtain some work in the institute, as a cleaner, or a cook maybe. I think maybe he needs to give her a Moldovan passport, so that she can work legally in the EU. We should have plenty of genuine Moldovan documents in Dublin. And tell her to find this Mickey Small, and persuade him to work with her, maybe tell him she's working for an American drug company. She should use her usual methods, sleep with him, buy him things, or drugs if that is his weakness, and then blackmail him if he is married. If he is not married, make him fall in love with her so that he will do as she orders. She should examine also whether he can find work in the institute, as a drug tester maybe? Comrade Jakovf will know in any case, she is our best agent for this kind of work, for sure.'

'And if he has the English condition?'

'He may be a gomoseksualist; that is possible, but unlikely. I don't believe there are many sodomit in Ireland, it is similar to Russia in that respect, although of course we do not have any such persons here at all, thanks God. But if he is, maybe she can blackmail him?'

'I believe that the English condition is legal in Ireland, Comrade President. There may not be an opportunity for blackmail.'

'Comrade Jakovf can find a way, I have faith in her and in her experience and her training. She will find a way.'

The others nodded, and the President continued.

'It is very important that we get this formula, Comrades. Our reputation will be greatly enhanced worldwide if a Russian company brings this vaccine to market, but conversely, we will look like the poor country cousin if America is first to the finish line. So do what you have to do, and remember that money is better than killing, always; it leaves less blood on the floor as we used to say when we were in the field together.

So, Comrades, fill your glasses and we will make a toast.'

Ambassador Kuznetsov poured water, and both men raised their glasses towards the screen. The President raised his glass.

'To Success, Comrades! And to Mother Russia.'

'Success, and Mother Russia! Za zdorov'ye!'

Chapter Twenty One

Miriam O'Hagan pushed herself up on one elbow and smiled at the man beside her in the comfortable bed.

'Better times a-coming, Billy Robinson, we'll be able to stop sneaking around like two grounded teenagers.'

'I don't know, Miriam, I quite like the whole illicit nature of it. And it beats the hell out of getting myself battered up and down Shop Street by Sergeant O'Hagan.'

'Jesus, don't mention my husband, it kills the atmosphere a bit. Anyway, are you just going to lie there, or can a girl get a cup of coffee in this house?'

Billy rolled out of the bed and pulled on a dressing gown, and spooned coffee grounds into the shiny coffee machine on the worktop in the modern kitchen. He took two mugs from a cupboard and filled them from the twin spouts of the machine, placing them on a small tray along with a small china jug to which he added milk from a carton in the fridge.

'No sugar, still?'

'The diet is still holding, so no thanks. And no biscuits either, I reckon they're my downfall.'

'I never complain, I like a woman with a bit of padding.'

'That's all right for you, you don't have to face the

corporate world every day, dealing with smartass executives with their judgmental attitudes to women. If you happen to add a few pounds, it doesn't matter; a white coat covers a multitude.'

They lay back in the bed and sipped their coffees contentedly. Billy sat upright with a start.

'I meant to tell you, I think there's an American spy in town. Do they know we've cracked the vaccine, do you think?'

'I can't see how they'd know, but who, where is this spy, how do you know there's a spy around the place?'

'I was on the lake early this morning, just pulling the boat on to the slip at the Doon Shore, when this Yank wandered over to talk to me.'

'Could just have been a tourist, there's always a few of them about.'

'At that hour of the morning? No, this guy was a bit more direct, asking probing questions. He had binoculars hanging around his neck too, I reckon he was watching me from the shore before I came in. He had fishing gear as well, but didn't seem to be interested in using it.'

'You thought there was something fishy about him?'

'Very funny, woman! But seriously, within a minute of stopping to talk to me he was asking what I did for a living,'

'Strange, all right. Maybe he was gay, trying to get a date?'

'He'd be wasting his time there.'

'Tell me about it! Unless you have a dark side?'

'No, what you see is what you get, with me. But he was definitely very nosy, he asked me what kind of jobs there would be in a place like Boyle, he couldn't figure how anyone around here could be driving a big car for instance, when it's mostly a farming town as far as he could see.'

'That red Tesla is too flashy, I'm always telling you that. You should drive an old Skoda, like me, I'm always what they call 'hidden in plain sight.' Nobody will notice that my car is parked just down the road from your house, but everybody knows when you're at home.'

'I like my cars, I don't have many vices.'

'Except me?'

'I don't see you as a vice. Anyway, I'm telling you, the Americans are here. I was in the café at King House for breakfast afterwards and Dorothy said there was an American guy staying at Frybrook, and he came in for coffee earlier. He was asking about the lab, wondering what that big building was. She thought it odd, he never mentioned the Abbey or King House or any of the usual historical buildings, just a plain old factory block that's a bit out of the way, off the tourist trail anyway.'

'So, they're on to us, you reckon?'

'Yeah, one of the girls who works in Frybrook was in the café this morning, apparently, and she said he asked about places for fishing but didn't seem to be listening to the answers, like he was going through the motions, she thought. She thought he might be a drug dealer, or maybe somebody trying to buy land without raising too many questions.'

'You don't get away with much in Boyle. You and I need to be more careful.'

'Nobody suspects us, Miriam, they know we have to meet regularly for work anyway. But the more I think about this guy, he's definitely sniffing around our operation.'

'Let him sniff away, and he can come out in the open if he has a big chequebook.'

'I thought you were going to run this one all the way,

subcontract the manufacturing, the whole works?'

'Part of me wants to do that, but realistically the big boys can steamroll us if they want. We have to go to them for manufacturing and distribution anyway, so we're probably better off doing the right deal with them.'

'But you got screwed last time, doing that, didn't you?'

'This time is different, we have the actual vaccine, and we have the data, a whole new approach that sidesteps mainstream research. What young Karen has done this time is extraordinary, real ground-breaking stuff. Although I wouldn't puff it up too much in case she gets a big head and decides to run to the opposition.'

'Kevin probably gave her the seed idea, in fairness.'

'True, to an extent, but Kevin is too timid to ever make it big time. He's a genius, but he has no confidence in his own ability. And he has a hang-up about a woman being better than him, you could see it last week at the meeting, he wasn't happy that Karen was getting the glory.'

'Do you think he leaked it to the Americans?'

'Maybe, we need to watch him carefully in any case. If you see him with this tourist, fisherman, whatever, move in immediately and interrupt the conversation.'

'I'll do that, Miriam, but he'd hardly be that stupid, to be openly seen talking to the guy. But his phone is on our account, I can check who he's calling, or who's calling him.'

'Check all the records while you're at it, any calls to or from the States particularly. Come on, we'd better get dressed, we have that meeting in two hours. Is everything going to plan with the testing and all that?'

'Yeah, Lucky seems happy as Larry in his little cell, he's eating well, and watching movies and box-sets. Mary has tried to infect him a couple of times with the virus, but no joy, as expected. Our next step is to put Mickey Small in with him for a few days and see if he can act as a vector.'

'But he's content enough? No cabin fever, no sign of him cracking up?'

'Not in the slightest. He loves watching movies and stuff. He can recite most of the lines in Moone Boy, he's watched it ten times at least, laughs his head off every time.'

'He's a real gent, but a bit strange in some ways. I had told Caroline to put him into Frybrook for a night or two, to give him a nice experience before he went for his spell in solitary, but he refused. Wouldn't hear of it.'

'Most people would jump at a night in a bit of luxury.'

'That's what you'd think, but he just wanted to get back to the lab. She reckoned he was afraid we'd change our minds and not give him the work, that he felt more secure once he was ensconced in his little room in the unit.'

'He's very content anyway, Caroline opened a bank account for him before we locked him in, and she shows him the transfers every week. I'd say that kind of money would be unheard of in Nigeria. Lucky will be fine.'

'And what about the other guy, Caroline's pet?'

'Mickey Small? He's a bit simple, I'm not even sure he is capable of giving informed consent, but needs must. He had a bit of a cold, so Mary Cohen got Doctor Mannion to have a look at him. He's a bit run-down, so he's back home for another few days, and Caroline has arranged for him to get three good meals a day in Clarkes all this week. She went in and cleaned up his house as well, it was in a bit of a state apparently, so she got some lad from out her way to give her a hand and they made the house look like new, got rid of all the rubbish, painted the place from top to bottom and everything.'

'A bit of a soft heart, our Caroline, under all that swearing and cursing!'

'Yeah. Anyway, Mister Small will be fit for active service by Monday morning. He's signed a contract and he's on the payroll from yesterday in fact, and he's sworn to secrecy obviously. But I think I'll tell her to bring him in today, get all our troops into the castle and pull up the drawbridge.'

'Might be safer.'

'I'd prefer to be looking at him than looking for him, once we get rolling on the next phase of the tests. She's warned him that if he says a word to anybody at all about the project, that's the end of it and he'll get no money, but if he's inside the building he can't talk to anybody anyway, so we'll be sure.'

'It's better to have him in house, Miriam. I'm sure that so-called fisherman is here for one reason, and a lad who's a bit pliable would be an easy way into the programme for him. Best to have Mickey somewhere safe, where nobody can get to him.'

'I know, I do believe you about the American spy, and I'm beginning to believe there's a Russian spy in town too.'

'You're kidding?'

'No, it all adds up now, they have somebody here, I'm almost certain. A woman, a beautiful blonde apparently, like in a James Bond movie. You couldn't make this shit up!'

'How did you find that out?'

'I was talking to Marius Albescu.'

'Pizza Marius?'

'Yeah, he told me about her. I was in there today, I dropped in his cheque for this month's account and he said there was a Russian woman in town and she was pretending to be somebody else.'

'How did he figure that out?'

'She was in his shop, asking questions about the town and about the lab. She said she was from Moldova, but he was suspicious of her accent.'

'Of course, he's from Moldova, isn't he?'

'Yes, but he didn't tell her that. He asked her where in Moldova, and she gave him the name of some town, and he said he'd heard of it from somebody he used to work with. He asked her if she knew some cathedral or other, he said his former colleague used to always talk about it and how beautiful it is. She said she knew it well and used to go to prayers there.'

'Maybe she did.'

'Except that he made it all up, there is no cathedral, and he reckoned she was Russian from her accent. He'd recognise the accent, Moldova has a lot of Russians in it I think.'

'He's a clever guy, Marius.'

'Yes, and he obviously values our custom, tipping me off like that. Jesus, you can do nothing in a small town!'

'Except what we've just been doing!'

'We're careful, and anyway we work together, so nobody would suspect anything. Isn't it kinda flattering though that the CIA and maybe the KGB or whoever might be taking an interest in my little business? If they are though, it means they're getting nowhere themselves, so I think they'll be willing to pay well for it.'

'How much is 'well,' in your book?'

'I reckon I'd ask for a hundred million, maybe take less, but not a whole lot.'

Billy gave a low whistle.

'Jesus, that's a lot of money, Miriam. Do you really think they'd pay that much?'

'It's not a lot in the context of a pandemic, governments

can conjure up money out of thin air if they need to. We saw that the last two times, we didn't charge them half enough, in hindsight. Anyway, I can drop my price if they pay me a royalty as well, maybe ten percent of the wholesale end-user price.'

'Is that not risky?'

'Risky? How?'

'You'd be better off with a lump, and not waiting on payments that might never arrive. Suppose another company comes up with a cheaper vaccine, for instance? You'd be left high and dry with damn all royalties coming, instead of taking your dealing trick when it's going.'

'There is that, but there's also the 'plan B."

'I should have known, what have you got up your sleeve?'

Miriam sat on the edge of the bed and brushed out her hair, securing it with a red scrunchie.

'This is strictly between you and me, Billy Robinson, okay?'

'Sure, of course.'

'No, I really mean it. This is very strictly confidential, and it is important for your future as well as mine. I want you to swear that you won't breathe a word of this, okay?'

'Absolutely, Miriam. You know me, I never talk out of school, or out of the bedroom for that matter.'

'I know that, that's why I trust you with this. I have a plan to make us both rich, very rich in my case but I'll leave you without money worries too, if I can make this work.'

'You have my attention now! What are you planning?'

'I built this company from nothing, Billy, as you well know. I even sold my car to start it off, if it didn't work out I would have been broke and up to my ears in debt. But it did work, I made a success of it. We made a success of it.'

'You, mostly, I'd have to admit that.'

'Anyway, I have a lot invested in it, a lot of my life, my blood, sweat and tears, you might say. But sometimes I ask myself what I'm doing it all for. A bad marriage, no kids, plenty of money in my pocket but no time to spend it and nobody to spend it with. So if the right exit comes up, I'm out.'

'You'd sell?'

'Of course I would. But first I want to sell the vaccine, then get a royalty stream that boosts the income of the company to a level where it's attractive to investors. At that point, I'd sell the lot, yes.'

'I'd never considered that you'd take that option, I don't know what I'd do without that place. I enjoy working there, to be honest, I like my life here.'

'Who's saying you'd have to go anywhere? The only assets the company will have are its patents, and its scientists. It's not like the building is worth much, maybe a million euro on a good day.'

'But surely you can't put a monetary value on the staff? They could walk away to a better offer any time they wanted to.'

'I've covered that base. I intend to reward the core staff very well, the current project team and people like Caroline and maybe Mary Cohen as well. I'll make them all millionaires, but I'll tie them in to a couple of year's contracts as part of that, hold back some of the money for a year or two.'

'So that would stop somebody like Kevin running to the opposition? You have this well thought out.'

'It should, among other things, but it will also mean that he has a stake in the best interests of the company. So unless somebody else is throwing an awful lot of money his way, leaking information won't a smart approach for him. But you haven't asked the 'what about me' question?'

'I wasn't going to.'

'But you were thinking it.'

'Maybe. So, what about me?'

'You have your secret share, so if the company is worth, say, another fifty million; that gives you two and a half million straight off. Plus I'll give you a slice of the vaccine sale, a bit more than the others because you're the team leader, and because, well, you know....'

Billy smiled and kissed her on the lips.

'I'm beginning to feel like a kept man!'

'You don't have to, love, I could never have done it all without you. But you'll be well looked after.'

'So what will you do, if you haven't a company to run?'

'I'd love to try doing nothing, for a while anyway. I have the Spanish house in Manilva, so I'd happily move there for a couple of years, soak up the sun and enjoy life.'

'Sounds appealing.'

'You'd always be welcome, but I don't want to be the one to drag you away from your beloved Lough Key. But I'm sure you'd find time to visit.'

'A few long holidays sound attractive, right enough.'

'Anyway, I'd better get out of here, you hang back for a while before you leave, and I'll see you in the boardroom at one.'

Chapter Twenty Two

Major Callaghan looked up in surprise as an aide tapped on his door and entered the office.

'Yes, Jessie?'

'The President wants to see you, Sir.'

'Okay, Jessie, I'll go there right away.'

'No, Sir, he's coming down here, he'll be here in a minute.'

'Oh? Okay, show him straight in, obviously.'

The Major tidied some papers on his desk and walked to the door, greeting his Commander in Chief as he approached.

'Come in, Sir. To what do we owe the pleasure?'

'I need to talk to you, Mike. And I don't trust that the Oval Office isn't bugged, you never know what the Chinese might be doing.'

'We've swept it, Sir, I would have no concerns about that side of things. If there's a bug there, then we're not doing our job, which I very much doubt.'

The President sat on the couch to the side of the Major's desk.

'I have to tell you, Mike, as one of the few people I trust around here, that somebody is leaking information that can only have come from my office. I've noticed it a few times over the last few months, small little things that ambassadors or reporters know that they shouldn't know, stuff that was discussed in my office and nowhere else, as far as I know. I'm just worried about security, you know?'

The Major got up from his desk and walked around to join the President on the couch.

'To be frank, Sir, if information is getting out from your close circle of advisers etcetera, it's more likely that somebody is telling tales. My guys have crawled over that office like bugs on a windscreen, and they check it every week to be sure that nothing new has been added. Same goes for your phones, they are checked and double-checked at least once a week, as is the aircon, the lighting, the power outlets, everything that has a voltage. So if your office is leaking, I'd look to all the people that are present at whatever meetings have had their details spread around.'

'That's an even bigger worry, Major. I mean, if I can't trust my own team, who can I trust?'

'Your own team is made up of people, Sir, and people talk. Especially civilians, Sir, if I may say so. They don't have the same code of secrecy as we have in the military.'

'Yes, to be fair I trust you completely, Major, and the rest of the core team. But I worry about a few of the others.'

'Like who, Sir? We can always run extra checks on anyone you have concerns about. We can follow them, check their phone records, that kind of thing.'

'Well, Vladimir, although he's been around the White House through a couple of administrations, but he's still foreign-born. I mean, on one level I trust him completely, he's been a key member of staff during the various medical emergencies we've had over the years, but when you start to look around, you obviously look at the foreigners first, don't you?'

The Major smiled.

'I would have no concerns about Vladimir, Sir, he's a naturalised American citizen, a Harvard scholar, and glittering career in pandemic medicine and he lives the American dream. Town apartment close to the office, nice home in Montgomery County, takes his holidays in the Hamptons, married to an all-American girl, kids in Ivy League colleges. Doctor Belyaev is one of us, I assure you, Sir.'

'Yes, but he was born in Russia. I know they're our closest allies, but it wasn't always that way. I don't really trust Zhadnyy, you know?'

'I think none of us trust Zhadnyy, but he's the old guard, isn't he? That job is more ceremonial now, I'm told; the younger guys run the country these days and he just turns up for the May Day parade.'

'I guess I worry too much, Mike. But could you keep an eye on him anyway?'

'On Vladimir, Sir?

'Yes. Can you run a check on him, see if he has any money in the bank he didn't earn, that kind of thing?'

The Major smiled.

'Sir, let me tell you something in compete confidence, which of course I know it will be, but we're ahead of you on that. I've had him followed for the last six months, not because he's a foreigner, but because I never fully trust anybody. And you'll be glad to know he checks out clean.'

'You had him followed? When?'

'For months, Sir, and we still do. Every time he leaves the White House, and every time he leaves his apartment.

And we found nothing, absolutely nothing. He's a simple man with no vices, Sir. No hookers, no drugs, nothing. He goes to church a lot, takes the same bus to the Eastern Orthodox place down on Edmund Street, he likes to go there several times a week for prayers and then he walks home, even if it's raining. He almost never deviates from that routine, never stops for coffee or anything, takes the same streets home all the time, an absolute creature of habit. Fit guy, too, some of the agents have trouble keeping up with him.'

'Can't they just use a car, or a bike?'

'Unfortunately his route home is mostly a one-way street, against the traffic, so that's not possible. But they manage to keep him in sight at all times, and he never meets anybody or talks to anybody. Vladimir is clean, I promise you.'

'Great, that's great news. That puts my mind at rest.'

'Anything else you want to discuss, Sir, my door is always open, obviously.'

The President relaxed somewhat, lounging against the back of the couch.

'Yes, there is one thing. Any update on that European laboratory, have we made an approach to the woman, or have we any more information?'

'Yes Sir, I'm in the middle of preparing a report for your eyes only, I'll have it for you in about two hours.'

'Great! But maybe you can give me the important bits right now?'

'Sure, Sir. Not a lot of hard progress, but we're lining up the ducks nicely. We have our guy in place in this little town, Boyle, and nobody is in any way suspicious, they just think he's a tourist who likes to fish a little. He's identified the guy, Mister Small, the aircraft specialist we're targeting as a special agent. Checked him out, lives alone in a nice cottage overlooking the river, cute place. Our man has been inside, it's spotlessly clean, newly painted. There's not a book or a paper in sight, no sign of a passport, or any kind of documentation other than utility bills, so he's obviously highly security-conscious. Our man had a few casual words with him in a bar where he goes to eat a couple of times a day, he seems well-liked there apparently. He runs a tab for food and drinks which is very unusual in Ireland, so he's obviously very trustworthy.'

'That's a positive, we want good citizens on our team. Any feedback on his abilities, any of his associates give any information about him?'

The Major consulted his notes.

'Yes, Sir. A lady called Dorothy, she runs a café in some historic building down the street, and our man asked her who the guy was when he saw him wander through there. She said he was an air accident investigator, last time she looked, but that he had 'a long CV and plenty of other strings to his bow.' Exact words, she was also very friendly apparently and had a very broad smile, according to the notes.'

'Excellent, excellent! You can't beat local knowledge, all the same. Let's hurry up and recruit him for Christ's sake.'

'Our man is waiting for his girlfriend to get out of the way, apparently, she's a Moldovan woman called Monica Macovei, beautiful blonde with 'legs to die for' according to the notes. She's apparently a bit besotted by the guy, so she's never far away from him. We're waiting until she's at work, or out of town, any chance to get to him without her noticing.'

'Remind me again, Major, where's Moldovian?'

'Moldova, Sir. It's a small country to the north of Romania, about to become part of Romania soon apparently, so anyone from there has a right to work in the European Union.'

'Isn't Romania a communist country?'

'No, Sir. A long time ago, it was part of the Soviet Union, but they got free of that and it is almost as capitalist as here. Apart from that dodgy preoccupation with providing free healthcare to losers, but all the Europeans have that obsession.'

'So, this chick, she's a tasty piece of ass? Good for him, guys like him always attract beautiful women. He's gone up in my estimation.'

'They sure do, Sir. But we're on it, we'll have him on the team by the weekend, I'd imagine.'

'Don't hang about, Major, we don't want the Russians or the Chinese getting to him, or to our scientist lady. I want that vaccine, and the sooner the better.'

Chapter Twenty Three

Vladimir Belyaev turned up his coat collar against the evening chill and pulled his broad trilby down over his ears, and strode quickly to the bus stop. He smiled to himself as he recognised the agent on his tail, an overweight, heavy-smoker who always struggled to keep up with him. He quickened his step and was amused to hear the man break into a puffing trot behind him, barely managing to catch the bus. At Edmund Street he skipped up the steps to the cathedral, quickly swopping coats and hats with Igor. His brother took up position at the top of the main aisle, bowing his head in prayer towards the altar as the agent puffed and gasped his way through the swinging glass doors.

The agent flopped gratefully into one of the chairs at the side of the church as Vladimir slipped out through the side door, walking briskly towards Wisconsin Avenue. The KGB man jogged past, giving him the usual hand-sign, and he walked briskly down Turnlaw Road and through the welcoming steel gate set in the yellow wall. In the shadows, Ambassador Kuznetsov shook his hand as he led him through the small door to the windowless corridor.

'Let's go down quickly, Comrade Belyaev, the President is expecting our call. He is not a happy man.'

They quickly took their seats and the junior officer opened the secure channel before withdrawing. They both pressed their buttons and their images appeared in picture at the top of the screen on the wall. A moment later, President Zhadnyy appeared, flanked by his two aides who wore the dress uniform of the KGB. It was clear when the President spoke that he was angry.

'Comrade Ambassador Kuznetsov and Comrade Doctor Belyaev, thank you for joining us. I'm afraid we don't have a good story to tell.'

In the basement of the consulate, both men thought it wiser not to interrupt. President Zhadnyy was renowned for his outbursts of bad temper if things were not going his way.

'I have learned, Comrades, that our Dublin office and your best agent, or so-called best agent, have between them managed to screw up a very simple operation. I mean, what did I ask you to do, Comrade Kuznetsov?'

The ambassador stammered a reply.

'In respect of this mission, Comrade President, you asked us to deploy Agent Vanda to a village in Ireland, so that she could infiltrate the laboratory that has the vaccine. I believe that was the brief.'

'And what was the outcome, Comrade Kuznetsov? Has the mission, this simple job that my most junior spy could have done before breakfast, has it been a success?'

'I don't know, Comrade President.'

The two KGB officers flinched as President Zhadnyy banged his fist on the polished mahogany desk in front of him. He leaned forward angrily.

'You don't know! You don't know? Well, I know, and would you like me to tell you, Comrades?'

'Yes, Comrade President.'

'Your people screwed it up, Comrades. Comrade Vanda has failed to recruit the guy she was after, and consequently we're no nearer to getting out hands on the vaccine. And do you know what is worse?'

'No, Comrade President.'

'The Americans are there, in theatre and with an active service unit that is obviously smarter than our people. And now they seem to have taken the guy, this Mickey Small, and made him disappear. So where are our people, Comrades? Where is the KGB in all of this, and why can nobody do anything right around here?'

Doctor Belyaev moved to calm the President.

'Are you sure the Americans have taken the guy, Comrade President? It would seem a dangerous play in a friendly country. We couldn't do that, to be fair, Dublin is our intelligence headquarters for all of Europe and we wouldn't risk eliminating a local citizen or even taking him prisoner. After all, if we did take him and torture him, for instance, we'd obviously have to end him, which would be risky.'

'We were never going to take him and torture him, Comrade Belyaev, was not our strategy to use Comrade Vanda to win him over, and to then deploy him into the laboratory or to generally find out information? So, why did she not do her usual tricks and take him to bed? Doesn't that always work?'

'I don't know, Comrade President. Any information I have is limited at this time.'

'Well mine isn't, so let me tell you, Comrades. Vanda was ready to move on him last night, she had spoken to him and was going to have dinner in the same restaurant, and then allow him to take her home to his house. But what happened?'

'We don't know, Comrade President.'

'Well, let me tell you. She went to the restaurant, and he never showed up. She waited, took her time over dinner, but no Mister Small. So she went to his house, looked through the windows but he wasn't there. Then she let herself in and checked the place, and do you know what she found?'

'Nothing, Comrade President?'

'Exactly, Comrade Kuznetsov. It was as though he did not exist. Apart from some bills for electricity, there was nothing. No passport, no bank details, absolutely nothing. Not even food in the refrigerator. He is gone, disappeared, vanished into thin air. The bird has flown, gentlemen, so I want you to do something for me.'

'Yes, Comrade President, whatever you wish.'

The President shook with anger as he banged on the desk.

'I want you to get to this woman and buy the vaccine from her, and I want it done right this time. We cannot afford to allow the Americans to get their hands on this formula, it is unthinkable. So, Comrades, unless you both want a new assignment in charge of the nuclear waste dump in Ozersk, I suggest you earn the trust I have so foolishly put in you both.'

The screen on the wall went suddenly dark, and the two men looked at each other with fear in their eyes.

Chapter Twenty Four

Lucky Oyeleye sat up sharply as he heard the tap on the door. Nurse Cohen poked her head around the door and half-smiled a greeting.

'Good evening, Mister Oyeleye! I have someone here that I want you to meet.'

She ushered a small, slightly unkempt young man into the room. Lucky tried not to let his surprise show.

'This is Mickey, Lucky. He will be sharing with you for a couple of days.'

'Yes, actually we have met.'

Mickey Small turned as if to leave, but Nurse Cohen's outstretched arm blocked his exit.

'Where do you think you're off to?'

'I'm not sharing with him, he might beat me up.'

'You've signed a contract, Mister Small, and if anybody is beating anybody up, it'll be me. Now, get in there like a good lad and shut up your moaning.'

Lucky held up his hands in a placatory gesture.

'I am not going to beat you up, Sir. All that other thing is forgiven, it is like my telephone sim cards, it is gone like water beneath the bridge. Please, sit down. You are most welcome to my home.'

Mickey Small sat down carefully on the edge of the bed, looking around with a degree of uncertainty.

'I didn't think I was coming in until Monday, why did you bring me in this evening? I was supposed to go to Clarkes, I had a date with a girl.'

'We'll bring you a nice dinner from Clarkes shortly, and sure the girl will be waiting in a couple of weeks when you go back, and you'll have loads of money in your pocket. You'll have no need of any more muggings, Mickey.'

'But why did you change the day? I don't like it when people change things. And I didn't tell anyone where I was going, they'll be worried about me.'

'Not my decision, Mickey. I just do what they tell me to do, and I'd say nobody will be too worried anyway, they'll be getting a bit of peace for a change. Now, let me show you how things work around here.'

She pointed out the kitchen and bathroom, and the way the audio and video systems worked, and opened and closed the cupboard door to demonstrate the food delivery system. At the mention of food her patient cheered up somewhat.

'Can I get the Moone Boy Burger? I do love that. And the big, chunky chips, and loads of ketchup?'

'I'll tell Caroline. Now, if you need anything, Mister Oyeleye will tell you anything I've missed. Any questions?'

'Yes, what do I have to do?'

'Nothing, just lie down and watch the television or listen to music. I'll come in every day and take a swab of your nose, like I did out in reception. That's all.'

'But what is that all about? Are you going to pay me for just lying here?'

'Yes, we are just checking whether you might catch a bit

of a cold from Mister Oyeleye here, although he doesn't actually have a cold, if you know what I mean.'

'But if he hasn't got a cold, how can I catch it from him? I thought he'd have to have a cold first?'

'Don't worry about the detail, you'll still get paid anyway.'

'So how long will I be here, trying to catch a cold that he doesn't have? That could take a while, I'd say.'

'We'll leave you here with Mister Oyeleye for a week, then we'll give you a room of your own for the next trial.'

'To see if I'll catch a cold from myself?'

'No, we'll give you a vaccine, and then we'll leave you there for a few days until the vaccine takes effect.'

'I don't like needles stuck in me, I hate that, actually.'

'We won't stick a needle in you, it's a vaccine you can drink in a glass of water.'

'I don't like water. Can I have it in Coca Cola?'

'If you like, yes.'

'That's grand, so. And I can go home then, with my wages? I have a date with a girl I met in Clarkes.'

'Not right away, but soon. There's another trial after that, just a few days. If that all goes okay, you can go home then, with six grand in your pocket.'

'Six grand? I'll be flying with six grand, I'll be able to buy a load of pints. So what's the next trial, after I drink the Pepsi?'

'I thought you said you wanted Coca Cola?'

'I changed my mind, I like Pepsi better.'

'Whatever you wish. The next thing after that is we spray a little sniff of a mist up your nose, to see if the vaccine stops you getting a bit of a cold.'

'And will it? Will it stop me getting a cold? I don't like getting colds.'

'It should do, that's the whole idea.'

'And then I get my six grand?'

'Yes. You'll be a rich man then, Mickey Small.'

'I will, surely. I'll be rolling in it, missus. I'll be the richest man in Boyle, so I will.'

'Just one thing, Mickey, before I go and leave you to it. In the case of an emergency, although that will never happen, but if it does, the doors will automatically unlock and you just follow the exit signs to get out. If for some reason none of that works, you break that little square of glass and the door will unlock and you can get out through the exit at the end of the corridor, under the green sign. Do you understand all that?'

'Oh yes, I do watch 'Air Accident Investigations,' I know all about it. Emergency lighting will guide me to the nearest exit, that's what happens. And if there's smoke I get down and crawl, I know all that.'

'Good. But also remember that if you break that glass and leave the room or the building for no reason, you won't get a penny of your wages and you will owe us for the accommodation and the food and everything. Do you understand all that?'

'Oh, I do, missus. I do surely.'

'Grand, so, I'll leave you boys to it, and your dinners will be here in half an hour.'

Chapter Twenty Five

Randy Corless sighed as the Sherriff waved him down. He braked and pulled in to the curb, and wound down the window as Kendall approached the truck.

'Mornin', Sherriff.'

'Where y'all goin' Randy?'

'I jest goin' ter the gas station, Sherriff, deliverin' some ice. Bill, he need some ice real urgent, this hot weather, folks uses a lotta ice.'

'How many ya got?'

'Sixty bag, Sherriff.'

'Y'all got fifty-eight bags now, Randy.'

'Nope, Sherriff, I got sixty. I done counted 'em two times, for ter be sure.'

'Read my lips, Randy. Yer got fifty-eight. I want yer to drop two bags to my wife.'

'Whatever yer says, Sherriff. Dang, but yer wife shore usin' a lotta ice these days.'

'Y'all mind yer own business, Randy, jest deliver the damn ice afore I start getting' curious about them tires a yourn. One a them lookin' as bald as a baby's ass.'

'I got it, Sherriff.'

'And while you're thar, clean up that kitchen for my wife.

Since I run that black woman off, place gone ter hell.'

'Kin yer pay me fer that work, Sherriff? I's plenty busy already.'

'Lemme see them tires, Randy. Reckon yer hafta leave that truck here until yer fix them.'

'Okay, Sherriff, I'll see to yer kitchen, this time.'

Randy drove angrily to the gas station and unloaded the bags of ice into the big freezer.

'Here ya go, Bill, fifty eight bags.'

'Not sixty? Sherriff Kendall usin' a lotta ice?'

'Damn right. I's in a mind ter tell him get his own damn ice.'

'I's often in a mind ter tell him get his own damn coffee, too, but he the Sherriff at the end of the day. Guess it is what it is, Randy.'

Randy put the truck in gear and drove slowly to the Sheriff's house. He picked both bags of ice out of the back and carried them to the door before ringing the doorbell. The policeman's wife blinked in the sunlight as she opened the door, slurring her words slightly as she spoke.

'Howdy, Randy, bring 'em in and put 'em in the icebox.'

Randy did as he was asked, looking around in surprise at the state of the kitchen. Dirty dishes filled every available space, and cooking pots and takeaway food containers were beginning to smell and had attracted a swarm of flies. He shyly broached the subject of the cleanup.

'Yore husband, Maa'm, he tell me ter give yer a hand with the vessels an' all.'

The woman bristled with half-concealed anger.

'My damn husband kin go ter hell, he was the one that ran off the maid, told me we can't git another one. How the hell am I expected ter keep house on my own, I don't got the time fer all that stuff. I'm married to the

Sherriff of this town, I don't do no dishes.'

'I kin give yer a hand, Ma'am, tek no time at all. Don't yer have one o' them machines fer washin' all the vessels?'

'Yeah, there one thar, but I don't know how to drive her.'

Randy pulled open the door of the dishwasher.

'I seen one o' them in a place whar we was doin' some work a couple year back. 'Taint complicated, my brother Buddy, he explain ter me how it work.'

'Then get her done, fill her with them dishes and get her started!'

Randy set to work, scraping food waste into bins and packing the dishes into the dishwasher. He poured the powder into the drawer and switched on the machine, smiling a toothy grin as it burst into life. He quickly cleaned off the worktops and brought the garbage outside to the trash cans. The woman watched from her armchair in the corner, sipping on a drink from a crystal glass.

'Damn, place looks better already. Shore didn't take you long, Randy. You do the housework at home too?'

Yes, Ma'am, shore do. I tries to keep on top o' her, so she don't git so bad.'

'You wanna do it every couple days, Randy? I'll pay yer ten dollars iffen you do.'

Randy shook his head.

'Sorry, Ma'am, I don't got no time, got ter work on the farm, an' other stuff.'

'Like yer moonshine? I know all about yer moonshine, Randy, my husband says you makes the best moonshine in the county.'

Randy shuffled his feet uneasily.

'We don't make no moonshine, Ma'am. We jest makes ice, that all.'

She got up and staggered to the refrigerator, adding a couple of lumps of ice to her glass and topping up the drink from a bottle that was chilling in the refrigerator door. Randy recognised the bottle as one of his own, and the smell of moonshine wafted across the room as she poured.

'You want a drink, Randy, a little drinkie?'

'No, Ma'am, thank you Ma'am.'

'This real good moonshine, Randy. I think you made this moonshine, didn't y'all?'

Randy mumbled and shuffled his feet.

'Maybe, Ma'am.'

'Call me Shirley; we friends, Randy.'

She lurched towards him, grabbing him around the neck for support. He could smell her perfume and the strong aroma of booze from her breath. Randy felt uncomfortable and tried to pull away.

'Ma'am, iffen Sherriff Kendall come in now he kill two of us, I reckon. He be real mad.'

She laughed, and hiccupped, dissolving into a fit of giggles.

'It's Shirley, Randy. And don' worry about my husband, he never come home until long after suppertime, he got a fancy woman over in the cathouse across the county line, though I don' know what he does to her, he can't get near a woman with that belly he got on him.'

Randy tried to break free, but the woman had a strong grip around his neck.

'Ma'am, I gotta go.'

'I let you go when y'all call me Shirley.'

'I gotta go, Shirley.'

'Y'all gotta call me Shirley darlin', then yer can go.'

'Okay. I gotta go, Shirley darlin'.'

'An' yer gotta kiss me, then yer can go.'

Randy kissed her awkwardly, and she clung tight before eventually releasing her grip. He backed away quickly and headed for the door. She laughed at his discomfort.

'It were jest a li'l kiss, Randy, ain't no harm in friends kissin'. Kin yer bring me more ice day after tomorra,' reckon I'll be all out by then. An' yer can help me clean up the kitchen. Darlin'.'

He heard her laughter as he ran to the door and jumped in the truck.

Chapter Twenty Six

Ambassador Kuznetsov placed his passport on the desk at the diplomatic counter at Shannon Airport, on Ireland's west coast. The woman spoke politely while flicking through the document.

'Will you be staying with us for long, Ambassador?'

'Just two nights, madam. I am meeting my counterpart in Dublin, there is a car waiting for me outside. I will be back in two days to continue my flight to Moscow.'

'Just killing two birds then? A pity to waste a stop-over?'

'Exactly. It's a social visit, really, to a former colleague. Not enough to justify a special trip, but as I was passing through from Washington I thought a little break in Ireland would be nice. A few pints of Guinness, and some of your lovely food, it is never a chore. And this country is not so unpleasantly hot as either Moscow or Washington at this time of year.'

'Yes, the humidity is a pure devil in them places, I hear. Have a nice trip, Sir, and welcome to Ireland.'

At the exit door he spotted the black Mercedes with the CD plates and walked towards it. The driver stepped out and opened the back door, taking his bag and stowing it in the boot. The Ambassador settled himself into the comfortable seat and reached out a hand to his colleague.

'Ivan Turgenev, thank you for coming to collect me. How is your posting here?'

'It is good, Igor Kuznetsov, a busy place with dismal weather but the population is welcoming to people of white skin and Christian origin. Not as busy or exciting as Washington, I imagine. You have done well since our days in the officer training college.'

'Believe me, Ivan Turgenev, I would exchange my position in America for your job in Dublin in heartbeat, I could happily live without having to deal with the idiot who runs the country over there.'

'Daniels? Can you believe that the Americans would elect such a clown to the highest office? A man of little education and with no record of service to his country, a seller of used cars, never in the army? In a country so big, you would imagine they could find one person of ability, but it seems not to be so.'

'We must bake with the flour we have been given, Comrade, otherwise we have no bread at all. So, how is the Dublin operation going for us?'

'It runs with no problems, Comrade Kuznetsov, we are able to run our European intelligence operation from here, the government in Dublin has no understanding of our business, or they don't care too much as long as we don't kill people and leave the bodies lying in the street.'

'Is the government still in our control?'

'No, we lost them in the last election, I think maybe they over-promised much and delivered little, although perhaps that describes all politicians, no?'

'But we must have gained some advantage by having them in charge for a time? As I remember, we spent a lot of money putting them there.'

'Yes, we got some law changes that will weaken their government for many years, and quite a lot of capitalist money driven out of the country too. So the overall reduced standard of living creates a good possibility for instability of course, which will help with our longer-term aims.'

'Dismantling the cursed European Union, you mean?'

'Yes, Comrade President Zhadnyy has that as his priority, he wants to return to the glory days of the USSR, his empire, as he sees it. But speaking of our beloved President, that is of course the reason for your visit?'

'Yes, I am one step away from the Gulag if I don't fix this problem. Is it far away, this village we spoke of?'

'No, maybe one hour and a half, maximum. We have good roads for most of the journey, then a slower bit for the last few kilometres.'

The driver accelerated as he joined the M18, following the signs for Galway and Sligo. The two passengers were silent for a while, before Turgenev spoke.

'You have a plan, for when we get there?'

'In broad terms, yes, but I will be guided by your local knowledge. Have your people arranged accommodation for us?'

'Yes, there is an excellent small gostinitsa in the village, it is called 'Frybrook,' it was originally the home of one of the local minor nobility.'

Kuznetsov smiled.

'Nothing is too good for the workers, Comrade. Is our colleague Vanda there now?'

'Yes, but not in Frybrook. She is in a cheap place, just down the street. Her cover is that she is a Moldovan woman who looks for cleaning work. Her operation name is 'Monica Macovei,' the same as the Romanian Minister who put many of our comrades in Romania into jail, if you remember.'

'Yes, the reformer, I do indeed remember. She locked up that guy, he used to look after the money for us when we worked in Dresden with Comrade Zhadnyy; I can't remember his real name. It is a good name for her to use however, we will none of us forget that woman, for sure.'

'So we will go directly to the place where we stay, and then we will go for a walk in their forest, it is small but very beautiful with a lake. Agent Jakovf will walk there too, and we can meet with her and she will give us whatever information she has about the target building.'

'Boyle Labs? I am interested to see this institute, for sure. So, Comrade Turgenev, what is your opinion of the situation, from what you have learned from Agent Jakovf?'

'I believe that the woman who owns the institute is what you would call in America a 'tough cookie,' so she will not be easily intimidated or persuaded about anything. In addition, because the Americans are in theatre, they may have already made an approach with an offer of money, so we cannot afford to be greedy. If she asks for some particular amount, we cannot easily offer something that is far less, for sure.'

'What about the American who is in position, do we know him?'

'We have information on him from our surveillance of their embassy in Dublin, obviously, but nothing of importance and nothing we can use to advantage. Our current information is that he is not a trained spy, that he is just a petty functionary who works for the CIA at a low level. His official role is as a cultural attaché, but he travels around the country a lot to gather information under the pretence that he likes to fish. His cover is really very bad, it is clear he knows little about fishing.'

'Not somebody to take seriously?'

'I would have thought this, indeed his methods are so amateur that my ten year old niece could see that he is a fake, but we may have been completely wrong about him. It may be that he is indeed a genius, that the stupid behaviour is a mere ploy to lull us into thinking he is an idiot. In any case it appears that he snatched away our civilian target, our aircraft guy, from under our noses. So he can't be entirely stupid.'

'Comrade Zhadnyy was not pleased.'

'Yes, that's an understatement and indeed our immediate problem. We must make amends on that front or we are all going to Ozersk. It's not just you and Comrade Belyaev that are under the gaze of our leader. Now that the focus has moved to Ireland, I am also under scrutiny since the game is being played in my stadium, so to speak. We are indeed all in this together, Comrade Kuznetsov.'

'I believe we are, although Comrade Belyaev is in the highest position we have ever achieved for one of our agents in America, so Comrade Zhadnyy may hesitate before removing him. For you and me though, our comradeship with him in Dresden and indeed after he moved to Leningrad will not save us if he decides to swing his cutlass.'

'Indeed, he becomes more ruthless every year. We must deliver this vaccine or life will not be worth living. In truth, I had hoped I would finish my service here in Ireland, it is an easy posting even if the weather is dreadful.'

'And I, in Washington. While it is not in any way like Leningrad, or as they now say, Saint Petersburg, it is an impressive city with much culture, for a capitalist country. The food is dreadful, but we manage.'

'Yes, 'dining for Mother Russia,' as we say here also when we must suffer the tedium of official duties in fine restaurants.'

'And it is possible to get good food here, in Ireland?'

'Oh, yes. But not in general in restaurants, many of them are the ubiquitous American-style places with processed rubbish, or Chinese takeaway places where they soak bits of cheap meat in some kind of yellow sauce they buy by the bucketful from some factory. If you avoid these, and are happy to pay a little more, it is indeed possible to find good food, yes.'

'And fine wines?'

'Not so much, but we have these shipped in from the European mainland, French reds and of course good German whites. We keep a good cellar at the embassy, you must come again when this unfortunate business is finished and we can celebrate over a good dinner.'

'Yes, I would be delighted, indeed. Although this problem has caused me to lose my appetite for the finer things in life for the moment.'

They fell silent for a while as the big car turned off the main road and wound its way down country roads and through small towns and villages. Ambassador Kuznetsov lay back and dozed intermittently, lulled by the swaying and the warmth of the car.

A hard left-hand bend jolted him into wakefulness, and he looked out the window as they passed down a suburban road. His host pointed out a large monolithic block of a building close to the street.

'There, that is Boyle Labs, we are in Boyle village-town now.'

'Ah, that did not take long. It really is a small place, and that building does not impress at all. Can it be that this is actually the centre of research that has led the world?'

'Yes, it is hard to believe, but that is the place. And now we are at our destination.'

The driver slowed as he crossed the bridge over the river, turning left into a small square. In the corner of the space a narrow gate filled a small archway, and he carefully threaded the big car through the opening and followed a driveway along the riverbank. A small mansion loomed ahead, with a welcoming array of large flowerpots framing the wide stone steps that rose to the elegant front door.

The driver slowed the car and brought it gently to a halt in front of the entrance, and the two passengers alighted and stretched themselves as they looked around. The evening sun silhouetted the house, casting long shadows across the graveled forecourt. Ambassador Turgenev pointed to the river that raced in a summer flood across the stony riverbed.

'This river is apparently good for catching of the trout fish, although at the moment it's probably too high for successful fishing. In the spring and autumn it is better, I believe. I intend to come back here for a weekend in September to try my luck. If I still have a job, that is.'

Ambassador Kuznetsov laughed sadly.

'And if I still have a job, I might come back and join you. It is certainly a beautiful place, very quiet and peaceful. What a shame we are visiting for a purpose other than leisure and enjoyment.'

'Yes, but we must be hopeful, always. We have to find this woman and make with her a deal that she will not refuse.'

The driver took the baggage from the car and climbed the steps to ring the front door bell. The two men followed him as the door opened and a friendly woman greeted them.

'Come in, you're welcome. Mister Kuznetsov and Mister

Turgenev, isn't it? Are you here for the fishing?'

Ambassador Turgenev reached for the woman's outstretched hand, kissing it and bowing politely in one fluid movement.

'I am Ivan Turgenev, and this is my colleague Igor. We are merely taking a few days to see this part of the country. I am the Ambassador to Ireland and my colleague works in the Embassy of the Russian Republic in Washington, he is taking a few days in Ireland as my guest. We believe it is always nice to take some time and see the best parts of the country where we are posted. And to meet beautiful people too, of course!'

The woman blushed at the attention. She ushered them into an elegant hallway and checked their bookings on a tablet on a small desk. She took two key cards from a drawer and gave them one each.

'Leave your bags there, gentlemen, and I'll have them brought to your rooms. Breakfast is from seven in the morning, and there are a number of excellent restaurants in the town that serve dinner. Clarke's is the nearest, just around the corner, and we have a facility called the Boyle Card where you can put your meals and drinks on your room bill, using your room keys.'

'Thank you, that is useful.'

'Your driver, does he need to stay with us too?'

'No, he has made other arrangements, but he may leave the car here if that is okay with you?'

'Certainly, that is no problem.'

The two men checked their rooms and changed into casual clothing, returning to the lobby a short time later. Outside, the driver stood by the car with the doors open. They slid into the rear seat and Ambassador Turgenev spoke to the driver.

'Boyle Harbour, where there is a walking path that leads to the Forest Park. Did you get the instruction from Agent Jakovf?'

'Yes, Sir, I have studied the location on the map, it is not far.'

The car drove along the main street and turned left at the partly-restored ruins of an ancient church, driving slowly down a slight hill and on to the outskirts of the small town, where the river ran briefly alongside the roadway for a while. The driver turned right and then left into a small harbour area, where a number of pleasure craft lay at their moorings. He got out and opened the doors for his two passengers, pointing to a broad path that followed the canal bank.

'This pathway leads to the Forest Park, gentlemen. Comrade Jakovf will meet you along there, she is in position about three hundred metres away and will emerge when you walk in that direction. She will have a map and will pretend to stop you and ask directions, in case you are being observed.'

The two men strolled along the pathway, enjoying the evening sunshine. They paused for a while to watch a couple of anglers who sat on folding stools, sleepily observing their floats drift on the mirror-like calm water, and wearing thin balaclavas to protect their faces from the biting midges that swarmed around their heads. As they resumed their walk Igor Kuznetsov nudged his companion's elbow, nodding towards the Lycra-clad slim figure of Vanda Jakovf as she emerged from the cover of some shrubs along the side of the pathway. She unfolded a map she was carrying and spoke to the two men.

'Excuse me, gentlemen, is this the right direction for Boyle?'

Ivan Turgenev gestured in the direction from which they had come, then spoke quietly to his agent.

'You have news, Comrade Jakovf?'

She spoke quietly in return, pointing to the map and back in the other direction as she spoke.

'The Americans are here, I believe they have taken Mister Mickey Small, the man we wanted to use. I had him on the hook but he disappeared. His house reveals nothing, it is clean and newly painted, and all the clothes in the cupboards are new and unused. It is as though he has disappeared off the face of the earth.'

'You think they have him imprisoned somewhere?'

'Yes, I have tried to follow the American who is here, but he has a car and it is difficult. When he walks in the town he just goes around and around in circles, going nowhere. I thought he would lead me to where they have Mister Small, but not so.'

'Where is he staying?'

'He is in a place called 'Frybrook,' it is in the middle of the town.'

'Yes, we know it, we are also staying there.'

'Oh my God, is that secure? Maybe you should move out?'

'It is fine, our laptops are encrypted if he finds them; it is not a problem. Do you think he has made contact with the director of the institute?'

'It is possible, but I have not seen evidence of it. I have a camera that watches the entrance to the institute, I put it there the day after Mister Small disappeared, and I check it each evening on my laptop when I get home. So far, it is only the staff that come and go, as well as the vans from the restaurants that bring food to the prisoners.'

'Where are you staying?'

'I have a small flat over the fruit shop on Main Street, you can find me there. The door to the side is the entrance to the flats, on my bell it says 'M McEvoy.' Monica Macovei is the name I use on this mission, ostensibly a citizen of Moldova, but many Irish mis-hear it as McEvoy, which is an Irish patronym.'

'Maybe he has approached her at her house? Do you know where it is?'

'Yes, she lives with her husband who is a policeman, on the road to Carrick on Shannon, near the circular church. He is there much, she not so much. I have also now placed a camera there, and I will check it this evening. But I think they will not go where there is a policeman living, they ask too many questions.'

'Can we maybe buy him? Most policemen are fond of money.'

'In Russia, yes, Comrade. But here, not so much. It might create problems. It is better I think to approach her directly, she must be expecting a call from us.'

'Yes, but where to find her?'

'She goes often to her colleague's house in a place called Greatmeadow, near the institute. He is her senior scientist.'

'Is she in a relationship with him?'

'I do not believe so, he is single and may possibly be a sodomit; there is no record of him having any interest in women.'

'So, what are his vices? Drugs, orgies with Englishmen? Gambling?'

'Nothing, he just likes to fish.'

'Perhaps we should talk to him? We could go to his house and tell him we want to speak with his boss.'

'I don't think that is a good idea, Comrade.'

'Well then, Comrade Jakovf, what do you think is the right approach?'

'At this point, comrades, I believe you should maybe go to the institute in the morning and ring the doorbell. Maybe the direct approach is the best one?'

'You are probably right, Comrade. Comrade Belyaev and I will go there in the morning. In the meantime, keep up with the surveillance, and let us know immediately if anything moves.'

'Yes, Sir.'

'And be careful, we do not want you to disappear like your almost agent.'

The two men continued strolling away from the road towards the Forest Park, and Vanda folded her map and marched swiftly towards the town. As she reached the carpark, one of the fishermen rolled his balaclava away from his face and packed up his rod and stool, reaching for his phone as he strode quickly towards the harbour.

Chapter Twenty Seven

Major Callaghan looked up from his desk as he heard a tap on his door. His aide looked around the door and spoke quietly.

'The President is here, Sir. He wants to see you.'

The officer stood up quickly.

'Thank you, Jessie, show him in immediately.'

President Daniels walked briskly into the office and motioned his Chief of Staff to resume his seat.

'No need to get up, Mike. I felt like getting out of my office and I'd prefer to talk to you here than there. You got any updates on the operation in Europe, in Ireland?'

'Good morning, Sir, I'm glad you called by. I was in the process of putting a report together for you. We seem to be winning that particular war.'

'We got our hands on it? Holy guacamole!'

'Well, Sir, that would be a little premature. But I do believe we have managed to close a deal with the head of Boyle Labs, our man on the ground has brought me up to date this morning on progress, and it's all good. It's Monday afternoon there now, they're about five hours ahead of us, and he was up late last night negotiating with the woman and her sidekick, her senior scientist, a guy called Billy

Robinson. They got agreement late last night, apparently it was a tough battle but her preference appeared to be to deal with us and not our Russian allies.'

'So, when you say it would be premature to say we've closed a deal, what hasn't been done?'

'It's just down to some additional testing, Sir. They have a few human lab-rats in the facility and they have given them various doses of the vaccine, and various strengths including a highly-concentrated solution, where they fed the guy enough of the product to vaccinate more than a million people, and he hasn't died yet anyhow.'

'So they have to do various tests on him, I guess, to see if it screws with his liver and stuff, like drinking a bottle of Bourbon at a sitting?'

'That kind of thing, Sir.'

'And where are the Russians in all this?'

'They got two heavy hitters in theatre, their ambassador to Ireland, a guy called Ivan Turgenev, we would know him from his KGB days. He's one of Zhadnyy's close confidants from their days in Dresden and in Saint Petersburg, a dangerous guy in his day but widely now seen as seeing out his last couple of years to retirement before moving back to the motherland.'

'They're taking this matter seriously, so.'

'Very seriously, Sir. The other operative in the field is none other than our local friend, Ambassador Igor Kuznetsov from the Russian embassy down the street.'

'Holy guacamole! I thought Igor was a friend of ours?'

'You know what they say, Sir, there are no friends in diplomacy, just strategic interests. President Zhadnyy must be taking this seriously if he has two of his most trusted lieutenants on the job. They also have Vanda on the ground in Boyle, from the embassy here, but she is operating on a Moldovan passport and using a false name. And of course there may be others that we don't know of or haven't spotted.'

'Vanda, yes, I remember her. Great-looking chick, blonde with legs to die for. I hope I didn't say anything inappropriate to her last time I stayed over.'

The Major didn't comment, but changed the subject.

'We had just one guy in field, Hank, but he's very good. He's staying in the same hotel as the two Russians, and has already gone through their rooms and used a memory scavenger to download the contents of their laptops, and we're analysing all that now to see if we can find out what they're planning. I've also taken the precaution of moving in a couple of other agents to cover our guy's back, and they are now in position as of an hour ago.'

'Excellent work, Major.'

'The two other guys have already spotted a number of cameras that have apparently been installed and are being monitored by Vanda, and they've intercepted the feed from these and diverted it to here, so that we can see what she's seeing.'

'I hope they're not using the local wi-fi network. I wouldn't like our guys to be caught doing surveillance in a friendly country. The Irish vote is very important to us.'

'No, Sir, they're using one of our own covert trucks, a motorhome actually with a satellite upload, and it's encrypted, of course.'

'Well done, Major. And when will we know we've got it in the bag?'

'I would estimate that we'll have it all wrapped up by the end of the week, Sir. Or at least enough of it for you to make the announcement.'

'That's what I like to hear, Major.'

'Thank you, Sir. And I assume you would like to know the detail, the cost and all that?'

'Of course, of course. The taxpayer dollar is important to us. What is the bill likely to be?'

'As we expected, Sir. Our man had authority for a hundred million, but he didn't have to put all that on the table.'

'That's good.'

'Unfortunately, there's a sting in the tail, Sir. She also demanded a royalty, based on the number of vaccinations issued. Worldwide.'

'Wow! So what were the terms?'

'Seventy million euro, Sir, that's about eighty-two million dollars. That's for a sole licence to use the vaccine and the technology associated with it. America will own the rights to produce this vaccine and we will be the only country that can manufacture it.'

'And what how much will the royalty be?'

'Five cents per shot, Sir. Could add up to another fifteen million in the USA alone.'

'But if we add it to the water, she can't track those, surely?'

'We'll have to put figures out for all the people reached, Sir, otherwise the WHO won't declare us as having sufficient bodies vaccinated to call us a safe country. So even if we only inject fifty million people, we're going to have to quote figures for a lot more. The contract is based on WHO verified figures.'

'Damn! I never thought of that angle. This broad sounds like a smart lady.'

'Smart, and lucky too, Sir. If the Russians hadn't been barking at our heels, we'd have done a better deal, but I told Hank not to come out of there without ink on a contract.'

'Don't be too hard on yourself, Major. Difficult times require difficult solutions. I'll ask Vladimir to put a proposal together to get Congress approval for the extra spend.'

'Is that wise, Sir? I know he's our most senior medic and we have checked him thoroughly, but Doctor Belyaev is Russian, after all.'

'I have no worries about Vladimir, Major. I appreciate your concern, but like you said, you've been keeping an eye on him and he's clean.'

'Yes, Sir, he is that. Anyhow, I'll have this report on your desk in an hour, with an abridged version for Doctor Belyaev, and you can take it from there. Is there anything else you need, Sir?'

'Yes, Major, I've been drawing up a strategy with my public relations people, I'm going to have a little event for the TV cameras where I get injected with the vaccine, so people know it's safe. And I'll do it somewhere that there are a lot of anti-vaxxers, out in the Boonies somewhere, with some hillbilly who can't put two words together, the common man, you know? Just to show them I trust the medics.'

'Sounds like a plan, Sir. You got a preference?'

'Well, there's that guy who hosted the dinner for the Klan last year, he's the Sherriff down in some hick place in Tennessee; he's the Grand Wizard or something of the local Klan gang.'

'Klavern, Sir.'

'I'm Sorry, Major, what's a hole in the ground got to do with it?'

''Klavern,' Sir, not 'cavern.' That's what they call the local gangs. Every Klavern has a Grand Dragon in charge.'

'Gotcha. Anyhow, I got the details of the guy someplace.'

'You gonna use him? He might be unwilling to be vaccinated, Sir. The Klan don't trust vaccines.'

'No, you're right, the Klan guys won't take it, but he's gotta have a contact with some dumbass hick from up the mountains who either isn't in the Klan or who'll do it for a fee. Or pretend to do it, if he likes. I just need a picture of a guy having a needle stuck in his arm at the same time they give it to me.'

'Okay, Sir, we'll get on it. Do you remember the name of the Police chief, or the town?'

'Corner Creek, I think it was called. The Klan boss was a real obese guy, something 'Junior,' but I guess there's just one Sherriff in a place like that.'

'I'm pretty sure we fitted our kit to the water supply there, that town name rings a bell with me. I'll check with our agents who did the job and I'll get back to you, Sir.'

The President turned to leave.

'Thank you, Major. And give my congratulations to your guy in Ireland, the guy that did the deal. It is very important to us, it would be a disaster if our Russian Allies were seen to be in control of our nation's health. So, thank him for me.'

'I'll do that, Sir. Thank you, I appreciate it.'

Chapter Twenty Eight

Lucky Oyeleye adjusted the mask over his nose and mouth as he walked back to the building from Caroline's office. He felt suddenly hungry, and he looked forward to his evening meal. He had ordered the steak and chips with the cheesecake for dessert, and he licked his lips in anticipation. Caroline used her card to open the door to the main building.

'Your wife is okay, Lucky?'

'Yes, indeed, Missus Caroline. She is happy that I am earning good money and that we will have a future when this is over.'

'I'm sorry I have to listen in on your calls, I don't mean to be rude but I have to be sure that no word of this project is shared with anybody, anywhere.'

'There is no need to apologise, I understand perfectly. These were the conditions under which I accepted this contract, and I have no complaints. None at all.'

'Thanks, Lucky. I wish all our testers were so understanding.'

'You mean Mister Small? He is difficult for you, I imagine.'

'No worse than many of them, but I certainly couldn't

risk letting him go to my office to make a phone call. I'm afraid Mickey has to stay inside the secure perimeter until his role in the process is no longer necessary.'

'He should be happy, I believe he is earning more money than he could dream of earning in any other job. His ability levels and language skills are limited, in my estimation.'

She laughed as she opened the door to Lucky's room and showed him in.

'You put that a lot more nicely than I would. He's basically a useless lump who wouldn't get a job anywhere, but sure wouldn't it be a dull world if we were all the same?'

'Indeed, it is true. He is pleasant enough, once you get to know him, but his view of the world is coloured by watching too much television and he has no real life experience. I believe there is some small piece of the puzzle that has become lost, as we say.'

'Or was never there! Anyway, are you all right for everything?'

'Certainly, although I wonder when the project will end?'

'You want to get your freedom? It can't be easy, locked up in solitary confinement.'

'No, that is not the issue, not at all. I can tolerate as much of this as is necessary, it is accumulating money in my bank account at a rate that I could never have dreamed of, to be honest. I now have enough money to buy a house for my wife and myself back home. It was more than I had imagined was possible when I came to this country.'

'So you want to see a bit of light at the end of the tunnel, a bit of certainty?'

'In the fullness of time, Missus Caroline. I can wait as long as you need me, it is all just adding to my security and my future. A couple of more weeks and I can buy a taxi back home, start my own business and be truly independent.'

'But you'd like to know? I understand that, but I can't really give you an answer to that at this point. It appears that we will need you for another three weeks at least, we have further testing to do and the result of those tests may require further testing to be carried out.'

'But I have not had any disease, no infections. I didn't even catch a cold.'

'Yes, I know, but you could have been a vector, a carrier for a virus that we exposed you to.'

'I felt well, at all times.'

'Yes, that is true. But it didn't mean you weren't infectious for a time.'

'So that was why you sent two different people to share my room, Mister Small and the English gentleman?'

'Exactly. So now we monitor them, take a series of samples from them over a given period, to see whether they have evidence of antibodies in their systems.'

'The presence of antibodies in their systems would show that they had been exposed to the virus?'

'You catch on quick, Lucky Oyeleye!'

'Thank you, I try always to understand what is going on. So, if they don't have the antibodies?'

'We will then vaccinate them with a new vaccine, and then we will again expose you to the virus and see whether you are a carrier. We know you have an immunity, but we will then check whether their bodies generate antibodies by exposing you to them.'

'So I can look forward to some company again?'

'Yes, for a couple of days each.'

'And then?'

Then we will expose them directly to the virus and see what their antibody response is like. After that, or in parallel with that we will administer the vaccine to you, and expose you to the virus again.'

'But you said I appear immune? I don't understand.'

'That will be a test to see whether you generate antibodies to the specific strain of the virus. Once we've gone through all those tests, and once we're happy that you are healthy and not a threat to anybody, you'll be free to go.'

'That makes the whole thing much clearer in my mind, thank you. Nurse Cohen explained it, but not in detail, and honestly she is not somebody with whom I feel comfortable when it comes to asking questions.'

The administrator laughed.

'Mary's bark is worse than her bite, she can be a bit blunt but she's a good nurse.'

'Oh yes, I am sure she is medically very competent. I got that impression from the first day I met her. But she is less empathetic, not so worried about people's feelings, I think.'

'Ah, Mary is grand, but I know what you mean. She doesn't suffer fools gladly. But you're happy now, everything clear?'

'Yes, thank you. I can rest easier now, and I won't bother you with any more questions.'

Caroline unlocked the door and headed out into the corridor.

'Ask all you like, Lucky. And enjoy your dinner.'

Chapter Twenty Nine

Shirley Kendall squinted as she peered through the windscreen of the big car, gunning the engine when she spotted the road that led up towards the mountain. She drove gingerly along the narrowing trail between the tall trees, slowing down as the tyres started to slide on the graveled surface.

She braked and backed up as she passed a narrow side road, hauling on the wheel and turning up the steep road that wound through the woods. She slowed to a crawl and steered around ruts and potholes as the roadway deteriorated and the undergrowth closed in and scraped along the sides of the vehicle.

She considered turning around, but then she spotted the old truck as she emerged from the woods and the vista opened up to give way to rolling small fields where a few scrawny cattle grazed and gazed at the strange car across a rusty barbed-wire fence. She pulled up behind the truck, beside a dilapidated small cabin where the two Corless brothers sat on rocking chairs on the shaded porch. Randy jumped to his feet in alarm as she emerged from the car and lurched unsteadily towards the cabin.

'Missus Kendall, Shirley, what y'all doin' here? Y'all broke down or what?'

She stopped and peered at Randy, and at the cabin.

'I come t'see yer, Randy, Honey. Why didn't y'all come by my house this week? I had a lotta housework needed doin', I thought y'all might have come by to help a girl out.'

'Tell the truth, Shirley, I was gettin' nervous 'bout it all.'

'Nervous, what you all nervous about, honey?'

'I gotten nervous about me an' you, y'all know what I mean.'

'About the kissin' and stuff? Ain't no reason to worry 'bout that, I never tell the fat guy.'

'Weren't the kissin' so much as the stuff, more the humpy-bumpty and stuff.'

'Didn't ya like it, honey?'

'Shore I liked it, course I did. Helluva lot better'n a cathouse, fer shore, an' it free. But if Sherriff Kendall come home and found us, we be dead, Shirley.'

'To hell with him, Randy, him comin' home every day with the smell of another woman offa him. Anyhow he ain't come near my room for a couple years; you could be in there, dipping the pump in the ol' oil well and he wouldn't notice a thang.'

Randy shuddered at the thought.

'Don't think I'd like to take that chance, Shirley. Don't think I'd like that kinda excitement.'

'You too scared of my husband, Randy. Jest relax and enjoy what we got, two consentin' adults having some fun. C'mon, take me to yo bedroom, show me round.'

Randy reluctantly led the way into the small cabin, past his brother who sat on the porch, swinging his legs. The woman saluted him as she passed.

'Hi y'all, I'm Shirley, I'se a friend of yo brother.'

'I'm Buddy, Ma'am. Yo welcome, I'm shore.'

She dragged Randy inside the cabin, swinging around in surprise as she took in the inside of the house.

'Randy, this place so clean an' nice, y'all got it fixed up real good.'

'Yes ma'am, we like to keep her clean, Ma allus tol' us keep the house nice, above everythin' else.'

'So, where y'all sleep?'

'Buddy sleep through thar, an I sleep in ma own room, back thar.'

'I'se gonna stay a while, Randy. I don' wanna go back to ma husband right now.'

'Damn, Shirley, I not so sure 'bout that. What iffen yo husband come lookin'?'

'We kin hide ma car back of yo barn, he never see it even iffen he come by. Anyhow, why he come lookin' up here, if he think I run off, he never think I come up the mountain.'

'I guess that true.'

'He don't even miss me, I reckon, not for couple o days anyhow. I wanna just stay here with you for a while. Kin I see yore bedroom?'

Randy lifted the latch and pushed open one of the heavy plank doors that led off the kitchen. Shirley cried out in delight as she threw herself down on the bed.

'Y'all keep the pace so clean, Randy, clean sheets an' all. Damn! C'mon in here an warm a gal up, we put a log in the stove.'

Chapter Thirty

The two men blinked in the bright sunlight once they moved outside the gloomy, brown-painted interior of Pushkin international airport at Sheremetyevo, on the outskirts of Moscow. Mafia taxi drivers jostled for their custom but fell back when they recognised the two men, apologising for any offence they might have caused. Several fawningly offered to bring them to wherever they wanted to go, at no charge, but both men ignored them and walked to the right to where the gleaming Aurus limousine stood by the kerb, its uniformed chauffeur polishing non-existent finger-marks from the door handles. As he saw the two men approach he snapped to attention and opened the doors for them, directing the porter to place their bags in the cavernous trunk. He slid into the luxurious leather driver's seat and started the engine, turning his head slightly as he pulled away from the arrivals area.

'The Kremlin, Comrades?'

'Yes, thank you, Comrade.'

'Comrade President Zhadnyy is expecting you at four, Comrades. I am instructed to take you to your rooms in the State Kremlin Palace first, and if you wish, I can drive you across to your meeting in the Great Kremlin Palace after that.'

Igor Kuznetsov spoke for both men.

'There will be no need, Comrade. Once you have delivered us to our lodgings, we will walk across the courtyard, it is a small distance and we are not yet old and decrepit.'

'Very well, Comrades. As you wish.'

The two passengers lapsed into silence, unwilling to speak openly in front of the driver. The car drove quickly along the VIP lane on the road to the city, and the motorcycle outriders cleared its path through the traffic lights on the way. In fifteen minutes the driver slowed and entered the Kremlin grounds through the security gate in the Borovitskaya Tower, the guards raising the barrier and dropping it immediately behind them. He drew up in front of the ugly, modernist façade of the State Kremlin Palace, where a guard stepped forward and opened the doors. His colleague brought out a brass trolley and loaded their bags from the car before pushing it into the building.

The two men followed the trolley and were intercepted by a uniformed member of staff who brought them to a separate passenger lift, rising to the third floor where she showed them into two generously-sized bedrooms with views across Red Square from the tall windows. Moments later, the trolley arrived with their luggage and the staff withdrew.

Ivan Turgenev caught the eye of his colleague and made a zipping motion across his lips. Igor Kuznetsov nodded and spoke briefly.

'I will meet you in the lobby in ten minutes, Comrade, and we can walk across to meet our beloved friend, Comrade President Zhadnyy.'

'Very good, Comrade. I look forwards to catching up with our old friend.'

Kuznetsov gave a wry smile as he left to enter his own room. Ten minutes later he re-joined his colleague in the lobby and they pushed through the tall doors to the warmth of the day outside. They waited until they were some distance from the building before speaking. Turgenev was the first to break the silence.

'How do you want to handle this matter? The bastard will be looking for weak spots in our position, he is sore about the licence going to the Americans, and he would have both of us shot in a heartbeat if he felt like getting revenge.'

'I suppose our early years together won't save us if he is having one of his tantrums.'

Turgenev laughed bitterly.

'I think we both know the answer to that one. Our best hope is one of solidarity, my friend, to both be on the same page and to hold that line.'

'I agree. I think we have to sell this as a success, a pulling of the wool over the eyes of Daniels and the Americans, while costing them a lot of money in the process. We must say that we have managed to have the Americans buy an empty bottle.'

'Yes, that is the best way. After all, we have managed to rescue an impossible situation. We had put too much emphasis on our attempts to recruit and insert our own spy into the institute, and Comrade Vanda clearly underestimated the American fisherman.'

'I agree, but we need to stay away from the failure of that part of the mission. Only a last resort must we go there, and if we do, it is to hang Comrade Vanda out to dry. He will not touch her because she is in the videos that compromise Daniels, and she cannot be made to disappear.'

Both men laughed at the reminder of the surveillance footage.

'Yes, if those tapes are to ever be made public, Comrade Jakovf will be needed to give the credibility, and she will have to still be in the KGB. So she is the one in the safest position, for sure.'

'It was funny, all the same, Comrade Jakovf naked with Daniels, it was like trying to get blood from stones, he was so drunk.'

'Yes, Comrade Jakovf reminded me of a cave woman, trying to start a fire by rubbing sticks together!'

'And the wood was damp!'

They paused and laughed aloud at the memory, before becoming serious again.

'Igor, we have a lot riding on this meeting, and it can go either way. So let us go into this battle as one person, if we die, we die together.'

'I don't think he'll kill us.'

'Not exactly, but is going to Ozersk for the rest of our lives a more attractive prospect?'

'I think it is important we do not antagonise him in any way. If he offers alcohol, we politely refuse. He has become obsessive about drinking these days, I hear.'

They lapsed into silence as they approached the Grand Kremlin Palace. A guard at the entrance checked the screen in front of his position and saluted before waving them through. They instinctively turned right, remembering the way from previous visits. A KGB Captain in dress uniform approached as they crossed the huge lobby. He brought his heels together sharply and saluted.

'Follow me, Comrades.'

At the entrance to the Hall of the Order of St. Alexander Nevsky, the officer opened the heavily carved door and waved them through.

'Please be seated on the far side, on the dais, Comrades. Comrade President Zhadnyy will join you shortly.'

A platoon of armed guards marched across the outer lobby and took up position outside the door. The two visitors walked across the polished marble floor, under the huge, glittering chandeliers, to where a row of ornate chairs stood on a slightly raised platform on the far side of the great hall. Unwilling to sit until the President was present, they stood nervously by the chairs, eyes on the door.

They swung around, startled by the noise as a small, hidden door opened in the near corner of the great hall. A KGB officer in fatigues uniform entered, followed by the bare-chested President wearing just tracksuit bottoms and sneakers. He walked briskly towards the raised dais and greeted the two men with outstretched arms.

'Welcome to my humble city flat, gentlemen! I have been looking forward to us meeting up in the flesh after such a long time.'

The two men mumbled a reply, unsure of the mood of their former comrade. Ivan Turgenev was the first to speak.

'It is good to be back in Moscow, Comrade President. And good to see you looking so fit and well, the years have been kind to you.'

The President accepted a proffered white T-shirt from his aide and pulled it over his head.

'No need for formalities here, Ivan, my old friend. It's great to see you, and you too, Igor.'

He hugged both of them and kissed them on both cheeks.

'Would you like a drink? Some tea, coffee? Or some vodka, maybe?'

'No Vodka, thank you. Tea would be good, Vladimir, thank you.'

The officer left the hall and they could hear him bark orders in the distance before he returned and sat discretely on the far side of the room. President Zhadnyy looked expectantly from one of his guests to the other, eyebrows raised quizzically.

'Well, my friends, what is this good news you have for me? I hope it is better than the fact that the damned Americans have acquired the licence to produce the vaccine for this new virus.'

Igor Kuznetsov cleared his throat and spoke, nervously at first.

'I believe that we, Ivan and I, we have managed a double-cross of the Americans that they never saw coming, that will make that idiot Daniels look like a fool.'

Zhadnyy laughed loudly, slapping himself on both knees.

'I think that past events have proved that theory beyond all doubt. Not even his own people think he is anything other than an idiot. Have you seen the video of him and our favourite honey-trap agent? Whenever we decide to release it, it will finish him. If we release it, of course, it may be more useful as a tool of persuasion.'

Kuznetsov permitted himself the slightest of smiles.

'For sure, that one will live long after we are all gone. I don't think I ever laughed so much, especially the part where she dressed him in her underwears. He looks like an English sodomit.'

When the laughter subsided, Zhadnyy snapped back into serious mode.

'So, Igor, tell me exactly what was achieved.'

The Ambassador sat forward in his chair and spoke in a firm voice, trying to ensure that the fear he felt wasn't evident in his speech.

'Having consulted with Vanda Jakovf, Ivan and I went to see the woman who owns the institute in the village-town of Boyle, in Ireland. It was our initial intention to buy the licence to produce the vaccine from this woman, from Miriam O'Hagan.'

'And you found that the bird had flown, that the Americans had beaten you to it?'

'Not exactly, Comrade. Yes, we found out that she had sold the vaccine licence, although not the intellectual property rights. She showed us her Swiss bank account with the money lodged just an hour earlier. A lot of money, as we mentioned in our memo.'

'So, all the Americans have is the sole right to produce this vaccine? They don't own it?'

'Exact. They can produce as much of it as they want, but they must also pay five cents a dose for every dose administered, not just in America but anywhere in the world. And they are also fully responsible if anything goes wrong, if there are any ill-effects from it, that kind of thing.'

'But they beat you to it, all the same. If I was a vindictive kind of leader I would send yourself and Ivan to Ozersk, would I not? Back in our younger days, we'd all have been happy to erase anybody who fucked up on such a grand scale. Other than our friendship over so many years, why should I let you out of this room alive?'

Igor Kuznetsov shifted nervously in his seat.

'I believe that we actually brought in a better result in the end, and a cheaper one too. Yes, Comrade Vanda was slow in getting off the mark and appears to have been overtaken by an American functionary that she underestimated, but once Ivan and I arrived in theatre we made a bad situation very good, and so it will prove. When this news breaks, the Americans will be humiliated, and the end result may be that it costs us nothing, or very little.'

'Explain?'

'We made an agreement with the director of the institute to buy the entire company for just fifty million euro, a small sum in anyone's language, and as much as half of that will come back to us in royalties from America alone. Other countries will have to pay us the same royalty when they buy the vaccine from the Americans, and we can of course produce as much of it as we like for our own home market and for China, and they won't have any control over that.'

Vladimir Zhadnyy sat back and considered what he had heard, his face impassive. The two ambassadors sat nervously in silence, afraid to make any comment that might kick-start one of his rants. Eventually he looked from one to another and smiled broadly.

'You have done it, my brothers. Truly, if you want a difficult job done, you send for one of the class of eighty-five from Dresden. I always knew you would solve this tricky problem.'

The two men relaxed and smiled. Zhadnyy called to the young officer who sat at a distance across the great hall.

'Moi horoshiy, good dear boy. Come here and serve the tea, my friends are dying of thirst.'

The man strode across the room, boots echoing on the polished floor, and stood with one arm behind his back as he poured tall glasses of hot, black tea. He saluted and withdrew when he had done. Zhadnyy raised a glass in a toast.

'Na Zdorovie, my friends. To success!'

The two men raised their glasses in response.

'Na Zdorovie!'

Zhadnyy pulled his chair closer to the others and spoke quietly.

'So, where do we go from here? I assume you have tied up this deal beyond any undoing by the woman, the director of the institute?'

Igor nodded.

'Yes, we paid the money from the account in Zurich, it is done and the papers are signed. The Russian government owns it, the business, all their intellectual property, even the buildings and the land. Also, the staff are contracted for two more years, if they leave before then they forfeit a substantial bonus.'

'Good, good.'

'So, fifty million is paid over, nobody can overturn that?'

'Forty million on paper, to be exact, ten million was paid in cash from the reserve in Dublin. And of the forty million, five percent of the overall total went to one account in the Isle of Man and the remainder to the director's account in Geneva. Apparently her chief scientist owned some small part of the company.'

'Excellent! And tell me, did you find out what happened to the guy who offered to spy for us? Is he working for the Americans, or did they make him disappear?'

'He has vanished, and nobody knows where he has gone. Agent Jakovf has been inside his house a number of times, her lock-picking skills are legendary as you know, but she has found no sign of anybody being there. He has melted away like the snow in spring.'

'They are ruthless, maybe not as ruthless as us, but they don't hesitate to kill whoever gets in their way.'

'It does not matter, Vladimir; we have a result, as they
say in Washington.'

'Yes, we do, for sure; that is good work. So, when should
we tell the Americans the good news?'

'Not yet, I think, not until they have announced the
arrival of the vaccine and claimed it as their own.'

Zhadnyy laughed loudly.

'I like it! Let us wait until the idiot Daniels has actually
had the needle stuck in is arm, then we release the story to
CNN or to the BBC. Then we will tell the world that the
vaccine that has saved America is developed by a Russian
company. I love it!'

They laughed and drank tea, the two ambassadors
relaxing for the first time in days. Zhadnyy was in high
good humour, and they swapped stories of good times
in Dresden and Saint Petersburg. Eventually the young
officer approached the dais and pointed to his watch. The
President stood up and made his apologies.

'It was good to see you, my friends, and to hear such
good news. I am enjoying the joke, and will enjoy it even
more when we humiliate that ignorant peasant in public.'

The two men nodded agreement, smiling at the thought.
Zhadnyy paused before leaving.

'I want both of you to go to Washington and work
together there for a while, the Irish won't notice that you
are missing, Ivan. There is something that concerns me,
and I want you both to put your heads together and think
about it, and deal with it. I need to be able to trust my
people there.'

Kuznetsov turned to him, nervously.

'What is the concern, Vladimir Zhadnyy?'

'Belyaev. Why didn't he tell us that the Americans had
bought the licence?'

'I don't know, perhaps he didn't know.'

'He's their chief medical officer, in charge of health for the entire United States of America. Why would he not know?'

Ivan Turgenev answered, thinking aloud.

'Either they didn't tell him, or they did, and he didn't tell us. My God!'

Zhadnyy nodded, his face serious again.

'If they didn't tell him, it means they are on to him. It means his cover is blown and we must take him out of there. But if they did...'

'You mean...'

'Yes, he's gone over to the West. In which case...'

'We understand, Comrade President, we will do what has to be done.'

Chapter Thirty One

President Daniels sat back in the comfortable leather seat in the dark green Sikorsky S-98 helicopter, looking down through the green-tinted armoured glass as the aircraft climbed steeply away from the White House. Major Callaghan pulled on his headset and plugged it into the armrest of his seat, motioning the President to do the same. Far below, they could see the second helicopter, a large King Stallion CH-53K, as it lifted off from the lawn and followed their flightpath. The President pulled the microphone stem closer to his face and spoke to the officer.

'The Press 'copter has just left the ground, we're on our way. This is gonna be a good day, Major.'

'Yes, Sir, I sure hope so, Sir. The medics are all in place in Corner Creek, and some of the TV satellite trucks are on scene as well. We're going to do the business on the steps of the Town Hall, the flags flying and all that kind of thing.'

'The Press know what it's about?'

'Not yet, Sir. We have the FDA approval, but we haven't announced it yet. You'll do that live on air, and then you get vaccinated. It's a hell of a story.'

'Holy guacamole! That's a real show-stopper. And we've got our hillbilly, our common man?'

'Yes, Sir. Fella with a limited amount of grey matter, local straw-chewin' Boonie, like something straight outa central casting, I hear. My guy on the ground says he even dresses in an old bib and brace overall, don't wear shoes in summertime. They don't come much more authentic than this one.'

'How did they persuade him to come down from the hills at all?'

'Five hundred dollars, Sir. And he insisted they don't give him the vaccine, just a shot of vitamins. Seems like the guy is an anti-vaxxer in the extreme, no way he'd agree to take a shot of the real stuff, says it makes your balls fall off. But for five hundred, he'll say anything we like.'

The President clutched at his groin in fear.

'Maybe he's right, Major. What if it does? Maybe I should go for the vitamin shot too?'

'That's all just crazy talk by the anti-vaxxers, Sir. Ain't nobody had their balls fall off last time around either, despite what they had been saying. You don't have to fear for the presidential testicles, Sir, if you'll pardon my expression.'

The president relaxed slightly.

'I sure hope you're right, Major.'

'I know I am, Sir. If it eases your mind, I'll be happy to get the shot at the same time, out of the same bottle, even.'

'Then I guess I'll take that chance, Major. How long before we get there?'

'Hour and a half, Sir. We need to get the story on the evening news all across the country, but we got plenty of time for all that.'

'It's a shame we couldn't have Doctor Belyaev there, I miss him at times like this, but there you go.'

'Yes, Sir. I know you and I have had some reservations about him, mostly because he was a foreigner, but he sure was an expert and he was a great guy for answering awkward questions from the press. It's damned unfortunate.'

'Did they find the driver of the car?'

'No, Sir. He disappeared completely, the car was stolen earlier just a few blocks away, from the garage of an apartment building. Seems the thieves captured the unlock data from the charger, very sophisticated trick that suggests an organised car-theft gang. Hit him so fast he never stood a chance, anyhow.'

'They got any DNA or stuff from the car?'

'Nothing. It was completely burned out. They used some kinda magnesium flare to start the fire, burned white hot. I'd imagine they'll never find the guy that did it.'

'We need to crack down on these car thefts, remind me when we get back and I'll tell Lucy's guys to do a bill, or whatever they do.'

'That's noted, Sir.'

The President stared out the window as the chopper flew out of the city and headed for Tennessee, the engine noise rising as the pilot picked up speed. He tapped the Major on the shoulder and pointed down to where they flew across farmlands and the occasional small homestead.

'They're our people, Major. Down there, that's where you find all the good folks who vote for me, that's how they live, working the fields and the factories. We gotta get closer to them folks, Major.'

'You mean, you want us to fly lower? We can't do that, I'm afraid, Sir. Security reasons, too many guys with rifles and machine guns. If they could see that this was your chopper, we'd be dead meat, Sir. Just takes one.'

'No, not that, Major. I get all that, we gotta balance our safety with the right to bear arms. I always support the second amendment, always did. Americans been carrying guns ever since the founding fathers did whatever it was they did, you know?'

'Of course, Sir.'

'No, what I meant was this stunt we're going to do now, we gotta use it to get closer to the people who vote, so we're seen seen to be ordinary folks, you understand me?'

'Yes, Sir. I guess that's what we're doing, holding this event in a little hick town off the main road that's off the main road, and then some.'

'Yes, but we're still holding it at the Town Hall, and for many people that's still a symbol of power. We gotta get closer to the people.'

'What did you have in mind, Sir?'

'Why don't we go to the house of the guy, the token redneck we got lined up?'

The Major consulted his small notebook.

'Randy Corless, Sir. That's the guy's name.'

'Randy Corless. Kinda has a nice ring to it, sounds like an all-American boy. He's a white guy, right?'

'Of course, Sir. We didn't want no controversy or anything. I reckon if we brought a black guy to the Town Hall steps in Corner Creek some people would be disappointed if we didn't have a rope organised.'

The President laughed.

'I figured that. So, this guy, he lives up in the hills someplace?'

'Yes, Sir. Him and his brother, they live on a small ranch up near the tree-line, on a gravel road. Not much of a place, a fairly weathered log cabin on thirty acres and some woodland. We had the FBI do a discrete check on them.'

'They're not very well off?'

'No, they don't even have electricity or running water, they live a very simple life. Their mother died a couple of years back, she used to keep them in line. They spend a lot of time sittin' on two chairs on the front porch, apparently, just shootin' the breeze and the occasional rabbit. They live well enough, a bit of hunting and trapping and they grow some corn and potatoes, and they get a small amount of welfare. I guess they do okay.'

'Sounds like an okay life, compared to a lot of city folks anyhow.'

'It's pretty basic, very hand to mouth, but I guess there's worse ways to live. Rumour is they make a little moonshine, but nobody was able to confirm that.'

'Probably just talk, it's a bit of a clitchy, isn't it? Hillbilly, moonshine, that kind of thing.'

'A cliché?'

'Yeah, that's it. They political?'

'No, sir, neither of them is registered to any party. Randy is a member of the local Klavern of the Klan, but it seems that he doesn't rightly know what it means, he just goes along with whatever the Sherriff says. A lot of the members are there just to keep that guy Kendall off their backs, he's the local Grand Dragon.'

'Yeah, I met him last year, not a guy you'd play golf with, but he fits the bill for this job. Real fond of hamburgers, by the look of him.'

'So, what were you thinking, Sir? About Randy Corless?'

'Oh, yeah. I figured we could go to his house and do the whole thing there. Imagine the TV ratings for that, the clip would be on RU-Tube for years!'

'I don't know about that, Sir. We got the town secured, I got about a hundred agents in place, but how would we secure half the mountain?'

'Simple, Major. We don't tell 'em.'

'We'd have to give them some warning, Sir.'

'No, we wouldn't. My car is there, right?'

'Of course, Sir. Plus several others, the decoy one with the flags and the other agency ones. We're landing in the backyard of the police headquarters and driving the couple of hundred yards to the town hall.'

'Then we just arrive at the town hall, tell our friend Randy to jump in, and tell the medics and the TV and press to follow us. Then we go to his house and get the doc to give us the vaccine on his front porch. Just me and my buddy Randy, sitting on the front porch, shootin' the breeze.'

'I don't know, Sir. I'm nervous about departing from the existing security plan.'

'Let me take the risk on that, Major. That's what we'll do, it will be television gold and we'll be on the front pages for days, and it will help swing the anti-vaxxers too.'

'I guess you're right about that side of things, Sir. But you have to understand my concerns.'

'We're going into battle, Major, and I'm leading the charge. Don't worry, what the hell could go wrong? Nothing, that's what. Relax, I got this.'

Chapter Thirty Two

Miriam O'Hagan stretched herself luxuriantly in the bed and laughed out loud.

'We did it, Billy, we're fucking rich! Make us some coffee, and see if you got any chocolate or sweet stuff in the fridge, this diet is doing my head in.'

'Coming right up.'

'We've done it, Billy. From now on we can go where we like, do what we like, money no object.'

'We could do that before, to a point. I'm exactly where I want to be, a few quid in the bank won't change that.'

'Are you saying you don't want the money?'

'No, of course not. It was a great result, in fairness, you played a blinder with the Russians and with the Americans. I just can't believe the amount of money involved, I can't even begin to get my head around it.'

'Me neither, if I'm honest. I never really had money, anything I made the last ten years I just ploughed it back into the business.'

'Well, now you don't have a business to plough it back into. When is the new management team going to arrive?'

'They have two months to put their people in place, but I can't see them waiting that long. I've told them I'm going on leave when we finish off the loose ends of the trial, so I'd say they'll be here in a couple of weeks.'

'There's not much to do if you wanted to get out of here earlier, I'm happy enough to mind the shop for you.'

'I might just do that. I've been to see my lawyers about a divorce, I don't think it will be much of an issue once I leave him his precious house, which I'm quite happy to do under the circumstances. I think I can probably afford to buy a nice house around here, somewhere to stay in the summertime.'

'You can stay here, for as long as you want. For good, if you like.'

'Is that some kind of proposal, Billy Robinson?'

'No, I know you aren't interested in jumping back into a marriage, and I'm happy enough with us just as we are. But my home is your home, I just want you to know that.'

'That's kind of you, Billy. I might even take you up on it for some of the time.'

'And the rest of the time?'

'The house in Manilva in Spain is just fine, it's big enough for friends and family to come and stay for a while, and not so big that it stands out as the home of the richest woman in Boyle. Or in Manilva, for that matter.'

'Will I be welcome?'

'Of course you will, my love. In fact, if you were happy to move away from your comfort zone here, I'd love you to come with me. But I know you well enough to know you are happy in Boyle, and I don't want to put pressure on you to leave your life here.'

Billy brought two coffees back and placed them on the bedside tables. He found two muesli bars in the cupboard and left one beside each cup.

'Sorry, I haven't done a shop yet this week, what with

all the excitement. I'll try to have some of your favourite brand in stock next time.'

He climbed back into the bed and sat with his back to the headboard, unwrapping the snack bar and biting off a piece.

'I appreciate it, you know....'

'The money? Think nothing of it, I wouldn't be where I am today without you.'

'Not just the money, I mean about not pressuring me to move to Spain. I might consider it, but I'd need to give it a lot of thought, I hope you understand.'

'I do.'

'It's not that I don't care about you. Quite the opposite, I'm mad about you, you know that. It's that I'm too old to do things on a whim anymore, and I really like living in Boyle. It's a beautiful environment, I have lots of friends here, and the fishing of course. I would find it hard to leave.'

'I understand, Billy, I really do. I moved here with the Sergeant because of his promotion, I didn't have any choice in the matter. I gave up my good job in the University to follow his career and ambitions, but nobody asked me what I wanted. I was a bigger fool to just accept it blindly, I should have dug my heels in.'

'It worked out well, all the same.'

Miriam laughed and sipped from her coffee.

'I suppose I can thank him for it all, in a perverse way, although he'll never know how much I made on the whole deal.'

'You're not going to tell him?'

'I'm not going to tell anybody, and you're not to tell anybody either, okay?'

'You don't have to worry about me talking.'

'I'm not, not in the slightest. In fairness, that would be a first, you telling anybody about your business, or mine.'

Billy smiled, idly studying the inside of his empty cup.

'No, I'll just carry on as before. I might even stay on in the job for a year or two, depends on how it goes. Do they know that I don't have to stay, that I'm not bound by the agreement?'

'Yes, the contract lists the staff that are tied to the business for the two years. So if they don't know, it's because they didn't read the small print. But the rest of the staff won't know that you're a free agent. I think it's better not to tell them, they might wonder why I did that.'

'I'll look after the wind-up of the tests anyway, make sure the guinea-pigs are checked over before they are released into the wild, that kind of thing.'

'If you would, that would be a help, although Caroline will be sure the paperwork is done. You'll just need to make sure the test results are noted properly, for the FDA approval and all that kind of stuff. How are the subjects doing anyway?'

'Lucky Oyeleye, the Nigerian guy, he's fine. Happy to stay there for years as long as the meter is running. He's earned himself about thirty grand so far and he'll get another six grand or so before he's done.'

'Not bad money for lying on a bed, in fairness. Although it's not a lot in the context of the development of a multi-billion vaccine.'

'It's an awful lot in Nigerian terms, apparently he can buy a house in his home district for about ten grand, so he's dead happy.'

'Sounds cheap.'

'Apparently the Naira has collapsed altogether, anyone with euros can do really well there. He's not so stupid, going home.'

'Yes, I guess so. What about our one-time Boyle mugger, how is he doing?'

'Mickey? He's calmed down a bit, getting to like the food and the unlimited availability of box-sets. He'll be okay, he just has to stick it a couple of weeks more.'

'Is his head okay? He's the one I'd be more worried about, he's a bit unstable, is he not?'

'He's fine, I'd say. He doesn't know what day it is or how long he's been there at this stage. In truth, I could probably let him out now and just bring him back every couple of days for bloods, but I'd prefer to be looking at him than looking for him.'

'So we're pretty much good to go with the paperwork, once they've been signed out?'

'Yes, I'd say the FDA approval will just be a box-ticking exercise, the American seemed very certain that the President could sort it out anyway. He reckoned they already have a date for it, they're planning to make the approval public sometime in the next day or so and then he'll pose somewhere an hour later and have them stick a needle in his arm.'

'He could just take it in a glass of water!'

'Nobody is going to know that side of it; that will be a covert operation I'd say, if it happens at all. They're also going to produce it as an aerosol, to just squirt it up people's noses, but a lot of it will still be produced as an injectable. There's something very reassuring about the image of a needle in an arm, isn't there?'

'Yes, especially in the arm of the most powerful man in the world.'

'They're going to inject Zhadnyy?'

Miriam threw a pillow at him and jumped out of bed to head for the shower.

Chapter Thirty Three

Ivan Turgenev and Igor Kuznetsov sat side by side at the table in the basement in Washington. The large screen on the wall was split into four, each showing a different television channel. The two men waited in anticipation of the announcement to come.

Two of the main American news channels were showing footage from a small Tennessee town, with flags flying above the Town Hall and a small number of people gathered around, almost outnumbered by press and media. The Presidential convoy wound its way through the couple of blocks from the local police station, led by a local police car with blue lights flashing. The convoy pulled up at the steps of the civic building and the doors opened, but the President did not emerge from the car. Secret Service agents and police kept the journalists at bay, as they scrambled to see what was happening.

The anchor on CNN appeared puzzled as she spoke to her reporter on the ground.

'What's happening there, Donie? Is the President getting out of the car, is he okay?'

The middle-aged reporter stood with his back to the cavalcade, microphone clutched to his chest and taking glances over his shoulder as he tried to make sense of the situation.

'There doesn't appear to be any panic, Erin. The President is calling to some man who was sitting on a chair on the steps. Can we get a camera on this, Sean?'

The camera zoomed in on a barefoot, weather-beaten, middle-aged man in a faded bib and brace overall, who had got to his feet and was walking hesitantly down the steps towards the Presidential car. The reporter started to speak, the surprise in his voice evident.

'The President is calling this guy by name, telling him to get in the car. Seems his name is Randy. The way he's calling him, it sounds almost like he knows him.'

'Try and get closer, Donie, see if you can throw some light on what's happening.'

The reporter fiddled with his earpiece and then spoke again, pausing occasionally as he get new information.

'The guy's name is Randy Corless, a local farmer. The President's people have just told us that he's going to visit Mister Corless' ranch and he'll make the announcement there.'

'And this is thought to be about progress on a vaccine on the Californian strain of the virus?'

'Yes, although the White House doesn't like the use of that term, as you know, Erin. They prefer to call it the China mutant, but it is the one that emerged in California and has been spreading eastwards. It is rumoured that a vaccine has been developed for this mutant.'

The reporter started to run as he realised the Presidential car was moving. He jumped on the back of a motorcycle driven by a cameraman with a camera headset, and they sped down Main Street in pursuit of the big, armoured limousines. He breathlessly continued his coverage as the bike rider wound up the throttle and pursued the cavalcade.

'Are you still hearing me, Erin? Can you still get our pictures?'

'Yes, Donie, loud and clear. We lost you for a second but we have picture and sound now. Do you know what is happening?'

'We're in pursuit of the Presidential limo, Erin, and the farmer, Randy Corless is definitely in the car with the President. As you can see, we've left the main street of Corner Creek and we're outside the town, and we've just turned up a road that leads up the hills, away from the main roads.'

'We've got you on the drone now as well, Donie. You appear to be driving through thick forest.'

'Yes, Erin, and the blacktop road just ran out, we're on gravel now and it's a bit loose for a bike.'

'Be careful, you guys, don't fall off, but try to stay with them. This is really unprecedented, Donie; I've never seen a President depart from the agreed protocols.'

'Yes, Erin, in all my years covering various Presidents, I've never seen it happen either. It's surprising, I'm told that the President's Chief of Staff, Major Mike Callaghan, is actually in the car with him, and Callaghan as you know would be a very safe pair of hands, normally. I'm surprised he went along with a stunt like this, it's very risky.'

'Yes, Donie, and from the pictures it seems they nearly lost control of the car there, at that hard left-hander.'

'They're not the only ones, Erin. That's not the best of bends for a motorcycle, the surface is very loose; we almost came a cropper there ourselves.'

'Do you know how much further it is to the Corless ranch?'

'No idea, Erin, we're coming out of the trees now, they're just on one side of the road from here on. You can probably see the cattle in the fields on my left, are you getting this?'

'Yes, we're getting it, Donie, and from the high-level aerial camera it looks like you're almost there. The Presidential car appears to be stopping at an old log cabin. We're not allowed to fly the drone below a thousand feet, but this is hardly the Corless ranch, is it? It doesn't look like anybody lives there.'

'We've just arrived as well, Erin, and I guess this really is the place. The car door is opening and Randy Corless has got out, as has Major Callaghan who is scanning the terrain. The Major has spotted me and has waved us forward, so we should be able to get our shots. Is our satellite van nearby, I'm worried about the link?'

'It's just a hundred yards behind you, those drivers on our roaming news team deserve a medal for the way they reacted to this change of plan. Well done to them all. What is it we're seeing now, Donie?'

'Well, Erin, you can probably see the President alighting from the car behind me, and he has stepped on to the front porch where another man appears to be sleeping in a chair. The Major has approached the man with his gun drawn, but I think that's just precautionary. It looks like the guy lives here and just dozed off.'

'He'll get a shock when he sees himself surrounded!'

'He sure will.'

'He looks a lot like Mister Corless, he could be his twin.'

'Yes, apparently he's his brother. He's just shaking hands with the President; he looks a bit shocked, right enough.'

'It's not every day the President of the United States drops in on you.'

'Sure isn't, Erin. This is incredible, the man who was in the chair has gone into the cabin and closed the door behind him, and the President and Mister Randy Corless have sat down in the two porch chairs. The President looks right at home, to be honest.'

'What's his plan, do you know?'

'He's asked us for one of our mikes, so as you've probably seen we've given him the hard-wired one from this camera. I'll keep talking on this mobile mike. I'm on the porch with the two men, Major Callaghan is directing the press outside and the Secret Service guys have fanned out into the woods and the fields.'

'Good work, Donie, you're at the head of the queue as usual.'

'The President is about to speak.'

The President stood and put his hand on Randy's shoulder.

'Ladies and gentlemen, thank you for coming all the way out here to my friend Randy Corless' ranch, in the heartland of our great nation. I decided to pay a call on Randy, a man who like many others is the backbone of our great country, growing the food we eat every day, working from dawn to dusk to feed our people, our frontline workers and our troops.

I wanted to make an important announcement, and I figured that making it in the White House was just too distant from my friends and the people who put their trust in me to manage the affairs of our great nation. So I came here, to Corner Creek in Tennessee, and to this mountain where Randy and his brother Bubba work so hard on our behalf.'

In the basement in Washington, the two ambassadors smiled in anticipation as they watched the screen. Igor

Kuznetsov idly nibbled on some nuts from a heavy glass bowl on the big conference table.

'Any minute now, Comrade. I see that our television cameraman is now in position at the home of the peasant in Tennessee, it will be wonderful to see the face of the idiot Daniels when he realises he has played a losing hand.'

Ivan Turgenev laughed heartily, pointing to the laptop screen where President Zhadnyy could be seen going through his notes.

'Our President looks very much a great leader, his suit is sharp and looks expensive. By comparison, Daniels appears to have dressed down to suit his company, he doesn't wear a tie and his shirt looks like he slept in it.'

'He looks like the idiot he is, but this will get better in a minute. I believe he is about to announce the approval for the vaccine.'

'Yes, but look at the breaking news banner on the laptop, this what the Russian national TV channel will be showing in a few minutes.'

Turgenev read the banner slowly as it scrolled across the laptop screen.

'American President announces FDA approval of Russian Vaccine on visit to typical American peasant home…'

The two men laughed loudly at the headline, as Turgenev continued to read from the laptop.

'Speaking from a typical rural home in America, a simple cabin without electricity or running water, President Daniels announced that a vaccine produced by a Russian-owned company is now the sole policy option for dealing with the Californian virus strain.'

They sat back as the CNN screen showed a close-up of President Daniels, baring his arm as he prepared to be vaccinated. The CNN reporter spoke in a hushed tone and was obviously very close to the action.

'And now the President will make an announcement.'

Daniels looked straight to the camera and spoke.

'Today, my fellow Americans, I can announce that the FDA has cleared this new vaccine for use against the Chinese Corona variant. Approval has been granted in the last few minutes, and I am proud to be the first citizen to receive the vaccine, the first step in our battle against this invader that has slowed our economy and taken away our freedoms. My friend here, Mister Randy Corless, in whose home we have enjoyed this nice visit, is also going to receive the vaccine. We, Randy and I, want to assure our fellow Americans that this vaccine is safe and that it will do the job. Let us all receive this miracle drug so we can get on with our lives.'

He rolled his sleeve up higher and the army medic stepped forward with two syringes. He quickly injected Daniels and used the second syringe to jab the farmer in his bare arm. The CNN reporter struggled between trying to commentate on what was happening and to listen to the voice in his ear.

'Donie, we're just getting some information on the wires, the Russian State TV company has President Zhadnyy on the news; he is congratulating Daniels on receiving a Russian vaccine. What's going on?'

'I don't know, Erin, the Russian crew has moved up beside me now and are asking questions of President Daniels, I'll try to find out more.'

In the basement in Washington, the two men could hardly contain their laughter. President Zhadnyy was on the State channel, speaking directly to camera, in front of the familiar backdrop of the Hall of the Order of St. Alexander Nevsky. Kuznetsov reached for the remote control and turned up the volume. Zhadnyy turned a page and resumed his speech.

'We are pleased to see that our allies, the great people of the United States, and their leader, our beloved friend Donald Daniels, will soon be safe from the harm of the Californian virus that is sweeping their nation. President Daniels has just received a vaccine that was developed by a Russian Company, Boyle Labs limited, a biotechnical company that has part of its research division in Ireland but that is headquartered here in Moscow and owned by Minet Industries of Moscow and Saint Petersburg. Russian-owned medical technology will save the American people from this disease, and for that we thank God and we are grateful.'

The news anchor picked up the story as the President shuffled his papers and placed them upside down on his desk.

'This is Oleg Lebedev, reporting from Moscow. Thank you, Comrade President Zhadnyy, and thanks to our experts who lead the world in medical science. Now we will go over to Tennessee in America, where our reporter Maxim is at the scene of the vaccination of the American President. Maxim?'

The reporter stood facing the camera, with the American President in soft focus behind him.

'Greetings from Corner Creek, a small farming village in the American State of Tennessee, where President Daniels has just announced Federal Drug Administration approval for the Russian vaccine that he has just received behind me here.'

'And that vaccine is to combat the Californian virus, or more correctly, the Californian variant of the Covid virus, is that correct?'

'Correct, Oleg. This Russian vaccine was made available

to the USA last week, and has today passed their approval process.'

'And why is the President being vaccinated in a small village? Would it not be more normal to do this in the White House, which viewers will know is like our own White House, but smaller?'

'Good question, Oleg. It appears that President Daniels feels at home among peasants, and this is a typical enough rural American home, with no water or electricity, although more of them do in fact have these facilities in recent years.'

'So this is basically a 'vozmozhnost foto,' a photo opportunity, as they call it there?'

'Yes, essentially. It is aimed it would appear at reassuring the peasants, many of whom are suspicious of anything coming from the government, including a vaccine that might save their lives.'

'So, not all American peasants will favour a vaccine?'

'No, Oleg, many of them will not in fact accept it at all.'

'And they are allowed to get away with that, Maxim?'

'Yes, Oleg. Law and order is largely absent in rural places in America, you will have seen the news reports showing heavily-armed civilians roaming the streets.'

'Yes, it seems like it is not the nirvana it is painted to be.'

The camera shifted focus on to the President, who was having his arm wiped and a small piece of cotton wool and surgical tape applied over the needle mark. The medic moved to Randy Corless and offered to do the same but he waved him away.

'Taint no more'n a lil thorn prick, ain't no need fer bandaging.'

The camera shifted slightly to show the cabin door opening. The secret service men froze, hands on their weapons, but relaxed when a blonde woman stepped out sleepily, stopping and looking in amazement at the crowd on the porch and in the front yard. She was wearing nothing but a towel, and the shock of seeing so many people caused her to drop it momentarily. As she grabbed at the towel and tried to cover herself, there was an angry roar from the crowd and her husband raced towards the cabin, drawing his gun as he ran.

'What'n hell yo doin' heah, Shirley? An you wit no clothes on, damn bitch. You comin' home wit me right now.'

He jumped on to the porch as quickly as his flabby bulk would allow him. The Secret Service men drew weapons and fired as one, and he fell back, his body lifeless from the impact of a dozen 38 calibre bullets.

Shirley tripped and dropped the towel again, screaming for Randy as she rushed to embrace him where he sat in shock beside the President.

In the basement in Washington, the two men stared open-mouthed at the screen, before bursting into laughter and calling for a bottle of vodka and two glasses.

Chapter Thirty Four

Miriam O'Hagan drummed her fingers on the table as she looked around the conference room. She poured a glass of water from the jug and sipped from it before speaking.

'Folks, I know things have been a little crazy these last couple of days, but trust me, everything will be fine here in Boyle Labs.'

Kevin Kelly picked up a newspaper and turned it around to show the others. The front page had a picture of a shocked President Daniels looking down at the body of a policeman, while the naked rear of a woman filled most of the background behind the President's head. The headline 'Who Shot The Sheriff?' blazed across the top of the page.

'Then how do you explain this? A headline like this doesn't do much for our reputation, we're supposed to be a serious company, not a circus.'

'Relax, Kevin. That was an unfortunate incident, but in fairness it couldn't be blamed on us.'

'But what about the whole debacle of the American President being made to look like a fool? Are we really a Russian company, I always understood that you owned Boyle Labs.'

Miriam raised her hands in a placatory gesture.

'Let's not get too hung up on who owns the company, Kevin. And there's no use worrying about that clusterfuck in Tennessee, who the hell could have foreseen that happening? Not me, anyway, but I have always acted in the best interests of all the people who work here, and there comes a time when I have to concede that we are a small fish in a very big pond. I'm not 'big pharma,' I'm just one person, a small niche player with a great team. I wouldn't have got to where I am today without you, all of you, and I'm about to acknowledge that.'

'So, do you own the company, or not?'

'No, I don't own any of it, as of last week. Boyle Labs is now owned by Minet Industries of Moscow and Saint Petersburg. The company still trades as Boyle Labs, but all the intellectual property, the income from existing contracts and all the licensing income resides with Minet. And as soon as the Land Registry does their work, they will own the very building we work in.'

Karen Doyle raised a hand tentatively.

'So, where does that leave us? Do we still have jobs here? I have a car loan, I don't want to lose my job.'

'There's no need to be concerned about that, Karen. All jobs are secure, including one or two I could justifiably have excluded from the agreement with Minet, but you will find that I have been more than fair with everybody.'

'It might have been fairer if you told us what was happening, so that we didn't see it on the six o'clock news.'

'Kevin, I had to do what I had to do, and there was a confidentiality clause involved, so stop whining and I'll get to the bit that will make you happy, the dividend for the team.'

Karen sat forward and smiled broadly.

'There's something in it for us? That would be brilliant.'

Miriam opened her briefcase and took out a bundle of envelopes that she spread on the blotter in front of her. She picked up the first envelope and turned to Billy Robinson.

'Billy, there's a cheque in here for three quarters of a million euro. Enjoy it. There's another quarter of a million coming to you in two years' time if you stay with the company until then.'

She handed envelopes to three of the other scientists and to Caroline.

'Same story for you guys, three quarters of a million now, and the rest in two years.'

There were gasps of delight from the staff. Caroline managed to find words to speak.

'Miriam, I'm overwhelmed, I don't know what to say.'

'You don't have to say anything, I told you all I'd make you millionaires if you stuck with me, and I'm doing that.'

She passed an envelope to Nurse Cohen.

'Mary, yours is slightly different, but I think it's fair. There's a hundred grand less in the initial payment, and a hundred grand more in the residual payment in two years' time. Okay?'

Nurse Cohen reddened as she accepted the envelope.

'I don't mean to sound ungrateful, Miriam, but why the difference?'

'I think you know, Mary.'

'No, I have no idea.'

'Are you sure?'

'Yes, I'm delighted to get this payment, of course, but why are the terms different?'

'What I'm doing here today, ladies and gentlemen, is to

214

reward loyalty above all. I promised you all that I'd make you millionaires, but I also asked you all to stick with me, to work in my interests and not your own.'

'I've always done that, Miriam.'

'I was hoping you wouldn't make me spell it out, Mary, but here's the truth of the matter. You live in Kiltycreighton, just out the road there. Nice, tight little community, all good people and great neighbours, right?'

'Yes.'

'But that didn't justify them all getting vaccinated on the quiet one evening last week, all around to your house for a vaccination party. You call that loyalty, Mary?'

The nurse reddened.

'I'm sorry, that was a lapse of judgement; I shouldn't have done it. How did you find out?'

'Let's say I have my sources, but I am still honouring my promise. Happy enough?'

'Yes, thank you, and I'm sorry, I really am.'

'Forget about it, it doesn't leave this room. Now, Kevin, you may wonder why I've left you until last.'

Kevin sat with his head dropped, looking at the table.

'I was wondering about that.'

'So, how much do you think I should give to you, Kevin Doyle? Same as the others, or more? Or less?'

He answered in a low voice.

'I don't know, Miriam. Whatever you think, I guess. You're the boss.'

'Do you know why I considered giving you nothing? Why my initial instinct was to kick your arse out the fucking door?'

'I don't know, Miriam.'

'You know too well, Kevin. If I wanted the American government to know my business, I'd have told it to them myself. You, Sir, have been running to their embassy in Dublin with stories, telling them what we're doing and all about the progress of our research. You almost scuttled the whole deal, you came pretty close to causing none of us to get a penny out of all the hard work that went on here, including your own efforts, I have to admit.'

Red-faced, Kevin pushed back his chair and got to his feet.

'I'll pack up my stuff. And I'm sorry, everybody. I was really stupid.'

'Sit down, you idiot. Nobody is going anywhere. Remember, I promised every one of you that I'd make you rich, and I intend to abide by that promise. You'll get your million euro, half now and half in two years' time. And you'll enjoy working for the Russians; as long as they never know you were an American spy, you'll be safe enough.'

'You'd do that, after what I did? And you won't tell them?'

'Of course I won't. And I forgive you, not because I'm feeling mellow, but because you inadvertently made the whole thing happen. You delivered the Americans right into a financial trap that couldn't have sprung without your leaks spurring them on. So, in a sense, we owe you one. But don't even think of pulling a stunt like that with the new owners, or you could find yourself at the bottom of the lake. They're dangerous people.'

Billy Robinson stood up and cleared his throat.

'Ladies and gentlemen, on behalf of the entire team, I want to say two things. Firstly, I have the job of telling the rest of the staff that the company is under new management, that the Russians will be coming next week, so no talking about anything that was discussed here today until I get a chance to do that. And secondly, I want to offer my thanks on behalf of the entire team to Miriam, who pulled off one of the most audacious financial coups in the history of the pharmaceutical industry, and who generously shared the spoils with the people who make the magic happen in our labs, every day.'

He turned towards Miriam and raised his water glass in a toast.

'To Miriam O'Hagan, one of a kind, and one of the best!'

Chapter Thirty Five

Mickey Small waited in the kitchen for the sound of the signal that told him that his dinner had arrived, and he opened the door to retrieve the tray with its covered plates. He lifted the plastic dome from the main course, smiling at the sight of the tall burger and the chunky chips. He took the tray back to the bedroom area and sat on the bed, propped up by pillows and with the tray on his knees. As he ate the food, he used the remote control to scroll through a list of episodes of 'Air Crash Investigations,' stopping on one from nineteen eighty-three. He watched this one a lot, it was about an Air Canada Flight between Montreal and Edmonton that had run out of fuel but where the pilots had landed safely on a disused airbase in Gimli, Manitoba.

Mickey liked this episode and could recite most of the lines by heart. It had a happy ending that pleased him, nobody had died and nobody was hurt. He sometimes wished that some of the other episodes had happier endings; all the deaths in other air crashes made him wonder sometimes if he should chose a different job and not become an investigator after all.

Mickey ate the Strawberry cheesecake dessert, watching

the part where the picnickers were walking around the runway, blissfully unaware that the Boeing 767 was heading their way. He knew that they would be fine, that they would run to the side just in time, but every time he watched he half-expected a different result. As he sat up, watching the screen intensely, there was a knock on the door and Caroline walked in.

Mickey paused the programme and smiled. He liked these short visits, Caroline was kind and chatty and he looked forward to their conversations each day. Over the last few weeks she was more upbeat than usual, her good humour almost infectious. Her presence already made Mickey felt better. She looked around and smiled her approval.

'You're keeping the place nice and tidy, Mickey. That's great, thank you, it saves me having to clean up after you.'

'Well sure you cleaned up my house for me, and painted it, and bought me new clothes and sheets and towels and everything. So I thought I'd better try and get into a habit of being tidy, like you said.'

'What are you watching, not Air Crash Investigations again?'

'Yes, I'm watching the one about the Gimli Glider, I like that one.'

'I've never watched any of those, I don't like the body count.'

'I like the ones where everybody is safe. I like happy endings.'

'You dirty fecker!'

'No, not those kind of ones, you're naughty, you are.'

'I try! Are you missing your house? I know it must get boring here sometimes, but it's important work you're doing here, and we appreciate it very much.'

'Well, it can be a bit boring, but the movies and TV shows are great, so it's not too bad. And the food is lovely, I had the Moone Boy Burger from Clarke's tonight, I'm stuffed.'

'Glad you enjoyed it. Look, just hang in there, the money is piling up and you'll have it all in another couple of weeks, at the most.'

'I don't understand why I'm still here, though. I mean, Nurse Cohen hasn't given me any injections or tablets or anything, she just comes in and looks at me and checks my pulse and stuff.'

'You'd prefer if we were injecting you?'

'No, no! I'm just wondering why you're still paying me a load of money for watching telly. I'm not complaining, I just don't understand.'

'It's very simple, Mickey. Do you remember the stuff that Nurse Cohen gave you in the glass of cola?'

'Yes, after they took me out of the room I was sharing with Lucky?'

'That's the one. That was actually a vaccine, it's just that they didn't inject it into you, they gave it in a drink and your body absorbed it that way.'

'I remember it, I thought it might make a taste in the Pepsi, but it didn't. So, what did that cure me of?'

'A vaccine doesn't cure anything, Mickey, it stops you getting a disease.'

'So, what disease have I not got then, because of the vaccine?'

'It's called the Californian strain of the Covid 25 vaccine, we just call it the Californian disease.'

'But I was never in California. Although I saw Chips on TV, it's an old programme about California. They didn't look sick, the guys on the motorbikes.'

'That was a long time ago, before this disease came along. We put you in with Lucky, to see if you'd catch it from him.'

'So, has Lucky got California?'

'No, he hasn't.'

'Then why did you think I'd catch it off him?'

'We were just checking. Then we exposed you to the actual virus. Do you remember the day that Nurse Cohen came in with the overalls and the helmet and all that?'

'Yes, she looked like she was going beekeeping. I laughed my head off at the sight of her, but she didn't think it was funny. She told me to sit still so she could stick the thing up my nose. The squirty thing.'

'That was when she tried to make you catch the virus, but she knew you'd be safe.'

'Because I had the vaccine?'

'Exactly.'

'But if she knew I couldn't catch it, why did she try to give it to me?'

'Just to be sure that the vaccine was working. Just in case it wasn't doing its job.'

'So, why am I still here, then? If it's all grand, sure I might as well go home.'

'Listen, Mickey. You were the first person in the whole world to get this vaccine, so we're just keeping an eye on you until we're sure there are no side-effects. You know, to make sure that it didn't make you even a little bit sick. We just want to be sure you're okay.'

'Okay. By the way, Caroline, what day is it? I kinda lost track.'

'It's Friday, Mickey. Friday the thirteenth of September, twenty thirty. And It's half seven in the evening. Well, twenty-five past seven, to be exact. Now, you know exactly what day it is, and what time.'

'Friday the thirteenth! I hope nothing happens to me, it's supposed to be an unlucky day.'

'There's not much can happen to you in here, Mickey; this must be the safest place in Boyle. I wouldn't worry about it, if I were you. Anything else you need?'

'Can I have the Moone-Boy Burger again tomorrow?'

'Of course you can, Mickey. You can have anything you want. Except a happy ending, like!'

She laughed as she left the room and closed the door behind her. She walked along the corridor and tapped on the door of the end room before entering. Lucky Oyeleye turned from his desk where he was sketching on a pad. He put down his pencil and smiled.

'Hello, Caroline, it is good to see you, as always.'

'Hi, Lucky. How is the drawing class coming along?'

'It is good, it helps me with the boredom. You get tired watching movies and TV shows, so it is good to have some kind of self-improvement exercise to do.'

'You have a real talent for the art.'

'I like it, actually. I never tried it before, but the videos show you how to approach it, and you learn by doing it. This is a starling, and this one is a thrush. They are the only two birds from this module that I recognised from my country, the others are all alien to me.'

'You don't have robins or blackbirds in Nigeria?'

'I've never seen them, apart from in English books, or on Christmas cards. A lot of our birds are more colourful, like parrots and other tropical species. But once I have mastered the technique on these ones, I can apply my skills to others, I hope.'

'You are missing home?'

'Of course, and I miss my wife of course. But it helps,

me being able to call her twice a week. She understands.'

'So, you still plan on going home when you leave here?'

'Yes, whenever that will be.'

'Well, Lucky, I can tell you that for definite now. You'll be finished the trial next week, on Thursday. Six more days, that's it.'

Lucky's face lit up with joy.

'My God, Caroline, that is wonderful news. I will be so happy to get home. Although Ireland has been very good to me, it has allowed me to fulfil my dreams in a way I never thought possible.'

'And all because of a mistake in looking for directions.'

'Yes, but maybe God was watching over me, he sent me here.'

'I wouldn't be much of a believer in God, Lucky. But maybe there's something in it. You have been responsible for saving a lot of lives with this project and your contribution to it.'

'I hope my part was useful, and I am grateful for the money I have got in return.'

'Everybody is happy, so. Anyway, I'll leave you to it and I'll see you tomorrow. Buzz if you need anything.'

She pulled the door closed behind her as she left, humming a tune to herself as she walked down the corridor and through the deserted reception area into the service corridor. She pushed the heavy fire door open against the wind and felt it slam closed behind her as she left the building. She hurried across the carpark to her office, grateful for the warmth of the cabin. She put the kettle on and started to sort through the pile of paperwork on her desk. Two hours later she felt her eyes become heavy, as the warmth of the office lulled her into a doze.

Back in Room six, Mickey Small finished his cup of

tea and threw the wrapper from the chocolate in the bin. His fingers were sticky from the chocolate, and he walked into the bathroom to wash them, splashing some water on his face as he did so. As he dried his hands and face he looked at the mirror, his mouth opening wide in shock as he looked at the face that gazed back at him. He shouted in shock at the image in the mirror.

'No, no! Jesus, what's happening to me? No!'

He panicked and ran back to the bedroom, pushing at the locked door. He remembered the instructions given by Nurse Cohen when he first came to work in Boyle Labs, and he frantically examined the small break-glass unit beside the door lock. He hammered at the glass with the remote control, and as it shattered he heard the lock click open. He pushed the door and ran down the corridor, crying in terror. He crashed through the fire door at the end of the corridor and ran out into the night. The crash bar on the pedestrian gate yielded to his push and he ran away from the building as fast as his legs could carry him.

His mad dash brought him across the railway bridge and down Elphin Street, as he ran even faster on the steep downhill towards the river. He barely noticed the flood that ran high as he crossed the bridge, but the icy blast of wind coming up the river made him conscious that he was wearing only the lightweight blue and white scrubs from the Lab. He ducked into the laneway behind Boles' store and slowed a little to catch his breath, turning left at the other end of the lane on Saint Patricks Street. He broke into a gallop again until he got to his house, where he scrambled around until he found the key under the big stone, his heart pounding as he closed the front door behind him. He sat on the floor in the corner beside the TV, hugging his knees and sobbing quietly to himself.

The alarm that buzzed at her desk woke Caroline from her doze. She quickly checked the panel and raced to the main building. A quick glance at Mickey's room and the broken glass told her of her worst fears. She hurried to the carpark and jumped into her car, driving quickly towards the centre of town. She scanned the empty streets for any sight of her missing patient, turning left in the centre of town to head to his small cottage overlooking the river. She breathed more easily as she saw a light in the sitting room of the small house, relieved that he hadn't met with some worse fate. She got out of the car and tapped on the front door but there was no answer. She moved to the window and tapped on the glass, and heard a faint response.

'Go away, I don't want to see anybody.'

'Mickey, it's me. Can you let me in, I just want to talk to you.'

'Go away. Go away.'

She knelt by the front door and pushed open the flap of the letterbox, and saw two eyes stare back at her, and the sobbing face of Mickey Small. She swore in shock at the sight that met her eyes.

'Jesus Christ, Oh my God! Oh my God, Mickey, what's happened to you?'

Chapter Thirty Six

Miriam O'Hagan sat on the comfortable chair on the terrace of her house in Manilva, overlooking the Straits of Gibraltar on the south coast of Spain. The night was balmy, the warm air loud with the sound of the cicadas. In the distance she could see the string of lights along the African coast, brighter around Tangier and thinning out as the settlements faded out to the east of the town. Off to her right she could see the twinkling lights around the yacht harbour of Sotogrande, and beyond that she could just make out the large, spot-lit Spanish flag that fluttered proudly above the rock of Gibraltar, the former British territory that marked the gateway to the Mediterranean. She smiled as she remembered her visit to the bank there the day before, and to the fawning change of attitude from the manager when he realised the extent of her funds.

She lifted her glass and silently toasted her good fortune. Her phone lay on the small cast iron table beside her and she picked it up idly, scrolling through the list of missed calls. She smiled again as she saw the numerous calls from her husband; he would find out soon enough where she had gone once the lawyers had all their ducks in a row.

She put the phone down again and took another sip from her drink, idly glancing at the silenced phone as it buzzed quietly with yet another call. She frowned as she saw Caroline's name on the screen; Caroline was unlikely to bother her unless it was important. She put down her drink and picked up the phone.

'Hi, Caroline. I assume this is urgent?'

'Miriam, sorry to bother you, but I have a problem.'

'There are no problems, Caroline, just solutions. Just tell me the solution and we can work back from there.'

The administrator sounded breathless, as though she had been running. She took a couple of deep breaths to steady herself and spoke in an even tone.

'Do you remember, at one of our team meetings a couple of months back, that Kevin raised a couple of reservations about the vaccine.'

'I never paid too much heed to Kevin, and you shouldn't either. He's a panicker.'

'He was right on this one.'

'What do you mean? On which one?'

'Mickey Small broke out of the unit tonight, smashed the fire lock unit and made a run for it, ran all the way home and he's locked himself in his house. Says he's not coming out again, ever.'

'He'll have to eat.'

'He left a note out for the 'meals on wheels' lot to bring him food. But that's not the problem.'

'Then spit it out, why did he make a run for it? Was the isolation too much for him? He is a bit loopy, we know that.'

'His skin, it seems to have been affected by the vaccine.'

'Then get a dermatologist, sort him out. It can't be

anything that a bit of cortisone cream won't fix.'

'I don't think that cortisone will turn a black man white.'

'What?'

'He's turned black, Mickey Small is now a black man, or whatever the correct term is. Black as the proverbial ace of spades. I looked through the letterbox and there he was, this black man looking back at me. Like Louis Armstrong, up close, or Sammy Davis Junior, more like. The only black man in the village, apart from Lucky Oyeleye and that priest fellow, although I think he's not here anymore.'

'Lucky is gone too?'

'No, he's still here, he's fine, happy as the day is long. The priest is gone, I think. I don't go near that lot and their church.'

'Sometimes, Caroline, I lose the thread with you. Slow down and take it from the top again.'

'It's very simple, Miriam. The vaccine appears to have turned Mickey Small black.'

'Black all over?'

'How the hell would I know, Miriam. I didn't ask him to take out his willy.'

Miriam laughed heartily.

'I know it's not funny, Caroline, but I just had an image, you know?'

'Sorry, I didn't mean to be rude. I'm just stressed out here. I didn't know who else to call, what will I do?'

'Did you tell anybody else about this?'

'No, I'm the only one on duty at the minute, we just have the two people in the secure unit. Had, I mean.'

'Then say nothing yet, this could be just a one-off, there's no reason to believe that this is a general side-effect, or indeed that it was caused by the vaccine at all. This might just be something that happened to Mickey, either as a rare side effect, or as a combination factor, you know, because of some underlying issue or some dietary issue from the past.'

'So I should do nothing?'

'Try to get Mickey back to the unit and have the doctor look at him. Have you told the new manager about it?'

'No, there are two of them, they just sit in the office all day and drink vodka. They don't seem to want to have anything to do with the business at all. It's strange.'

'Then say nothing, this might be nothing to worry about, but try and persuade Mickey to come back in, in case anybody sees him if nothing else.'

'Thanks, Miriam. I know it's nothing to do with you anymore, but I didn't know who to call.'

'That's fine, and stop worrying. This is all probably nothing.'

'But what if it isn't?'

'We don't even want to go there, girl. I don't even want to think about it.'

Chapter Thirty Seven

Major Mike Callaghan awoke from his sleep in the cot in the room off his office as his phone rang. He grabbed the phone and quickly tapped the green icon when he saw the caller ID.

'Callaghan here, Sir.'

The President spoke quietly, so that the Major could hardly hear what he was saying.

'Major, can you come to my quarters immediately? This is an urgent matter, please use your pass card and don't ask anybody's permission to come in, and try not to be seen.'

'I'll be there in five minutes, Sir.'

Callaghan grabbed his clothes and dressed quickly, wondering why the President would need to see him at four in the morning. He quickly checked his phone to see whether some international crisis had occurred, but there appeared to be nothing out of the ordinary happening anywhere. He slipped along the corridor to the Executive wing, using his card to access the small service elevator that took him quickly to the second floor lobby. He tapped the card again on the lock at the entrance to the bedroom suite, using his fingerprint to verify his access permission. The President was waiting in the lounge area outside the bedroom, sitting in an armchair with a white towel over his head. He lowered the towel slightly as he heard the door open, quickly replacing it as the Major entered the room.

'Thanks for coming over, Major, and my apologies about the hour, but this is urgent.'

'No problem, Sir.

'You want some coffee, there's a pot on the tray there. I ordered some, I couldn't sleep.'

Major Callaghan poured himself a cup of coffee and waved the pot in the direction of the President, who was still seated in the armchair, the towel covering his head and hands.

'You want some, Sir?'

'Coffee? No thanks, I had some already.'

Callaghan sat in silence for a few minutes, sipping the hot coffee and wondering at the purpose of the meeting, but he knew better than to ask questions. Eventually, the President spoke.

'I guess you're wondering why I called you over.'

'No, Sir. I figured it was urgent.'

'Yes, it is. I don't know what to do about this problem, and I don't know how it happened.'

'The problem, Sir?'

'Yes, Major. I don't understand it, it's come as a shock.'

'Yes, Sir.'

'So, the question is, what do I do now?'

'I don't know, Sir.'

'Do you know what I'm talking about, Major?'

'Not exactly, Sir.'

The President slowly peeled the towel from his face and looked at his Chief of Staff. Major Callaghan carefully put the coffee cup on the table and looked in astonishment at the sight before him.'

'What's the matter, Major? Cat got your tongue?'

Major Callaghan wiped his brow with the back of his hand, looking away from his boss and then looking back in astonishment.

'Goddamn, Sir! What'n hell happened to you?'

'Damned if I know, Major. I was looking a bit grey when I went to bed last night, I thought it was that I was working too hard, or too much booze or something. Then I got up to go to the bathroom half an hour ago and when I took out my…'

'I get the picture, Sir.'

'I thought it looked a bit black, I thought I'd caught one of them STDs, you know? Although I'm real careful. I gotta be, in this job. Then I looked at my face in the mirror. Holy guacamole!'

'You been feeling all right, Sir, lately?'

'Sure, never better. Feeling good, eating right, not even drinking as much as I used to. What the hell is happening to me, you ever see this before, a white man that turned into a black man?'

'Never, Sir.'

'You never saw nothing like that in the army, a guy turning black?'

'Never, Sir. We did have a white African American in a unit once, but he was like that from he was a kid. Albino, the medics said. But it wasn't that he started out black and turned white, nothing like that. Born that way.'

'You reckon I got black blood in me, from way back, maybe? Just took until now for it to show up?'

'Could be, Sir. But the truth is, I don't really know. Have you called the medics?'

'No, and we don't have a new CMO, we never appointed one since Vladimir was killed. I think they got a shortlist, but they have to check them out before they send them to me.'

'I'll follow up on that, first thing. We gotta get you checked out.'

'Good. Although I feel good, I don't feel sick or nothing. Maybe I picked up some bug though, something that just affected my skin.'

'I really don't know, Sir.'

'Or maybe I got exposed to some chemical? You remember we went to that chemical plant a couple of weeks back, could have been something there.'

'That was a food plant, Sir. They make breakfast cereal.'

'Oh, okay, but there were a lot of chemicals in big tanks, it might have been something I got exposed to there.'

'It's possible, Sir, but I was with you all the time, and I haven't turned black.'

The President peered at Callaghan closely.

'No, you haven't. It's very strange.'

The Major felt a chill as a thought occurred to him. He spoke, hesitantly.

'I wonder...'

'Yes, Major, spit it out. You thought of something?'

'It couldn't have been the vaccine, Sir, could it? The California vaccine? I mean, the vaccine against the Chinese virus that came in through California?'

'That goddamn vaccine! I was trying to forget about that damned episode, we were made to look like a laughing stock in front of the whole world. Damned Ruskies, you can never trust them, my Daddy used to say that all the time. You think they're your friends, but they're working away behind your back, trying to pull a fast one.'

'But could it have been that, Sir? Is it possible that the

vaccine has a side effect in the occasional case, to make the skin turn black?'

'How the hell would I know, Major? I'm not a goddamned medic!'

'Sorry, Sir. I was just thinking out loud. But it's something we have to check out.'

'It hasn't turned you black, Major, so that's screwed that theory.'

'I didn't get it just yet, Sir. I changed my mind, I didn't take it on the day in Tennessee in case of any side effects. I was on duty and I couldn't take any risks for safety reasons.'

'Can we check out the farmer guy, the one with the naked girlfriend? He got his shot the same time I got mine.'

'No, Sir. He just got a shot of vitamins. He didn't want to get the vaccine at all.'

'Get down there anyhow and check him out in the morning, take the chopper as soon as it's light, This could be something I picked up in that place, they didn't even have a goddamn bathroom, just a long-drop outhouse, I had to hover. Check all the angles.'

'I'll do that straight away, Sir. If there's anything amiss down there, I'll find it.'

'But what do I do in the meantime, Major? I can't show my face outside of here. If the folks out there thought they had elected another Obama to this job, they wouldn't be happy. They'd think I was coming to take away their guns, or make them take free medical care.'

The Major thought for a minute before speaking.

'A couple of things, Sir. First, you gotta cancel all appearances, just do radio work or voice communications only. We can arrange for some speeches to be written to match the facial movements on older press briefings, and you can voice them over the tapes.'

'Like we did at New Year when my wife gave me the black eye?'

'Exactly. I'll get Billy to work on that straight away, he's reliable and he won't know what it's about anyhow. That should buy us some time until the medics give us some clue as to what's happened to you. We just need two days, then we're at the weekend and we got two more, so with any luck this will have faded away and you'll be fine, or they'll be able to treat it.'

'They gotta treat it, Major. The idea of being a black man in America isn't very appealing, to be honest.'

The Major paused again before speaking.

'We also gotta look at the worst case scenario, Sir. We have to plan for all eventualities.'

'You mean if I stay black? That would be about as bad as it gets, right enough.'

'That ain't the worst case scenario, Sir, not by a long shot.'

'What do you mean?'

'If it really was the vaccine, and this side effect is the norm, we are looking at a country that is mostly populated by black people, Sir.'

'Holy guacamole! Goddamn! America is a white country, always was. If everybody is black, where does that leave us?'

'It's not a scenario we ever war-gamed for, Sir. Short answer, I don't have a clue. But we need to start thinking about it, and real quick.'

'Can we stop the vaccine programme?'

'A bit late for that, Sir. Most of the population has been covered already, the use of nasal sprays meant the army and the National Guard was able to administer it quickly, and the water treatment plan has delivered it to the rest. I'd imagine there aren't a couple of hundred thousand people in this country that haven't been reached by the vaccine at this stage.'

'Major, this is turning into a right clusterfuck. Apart from the effect on my own life and career, the knock-on of something like that is going to be unbelievable.'

'True, Sir. The social implications will be extraordinary, although not necessarily all bad. No more race riots, I guess.'

'I wasn't thinking of that, Major. Can you imagine the effect on property prices? Who will want to live in a black neighbourhood?'

Chapter Thirty Eight

Miriam O'Hagan strode quickly across the tarmac at Ireland West Airport, a small regional airport outside the village of Knock, near the country's Atlantic coast. She waved to Caroline who stood in the airport lounge, looking through the floor-to-ceiling windows at the arriving passengers. As Miriam came through the door she turned left and fell into step beside her former colleague. Conscious of listening ears in the small building, they didn't speak until they were inside Caroline's car. Miriam looked at the plush interior of the electric Mercedes and smiled.

'I'm glad to see you didn't save it all for a rainy day! Nice wheels!'

Caroline smiled briefly, then her face became serious again.

'I'm glad you're back, Miriam, even if it's only for a few days. I really don't have anyone to discuss these things with, I don't really trust Mary Cohen after the vaccination stunt.'

'Ah, Mary is just a kind soul, no more than yourself. I don't think she had any motivation other than to do a favour for her neighbours. Who's to say either of us wouldn't have done the same, if the situation was different?'

'Maybe, but it was a breach of trust all the same. I don't think I'd have done it, it could have jeopardised the entire project if it had gone wrong at the time.'

'What do you mean, 'at the time?' Are you saying it has gone wrong now?'

'You were always quick on the uptake, Miriam. I'm afraid it's now part of the overall problem. We're not just dealing with a black nut-job who thinks he's an aircraft engineer, we have a few other black faces in Boyle, and they didn't arrive on the Galway bus.'

'Jesus! Mary's neighbours?'

'I'm afraid so. That's why I've called this meeting tonight in Mary's house, I don't want the two Russians to get an inkling of this, until maybe we can reverse it or something. I really don't know what to do.'

'Speaking of Russians, how are you getting on with the new management team?'

'A pair of idiots, as far as I can see. They don't have a clue about running a lab, Billy is doing that, with a bit of help from me on the admin side. And Karen is frantically trying to get her head around the science of this mutation, the darkening of skin in some of the vaccinated people. Kevin is helping with that side of things, and in fairness to him he seems to have learned his lesson from the public dressing-down you gave him.'

'Taking care of his money, more likely. He's not a bad lad, but I'd also say he's just afraid he won't see his residual payment at the end of two years if he slips up again. Anyway, if he's burning the midnight oil along with Karen, and there's a solution to this, they'll find it. So the Russians don't engage with you at all?'

'Hard for them, they hardly speak a word of English,

and they seem to be drunk a lot of the time. I'd say the Russian government has no long-term interest in the lab, they're just harvesting the royalties and maybe laundering a bit of money through the place. Lolek and Bolek we call them, they seem to be just two nominal directors, maybe sent here as a punishment. They know fuck all about running a laboratory anyway, Kevin had to physically keep them out of the clean room one day, they were poking around and he was afraid they'd contaminate the place. Two stupid yokels.'

'You could be right about that. Are Kevin and Karen coming along tonight?'

'Yes, they'll be there.'

'What's the story with Mickey Small, is he all right? I have a bit of a conscience about that lad, I'm not so sure he was able to give informed consent for the tests.'

'His IQ is near enough normal, I'd say, he's well able to get along from day to day. It's more that he lives in a fantasy world, he's just a bit of a dreamer. But he's not stupid; he knows his rights and all that, he has the meals on wheels bringing him his dinner every day, and Lonely Alone bring him his groceries and probably pay for them as well. Some other scheme pays his electricity bill and his TV subscriptions, so our Mickey lives high on the hog without dipping into his own money.'

'Still, he can't stay locked up in his house forever. Somebody is bound to notice that he's a bit off colour.'

Caroline laughed.

'That's one way of putting it, all right.'

She turned the car towards Boyle and they lapsed into silence for a while before Miriam spoke again.

'What's the plan for tonight? Have we an agenda, apart from talking for a couple of hours about something we know already, that this is a bit of a fuck-up.'

'I hadn't thought about it too much, or about what we can do about it. I suppose there's two sides to it, two angles. The first is the technical side, whether we can find some way to reverse the effect on people's skin, and the other is how we can keep this covered up until we do that.'

Miriam thought for a few minutes before answering.

'I'd say this is a lot bigger problem than just a few black faces in Kiltycreighton, Caroline. I mean, if Mickey and few of Mary's neighbours have darkened up, then half of America can't be far behind. From the news reports, I think they've rolled the vaccine out faster than any vaccination programme in history. They trained up the army and the National Guard to administer the nasal spray, and God knows what else they've done in terms of adding it to the food chain or indeed maybe to bottled water or something. They're claiming to have seventy five percent of the population vaccinated, which is phenomenal. But if half of them turn black, and the other half already are, you're looking at a country that will end up with an almost entirely black population. The societal implications of that are something the world hasn't even considered.'

'But it's unlikely to affect everybody, is it? When Kevin raised this a couple of months ago, he said it might affect an occasional person.'

'We're in unknown territory now, Caroline. If all the people in Kiltycreighton turn black, that's statistically significant, it means that it's likely that this side-effect is widespread, not just an aberration.'

'I think they have.'

'All of them?'

'I think so. They're all keeping indoors when anybody is around. As you know, the townland is just one road and it's a dead end, so there's only one way in and out. The lad who lives in the first house has rigged up an alarm so that any car or person entering the road sets off an alarm in every house, so they can all get indoors. It's usually just the postman, or the binman, and the kids are off school now anyway, so nobody has noticed so far.'

'So have you seen Mary? Is she black as well?'

'Yes I saw her, she's fine. She didn't inject herself at the time, she was going to wait until we all did it at work, so she looks the same. We'll see her in a minute anyway.'

Caroline slowed and took a hard left turn on to the Ballymote Road, driving carefully uphill towards the mountain. As she crested the rise half a mile further on, she indicated and turned left again down the narrow cul-de-sac. The car glided along the leafy lane, triggering an almost imperceptible blink of light from a box on a roadside pole. She pointed over her shoulder as they passed the electronic box.

'That's the alarm, every house on the road will know now that there's a car on the way.'

Caroline turned up the steep driveway to Mary Cohen's house, pulling up at the front door as the nurse opened it and came out to greet them, leading the way into the large hallway and taking their coats before ushering them into the sitting room where the other team members sat around on chairs and on the floor. A large coffee table held plates of sandwiches and pots of tea and coffee, and their host waved her hand in its direction.

'Food and drinks, everybody, help yourselves. I have something stronger if anybody wants it.'

Miriam took a mug and poured herself a coffee, helping herself to a couple of titbits from the tray of food. She sat on a small chair in the corner and surveyed the room.

241

JOHN MULLIGAN

'Well, folks, I guess I have to eat a bit of humble pie. Your concerns appear to have been well founded, Kevin.'

Kevin Kelly shook his head sadly.

'I wish it weren't so, Miriam, but to be honest I never considered this outcome to be other than a possible outlier, statistically speaking. I certainly never considered the possibility of it being a one hundred percent risk for all recipients, I was more thinking of one in a thousand, or one in ten thousand, something of that order. I might have had reservations about going into production with minimal testing on humans and just relying on computer modelling, but I never considered this.'

Billy Robinson stirred from his position on the floor by the window.

'Where does this leave us, now that it's a reality? I mean, this isn't just some theoretical exercise, we have twenty or so black people living in Kiltycreighton, I don't think there was ever a black person on this road, except for that priest who was here for a while maybe. But what are the implications for the company and indeed for all of us as individuals?'

Miriam sipped her coffee thoughtfully.

'The company is fine, except maybe for reputational damage, but the risk for this is carried entirely by the government of the United States. With regards to individuals, you all just work there and no liability can attach to you. Where this leaves the vaccination programme worldwide, I don't know, quite honestly. Although I hear that the US has rolled out this vaccine to most of the population.'

Karen Doyle raised her hand before speaking.

'The thing is, I have checked everywhere, and there's no mention of anyone in the US turning black because of

242

this, Miriam. Not a whisper, anywhere.'

'There are a couple of possible reasons for that, Karen. Firstly, it's possible that Irish people have some genetic predisposition to being more receptive to this effect of the vaccine. We are a bit inbred as a small island nation, after all, and there are some genetic defects that are more common here because of that. The other angle is that thanks to Mary here, the people of Kiltycreighton were the first in the world to get the vaccine, so maybe the tsunami of blackness is yet to descend on the land of the free.'

Mary reddened, and muttered an apology.

'If I could take it back, I really would. I never thought this could happen. I mean, I know I was there when Kevin mentioned it, but I thought it was a really long shot. And now I have to stay indoors and avoid my neighbours, and maybe they'll sue me or something.'

Caroline smiled wryly.

'No use crying over spilt milk, and no use worrying about the neighbours. After all, can they definitely blame it on the vaccine? Particularly since you didn't officially give it to them?'

Kevin pondered the question before speaking.

'Good point, Caroline. I don't think it's possible to actually tie in this colour effect to the actual vaccine. After all, we don't even know for sure ourselves that the two are linked. It might be something else entirely, something in the water for instance. Are they all still getting their water from wells along this road, or is there mains water?'

'Mostly mains now, I think.'

'Well, maybe not the water, but it could be some other phenomenon. Although to be honest it's probably the vaccine, but it would be hard for a court to prove that, is all I'm saying.'

Billy Robinson smiled from his place by the wall.

'We could be worrying unduly, too. Maybe this is just a temporary phenomenon? Any ideas on that, Kevin, or Karen?'

Karen looked at her colleague who motioned her to speak.

'That is definitely a possibility. After Mary told us about the black thing here in Kiltycreighton, Kevin and I did some computer modelling on the possible cause, the timelines and all that. One outcome was that the effect faded away after varying times, from a month to a year depending on what figures we used. But there's no hard science in that, just statistical analyses of various outcomes.'

'So you're saying?'

'I don't know, Billy, that's the honest answer. But it is one possible outcome. Or more correctly, it emerges as a result in around ten thousand outcomes.'

'That sounds hopeful.'

'Not really, that's out of several million permutations.'

Miriam held up her hand to get attention.

'So, what we have here is an aberration, something outside the mainstream of predictability, is that a fair summary?'

'Yes.'

'And equally, a natural reversal of that over time is also a possibility, of the same order as the original effect?'

Kevin and Karen nodded their assent.

'So, basically, the original accidental or unintended effect, if we can call it that, was something we couldn't really have predicted, despite it featuring as a statistical possibility out on the edge somewhere. And the reversal of that effect lies in the same mathematical area, would that be a fair way of putting it?'

Karen nodded.

'You summed it up pretty well, Miriam.'

'Then there's nothing we can do, folks, except keep our heads down and say nothing. The two Russians own the lab, so if this thing does start to feature in the USA, we let them deal with it. And in the meantime, the thinkers among you might also look at whether there is some pharmaceutical way of reversing this skin tone issue.'

Billy Robinson smiled.

'You're right about us keeping our heads down, Miriam. But the other idea, coming up with a treatment for black skin? That has ethical issues way beyond where my mind can even go. Can you imagine it, black people in America taking a pill to get a better job, or to get into Yale or Harvard?'

'Hang on, Billy, plenty of black people go to Ivy League colleges.'

'Yes, but statistically, white people have a better chance of getting in, and of getting the good jobs when they come out the other end and qualify. Being black is no fun, in America or anywhere.'

'That's a debate for another day, Billy. But for now, we can talk around this forever and we won't solve it. I suggest we just do as we more or less agreed, and keep shtum.'

'Whatever you say, say nothing?'

'Exactly.'

Mary opened the window slightly to ventilate the room. The sound of reggae music could be heard in the distance. She smiled.

'A few of the neighbours, they made steel drums out of old oil barrels and they started playing Caribbean music. They reckon it's all part of their heritage now.'

Miriam suddenly remembered something.

'What about Mickey Small, how is he doing? He's the

most likely one to break cover and show himself, the neighbours here will probably stay hidden for a while anyway. But I can't see Mickey staying in that little house for ever.'

Mary laughed.

'Don't worry about our mugger turned airplane engineer, I spoke to him a couple of hours ago. Our Mickey has plenty to occupy himself these days.'

'Do tell, has he found a hobby?'

'He's got a live-in girlfriend, a fine-looking young woman from somewhere in Eastern Europe. Her name is Monica McEvoy. They're in love, apparently; Mickey won't be leaving the bed for weeks.'

Chapter Thirty Nine

President Daniels sat in the shadows in the shuttered Oval Office, the bright desk light pointing away from him towards the members of his team who sat on the two couches that were positioned facing each other at right angles to his desk. Major Mike Callaghan sat nearest to the President on his left side, sharing the couch with Brad Brady, the new Chief Medical Officer. Lucy Martinez, the Attorney General, sat opposite, a pile of files on the couch beside her. The President pointed to his Chief of Staff.

'Fill the others in on this, Mike.'

The Major got to his feet and addressed the room.

'First thing, folks, everything you see or hear in this room is classified to the highest level, which is rated as Top Secret. In case any of you doesn't know, I'll spell that out. Top Secret applies to information, the unauthorized disclosure of which reasonably could be expected to cause exceptionally "grave damage to our National Security. In other words, disclosure of anything said or seen in this room is a crime against our Nation and will almost certainly mean spending a long time behind bars. Have I made myself clear?'

The others nodded assent. The President took a towel

from his head and dipped the reading light so that it didn't glare in the faces of his audience. There were gasps from the other two team members, but they didn't say anything. The Major continued.

'As you can see, President Daniels has been afflicted by some disorder that has resulted in him taking on a Negroid appearance.'

The Attorney General raised her hand.

'Come on, Major, you cannot use that term or any other racist terminology in this office.'

'I'm sorry, Ms Martinez, no offence meant. He has taken on the appearance of a black man, if that's the term preferred by coloured people.'

The Attorney General interrupted again.

'Coloured people, Major? Do you mean African Americans and Hispanics?'

'No, not Hispanics. No offence intended on your people, Ms Martinez.'

'My people, Major? I'm an American, fourth generation Californian.'

The President stood up and banged the desk with his fist.

'For God's sake, Mike, Lucy, can you cut the damned crap and get on with it without getting bogged down in, in, what's the word?'

'Semantics?'

'Yes, Lucy, seaman tricks. Can we just all agree to disagree for half an hour until we try to get our heads around this problem?'

The Major raised his hands in a placatory gesture.

'I'm sorry, Ms Martinez, I guess it's just man-talk; we're used to using that word in private, it don't mean anything, we'd never use it in public where it might offend.'

'It offends me.'

'Okay, okay, let's just call them 'people of African appearance'.'

'That doesn't cover it; nearly half of South Africans are white.'

'So, what do I call them, then?'

'Americans? They're Americans, after all. All equal under God, according to the constitution.'

'But how do I refer to skin colour?'

'Just refer to skin colour if you must, but don't apply it to any sector of society.'

The Major shook his head and resumed talking.

'Anyhow, the President, as you can see, is suffering from a darkened skin, he has turned black all over.'

'Suffering? You think one person's skin colour is something to be suffered, compared to a privileged white male maybe?'

The President banged on the desk again, angrily.

'Holy guacamole, Lucy, can you give it a damn rest? I'm a black man sitting in the Oval Office, elected here by folks who thought different. I want to know what the hell to do about that, not about whether it makes me a less good person.'

'I just don't see that as a problem, Sir. We had a black man in the job back in twenty seventeen, and he'd been there for two terms at that point. And we had a black woman in twenty-five. The world didn't fall apart while either of them were in that chair.'

'That's debatable.'

'Maybe, Sir. But all I'm saying is that it shouldn't matter what colour your skin is. You look rather well, in fact. Being black suits you.'

The President took a deep breath before speaking.

'Carry on, Major.'

Major Callaghan looked at the Attorney General and shook his head before continuing.

'Like I was saying, the President's appearance has changed somewhat in recent days, and we need to get to the bottom of it. Do you have any ideas on this matter, Doctor Brady? Welcome to the team by the way, we haven't really had time to talk since you were appointed to the CMO role.'

Brad Brady stood up to speak, hesitantly at first.

'Mr President, Major, Ms Martinez, my speciality was general practice, I don't have a dermatology background, but I'd say this is a very unusual complaint. I've never heard of anyone's skin turning black, except to some degree in persons of mixed race whose skin tone was maybe lighter before puberty for instance, but who might have darkened up a shade after that. But I understand that there is no mixed-race background in your family line, Sir?'

'Damn right, Brad. My folks go all the way back to the time of the founding fathers. We sold pickup trucks to the dust-bowl refugees, we're all-American, white as they come.'

Lucy Martinez shifted in her seat and sighed audibly, but refrained from comment as the doctor continued.

'Anyhow, Sir, I understand from Major Callaghan that your first suspicion was that this was a reaction to the Californian Virus vaccine.'

The Major nodded.

'Yes, Brad, that was our first thought on it, that it might have been some side-effect of the vaccine against the Chinese variant of Covid-25 that came in through California. The President, as you know, was the first person in the country to receive the vaccine.'

'Yes, I saw that on TV. Along with a farmer, the one with the naked girlfriend.'

'We'd prefer to forget that episode, Brad, so please don't mention it again. But that's only partly true, the farmer didn't get the vaccine, he just got a vitamin shot. He's an anti-vaxxer, a lot of them are in that part of the world. We just gave him a shot for the TV cameras, a PR exercise. We paid him to be there.'

'Then you'll know, if he didn't get the vaccine it means he's your control.'

'Yes, that's what we thought, Brad. I went down there yesterday, I flew to Corner Creek in the helicopter and met the new Sherriff, a lady called Polly Ammery, a pretty likeable individual. She used to drive a speed-camera car but when the other guy got shot they made her Sherriff, she was the only one who could write the answers to the test.'

The President interrupted.

'Major, cut the gossip and get to the point, okay?'

'Sorry, Sir. Anyhow, I spoke to the Sherriff and asked her about Randy Corless, that's the farmer we spoke of. She said he'd moved out of his cabin and was living with the dead guy's widow, a Shirley Kendall, in her house in the hills outside the town. She said neither of them had been seen since Sherriff Kendall's funeral, but that they were still alive because they were known to be getting their groceries delivered. She had gone to their house a couple of times to check if they were okay, given that the lady is a police widow and therefore entitled to support from the Police Department, but Shirley just spoke to her through the door and didn't come out.'

'So you didn't get to see them?'

'I don't give up that easy, Brad. I borrowed a police cruiser and drove up there, followed the directions that Sherriff Ammery gave me. I parked up outside and knocked on the door.'

'She let you in?'

'No, not at first. Then I told her I'd blow the door off its hinges, so she opened it. The shades were all drawn, then as my eyes got used to the light I realised that both of them were, had the same kind of skin as the President, if you know what I mean.'

'Both of them were black?'

'Yes, Brad, ain't that the truth. She looked completely different, I wouldn't have recognised her at all, it's amazing how much difference the, ah, colour makes.'

'Him too?'

'He was even more changed, he was wearing a suit that was too big for him, and some fancy leather shoes. Last time I saw him he was dressed in overalls, with bare feet. I guess he was making use of the contents of the late Sherriff's closet.'

'Then there you have it, neither of them got the vaccine, so it isn't the vaccine that's causing the problem.'

'That's before you look at the full story, Brad. You see, we've been adding the vaccine to the water supply in Corner creek since a couple of days after the President was there.'

The Attorney General jumped to her feet.

'You've been doing what? Are you crazy, Major? You can't add a vaccine to the water, that's against every rule in the book. That's the kind of stuff they do in North Korea.'

The President smiled wryly.

'Are you saying there's anything wrong with people from North Korea, Lucy? I thought we were all equal, and all that stuff?'

She sighed in exasperation.

'Don't misquote me, Sir, with respect. But we can't just add stuff to the water supply, it's not ethical.'

'It's not ethical allowing people to die from this Chinese virus either. Sometimes you gotta pick the lesser of two evils.'

'I've never heard anything like it, Sir. I really haven't.'

'Then it's just as well you weren't in the job when we did 'Operation Reduce,' I guess.'

'What's 'Operation Reduce?''

'We'd best not go there at this point in time, Lucy. Carry on, Major. You were saying?'

'Thank you, Sir. Like I said, both of them had turned black, got black skin anyhow. So I figured it was the water, but now I ain't so sure.'

'Why is that, Major?'

'Well, you see, Brad, I checked all that. Their house isn't on the mains supply. When the late Sherriff built the place, there weren't no utilities up there except the electricity. He had a deep well sunk, and put in a septic system for the sewage. So they ain't getting water from the mains.'

'Maybe they got it in his last place, the cabin we saw on TV, the time that….'

'Nope, same thing there. They don't have mains water in that cabin either, not even electricity. It's pretty basic living, up there.'

'So, didn't the farmer have a brother or some other relative that lived there?'

'Yes, a brother, fella by the name of Buddy. I went up to see him as well, after I'd left the happy couple. He was just sitting on the front porch, same as last time I saw him, but with one exception.'

'He was black too?'

'Yes. As the ace of spades.'

The President stood up and began to pace the room, around and around the oval rug with one foot on the rug and one clumping on the hardwood floor. He pointed at the doctor with the index fingers of both hands.

'So, you're the doctor, Brad. Can you tell us how that can have happened, how none of the three of them took the vaccine but all of them have got the skin colour change? Does that sound like a vaccine side-effect to you?'

'I think we can definitely say it isn't down to the vaccine.'

'So, what is it?'

'It is obviously contagious, to a greater or lesser degree. Either you carried it there and spread it to the two brothers and the woman, or they already had it and they gave it to you. Those are the two possible scenarios, there's no other logical explanation.'

'Chicken and egg kinda situation? Hard to tell which came first?'

'Yes, Sir, you could say that, I guess.'

Major Callaghan interrupted the musings of the two men.

'So, Brad, can you drill down into this further? For instance, if the President caught it on a Monday, and the Corless brothers caught it on a Tuesday, does that necessarily mean the President is the spreader, in a manner of speaking?'

The Attorney General raised a hand as if to stop the conversation.

'You don't have to answer that, Doctor, if it implies blame on behalf of the President.'

Major Callaghan sighed in exasperation.

'Ms Martinez, can we drop the legalese for a minute? We're just chewing the fat here, trying to make sense of how something might have happened, we're not trying to find anybody guilty or innocent of anything. This is just war-gaming, postulating scenarios and trying to knock them down.'

'It's my job to protect the interests of the Oval Office, I can't allow the President to be accused of anything.'

'Okay, we'll discuss somebody else, some fictional character who isn't the President, is that acceptable.'

'Yes, that would be better, thank you.'

Major Callaghan took several deep breaths before continuing.

'Okay, Brad, let's take it from the top again. A random guy goes to Tennessee, and a month later he's got dark skin. His three closest contacts during that visit have also turned black, and what I want to know is whether it is possible to determine who gave what to who?'

'Whom, Who gave what to whom. And why is it always a random guy, why is the default position always a man?'

'Because the random person was random, Ms Martinez, okay? She could equally have been a woman, or a person of whatever variant of gender happened to randomly come to the top of the heap. You happy with that?'

'Yes, I guess so.'

'Okay, Brad, what's your view on the position of our random person in that mix?'

The doctor pondered the question for a moment before responding.

'First of all, Major, I want to make it clear that I'm not an expert in infectious diseases, I come from the general practice side of the medical world, but I've been around sick people long enough to have learned some stuff about them. So, in my opinion, it's not always possible to guess who was the one that left the smell in the shithouse, if you'll pardon my use of the expression.'

'Back to square one?'

'Reckon so.'

The Attorney General interrupted the conversation.

'But you must have some theory, some possible explanation?'

'I'm just a regular doctor, but it strikes me this is a puzzle of logic as much as it is a medical issue. So I do have a thought on it, yes.'

The President spread his hands, palms upwards.

'So, shoot, Brad. We're all just trying to figure this out.'

'Well, Sir, the way I see it is this. It seems clear it isn't the vaccine, and women and men and maybe others are catching it from one another in ways not yet understood by us, maybe what we're dealing with is a new virus altogether, one that acts on skin colour? That's how I see it, anyhow.'

'You think it's a new pandemic, or the beginnings of one?'

'Sure looks that way, Ms Martinez. That could be it, a new disease or a mutant of an existing disease.'

'I'd hesitate to use the word 'disease' to describe one's skin changing to black. That would imply that persons of colour other than white are diseased.'

'So, what is the correct term for turning black, Ms Martinez?'

'It's a condition, Doctor, not a disease. Nobody who acquired the condition is sick, their outward appearance is just different, that's all. It's no big deal.'

The President paused in his pacing.

'Might be no big deal to you, Lucy, but it's a hell of a big deal to me. I got into bed beside my wife last night and she woke up and screamed, but then she told me to be quick because her husband would be home soon. I guess she was kidding about that bit.'

'Then the problem lies with her, Sir, with prejudices she acquired from her childhood, most likely. She'll get over it.'

'It is what it is, Lucy. White folks are scared of black folks, and that's just a fact of life. But my concern is about this new disease, condition, whatever we want to call it. If this thing is spreading, and it seems like it is in one small town anyhow, then there's a possibility that before too long everybody in America will be black. Would that sum it up, Brad?'

'I guess so, Sir. It don't bear thinking about, to be honest. I mean, everything we think of as normal won't be normal any more, I can't get my head around it.'

'What do you think, Lucy? What are the implications for America?'

'I guess I don't see it as a big issue, Sir. If the doctor is right, and this condition spreads to the entire nation, I would honestly see that as a good thing. We would have achieved what Martin Luther King dreamed of, all those years ago. What I recall he said was 'we might all have come on different ships, but we're in the same boat now.' We sure will all be in the same boat then, Sir, for the first time in our history, and I don't have a problem with that.'

'But what about our laws, won't we all be at a disadvantage then, if we're all black?'

'At a disadvantage to whom, Sir? If we're all black, the playing field will be level.'

The doctor raised an index finger in a cautionary stance.

'It's unlikely that everybody will be black, that's the thing. Any pandemic will have a few exceptions, as I recall reading in one of our medical magazines. Suppose half of one percent of Americans don't succumb to the dis.., the condition? That's still a whole lot of white folks.'

The Major interjected.

'That's one and three quarter million, more or less.'

'Thanks, Major. I hadn't even thought of a number that big, but you obviously got a head for the math. So, like I said, we might end up with a white elite that runs things, and the rest of us gonna have to knuckle down to them.'

The President made a patting motion with both outstretched hands to signal his intention to close off the discussion.

'Okay, folks, we got ourselves a helluva problem, that's for sure. But we're the adults in the room. The four of us, we're the people in charge of this great nation, we're the pick of the crop, and it falls to us to solve this problem and show some leadership. So here's what we're gonna do.

First, Brad, get our scientists to analyse this new disease, don't listen to the doubters who try to suggest it came from the vaccine, because it clearly didn't. And maybe we might eat some humble pie and go back to that lab in Ireland, the one that the Russians seem to own, they obviously got the best scientific brains. Ask them to find a way to reverse this condition, and give them whatever money they need to do it. And Lucy, we urgently got to prepare for the worst case scenario.'

'Which is, Sir?'

'That the condition is permanent. We need to shuffle up some of our laws and statutes to take account of the fact that we may all be black, or most us anyhow. We gotta do whatever it takes. We can't have a situation where a white minority rules us black folks with laws that ain't made for black people.'

'You want me to end discrimination, Sir?'

'Yes, I'm afraid so. That pretty much covers it, Lucy, we need to put an end to discrimination.'

Chapter Forty

Ivan Turgenev and Igor Kuznetsov exited the terminal at Sheremetyevo, emerging from the gloomy, brown interior into the bright sunshine. They looked around for the car, surprised it wasn't there. A policeman stepped in front of them as they walked towards the VIP area of the carpark.

'Gentlemen, I have been asked to collect you and bring you to the Kremlin. Bring your bags and put them in the back of the car, please.'

The two men reluctantly took the bags from the porter's trolley and loaded them in the trunk of the police car. The officer got behind the wheel, pointing with his thumb at the rear seats. They got in to the back of the car and barely had time to close the doors before the car moved off, the driver blipping the siren to clear his way through the slow-moving traffic around the carpark.

The policeman looked back at his passengers.

'Excuse me, Comrade Igor Kuznetsov, aren't you one of my old neighbours?'

'I don't know, where do you live?'

'There was a Kuznetsov family on our landing when I was a boy, in Leningradsky Prospekt, the fifth floor. There was an older boy, Igor, who went away to the army when I was small, I remember him coming home in his officer uniform; he brought candies for all the children on the landing.'

'I lived there, for sure, but I'm sorry, I can't remember the names of all the children on that landing.'

'Then it must have been you, I'm glad to meet you again, Igor Kuznestov.'

'And I you, but you have the advantage on me.'

'I'm sorry, I am Aleksandr Artyomov; my father was of the same name. He drove the tram on our street, the number 904.'

'Ah, now I remember, he had the uniform and the cap, and the leather satchel; he always looked smart. Is he still living?'

'No, sadly, he was killed by the 144, driven by his friend Oleg. He had drunk a lot of vodka one day and did not see the tram coming, I think.'

'I'm sorry to hear that. It all seems a long time ago.'

'It was, in the early eighties, I was still a child. A lifetime ago, for sure. But I don't live there anymore of course, we were moved to the suburbs after my father died, they wanted the apartment for some friend of the government, I believe.'

'Yes, Everybody wants to live on Leningradsky Prospekt nowadays, it's not the home of the workers these days.'

'It is long time since you were back in the Mother country?'

Turgenev answered for both of them.

'No, we were here a number of weeks ago, just before the summer. Was it a hot one, this year?'

'Yes, August was very hot, and very humid. But now in September it is better, very pleasant.'

'Do you stay in the city all the summer, Aleksandr, or do you go to the country for a spell?'

'In this job, you have to stay when it is necessary, but I did get away to my wife's family dacha for a few weekends, to help with the growing of the vegetables. Although of course officially there are no dachas anymore, not since twenty seventeen, but you understand ....'

'Yes, it is good to get away, and where would we be without the vegetables we pickle for the winter?'

'You had a dacha, comrade Turgenev, when you lived in Russia?'

'Yes, but that was of course before the law of seventeen, when it was allowed. Now, it is more difficult, our dear President does not approve of the ownership of private homes, they must all belong to the State.'

Kuznetsov grunted.

'Except when he is the owner.'

Turgenev laughed.

'My friend, he jokes a lot. He means no disrespect to our President.'

The officer smiled.

'Don't worry, I know how he feels, many of us feel the same, but what can you do? You are both ambassadors, I am told? That must be interesting.'

'Yes, he in Ireland, I in America.'

'I often thought it might be nice to live in America, but when you see the news reports, it is a grim place. All the shootings, and the poverty, it cannot be easy.'

'Sometimes the news does not tell the whole story.'

'Yes, I understand with the foreign media, but our own State television also shows much of the problems there too. Houses without the basics, no water or electricity, it is terrible. You feel sorry for the workers there.'

'Many of them do okay.'

'I know that some do, my cousin is there, he owns a

gasoline station in New Jersey. It is hard nowadays, he tells me, they use many electric cars there now, but he manages okay.'

'You were never tempted to join him?'

'I thought about it, my wife and daughters say sometimes it would be nice, but the opportunities are better here.'

'In the police job?'

'Well, you know how things work here....'

He drove in silence for a while, drumming his fingers on the wheel as the traffic slowed. He switched on the siren and moved to the VIP lane, moving quickly towards the city centre. As the traffic began to flow he spoke again.

'I didn't mean any disrespect to the government, you know? We all love to complain, but this is still the greatest country in the world. You must know that, you have seen other places?'

Kuznetsov gave a reassuring laugh.

'We have, for sure. But don't worry, we are all friends here. Old neighbours count for something, still.'

'They were better times, back then. We had little, but we were happy.'

'Indeed.'

Warming to his passengers with the conversation, the driver turned towards them as he paused at the lights at Tverskaya Street.

'Gentlemen, I ask you to be careful. I am told that the President is angry with you for something. And please don't tell anybody I told you this, but he has apparently become more erratic of late. He stays in his room, and has his meals delivered outside, very strange behaviour. So be careful, do not upset him, you know the rumours about people who have upset him in the past.'

'Thank you, but we have no concerns, we were classmates of his in the military, many years ago.'

'Please, many others who were close friends of his have reputedly disappeared because of some falling-out. Just don't upset him, you are good people.'

The policeman saluted the guard at the gate in the Borovitskaya Tower and the barrier briefly raised before dropping behind the patrol car. At the State Kremlin Palace he pulled up by the main entrance and got out of the car, opening the rear door. As the two men retrieved their bags from the trunk he saluted them.

'Go carefully, my friends. I pray for you.'

Inside the building a solitary uniformed staff member handed them two keys and pointed towards the stairs.

'Rooms 205 and 207, and you are asked to see the President at three-thirty exactly, the usual place, according to my instructions.'

They lugged their bags to the stairs and walked up the two flights, following the numbered signs on the wall to find their rooms. Igor Kuznetsov opened his door and smiled wryly.

'A view of the service yard, how nice!'

Ten minutes later they left the building and walked swiftly towards the Grand Kremlin Palace. The guard led them to a side door that entered directly into the Hall of the Order of St. Alexander Nevsky, which was shuttered and almost completely dark. They stood just inside the door, letting their eyes get accustomed to the gloom and wondering what to do next. Before they could speak, a familiar voice rang out from the far side of the room.'

'Friends, come here, towards the stage.'

They stumbled in the direction of the President's voice; they could just make out his presence by the sliver of light that peeked around the giant, ornate shutters on the big stained-glass windows. They felt their way past a number of straight-backed chairs and stood before the platform. They could see Zhadnyy's silhouette as he sat in a large, wing-backed chair. When he spoke, his voice was even, with no trace of any emotion.

'Sit down, Comrades.'

They carefully took their seats on two chairs on the lower level, looking slightly upwards to where the President sat. Neither of them spoke as they waited for Zhadnyy to say something. They could hear his heavy breathing as he appeared to compose himself before speaking. Finally, he cleared his throat and spoke quietly.

'We go back a long way, the three of us, don't we?'

Ivan Turgenev glanced at Kuznetsov before answering.

'Indeed we do, Comrade President. A lifetime, for sure.'

'Long enough for me to trust you to do a good job, would you think?'

'Of course, Comrade President.'

'Then tell me, Ivan Turgenev, how it is that the two people I trusted most with a simple job could have fucked it up so badly? Can you explain how a task I could have safely given to a schoolboy from the Pavlovsk Gymnasium could be mishandled by two of my most senior people to this extent? Can you explain that to me, Igor Turgenev? Because I cannot understand it, myself.'

'We did our best in a rapidly changing situation, Comrade President.'

'Your best? My God, if that is your best, I fear for what is your normal, or God forbid, your worst. And what about you, Kuznetsov, you are very silent for a change, can you tell me what went wrong, why you and your fine-dining colleague screwed up so magnificently?'

'I have no answer, Comrade President. Who could have predicted what would happen?'

'Who could have predicted? Do you know the two idiots I sent to Ireland, the two nephews of General Morozov who needed to disappear from the police for a while? They were able to tell me what was predicted, they photographed notes of a meeting where one of the scientists in that institute predicted exactly this outcome. Now, if two intellectually uninspiring morons like those two were able to find out that piece of information, how come my two best people missed it? Can you tell me that, Comrade Kuznetsov?'

'I don't know, Comrade President. But surely it doesn't matter? I assume you are referring to the fact that some Americans appear to be turning black?'

'And you think that doesn't matter to us?'

'Hardly, Comrade President. After all, half of Americans are already black, they even had two black presidents in recent years. I would imagine that a shift in the percentage of black citizens in America is of little concern to us, except perhaps as an opportunity for us to incite some disruption of civil society there.'

'Were you born stupid, Comrade Kuznetsov, or has living in America dulled your brain? Do you understand nothing?'

'I'm sorry, Comrade President, I understand that the current situation with the effect the vaccine is having on Americans is not how we would have planned it, but I fail to see how that is of any concern to us. After all, if the vaccine is the cause of the problem, and the best information we have is that it is not, then that is a problem for the Americans. We haven't vaccinated anybody here, the Russian people are strong and healthy and are less susceptible to the Californian virus than the badly-fed Americans. It is not a problem.'

'Even if their President is now black?'

'But that is not the case, he was on TV earlier today and he is as white as you or I.'

President Zhadnyy snorted angrily.

'That piece of TV is a fake, our intelligence services deconstructed it an hour ago and it is simply a speech that has been dubbed over an earlier appearance. We have the video from two months ago and it is exact in every detail, except for the words spoken. Daniels is afraid to show his face, which can only mean one thing.'

'That he is black? Maybe he is just sick?'

'Do you really think so? Really?'

'I accept you are probably right, of course, Comrade President. But I still fail to see how it is our concern. After all, the American Government is one hundred percent liable for any ill effects from the vaccine. Although, I would concede, this may be why they are describing this blackening of skin as a new virus and not as a side-effect of the Boyle vaccine.'

'The vaccine from the Boyle vaccine laboratory, the one that is one hundred percent owned by the Russian people? That Boyle vaccine?'

'Yes, Comrade President.'

'The one that cost us fifty million euros?'

'Yes, Comrade President. But we will get much of that back in royalties.'

'If they pay. If they realise that the vaccine is what turned their President black, then what chance do you think we have of collecting that money?'

'I understand they have already decided that the vaccine is not to blame, Comrade President. Their Chief Medical

Officer has already stated that some discolouration of skin is a side effect of a new Chinese virus.'

'Ah, yes, their new Chief Medical Officer. And why, tell me, did none of our people get this job? I thought you had arranged for all three of the shortlisted candidates to come from our pool of sleepers, from the people we have spent millions of dollars on over the years, waiting for a time such as this?'

'We had three candidates on a shortlist of three, Comrade President. I fail to see what else we could have done. President Daniels appears to have decided that he didn't like any of them, and he appointed his own family physician to the role.'

'Yes, a small-town clown whose father had to pay a bribe to the medical school to allow him to pass his exams. But a clown who crucially is not our man, he is a loose cannon who is capable of anything.'

'Do you want us to remove him?'

'Maybe, but not just yet. It might attract attention if two people from the same role were to die in an accident within months of each other.'

'We can make it look like the job got too much for him, we could throw him off the Dumbarton Bridge.'

'You did that already with the embassy driver that was talking to the Americans, you can't go back there again for a while. You'll just have to have him mugged and stabbed, I understand he lives in a suburb that has many murders. It should be simple, but maybe that is too difficult for you, you are getting too used to the lazy American ways. Maybe it was time you had a new posting?'

'I had hoped the American one would be my last, before I retire, Comrade President.'

'You would want to improve your performance very

much. And what about you, Turgenev? Are you getting too fat with your easy life in Ireland? Is it beyond your capacity to erase a stupid clown in an American city?'

'No, Comrade President, I would have no issue with that. I have never shirked from my duty, and killing this clown would not be a problem for me, but I do not think his erasure at this point is a good idea. Better to turn him, I would think, or compromise him in some way so that we can better control him. An idiot in the job is useful, and a better option than having some clever guy who can actually think for himself. There are now two clowns in the Oval office, Daniels and Brady, and that can only be a good thing. We already have enough on Daniels to absolutely control him fully if there is need. We can collect some similar information on Brady, it will not be a problem, I think.'

'I am disappointed in you both, but old friendships count for something, once they are not abused by inaction and a forgetting of duty and loyalty. So I give you both one last chance, but once chance only, to put this to rights. Firstly, I want you to go to Boyle village-town and find out more about what happened with this vaccine, why it made people black. You, Ivan Turgenev, will stay in Ireland because you have a legal right to be there as Ambassador, and you will take personal charge of the project and of the institute, although ostensibly the two fools will be running the place. Igor Kuznetsov, you will initially spend a few days in the village-town with your colleague and try to get to the bottom of this thing, and then you will resume your duties in Washington, for the time being in any case. You must 'dig the dirt' as the Americans say on Doctor Brady, but also put an assassination plan in place for him in case we need to eliminate him. You need to rehearse the plan until it is foolproof, so as to be ready at a minute's notice to carry it out. Do you both understand me?'

'Yes, Comrade President.'

'And find Vanda Jakovf, I understand she has either been taken or has defected. Put her back on the rails, or end her.'

'Yes, we will do that.'

'And most of all, and this is very important, you have to make sure that the scientists find a way to reverse the blackening of the skin. This above all is the marker on which your performance will be judged by me. We can't have a country with black Russians, we are a white race and not a black one.'

Igor Kuznetsov smiled.

'That won't happen in any case, Comrade President. Nobody in Russia has been given the vaccine. Apart from the sample we arranged to deliver to your office for analysis, there is none of it in this country and so nobody in Russia will be affected.'

The President stood up and moved towards the window.

'And what do you think I did with the sample?'

The two men gasped in astonishment as Zhadnyy opened the shutter and allowed light to flood into the room.

Chapter Forty One

Shirley Kendall peeked out between the drawn curtains before letting them fall back into place. She called to Randy where he lay on the couch in front of the TV.

'Honey, I'm gettin' tired of sittin' in the house all the time. There ain't nobody around, kin we go out someplace?'

Randy sat upright, rubbing sleep from his eyes.

'Guess we could go see Buddy, he might need some help with the ice business.'

'I was thinkin' more like goin' to town, not to Corner Creek, maybe down to Woodtown, look at the shops or sumpin.'

'I don't go to Woodtown, it all black folks there, we not welcome in Woodtown.'

'But we black folks now, Randy, we fit right in.'

'Yeah, but we not real black folks, Shirley, we jest got us black skin. Inside, we white.'

'Like an Oreo, we white inside. But nobody know that, we look like black folks.'

'Okay, we go down to Woodtown, but what we do there? Ain't much there, I hear, just a couple stores and a church. Corner creek got more stuff than Woodtown.'

'They have a church supper thar on Thursdays, I often

usedta pass thar comin' from Ma's place when she was livin', I hear them singin' an shit. We could go to the church supper, mebbe hear the preacher after.'

'But ya gotta bring food to a church supper, we don't have none fixed.'

'Y'all can pay five dollars, eat all ya want.'

Randy brightened at the mention of food. He got up from the couch and put on a black leather coat. Shirley gasped in delight.

'Randy, honey, y'all look real smart in that coat. Ma husband never could fit in it, not fer a long time. Y'all look like a preacher yourself. Let me get a nice dress and we go to the supper; that be real nice.'

They looked around furtively as they dashed out to the car. They met no traffic as they drove down the hill and turned right on Main. As Randy drove slowly along the wide street towards the town limits, Shirley looked around in wonder.

'Randy, lookit all them Blacks. Ain't never seen Blacks in Corner Creek, not since I was a kid.'

'Mebbe since the new Sherriff took over, mebbe Miss Polly Ammery like Blacks.'

'Y'all wanna know what I think, Randy? I think them ain't Blacks, them good Christian folk what get the same disease we got, them all white folks that gone black.'

'Y'all think other folks got this black thang?'

'Reckon so, Randy.'

'Then it ain't so bad, Shirley. Iffen other folks got the black, that mean we ain't alone. I feel better already 'bout it all.'

'How you think we got it, Randy, from our lovin'?'

'Nope, Buddy got it too, and looks like other folks too. And that army guy from Washington, he was mighty interested in it, so mebbe it a disease is goin' round.'

'Hope it gets better soon, anyways. I don' like bein' no Black, Randy.'

They passed by the gas station and Shirley pointed to the man who sat on a small stool out front.

'See thar, Randy, that looks like old Bill what owns the gas station. I reckon he caught the disease an' all.'

'Shore looks like him, right enough. Mebbe we oughta pull over?'

Randy pulled across the road and drove in beside the pumps. He got out of the car, hesitantly at first, looking for any sign of recognition by the man on the stool.

'That you, Bill?'

The man turned slowly to face Randy.

'Who'n hell I got here? That you, Randy? You shore look different.'

'I got the black, couple weeks now, Bill. Don' rightly know whar it come from. Woke up one mornin' an' I was black as Tom Schmidt's dog. Shirley, she turn black nex' day, Buddy too. Figgered it some kinda disease or sumpin.'

'Same here, week after the President was here, I look in the mirror to shave, seed this Black lookin' back at me. Damn near shit maself, thought it were a holdup.'

'We the only ones in town, Bill?'

'Hell, no! Half the town got the black now, I reckon. Folks stayin' inside to avoid her, but they still catchin' her. Folks down in Coney County too, they all turnin' into Blacks. Helluva note.'

'What we gonna do, Bill? We can't hold no Klan meetin' iffen we all black. An we can't go noplace lookin' like this.'

'Reckon we oughter hold a Klan meetin', we gotta elect

a new Gran' Dragon anyhows.'

'Reckon you're right. But how we goin' do that with Sherriff Kendall gone?'

'Kin ya go up ter the Moore ranch an' ask Mister Moore to call a meetin'? He live up near your place.'

'I ain't livin' thar right now, I'se livin' wit' Shirley. But I call him. I got his number someplace.'

'That be good, mebbe he got some idea 'bout all this black thang. An' kin ya bring me some ice when y'all back at yore place? I need a lotta ice these days, folks is all drinkin' at home since they got the black.'

'I do that, Bill, fer shore. I brin' ya a loada ice tomorra.'

Chapter Forty Two

The Oval office was dark, the heavy curtains drawn. Lucy Martinez' face was lit by the glow from her laptop as she sat in an upright wicker-seated chair beside the Resolute desk. She sat with her arms folded, waiting for the President to say something, but he appeared lost in thought. Major Mike Callaghan sat at the other corner of the desk, a small tablet and a couple of printouts on the polished oak surface in front of him. Like the Attorney General, he sat in silence and waited. He caught the quizzical expression on her face and smiled slightly.

President Daniels sighed heavily and looked at his two aides, appearing to notice them for the first time. His face was impassive behind a layer of white makeup that gave him the appearance of a Halloween movie character, and black streaks had begun to appear where perspiration ran down the sides of his cheeks. He sighed again.

'Damn this damn thing, it looks like it ain't goin' to go away any time soon. Looks like I'm stuck with being a Black for a long time, maybe forever.'

The Attorney General made to speak, but he silenced her with a raised hand.

'I know, Lucy, I ain't allowed to use that word. But I'm a

Black now, so I can call myself a Black if I want, okay?'

She took a deep breath before responding.

'I guess that's fine by me, Sir, as long as you confine that term to yourself. I guess I can't have any argument about it in that context.'

'Fine, then let's not refer to it again. At least the Doc isn't here, he seems to like stirring that pot.'

Mike Callaghan smiled.

'Sure does. That was a surprise, Sir, if I may say so, appointing Brady as CMO. Didn't the three on the list make the grade?'

'We had concerns, Mike. All three were of Russian birth, although they were all American citizens of course. But I figured that it was time to put a real American in the job this time, ya know? We needed somebody folks could identify with, and I've known Brady Senior a long time. He was our family doctor, growing up. So I asked Brady Junior to step up to the plate.'

'He doesn't appear to have much specialised knowledge, Sir.'

'I know that, Lucy. But we don't necessarily need an expert in that job, more a guy with a good bedside manner. We gotta have folks in high-profile jobs that people trust, and they'll trust Brad Brady, for sure. He talks a good talk, that's what's important. We can buy the knowledge, but we need a good ol' boy to deliver it, sometimes.'

'We could be open to a charge of racial discrimination, Sir, if we passed over some well-qualified people in favour of a less-qualified guy who was picked because he was American born. And white.'

'We could, if this conversation ever went outside this office, Lucy. But I don't need to remind you of the classification that goes with anything that is said within these four walls. Or one wall, to be exact, I guess; there ain't no corners in the Oval Office. Do you know that never occurred to me before I got this job? You learn new stuff all the time. Anyhow, I asked you to give me a list of how us Blacks are at a disadvantage in the U S of A, and how we might fix that.'

'I've prepared a list of sorts, Sir, but it isn't as simple as it might sound.'

'Why not? Surely if there are laws that need changing to make it fairer for black people, we just write them and pass them, and we're all fixed?'

'Well, first of all, it's not all that easy to actually tabulate the problem as a list of stuff that needs fixing. A lot of discrimination is subtle; a woman goes for a job, her CV is good so she makes it to the interview, but as soon as the interviewer sees her face it's all over. The interview goes ahead as planned, but she was never going to make it. Same can go for a white woman or man too, but the statistics show the bias against people of colour.'

'So, what are the issues as you see them? You're close to this legal shit, gimme your own view.'

'Well, Sir, I can do that, but not as Attorney General. I can give you my informed legal opinion as a private citizen, but I can't give official advice based on my own views.'

'Okay, shoot anyhow.'

'That thing about CVs, you could immediately outlaw putting people's pictures on CVs, simple enough way to at least give people half a shot at a job.'

'Sounds good, I guess. Anything else?'

'Well, Sir, simple stuff really. Like solving the problem of gentrification of traditional black neighbourhoods, pushing up prices so lower paid families have to move out, and we know most of the lower-paid are black.'

'So how do we fix that? Surely if black folks can afford the rents, they can stay?'

'Yes, but they begin to feel like they don't belong, too many white folks, and shops and restaurants get expensive.'

'But it's like that for the first few white folks who move into a black neighbourhood, surely?'

'Yes, you could say that, Sir. But they know it's all going one way, they just gotta wait it out.'

'So, what's your solution?'

'Fix rents and property prices in lower-paid neighbourhoods, or penalise high rents with big taxes on owners when the black/white ratio shifts away from a balance that mirrors society as a whole.'

'I guess that could be done. So what else you got?'

'Employment, I guess. In theory, there should be a fifty-fifty split in all jobs, and at all grades within those jobs. Or better still, a split between black and white that reflects the existing societal ratio at any given time. That should also apply to the divide between women and men, obviously.'

'But you can't force employers to hire according to skin colour, or because somebody doesn't have a dick.'

'You can, with taxes. Tax the hell out of any company whose employee profile doesn't match the relative ratio of white to black people in society. Or women to men as well.'

'Racy ho?'

'Ratio, Sir. The number of black people compared to the number of white people at any given time.'

'Okay, I guess. Anything else?'

'How long have you got? The list goes on and on. But what's more important is the stuff that you can't list, the subtle, nuanced behaviour that allows discrimination to happen. It starts in early education; kids aren't racist, they have to learn it from adults, but segregating them in the classroom is how you start that.'

'So, lemme get this straight, what you're saying is that we need a full overhaul of the way we do pretty much everything?'

'That's about it, Sir.'

The President started to pace around the perimeter of the office, one foot silently shuffling on the blue rug and the other clumping on the hardwood floor. He lapped the office twice before stopping and pointing to Major Callaghan.

'What you reckon, Mike? What's your experience in the army, for instance?'

'Well, Sir, I guess the black man always gets the shitty end of the stick in the army. Like when it comes to who goes into battle on the ground first, that'll always be the black infantrymen. And if you look at kills among our own ranks, that's going to be more blacks than whites. Add in Hispanics to the black casualties, and for sure the white guys do better.'

'Damn! I never knew all that. Or maybe I just didn't care. I guess you only get concerned about black problems once you're black yourself. So, what would you do about it, if you were in my job?'

'Reckon I'd look to the constitution, Sir. Isn't that the paper that runs the whole show? I guess there oughta be something in it that guarantees that all folks get to shoot at the target from the same place.'

The President shuffled around a few steps until he was facing the Attorney General.

'Can that be done, Lucy? Can you put words into the constitution to fix it? Damn, if it's that simple, we could do it right here, you write it up and I stick it into that ol' paper.'

'I'm afraid it's not that simple, Sir. Firstly, those protections are already there, in theory anyhow, but they just get ignored. And they were written at a time when there weren't so many black people about, when they had just been freed from slavery and were happy enough with that.'

'So, we need to write some stronger stuff in there?'

'Yes, but that would take a constitutional amendment.'

'Then let's make one of them.'

'It isn't as easy as that, Sir. There have been just thirty-three amendments to the Constitution since it was written in seventeen eighty-nine.'

'Like the second amendment, the right of the people to keep and bear arms? Was that a change to the original paper?'

'Yes, Sir, the constitution was amended to make sure folks could keep their guns.'

'It was changed, is that what you're saying?'

'Yes, Sir. Changed, amended, same thing.'

'Damn, so that's what 'amendment' means. I never figured that out before. I wish they'd use normal words, not this Harvard shit.'

'Yes, Sir. But like I said, it's not that simple. There are around two hundred attempts to change the constitution every term, but most of them never make it. It's a rare event, to be honest.'

'So, how do we do it, do you just write it and I sign it? I got all kinds of stamps and shit here in this drawer.'

'Not exactly. We need either Congress to do it, with a two thirds majority in both houses, or we need a state convention with two thirds of the legislature in each state to pass it. And then it has to be ratified by the legislature of three quarters of the states.'

'Ratified?' What is that?'

'To, ah, give it formal approval.'

'Okay, I got it. Which one is the easiest?'

'Neither could be described as easy, Sir. The only amendment to be ratified through the state convention method was the twenty-first amendment in the nineteen thirties. That one repealed the eighteenth amendment, the one that established prohibition. It doesn't happen often, Sir.'

'So, the Congress road is the one to take?'

'I guess so, Sir.'

'Okay, Lucy. You get your team together and write the words, and we'll meet again next week and see how we can make it happen.'

'Understood, Sir. Are we done for today? I need to get working on this.'

'Sure, Lucy. Major, can you stay behind for a while? We got other stuff to do.'

Chapter Forty Three

The two diners sat in the shadows at the small table at the rear of the restaurant, each silently perusing the menu. Lucy Martinez placed hers on the table and raised her glass.

'Here's to your health. I know what I want, how are you doing with it?'

'And to yours. I don't know, I don't often eat Mexican food, but it all looks good. I think I'll try the Cemita Poblana, I had it once and it was real good.'

'Starter?'

'No, I think I'll leave room for some Churros at the end. But you go ahead.'

'Maybe you'd like to share some guacamole to start? It's a small enough portion, just to give us something to nibble on while we're waiting for the mains.'

'Okay, I guess since he pays our salaries, we gotta have some loyalty to the 'holy guacamole' guy!'

She laughed and waved to the waiter.

'I'm glad to see you haven't drunk all the Kool-Aid, Major. It pays to have a healthy degree of cynicism about one's job, I think, particularly when we work for the government.'

'I like to think I'm my own person, Miss Martinez. I

respect the President because he holds the highest office in the land, but I don't necessarily believe all he says.'

'I have to say when I first met you I thought you were a white supremacist, Major. But then I began to see the real Mike Callaghan under all that. Is that a fair assessment?'

'I'm a soldier, Miss Martinez. Quite often that involves using camouflage, not standing out against whatever background you happen to be stood in front of. Saves you getting shot.'

'So, you work with a bigot, you gotta appear bigoted?'

'If you want to move things, yes. I could get nowhere with our friend if I appeared to be always pushing him back; it's easier to let him think his views are being listened to.'

'And are you managing to move things?'

'Damned if I know, but at least things aren't going backwards too much. We might not be winning the war, but the casualty numbers are low enough so far.'

'Anyway, what I'm trying to say is that I don't dislike you, despite our occasional spats in the Oval Office.'

'That's mutual, Miss Martinez. You certainly bring a certain level of smarts to the debate in there.'

'You should call me Lucy, Mike. You don't mind if I call you Mike?'

'You can call me anything you like, Miss Martinez. Lucy. I guess we should drop the formalities now that we're working closely together.'

'Damn! And here was me thinking you were asking me out on a date. Are you saying this is a working dinner?'

The Major laughed, his blushes saved by the arrival of the waiter. They ordered the food and he sat forward to speak quietly.

'Look, Lucy, I wanted to talk to you outside the office. I got concerns, to be honest.'

She raised her eyebrows at the comment.

'Concerns? About HG?'

'I think it might be an idea to refer to him as such, walls can have ears. HG, I like it.'

'So, what concerns you, Mike?'

'I don't know, exactly. I just got concerns he is struggling to manage.'

'I disagree. Let me put it how I see it. He's a fucking idiot, I don't understand how he got to be the top dog. I wouldn't give him a filing job.'

'You're being forthright, Lucy.'

'I'm not known for talking in riddles, Mike. Let me get one thing straight, I have to trust you before we broaden this discussion, but I think I can do that. You have a reputation as a straight guy, and your military record is impeccable.'

'You've been checking?'

'Haven't you?'

The Major laughed.

'I must admit, I have. Working-class parents, scholarship to Berkley, first in the USA in your final law exams, a glittering career as a public defender and then as an international human-rights lawyer, you are about the best qualified person back in the big house. Maybe the only qualified person, if it comes to that.'

'You didn't do too bad yourself. Congressional Medal of Honour, top instructor in West Point, a reputed workaholic who often sleeps in the office, picked by HG as his Chief of Staff and national security advisor because you once lived in his neighbourhood and because you thumped some kids that were bullying him when he was still at school.'

'Don't believe all you read in the papers.'

'How the hell did he get selected to run?'

'It was an accident. He wasn't even an active member of the party. He had sold a pickup truck to a local party bigwig who had defaulted on the payment, and he went along to the convention to try to collect his money. He had a few beers while he was waiting, got a bit drunk. Then when they passed the microphone around for questions he stood up and grabbed it, and sang the national anthem. He's quite a singer, great voice when he's had a few beers.'

'Yeah, I remember he sang it at his inauguration, he was really good, to be fair.'

'Yeah, he brought the house down at the convention too. Then the guy that owed him the money proposed they wind up proceedings there and then and put Don forward, and that's how it happened. The debtor never paid the bill and got to keep his truck, but he put Daniels into the Senate, and the rest, as they say…'

'Is history. Wow! Things are often as random as that, I've seen it in the legal field too. Lawyers who could hardly spell, suddenly made into judges because somebody died or got in trouble somewhere, and the spare wheel got put on the wagon.'

'Did you ever notice how he sings the first line of the National Anthem?'

'Oh say, can you see, by the dawn's early light?'

'Yes, but next time you hear him sing, listen carefully. He runs the first two words together, just one word. Somebody once told him that the anthem was written by a guy who was explaining stuff to his Mexican gardener.'

'I don't get it.'

'He sings 'Jose, can you see.' Listen for it, next time.'

'You're kidding me! Every kid in middle school knows that's an urban myth, a silly joke.'

'I wish I was. I even tried to tell him but he told me I had it wrong.'

'Jesus, this is worse than I thought. We're working for a madman.'

They picked at the guacamole, scooping it with tortilla chips. The Major was serious as he spoke.

'The thing is, Lucy, I don't have anybody I can confide in. But it occurred to me the other day when you were speaking at our meeting that you weren't taking HG's utterances too seriously. I thought I detected a bit of eye-roll.'

Lucy laughed.

'I didn't think it was that obvious, but yes. Like you, I have concerns, to be honest. But I also see an opportunity here, a chance to make our country a lot better, to turn this debacle into something good.'

'Debacle? You mean the black virus?'

'Come on, Mike. You don't really think this blackening thing is unrelated to the vaccine, do you?'

'That's the official line.'

'Don't bullshit me, Mike, please. It's too much of a coincidence. If this is a virus, how come it hasn't appeared anywhere else in the world? How come it just arrived here a few weeks after the President got vaccinated? I know the official line is bullshit, I just can't prove it, but I think you know.'

'What makes you think I know different?'

'If the blackening is caused by a virus, why did you need to go back to Tennessee yesterday? What was all that about? And why did you invite me to dinner? That was from left field. Come on, Mike, spit it out, you'll feel better. And it's safe with me, I promise you. We're coming from the same place, we are both patriots, our concern is for our country and the people in it.'

'If you break trust with me, we're probably both going to jail.'

'I know that. Remember that I'm trusting you too, just by being here.'

The Major chewed on his Cemita and washed the mouthful down with a sip of wine before speaking.

'Okay, it is bullshit. The blackening isn't a new virus, it's a side-effect of the vaccine, as far as I can tell.'

'Jesus! Does HG know?'

'No, he doesn't. And I'm not going to tell him. That would open the biggest can of worms you ever saw, Lucy. You think Watergate was big, this shit would blow that away.'

'Maybe I shouldn't have asked? I might be better off not knowing some of this.'

'Too late now, Lucy. I went back to Corner Creek yesterday, there were a few things that bothered me. I went to see Randy Corless.'

'The farmer guy?'

'Yes, he lives with his new girlfriend in her house. She's.....'

'The widow of the Sherriff that got shot on TV?'

'Yes, that's the one. Anyhow, I got the Sherriff to drop me off at their house and then I asked Randy to drive me up to his brother's place. I was trying to figure out the whole thing, how the hell he and his brother and his girlfriend could have got the blackening if they weren't vaccinated, assuming it wasn't a new virus. That was the puzzle.'

'But nobody in Corner Creek got vaccinated, isn't that what you told HG last month? They all refused the vaccine when the army guys turned up, didn't they?'

'Yes, but we had added it to the water supply there, the pumping station supplies all the towns along that valley. And a lot of those folks now 'have the black,' as they put it.'

'But we went over all that, along with Doctor Brady. The houses on the hill, and the farmer's ranch, they don't have mains water, they use wells, right?'

'Exactly. But I missed something the first time I was there, something obvious now I've spotted it. I got a ride up to the ranch in Randy's pickup truck, it's an ancient Ford. I noticed he had built a big box on the bed of the truck, made of those insulated panels you use in factory buildings. I was just making conversation, I asked him what he transported that needed keeping cool.'

'And what was that?'

'Ice. His brother and himself, they make ice and sell bags of it through the store on Main Street. They got them a big ice machine they found in the dump and fixed it up, and they got a business making ice cubes.'

'But they don't have mains water? Or electricity?'

'They do. But it's an unofficial tap into the mains, in both cases, so they don't pay for it. I got that out of Randy, I had to promise I wouldn't tell anybody. So I guess I lied.'

'His secret is safe with me. So you reckon the Corless brothers have unwittingly been vaccinating all the people in Corner Creek, with their ice?'

'And in a few other towns as well. The store on Main Street is pretty popular, for another reason, they also sell a lot of moonshine through the place, which brings in a lot of customers who buy other stuff, like ice. Proper pair of entrepreneurs, the Corless brothers.'

'Holy guacamole!'

'As our boss would say, yeah. Are you having dessert?'

'No, I'm done, thanks.'

'Me too, that was filling. Coffee?'

'No, but why don't we have a coffee in my place? I assume you're not going to ask a girl to walk home alone this time of night?'

'I haven't walked anyone home in a while, I'm kinda out of practice.'

The Major called for the bill and paid with his phone, standing to help his colleague with her coat. They emerged into the still warm autumn evening and strolled slowly down E Street. He took her arm and guided her across the street towards 10th Street. She smiled in surprise.

'You know where I live? You been checking up on me?'

'I know where all the senior people live, it's my job to be aware of security issues wider than the White House. I need to know you're all safe.'

'That's a consolation. Although it should probably worry me too; do you bug people's homes?'

The Major laughed.

'No, we don't take it that far. Unless we have a suspicion, of course, then all bets would be off, I guess. But I never had any concerns about you, to be fair.'

She linked her arm through his and looked up playfully.

'Maybe you should have? Don't you know I'm a woman on a mission?'

'What kind of mission is that?'

'Like I said, to make this a better country, for everybody who lives in it.'

'A lot of people have tried that one, and didn't get far. Isn't this your block?'

'You know too much, Mike Callaghan. Are you coming up for that coffee?'

'I guess that's an offer I can't refuse. So, what's your plan, to make this country better?'

'I'll tell you all about it when we're safely behind closed doors. This blackening thing might just be the best thing that ever happened to the USA, but it will need some help from you, and from me.'

'Sounds like a big responsibility for two people.'

'Who else is there, Mike? You and I are the only two adults in the room at this point, unless you count HG and the Doc. And I'm afraid I don't rate either of them.'

Chapter Forty Four

Jacob Moore fiddled with his white hood, aligning the eye-holes with his eyes. His white robes and white gloves reflected the dress of everybody in the room, except for Randy Corless who had forgotten to bring gloves and who kept his black hands tucked into the folds of his robes. The Deputy Grand Dragon tapped on the table with his gavel to get the attention of the meeting.

'Brothers in arms, I'm glad to see you all here in such numbers. This is the best turnout I've seen since back in the day when the Blacks started to revolt and look for rights and shit. I want to advise you all that I have spoken twice this week to the Klud who advises this Klavern on spiritual matters, and he advised me that as Deputy Grand Dragon I must assume the role of Grand Dragon until the end of the year, following the tragic loss of our leader, Homer Kendall Junior, may God bless his immortal soul. Before the end of the next quarter year, we must elect a deputy Grand Dragon, but there is no urgency about that tonight.

So, as Grand Dragon of this branch, I want to welcome you all here. As is traditional, I must ask, is everybody here a native-born, white, Gentile American citizen?'

There was silence from the floor. Jacob Moore asked the question again.

'I must ask, before we can proceed, is everybody here a native-born, white, Gentile American citizen?'

The response was some shuffling of feet. A stocky man in the front row raised a gloved hand. Jacob Moore pointed to the seated figure.

'State your name, and your business.'

'Bill McCauley, Jacob. I just wanna say what everybody else is wantin' to say. I sure am a native born, American citizen, like my pappy afore me an' his pappy afore him. My great, great granddaddy owned a forge on Main Street, an' all my ancestors since then lived on the same lot, where I got the gas station and general store today. So I'm as native born as any man here, so help me, God.'

'Howdy, Bill. So, state your business, like I said.'

Bill McCauley peeled off his hood to reveal his black face, to gasps from the crowd.

'This is my business, Jacob. I got the black, I done turned into a Black and I don't know how to fix her. An' I reckon I ain't the only one; half my customers already got the black, and I ain't seen the rest of 'em for weeks, they stayin' home. We got us a mighty big problem, Jacob, ain't no use pretendin' we don't.'

The room erupted into babble of conversation. Jacob Moore banged the table to restore order.

'Brothers in arms, we will have one voice at a time. I'm sorry you got the black, Bill; that sure is a devil's curse. I been hearin' that others got it too, but thank God the contagion has stayed away from my family.'

He took off his hood to reveal a well-tanned but still obviously white face.

''So what do we do with you, Bill? We can't have no

Blacks at our meetin' anyhow, I'm sorry to have to tell you that. I'm goin' to have to ask you ter leave.'

The older man stood up, angrily turning to address the crowd.

'I bet a sack load o' beans there ain't no more'n a handful of white folks in this room, right now. Why don't y'all take off ya hoods?'

The Grand Dragon banged the table again.

'That's a sacrilege, Bill, an' you know it. You can't ask a Klansman to take off his hood, it be against all that's holy. We all equal here, the hood signifies that, and it also protects us from retribution by the Blacks, saves our families from bein' raped an' pillaged. We whited and we united. The hoods stays on.'

Bill McCauley dropped his hood on the ground and peeled off his robes, throwing them to the floor angrily. He pulled the white gloves from his hands and added them to the pile of white cloth.

'I'm done with the Klan, it don't make no kind of sense no more. I'm the same person I was last week, excep' now my skin is black, but how does that make me different? World looks exactly the same as it did las' week, or las' month. How am I different, Jacob? What the hell has changed, inside this damn skin o' mine? Kin yo answer me that?'

'I tol' you, Bill, y'all ain't welcome here no more, not since you gone and become a Black. I'm real sorry 'bout that, Bill, y'all a good man, but you not a white, Gentile American citizen no more, like the good book says, which mean you can't be a member of the Klan no more. So can y'all kindly leave the meetin' without any more talkin' 'bout it?'

Randy Corless stood up and waved his black hands in the air.

'Bill's right, Mister Moore. There a lot more Blacks in this room than y'all think. I'm a Black now, ma woman a Black, ma brother a Black and most of the folks I seen around the town the last week, they Blacks too.'

Randy took off his hood and held it awkwardly in his hands.

'See, I as black as ol' Bill, here. I been a white, Gentile Christian all ma life, like the good book say, but now I be a Black, can't rightly say why. But that's it, guess by what you sayin' I gotta leave along with Bill. But I reckon everybody that's a Black under them hoods, they oughta leave too. Bill McCauley is my friend, I can't see him done wrong. I'm just sayin.'

The Grand Dragon banged the table angrily.

'Then get the hell out, Randy, and bring yo other Black friend with you. I know you a long time, since you were a little kid, but I never figgered you for a Black. Bill neither. But the good Lord he seen fit to make Blacks out of the two of you, so I gotta accept that. Now, get the hell out.'

Randy shook his head.

'I'm sorry, Mister Moore, but I ain't leavin', an' Bill ain't leavin', not afore we get somebody tell us what the hell is happenin' here, an' until all the Blacks in the room goes too. Why we got the black, and why half the town got the black, and where we stand now that we Blacks. Y'all gonna burn us out now we black? Y'all gonna lock up the kids when y'all see us comin?'

'You challenging my authority, Randy? Did you not say the prayer when we started, same as every God-fearin' man here? We avow the distinction between the races of mankind as same has been decreed by the Creator, and we shall ever be true in the faithful maintenance of White Supremacy and will strenuously oppose any compromise thereof in any and all things. Amen. That what we all said, includin' you, Randy. Don't fly in the face of God, get the hell out.'

A voice from the back of the room shouted 'hang the Blacks.' The Grand Dragon moved to quell the shouts.

'Won't be no hangin' here, not tonight. These men may be Blacks, but they our neighbours too, and once they don't start behavin' like Blacks they welcome to live in peace beside us.'

Randy turned angrily towards the crowd.

'Who the guy that say I oughta be hanged? Show ya face, if y'all a man an' not a lil pussy.'

There was a titter of laughter from behind the hoods. One voice spoke up.

'Reckon y'all not so dumb, Randy Corless. I reckon the fella that said that oughta take off his hood. If he a man, that is.'

There was some muttered assent, and suddenly a man was pushed in the back and made to stand up. His assailant pointed to the robed and hooded figure.

'Here's yer hangman, Randy. Reckon this is the fella wants to see a hangin.'

Randy angrily rushed at the man, who backed away but was unable to move far, surrounded as he was by the packed crowd of hooded men. Randy grabbed at the hood and pulled it from the man's face. The crowd let out a low roar. Randy pointed triumphally to the hapless, black-faced man.

'Thar ya go, Mister Moore. I tol' y'all, the room is full o' Blacks. Reckon you the only white man here. Tell 'em all take off their hoods. Tell 'em!'

Before the Grand Dragon could respond, a number of men began to slowly take off their hoods. As black face after black face was revealed, more and more of the attended gathering followed suit. Jacob Moore took a long drink from the glass of water on the table, refilling the glass from the pitcher with shaking hands, and drinking again before he could speak.

'May God have mercy on this here town, and all the good folks all around. I don't know why God has chosen me to avoid this pestilence, but chosen me he has. Like it says in our good book, we have held the line since eighteen sixty-five against the heathens, unbelievers and every kind of racial contamination since our forefathers stood aghast and pale, wondering at the meaning and purpose of the gathering gloom after the South's defeat by the Union of evil. But now the line has broken, the heathens are at the gate and they walk among us. They have taken our form, made themselves in the image of Christian folks, and we can only pray to God, our good and white Christian God, for help against this darkness.'

Bill McCauley sat down again and the rest of the gathering followed suit. He spoke quietly, so that people at the back had to strain to hear his words.

'What do we do, Jacob, apart from prayer? How we gonna fix this thing, kin we call in the Federal government an' ask 'em for help?'

The mutterings from the crowd gave Bill his answer to that proposal. When he spoke again, his anger and frustration was clear.

'God damn it, we're all the same folks we were last year, or last week, we're just a different colour. Kin we not live the same way we allus did, just neighbourly, forget about the colour of our damn skin? What the hell is wrong with that?'

'It ain't that simple, Bill. This is a white town, we kept it clear of Blacks since the Founding Fathers passed through, and we ain't gonna let our standards drop just because some pestilence has struck some of our people.'

'Damn near all of our people, Jacob.'

The Grand Dragon drank deeply from the glass of water.

'No, Bill. I ain't black, an' even if I'm the last man standing, I will hold the line according to my responsibilities as Grand Dragon and according to the good book. We ain't gonna let this become no Black town. Can you imagine how that would be? Can you imagine if your daughter came home an' said she was gonna marry a Black?'

Bill McCauley shook his head sadly.

'Too damn late for that, Jacob, she already has. My son in law got the black last week, my daughter and my grandchild too. We all Blacks now, Jacob. We all Blacks now.'

Chapter Forty Five

Caroline and Billy sat on one side of the conference table. The two managers sat across from them, bleary-eyed and unshaven. Beside them, two older men sat stiffly, dressed in finely-tailored suits and carrying an unmistakable air of authority. One of the older men spoke first.

'Good morning, I am Ivan Turgenev, and this is my colleague Igor Kuznetsov, we represent the government of the Republic of Russia who are the ultimate owners of this facility, as you know. Doctor Robinson, we have already had the pleasure of meeting when we negotiated the purchase of the company. And you have already met our colleagues, the Morozov brothers.'

Billy Robinson nodded.

'Welcome back to Boyle, Ivan and Igor, I'm glad to see you. And we've met your colleagues, of course, although their lack of English and our lack of Russian can lead to communication problems. Now, what can we help you with today? You will appreciate that we are very busy on a number of projects.'

Turgenev sat forward, elbows on the table.

'We appear to have a problem, Doctor Robinson. Our information tells us that a number of persons vaccinated with the new product have developed a skin disorder. Are you aware of that?'

'I had heard it, but I don't have any verification that it is a definite thing. Can you give me some hard facts, all I have are some vague rumours.'

'We have some hard facts, the farmer who was vaccinated along with the American president has experienced a change of skin colour, and there is a story circulating in diplomatic circles that the same condition has affected the American President, no less!'

'I saw him on the TV news last night, he seemed normal enough to me.'

'Perhaps, but we are sure about the farmer and his brother. The story circulating in official circles is that the skin condition is unrelated to the vaccine, that it is a separate pandemic, or the beginnings of one. Obviously it would be an international disaster if the entire population of the western world was to turn black, would you not agree?'

Billy smiled across the polished table.

'I wouldn't, to be honest. I don't really care too much about the colour of somebody's skin, and I think the world would quickly adjust to any such change. After all, less than half the world's population is what we refer to as white-skinned.'

Kuznetsov shook his head sadly.

'Nonetheless, it is important for those of us who live in Europe, and in that I include those of us who live in my own motherland, to be conscious of our heritage and our history of attack by the Barbarians over the centuries. White skin is the way we recognise those of us whose bloodlines run back to the dawn of time in this great civilisation. While of course we respect the right of black people to have a place, the rest of us are the inheritors of these lands and to be seen as otherwise would be disastrous.'

Billy stared at the speaker in amazement, then relaxed and smiled.

'I suppose we will have to agree to differ, Igor. So, what exactly is your concern?'

'We know the skin blackening is caused by the vaccine, and it is not simply a new virus as the Americans are telling us. However, we are not going to make that public, and it is all our interests here in this room to keep that information to ourselves. What we need you to do is to firstly figure out why exactly the vaccine is causing this effect, and then find a way to reverse it.'

'We're running a business here, Igor, or we were the last time I took instructions from the then owner. We're scientists, Caroline is an administrator, and between us we solve problems and stay in business. It's a balancing act, as you can appreciate; there are often areas of research we'd like to pursue, things that come up in the course of other research, but we only go places where somebody pays us to go places. Part of our salaries is comprised of bonus payments, so you can understand that there is an incentive not to go off on any kind of personal scientific adventure. We stick to the job in hand, as we say.'

'So, you are saying you will need more payment to do this work?'

'I'm saying that your managers will have to manage, or hand over control of finances to the people who are actually doing the work. If we need our best scientific brains to be free to solve this little problem, they don't need to be worried about deadlines for testing sewage samples.'

'You need more money?'

'Yes, if we have funding we can bring in contract staff

to carry out routine work, freeing up the main team for your project. But we'd also need to be funded to provide incentive. You know, there has to be some reward for any solution, but we can't necessarily expect the 'live horse and you'll get grass' system to provide that reward. There have to be some guarantees, and some front-loading of payments too.'

'This thing, 'live horse and you will get grass,' I do not understand.'

'Sorry, that's an Irish expression. It means that you promise the horse that the seed you have planted will give him grass, if he waits. But of course it doesn't pay the bills while he is waiting. And maybe when the grass grows, the farmer mightn't want the horse to eat it all, or indeed any of it, but the horse will have done all the ploughing to prepare the ground for growing the seed.'

The two older men looked at each other and laughed. Kuznetsov pulled a silver pen from the spine of his leather-covered notebook and used it to write down the phrase.

'It is very good, we don't have such a saying in Russia, although the horse is also an important part of our culture. We do say that 'a tomtit in your hand is better than a crane in the sky,' which I suppose means something similar. If you don't have it in your hand, a promise for the future means little. So you want to be paid to do this work, before and after? Is that the essence of what you say?'

'We want resources, Igor, mostly. We need to be able to hire new staff for basic work in order to free up our experienced scientists for this project. And yes, we would need some token of good faith, an upfront payment plus a pay raise for the duration of the project, the front-end payment to be deducted from an agreed bonus when we deliver.'

'If you deliver.'

'You gotta have faith, Igor. If we didn't believe we could do it, we wouldn't even begin. You have to remember that this is just a puzzle to be solved, a giant crossword where we don't have all the clues, but that is what we do, all the time. Believe in the process, Igor.'

Kuznetsov spoke to his two managers in Russian, and they nodded furiously, not speaking at all. He glanced towards Turgenev who nodded assent, and then turned to Billy and Caroline.

'Very well, you will have the resources, immediately. How much do you think it will take to carry out the additional research?'

'I already gave this some thought. We are fully stretched already, and we are probably looking at six months to a year to crack this problem, so we'd need to budget for additional staff to cover the ones I would redeploy to this job. Plus we'd need quite a bit of additional equipment, a lot of it is Swiss and is very expensive.'

'You've put a figure on it?'

'Yes, approximately ten million euros, more or less.'

The Russians spoke together in their own language before Igor turned to speak to Billy.

'It sounds like a lot of money, but I accept that this is an extraordinary set of circumstances that maybe requires an extraordinary response. Is there any way that figure can be reduced?'

'On the contrary, that may not be enough, but we would try to work within those limits, or even below them obviously if we have luck on our side.'

'And how would that money be paid?'

'Some of it in cash, if possible, the remainder to a bank account in the Isle of Man where we can access it quickly when we need to pay bills.'

'Very well, you shall have it. But there are a number of things I need from you.'

''Sure, if we can help, of course.'

'An Irishman called Mickey Small, he was here, working for you?'

Billy sat upright in his chair, looking to Caroline in astonishment.

'What about him?'

'Did he work on this project?'

'Yes, but why is that of concern to you?'

'Do you know where he is, right now?'

'Yes, I do; he's not far away. Caroline was speaking to him within the last hour.'

'And the Moldovan woman, Monica Macovei? Is she working for you?'

'Monica? She's not Moldovan, she's Russian. And no, she doesn't work for us, she never has.'

'But you know where she is?'

'Of course. But why is that of concern to you?'

'Nothing, not of any concern, just wondering. But you must bring Mickey Small back to work on this project, we believe his input will be crucial to the solving of it. It will be a condition of our agreement with regards to the extra money.'

'I'm sure we can arrange that, but obviously it depends on whether or not he wants to work with us.'

'Then I won't delay you any further. Shall we maybe meet here tomorrow morning at the same time, and discuss the detail. In the meantime, you will make every effort to bring back Mickey Small and also to locate Monica, we would like to talk to her.'

'We can't promise anything, but we'll try.'

The four Russians left the room and Billy looked at Caroline in amazement.'

'How the hell did they know that Mickey was the key to our research? He was the first person to turn black, but I thought we were the only ones who knew that. Did somebody tell those two so-called managers about him?'

Caroline shook her head vehemently.

'Not likely, Billy. For a start, they don't communicate with anybody around here, and in any case they have very little English.'

'They must have some way of knowing, I wonder if they have the place bugged. I nearly fell over when they said that Mickey was the key to the project. They obviously know a lot more than we thought they knew about the whole process, and about his role in it. We'd better get him back in here quickly, and keep him locked up as far as possible.'

'He won't go anywhere without his new girlfriend. They're infatuated with each other. She thinks he's 'refreshing,' he told me. He told her that every man she ever met wanted something from her, but Mickey just wants to sit and look at her, and she likes that.'

'Sounds a bit creepy.'

'I know, but not the way she said it. He adores her, and she loves it.'

'Do you think she'd come in with him, stay here while we figure out a way to change him back to his normal skin colour?'

'I reckon she might; I'll ask anyway. We could probably put them on a salary each, and give them the big room at the end, beside the lobby. That might be less claustrophobic than one of the standard rooms.'

'Mickey is smart enough, he'll want the full testing rate, which means she'll want it as well.'

'I'll try to negotiate that once I get them inside the building.'

'If necessary, we'll have to give it to them. Anyway, what the hell, the Russians are going to be paying for it, why am I worried about costs? But we could use Monica in a trial, give her the vaccine, maybe a tiny trace dose, and see if she turns a little bit black. That might give us some reference point data on the change, to give us somewhere to draw a baseline. Because between you and I, Caroline, I don't know where the hell we can start with all this, I really don't.'

Chapter Forty Six

Donald Daniels sat morosely behind his desk, idly twirling a pencil between his thumb and forefinger. Mike Callaghan leaned back in his chair, waiting for the President to speak. Doctor Brad Brady sat nervously in the other wicker-seated swivel chair, looking to the Major for a cue.

The President seemed to suddenly come back to earth, dropping the pencil and jumping to his feet to start his usual lopsided pacing around the room, one foot almost silent on the soft, oval rug and the other clumping loudly on the hardwood floor. He paused, facing Brady, fixing the hapless doctor with an intense stare.

'Well, Brad, whatcha got for me? How are we doing, out there?'

'With the vaccines, Sir?'

'No, Doc, I know we've vaccinated pretty much everybody by now, that's not my concern. The black, what about the black? You figured out how to fix it yet?'

'No, Sir, we haven't. But we're working on it. Although I'm having trouble convincing the scientists that they need to look at the probability this is a new virus that's causing this. A lot of them are blaming the vaccine, although not publicly of course.'

'Idiots! They're wasting time, chasing a non-existent side-effect of a jab when any fool can see it couldn't be the cause.'

'Yes, Sir. And it's going to get worse, this black thing is spreading. Nearly the whole state of Tennessee has gone black now, most likely all coming from the initial outbreak in Corner Creek, where you seem to have caught it. It's out of control, Sir. California too, Los Angeles seems to be full of black people now, not a white man to be seen on the streets there.'

'Anywhere else got a major problem?'

'Pretty much everywhere, Sir, although the ban you put on reporting it has helped stop any kind of panic, for now anyway. Cases are starting to appear all over the country, and a lot of them are in towns where the anti-vaccine sentiment is strong. In fact, many of those places have some of the biggest outbreaks.'

'So it isn't the vaccine anyway. That's a relief, we'd have been on the hook for trillions of dollars in damages if that was the cause, so I guess that's something.'

The President turned his attention to his chief of Staff.

'Well, Mike? Any news on the international situation?'

'A mixed bag of stories, Sir. It's a reasonable guess that Zhadnyy has gone black, he's apparently disappeared from view over the last few weeks, most unlike him. Any public announcements from him are done on radio now, apart from one fairly crudely dubbed piece of video that was on State Television earlier this week. It looks like they are doing what we did, but with a lot less finesse. It wouldn't fool anybody.'

'So how the hell did he catch it?'

'Damned if I know, Sir. We're trying to figure that out. I know he had a visit from a few of his top ambassadors recently, including our own friend Igor Kuznetsov, down the street here in Wisconsin Avenue. They were picked up at the airport by a Kremlin cop who is on our payroll, so we knew they had gone to see Zhadnyy almost before Zhadnyy did. He could have caught it from them.'

'Has Igor turned black?'

'No, Sir, but he could be carrying it, maybe. He just arrived back in town yesterday, and our guys report he looked normal. Apparently he stopped off in Ireland, to spend some time with Ivan Turgenev, their ambassador there. Both of them are heavy hitters, as you know, former colleagues of Vlad when he worked in East Germany.'

'I didn't know Zhadnyy worked in Europe?'

'He didn't, Sir, not really. East Germany was a Russian satellite state then, it was part of the Warsaw Pact before reunification.'

'What did it reunificate with?'

'With West Germany, Sir. The two parts of Germany reunited when the Berlin wall came down.'

'I guess they had to take down the wall to join the two bits back together; that makes sense. There's some crazy shit happens in those places, for sure.'

'It's all a bit complicated, Sir.'

'Yeah, it sure is. I thought Germany was in Europe, it can all be very confusing. I didn't know the Germans were communists, either, even if it was back in history. I guess I gotta be more careful in dealing with them. Why the hell can't they leave the borders alone in those places anyhow? It makes it hard for us to keep track.'

'I guess every country has done that at some stage, Sir.'

'Except the USA.'

'We've done our share of border moving, Sir.'

'No we haven't, Major. America is America, always was and always will be.'

'Yes, Sir, I guess. Anyhow, they spent a few days in Ireland.'

'The Germans?'

'No, Sir. The two ambassadors, Ivan Turgenev and Igor Kuznetsov. They paid a visit to Boyle, spent all their time there.'

'Boyle, is that the place where we got the lab?'

'Yes, Sir, but we don't have the lab, the Russians do.'

'Oh, yeah, right. Smartass bastards, they're supposed to be our allies. Never trust a Russian, my Daddy used to say. He was damn right!'

'Yes, Sir. Anyway, they spent a few days there, having intense discussions with the managers apparently. We don't know the detail, but we're working on it.'

'You think they know about the black skin thing? Maybe they're trying to find a fix for it?'

'Well, if Zhadnyy has it, then they know about it. And indeed I have no doubt their spooks here have some information on the Tennessee Virus situation at this stage. There's a lot of rumbling in Tennessee about what the folks down there call 'the black,' and we can't keep a lid on it for much longer. So you can probably say, they know about it, Sir.'

'So, you think they're trying to find a fix, with the place in Ireland?'

'Maybe, Sir. But our guy got there before them, and made a deal with the local Irish staff. Or specifically, a guy called Billy Robinson. Doctor Robinson is their chief scientist, and he's effectively running the place now that the former owner has cashed in her equity.'

'Pity she had to leave. She sounded like a great broad, I'd have liked to meet her. Nice ass, too, I like a broad with a bit of meat on her.'

'Yes, Sir. Anyway, our guy made a deal, they are going to divert some resources to our project, without the Russians knowing about it.'

'Excellent! That's damn generous of them. I like the Irish; the Irish vote is very important to us, you know.'

'It's not all about being generous, Sir, although there is some element of that. The Irish would have a natural affinity with the USA; they wouldn't really trust the Russians, I gather.'

'Damn right. My Daddy always used to say, 'never trust a Russian,' and he was right.'

'Apart from that, Sir, we had to front-end a certain amount of money to help them co-operate with us. Doctor Robinson pointed out that the new management team are very cost-conscious. The Russians have two guys in situ who watch everything, he said, so there is no way he can divert resources over to our project. They watch every penny, apparently.'

'So he needs funds, to hire people and stuff?'

'Exactly, Sir. He needs extra people, paid off the books in cash, as well as some extra equipment that is apparently very expensive. So in fairness we had no choice but to pay up. These guys are on our side, but that comes at a price.'

'How big a price?'

'Ten million euro, Sir, that's about twelve million dollars. Half in cash, and half paid into some Isle of Man bank account. We've paid it over already, so they're working busily on our behalf as we speak. I got faith in those guys, Sir.'

'Damn! That's a high price to pay, but I guess it's a lot cheaper than the alternative.'

'Paying out compensation here?'

'No, not winning the next election, Mike. That's the high-stakes risk here, let's not forget that. We can't serve our country from the side-lines, we gotta be out there, on the field.'

'I guess so, Sir. I have some additional news as well, Sir. The guy that wanted to work for us in Ireland, the aircraft investigator guy, we've found him and he's alive. Doctor Robinson's assistant, a lady called Caroline, she located him and has him on board. Robinson says he's crucial to the success of the project.'

'Excellent, Mike.'

'And another thing, Sir. We've also located Vanda Jakovf, the Russian lady who used to work down the street in Wisconsin Avenue.'

'The tall blonde with the great legs?'

'Yes, Sir. We got her, she's come over to us. Or at least she's come over to Doctor Robinson's team, she wants nothing more to do with the Russian government.'

'What the hell does she mean by that? They must have pissed her off.'

'Damned if I know, Sir. Anyway, she's living in Boyle under an assumed name and now she's Mickey Small's girlfriend. They've moved into a room in the Boyle Labs facility and are actually living there, on site. We've got her, Sir.'

'Great news! Anything from Lucy Martinez? You speak to her recently?'

'Not since our meeting here the other day, Sir, apart from one brief phone call. Her team is working on a constitutional amendment along the lines of a proportional representation for black people in all walks of life, related to the proportion of black people in the population.'

'I don't understand that, what does that mean exactly, proportion? I thought that was about the amount of food you eat, or the size of a slice of pie.'

'It's a ratio, Sir. Imagine that across all of America, there were say seventy black people in any group of a hundred.

Then any employer would have to employ seventy percent black people, and thirty percent white people.'

'Why only thirty percent white folks?'

Because that would reflect the percentage of white folks in the population as a whole.'

'I don't quite understand that, math was never my strong point. You understand that, Brad?'

'Yes, Sir. I got it.'

'I'm glad somebody does. So, Mike, you reckon we gotta employ seventy percent black folks in every job from now on?'

'Assuming that's the proportion, Sir. Could be more. Could be a hundred percent if everybody catches the black.'

'In every job? Even the top jobs, the CEOs and all at that level?'

'Yes, Sir, that's the plan.'

'Damn, sounds scary to me. In the banks, too? Black folks in charge of the money?'

'I don't see why not, Sir.'

'Holy guacamole! You think our Lucy is a safe pair of hands, Mike? She's not a bit of a screwball? Last day she was in here she was as angry as a bag of coyotes, you remember that?'

'I guess, Sir.'

'Maybe she's not always like that, might have been her period or something. That's the problem with women, too damn touchy. Nice ass though, a lot of Latinos have great asses.'

'Miss Martinez has a great reputation in her field, Sir.'

'That's what I'm told, everybody speaks well of her, even the opposition. So I guess she's okay. Nice figure though. I can never rightly hear what she's saying; I just get lost, looking at that perfect figure.'

Chapter Forty Seven

Randy Corless finished unloading the bags of ice into the freezer at the gas station. He filled a coffee from the machine and brought it outside to where the older man sat on a plank that was laid between two crates in the shade of the overhanging roof. He sat down beside the store-owner and swallowed a mouthful of the strong brew.

'You all set, Bill. A hundred bags, she don't hold no more anyhows.'

'Much obliged, Randy. I'll get yer money in a minute, jest takin' a lil' time out here.'

'Ain't no hurry, Bill. Tomorro' iffen ya like.'

'Nah, I get her in a minute. Labourer is worthy of his hire, like the book says.'

'Book says a lotta stuff, Bill, but I ain't so sure no more. Reckon I'se all done with the Klan anyhow, no matter what the book says.'

'Me too, Randy. I learned me a good lesson that night, mostly 'bout who my friends is. I thank y'all kindly fer stickin' up fer me, I was on ma own fer a while thar, like a Black at a lynchin. Weren't a nice place ter be. Made me kinda unnerstand how a black boy feel in a white man's world, never thought much about that afore.'

'Got kinda nasty, fer shore.'

'Thanks fer the support anyhows, you allus been a good friend ter me.'

'Ain't nothin', Bill, you'd have done same fer me.'

'What we gonna do, Randy?'

''Bout what, Bill? The black?'

'Yeah, 'bout the black. What iffen it don' go away? What iffen we stay Blacks? Y'all thought 'bout that?'

Randy scuffled the dust with his toe, taking long sips from his coffee. He sighed deeply.

'When I got her, first, I thought the world end was comin' like it say in the book. Thought we was all headin' up ter see the Saviour an' the rapture an' heavenly music an' shit. Then after a few days I got used ter it all, and y'all know what? She ain't so bad. Bein' a Black ain't the end o' the world, it jest mean yer skin is different, that all. After that, it don' mean shit.'

The older man laughed.

'Y'all got a way wit words, Randy Corless. An' folks usedta say you was the dumb one, but yer ain't, not by a long shot. Y'all got this shit figgered out, I reckon.'

'It like this, Bill, folks like us, we all Blacks anyhow. Folks around here, poor folks, jest don't all got black skin, but we all Blacks jest the same. We do the fetchin' an' carryin' an' guys like Kendall do the hollerin' same as always.'

'Guess y'all got it figgered, Randy. We shore works like Blacks, and fer Black pay, mostly. Least Kendall don't do no more hollerin' anyhow, an' y'all got his house an' his woman.'

Randy laughed.

'She a fine woman, a lot better 'n goin the cathouse, fer shore, an' she smell better too. Guess my penny landed right side up that time. An' I don't care what colour she is, she all the same when the lights is out.'

Bill McCauley pondered for a while before speaking.

'What iffen we never go back to white, Randy? What y'all think?'

'Let me tell ya sumpun, Bill. I ain't so worried about the black no more. Tell the truth, I likes bein' a Black. Don' rightly wanna admit that aroun' here, but she ain't so bad. Reckon I was allus a Black, 'cept ma skin was white, but I was a Black in how I was the last man in the line fer everythin'. Now I don' care 'bout that, I got the black, but nothin' else changed.'

'Reckon I got used ter bein' black, Randy, but I'm not shore I likes it too much. Don' think I kin say I likes her.'

'See here, Bill, me an' Shirley, we been goin' down to Woodtown every Thursday, meetin' black folks thar fer the church supper. First time, we pay five dollar each, had some real good vittles, met some nice folks. Nex' time we brin' some our own vittles', share 'em around, it were real nice. Ladies thar, they teach Shirley how they makes some o' the food, an' so we been eatin' real good when we home too. Buddy, he putting on weight.'

'But Woodtown is a Black town. Folks from Corner Creek don' go to Woodtown.'

'That's the thang, Bill, the folks in Woodtown is real nice, God-fearin' folks that likes ter share good food with other folks. An' we Blacks too, we welcome thar. Sometimes it ok ter be a Black, iffen yer friends is all Blacks too.'

'An' yer reckon it ok ter go thar? Safe, an' all?'

'Shore is, we take yer thar nex' Thursday, iffen y'all like.'

'Mebbe I do that, Randy. Sounds good, shore does. Mebbe all I gotta do is accept that I'm a Black, and that's okay.'

'Y'all got it, Bill. It okay to be a Black, ain't nothin' wrong with it. We all the same colour inside. We bleed, we all bleed the same.'

Chapter Forty Four

Lucy Martinez sat up in the bed and pointed the remote control at the TV screen on the wall. She scrolled through the channels to reach CNN, and turned up the volume slightly to hear the commentary. Mike Callaghan emerged from under the light duvet and rubbed his eyes sleepily.

'What's on TV that's so urgent? I've just had the best night's sleep I've enjoyed in years.'

'Must have been all that exercise. I have to admit I slept pretty well myself.'

'I guess that explains it. What's happening in the world?'

'As long as they don't report that the Attorney General is sleeping with the White House Chief of Staff, I guess we're okay. But it looks like this black story is growing legs. The genie is out of the bottle.'

'We can expect a call from HG this morning, I guess.'

'Yes, we'd better get dressed and get to the office pretty soon. Look at the feed from Texas! A lot of people around Huston and Dallas seem to have crossed the colour divide.'

'They sure have. But relax, Daniels won't be up yet, he was at another Russian party last night, along with Brady. Neither of them will have made it home, Igor always runs a

316

late-night bar at his soirées, and then makes the guesthouse available so that guests can sleep it off. Our man won't appear for another two or three hours, I reckon.'

'You reckon the Russians take any advantage from having a drunk President sleeping in their embassy, Mike? It sounds like a major security risk to me.'

'I guess they do, but they can't get much out of HG, he doesn't know too much in the first place, and he doesn't understand the significance of anything he does know.'

'But he knows about the black effect. They might get the detail of that out of him.'

'I reckon they already know more about that than he does. Don't forget it's their vaccine that has caused it, so they know all about it. He only knows what we shared with him, which isn't all that much.'

'I wonder why they wanted Doctor Brady to go to their party. Somebody on his pay grade wouldn't usually be on the front page of the diplomatic circuit guest-list.'

'They said it was a mark of respect to his predecessor; Belyaev was a former Russian citizen. Sounded thin enough to me, I'd say they want to get to know him in case this whole vaccine thing blows up in everybody's faces, they'll be protecting their little research company in Ireland. They want to be on friendly terms with him so he will pick up the phone if they need to reach him.'

'You want coffee?'

'Thanks, Lucy, I'd love some. How you been getting on with the constitutional amendment? I was going to ask you last night but I didn't want to spoil the atmosphere. We talk too much about work, sometimes.'

Lucy put two cups under the spouts of the machine and pressed the red button.

'It's normal that we would talk about work, it's what

we've mostly got in common after all. So let's not worry about that too much, I don't care what we talk about; what's important is that we talk, it's good.'

'I guess I ain't the most talkative man on the planet. I spend too much time on my own, I think.'

Lucy laughed as she took the two cups of coffee and carried them back to the bed.

'A man who doesn't talk much! Ain't that something different?'

'Okay, I guess it's a man/woman thing, men don't say too much, and probably don't listen much either.'

'Some women too, in fairness. Anyway, you asked me about the amendment. It's essentially ready, I have a constitutional lawyer just tidying up the language to make it watertight.'

'Can you sum it up, just give me the general picture?'

'We are calling it the 'equal access' amendment. Essentially, it says that everything in society must be equally accessible to every citizen, regardless of colour or gender, and that the level of access shall be measured as a relationship to the proportion of persons of any particular colour or gender in society at any given time.'

'Sounds complicated.'

'Not really. It means that if there are equal numbers of black and white people in society this year, then employers must employ equal numbers of black and white people. Same goes for men and women, and no question about religious belief is to be asked of anybody in any situation, ever.'

'Seems a bit difficult to manage? If it was just black or white, it would be easy, but add in gender and it gets complicated, mathematically.'

'Then the proportional thing comes into play, there

will have to be an algorithm developed that is constantly updated with statistical data from a recognised and reliable source, we envisage the Federal Census Bureau having that responsibility. They would produce a calculator every year, and all employers, housing providers, educational establishments, etcetera would have to work with that.'

'It seems complex. I guess this equality thing ain't so simple as it sounds at first. I mean, in theory all we gotta do is ignore a person's skin colour, religion, and gender and we got us a fair society.'

'Unfortunately, Mike, it isn't that simple. It sounds fine in theory, but without enforcement you get nowhere. Look at the issue of women in the workplace, equality has never happened anywhere without quotas, which are inherently unfair in themselves at a micro level. If you are a guy and you're the best person for a job, but a woman gets it because the quota says a woman must be employed, that's unfair on you even if it is necessary in order to level the field overall.'

'Yeah, I get all that, and I don't have a problem with it on a big-picture level. But like you say, if I'm the guy that missed out on a job because I have a dick, it don't feel fair.'

'Although women and brown and black-skinned people have had to put up with it for generations. It's hard to get it all right, but we have to start someplace.'

'And you reckon that this amendment will do that?'

'It will, but not necessarily because of the complex, three-dimensional quota system that drives it. What I want to see is a level playing pitch, which can come about this way, over time. After that, people will have become used to seeing women and people of colour in top jobs, regardless of difference. It will have normalised equality of access to jobs, to housing, to education. When something becomes normal, there is no longer a need to force it to be normal; it will become part of the culture. What was it they used to say? 'If you can see it, you can be it.' Once kids see that colour or gender isn't an issue, it will cease to be an issue, and prejudice will just gradually fade out of society.'

'I get your thinking, and I guess it's worth a shot. And there might never be a better time to do it. With an idiot at the wheel, anyone who can drive a bus can decide where it's going.'

'Ever thought of being a speechwriter, Mike? You got a turn of phrase that is funny, but right to the point.'

'I leave that to the guys in the public relations office, although sometimes I tweak their stuff so HG can read it. So, once this amendment is written, what next? He did tell you to go ahead and make society more equal, so you got a free run.'

'Biggest problem will be getting it past Congress. You got any ideas?'

Mike drained the last of his coffee and sat forward.

'I have an idea, but I'm not sure you'd like it.'

'Try me.'

'Biggest problem, as I see it, is that the folks on Capitol Hill are mostly white.'

'That is a hurdle we have to overcome, right enough. There's nothing in this for them, they're the epitome of white privilege. It's going to be a hard sell with those guys.'

'But what if they were mostly black?'

'From the vaccine? That won't happen, Mike. I know these people, most of them are anti-vax, and they all live in the same neighbourhood mostly, here in the downtown. So they aren't affected by the water treatment Vladimir put in place in Klan areas.'

'But what if they were? What if we put the vaccine into the pumping station right here, on Independence Avenue? The old Adams County station still pumps all the water into the downtown, including the White House and all the buildings on Capitol Hill. It also pumps to all the apartment buildings for a mile around, where pretty much all the staff and the Members live when the Houses are in session.'

'You could do that?'

'I could do it today, if I wanted to. I can give the clearance to access that pumping station. As you can imagine, it's locked down pretty tightly in case of terrorist interference, but I can put an agent in there, no problem. Takes about fifteen minutes to fit the kit, and we got plenty of it, and plenty of the vaccine too.'

'So do it! Let's do this, Mike, we can change the world, just by doing this thing. Can you imagine if both houses were entirely black? This amendment would pass in a heartbeat.'

'Sure would, but there's a small problem.'

'I really don't see a problem, quite honestly. But spell it out for me.'

'You and I, we'd be black too, Lucy. Are you okay about that? You think life was tough as a Hispanic woman, have you any idea what it will be like when you're black?'

'Same goes for you, Mike. How many black men would get the Chief of Staff job under somebody like Daniels, do you think?'

'I guess they can't fire me when it happens. I honestly don't care about my skin colour, I'm just worried about you.'

Lucy snuggled up to him in the bed and smiled mischievously.

'I always had a fantasy about sleeping with a big,

handsome black man, and maybe this is my best chance. I can handle it, Mike, don't you worry. Let's just do it, let's try and change the world for the better. How many people ever get to do that?'

Chapter Forty Nine

Billy Robinson checked the door viewer before answering the doorbell and welcoming Karen to his home. She raised a hand in greeting as she entered the living room.

'Hi, guys, sorry I'm a bit late.'

Billy motioned her to a seat by the fireplace.

'Park yourself there, Karen. Tea, coffee?'

'Just a glass of water, Billy, thanks.'

'Okay, help yourself. If everybody else is okay for drinks, I'll begin.'

There were murmurs of assent from the others in the room.

'Right, I asked you guys here, the core team, because it's away from the lab and we can all talk freely. I know a lot of you aren't too keen on sharing everything with our two friends. There are a few developments you need to be aware of, or that some of you are aware of but the others need to know. Can I start with you, Caroline? Maybe you'd bring everybody up to speed on the situation in the secure unit?'

The administrator took a sip from her coffee before speaking.

'Thanks, Billy. Okay, we have a number of test

individuals in the unit. We have Mickey, of course, and the lovely Monica McEvoy, although her name isn't actually McEvoy but she prefers us to use that. Her role up to now was simply to stick like glue to her man, she's completely smitten by the guy, but I suppose there's no accounting for taste.'

Her comments were greeted with laughter. She waited for silence before continuing.

'Monica doesn't really have a role, although we are paying her, but that may be about to change, which Karen will deal with in a minute. As well as those two, Mary managed to bring in two of her neighbours from Kiltycreighton, two students who are worried about going back to college next month with black skin and who are hoping we can fix their little problem. Although one of them is wavering a bit today, she thinks that being a black woman in a west of Ireland College might give her a novelty value. She had been thinking of becoming LGBTQQIP2SAA, but she now thinks that simply being black might be more cool.'

Billy shook his head in puzzlement.

'What the hell is LQBG2, whatever?'

Caroline read carefully from her notebook.

'It stands for 'lesbian, gay, bisexual, transgender, questioning, queer, intersex, pansexual, two-spirit, androgynous and asexual.' Kinda catch-all term for every occasion, if you like.'

'But now she reckons black is better?'

'Seems so. Or maybe she just has trouble learning the acronym. I know I would. Anyway, like I said, she's wavering. But the other guy just wants the black to go away, he plays a lot of football and he is afraid he won't get picked for the college team if he is black. There's never been a black guy on the team, apparently.'

'There was, Caroline, back in my day, but he was brutal. He just got picked because he was black, a sop to inclusion, but he was the worst goalkeeper ever. We lost by twelve goals in the first match in the first round. Turned out he was actually really short-sighted, but he didn't know; he just thought life was blurry for everybody. He might have made people less supportive of inclusiveness in the club in the years since then. Anyway, any other news from the unit?'

'That's about it, We've carried out all the tests as we were asked, so we're just doing the bloods as required and generally monitoring the individuals for the usual, physical and mental issues. Karen will maybe fill you in on the details?'

Karen shifted in her chair, sitting forward to address the small group.

'Like Caroline said, we're running a whole gamut of tests, as well as treating the black-skinned individuals with a range of basic treatments like vitamin shots etcetera. We've also been doing analysis on the transition phase between white and black skin, but we are at a disadvantage in that we don't have any data from that phase; we weren't expecting Mickey to turn black, so we didn't monitor him on a micro level, hour by hour, like we should have, in hindsight.'

'So we need to actually give somebody the vaccine, and monitor the stages of their transition to black skin?'

'Exactly, Billy. But ethically, we can't do that, because we know that it will turn them black. We can't take a white-skinned person and deliberately give them something as life-changing as that. Or we couldn't, until yesterday.'

'What's changed?'

'Monica, she told us she wants to be black, like her

man. She said she hates her horrible, pale skin, and those are her words. She said she wants the vaccine, so that she and Mickey can walk out proudly as a black couple to their new life when this is over.'

'So, did you get a consent form signed?'

'Yes, we did, but we haven't given her the vaccine yet.'

'Why not?'

'I'll let Kevin explain, it was something he came up with in trying to find a cure for this skin thing, a side issue, if you like. Anyway, I'll let him explain.'

She motioned to her colleague who was sitting on the end of the long, low couch. He stood up and positioned himself with his back to the fireplace before speaking.

'I'll keep this simple, guys, or we'll be here all night. Basically, Karen and I have been batting this thing over and back between us, trying to find a rational explanation for all the effects of the vaccine protein at every stage of the process. It was actually a joking remark made by Karen that triggered the thought process in me, when we were talking about why Mickey might have turned black instead of just getting a bit brown.'

The others became noticeably more interested. Kevin continued, knowing he had their attention.

'She said we could very well find an alternative to spray tan, you know, fake tanning products. Every white woman on the planet, not to mention man, wants to be brown instead of white. It's just being black that doesn't attract them, but they're very interested in going half way.'

Billy interrupted, excitedly.

'So you looked at how somebody could be brought to some kind of half-way stage without progressing to black? You wanted to see if you could stop the process half way?'

'Exactly. Once we talked about it, we realised that there

might be a way of pausing the process, initially as a way of studying the transition.'

'A kind of freeze-frame analysis of the transition, by pausing at a certain point?'

'Or points. Yes, that was the thinking. But obviously how to do that was then the problem.'

'But you've figured it out?'

'I can't say for sure, but I think we may be getting there. Our thought process brought us back to basics again, back to where we first postulated the vaccine model. We looked at the DNA and the tiny point of difference that determines skin colour, and we then looked at the marker for slightly sallow skin and other different skin tones that occur naturally. A lot of the information was there in research material, once we looked for it.

Then we looked at the differences between black and brown skin from a DNA perspective, to see whether a light tan for instance is some kind of a half way stage to fully black.'

'And is it?'

'It is, and it isn't, if you'll pardon the answer. In general, you can't say that somebody with a light tan-coloured skin is half way towards being a black person, or vice versa, which was obviously our focus. But there are also some possible permutations that we were able to apply to the way we fabricated the initial vaccine, and we think we have come up with an adjustment that can give us a tan colour and stop any further progression. However there is a problem, we think. As far as we can model the various outcomes, a second dose, or an overdose, would actually push the recipient all the way to black.'

'So it can't be given as a nasal spray, or as a drink additive?'

'Exactly, Billy. It would have to be given very precisely, by injection only, and related to body mass. A nasal spray would be out of the question, certainly.'

'So any hope of reversing the syndrome in the USA for example would present an enormous logistical challenge? Maybe an impossible one?'

'Yes, but we're jumping ahead of ourselves a bit here. We are still looking at altering skin tones from white to brown, or black. We haven't been able to figure out how to reverse the process. Not yet, anyway.'

'Okay, Kevin; that sounds incredibly interesting to this geek at least, so all I can say is that you keep chasing that line of research and see whether you can progress it. Anything to add to that, Karen?'

Karen shook her head thoughtfully.

'Not really, but we do at least have a number of good cards in our hand. Firstly, we know that our next objective is to get from a white to a tan skin, and we think we have a route to that. More importantly, we have a willing volunteer who wants to try it and who is actually happy to go black if we overdo it. We are unlikely to ever get our ducks lined up in a row like that again, particularly with the volunteer. I know I wouldn't accept a vaccine if I knew it was going to turn me black.'

'I wouldn't worry about it, to be honest. I don't really care what colour my skin is in any case. I could still live my life the same as I always did, regardless.'

'Maybe you could, Billy. But then again you don't have to struggle to get a job, or rent an apartment, or face up to any of the struggles that black people face, every day.'

'True. But I'd prefer if society put some effort into changing the problem instead of worrying about the colour of people's skin. Although I accept that isn't going to happen.'

'It might, if most of America turns black. I'd say they won't be long reforming their systems if they find they all look like Snoop Dogg.'

'Or Michael Jackson!'

'It might come to that, Billy, a big boom in skin whitening treatments and all that.'

'That's a whole new ball game, let's stick to the job in hand. Everybody okay for everything else, you've got all the resources you need?'

There was a chorus of yesses.

'Okay, then, we'll call it a day, or an evening. I'll be missing on Monday by the way, I'm taking the weekend off and I won't be back until Monday night. But my phone is always on, if any problems arise. Have a good weekend, everybody.'

Chapter Fifty

President Donald Daniels paced angrily around the Oval Office, firing questions at his three assistants. Mike Callaghan caught Lucy Martinez' eye and tried not to smile at the peculiar gait of the politician, as he clumped around with one foot on the rug and one of the hardwood floor. The President eventually stopped his lapping of the office and slumped into the chair.

'This damn thing is driving me crazy, what the hell are you guys doing about it? And now the story is out there, and people are openly saying their President is black. Somebody even generated a video of me with black skin, giving the State of the Union address last year. How the hell did they do that, Major?'

'It's apparently pretty simple, Sir, once you know the technique. Any teenager could do it, and apparently did, in this case.'

'Some kid made a laughing stock of me? Was he arrested?'

'It's not an arrestable offence, Sir.'

'Damn well should be, I'm the Goddamn president of the United States of America, folks gotta show respect. Can we change that law, Lucy?'

'I don't believe so, Sir. It's just satire.'

'It might be sat higher to you, but it's disrespect to this office, that's what it is. We need to look at that. Now, what is happening with this thing, the changes to the amendments and shit?'

'It's an amendment in itself, Sir. We're calling it the 'equal access' amendment, as you know, and it's ready to go to both houses pretty much right now.'

'And it gets rid of any discrimination against us Blacks, right?'

Lucy frowned but Mike Callaghan's glance meant she didn't react to the President's choice of words.

'It will remove all discrimination, Sir. Not just against black and Hispanic people, but against women too.'

'I ain't worried about women, present company excepted, I just don't want to be no second class citizen in my own country.'

Lucy smiled and sighed.

'This amendment will take care of that, Sir, once it has been passed.'

'Then why the hell are we waiting? Let's get it to Congress, let's get it done with!'

'We're just doing some extra checking, Sir, just to be sure it's all watertight. But we're almost ready to go.'

'When, Lucy? When?'

'Let me consult with my legal team and get back to you tomorrow morning, Sir. I can put a definite date on it then.'

'Great! That's what I like about you, Lucy, you're able to put a time on stuff. I get a pain in my ass with all the people in this building who can't give a straight answer. I mean, something like, do we bomb Arabland? That's pretty simple, we do or we damn well don't. But try asking that question of the Airforce!'

'In fairness, Sir, doing some paperwork doesn't rate with killing a load of people in some place in Africa or Asia.'

'Foreigners, Lucy. Not Americans. There's a difference.'

'As you wish, Sir. I've gotta go, if you don't need me for anything else. I'll pass the final timeline to Major Callaghan later and he can brief you on it, if that's okay?'

'Sure, Lucy, you run along.'

As she left the room the President turned to Doctor Brady.

'Dammit, Brad, can nobody help me with this thing? I wasn't born a Black, I never wanted to be a Black and I sure as hell don't want to be a Black now. Surely there's some quick way to fix this.'

'Everybody is working on it, Sir, but we have a problem. A lot of the scientists refuse to let go of the vaccine as a possible cause. They're wasting a lot of time when they could be chasing the source of this black virus.'

'Damn eggheads, they never learn. Theories about this, theories about that, they never knuckle down and do some real work. Tell them their research money depends on finding the cause of this virus, that'll sort them out real quick. Don't take no crap from these guys, Brad. Kick some ass!'

'Yes, Sir. I'll go back to them again and lean a bit harder, like you said,'

'You do that, Brad. Holy guacamole, Lucy sure does have a nice ass. What did she say about the change to the amendment, Mike? Damn, I can't concentrate on a word she says, what a broad!'

'She said she'd have a definite 'go' date for the amendment tomorrow morning, Sir. She's going to come back to me with that and I'll brief you then.'

'Okay, guys, get to it, let's try to make some progress someplace. The black story is all over the place now, and sooner or later somebody will realise that the videos we're putting out are fake. That's when the shit will hit the fan. Goddammit, they could come in here and lynch me, they won't like the idea of a Black in this job, let me tell you.'

'They got over it before, Sir. Twice, in fact.'

'Yes, Major, but they elected me to get rid of Blacks out of government, there was too much liberal shit about healthcare, and taking away people's guns. People voted for decent, American values, Major, not for Black shit and free healthcare for communists. This is the land of the free, Major, don't you forget that.'

'Except free healthcare, obviously, Sir?'

'Absolutely, Major. Let them keep that commie shit in Europe, along with their little gay single-shot pistols. Bunch of Goddamn homosexuals, those Europeans.'

'Except the Irish, Sir?'

'You betcha, Major. Ain't nothing queer about the Irish. The Irish vote....'

'...is very important to us; yes, Sir.'

'Speaking of the Irish, Major, do we have any information from that place, where the lab is?'

'Boyle, Sir? Yes, I got an update from our guys there early this morning, they're five hours ahead of us so it was lunchtime there.'

'Holy guacamole, are the Europeans ahead of the US of A? That don't sound right, can we change that?'

'I'm afraid we can't, Sir, it's not in our gift to do that.'

'Damn. Anyhow, what news have you got?'

'Nothing to give us any comfort, Sir, I'm afraid. They're apparently working on it, but our mole has gone silent, we're getting nothing from him at all. Says it's more than his job's worth, that they know he was talking to us and he's afraid the Russians will find out and kill him.'

'Can you not throw some money at him?'

'Money won't fix it, Sir, the guy got some kind of a shock and he's clammed up. But we have our deal with the plant manager, Billy Robinson. He's talking to us but our guy says he is as wise after he's talked to him as he was beforehand. Billy talks a lot but says nothing. A lot of ifs and buts and maybes, but no hard facts at all. He has said they're half way to understanding the kernel of the problem though.'

'A kernel? Like an army officer? What the hell has a soldier got to do with it?'

'It's a figure of speech, Sir. It just means the important bit of the puzzle.'

'Major, how often do I have to tell you….?'

'Sorry, Sir. No Harvard language. I got that, Sir.'

'So if they're half way there in three weeks, does that mean they'll fix it in three more?'

'I sure hope so, Sir. But apparently it doesn't work like that in science. They might be half way to the wrong place, in a manner of speaking, so they might have to turn back and start again if they find they're getting nowhere.'

'I wonder why we pay these guys at all. Why the hell would they go off in the wrong direction to start with? Holy guacamole, if I tell the kids to go to school they're not going to go to the mall, are they?'

'I guess not, Sir.'

'Mike, I need you to take a more active role in all this shit. You're the kinda guy that kicks ass, that gets things done. I want you to go back to that place in Tennessee, interview all the folks around there and let's see if we can find the messy centre of this whole thing, okay?'

'The epicentre, Sir? You think it came from Tennessee first off the bat?'

'I reckon the damned Chinese put it there when they heard I was gonna go there to take the vaccine for their last virus. I been thinking, okay? We know the Chinese are jealous of our country and our freedom, and the way we're all bigger than them too. You ever see a big Chinaman?'

'Not too often, Sir.'

'There ya go! They're trying to cut us down to size. I saw a movie one time about some Black tribes in Africa, one of them was real tall people and the other was all small people. When they went to war, you know what the small guys did?'

'No, Sir. I haven't seen that movie.'

'They cut the legs offa the tall guys, with like big swords and shit. Cut 'em down to size; that was their plan. So, now do ya get it?'

'No, Sir.'

'It's simple. That's what the Chinese are trying to do to our great nation. First they tried to kill us off with Covid 19, but they didn't succeed. Then they came back with Covid 25, and that didn't do it either. Then they came back with another one, the one they sent to California, and when they saw we were able to bat that one right out of the park they made another one, but this time they tried another way. You see, they knew we were having a problem with the number of Blacks getting bigger and the number of Americans getting smaller, so they figured a way to pull us down by making us he same as Africa. They want to cut us down to size by making us the third world. You agree with that, Brad?'

'Sounds about right, Sir.'

'And you, Major? You think I got it figured out?'

'I guess that's why you're the President, Sir, and I'm just the Chief of Staff. I just follow orders, at the end of the day.'

'Thank you, Major. I like that I can always rely on your support, so get out there and try to fix this thing. And keep me posted, I need to know in real-time what's going on. Apart from you and Lucy, nobody tells me shit around here; they need to remember that I'm the President of the United States, not the idiot who takes out the garbage. Although he's a smart guy, to be fair, he gives me a lot of good advice. Or he did, before I had to put him on nights when I got this black shit. I couldn't have him coming in here and seeing that I'm the same as him, he might think we were kinfolk.'

Chapter Fifty One

Billy Robinson smiled contentedly to himself as the plane started its descent. The lights far below were sharp and clear, even from twenty thousand feet, and he could pick out several towns along the shoreline. The plane made a long, slow curve out over the Mediterranean before making its final approach to Malaga Airport. It flew low over the water and the beach and the brightly lit stores in the retail park before making a smooth touchdown on the northerly runway and cruising to the end before turning off along the taxiway.

He felt a blast of warm air as he exited the front door and started to walk down the steps. He was sorry he had brought his jacket, it suddenly seemed like an unnecessary encumbrance. He joined the queue for passport control and medical screening and quickly passed through both to emerge in the small plaza outside the terminal doors.

He spotted the car as it cruised slowly along the concourse, and waved to Miriam as she searched for his face among the crowd. She pulled over and he slid into the front passenger seat, throwing his jacket and weekend bag into the rear seat. He kissed her quickly as she moved away from the kerb. She squeezed his leg and smiled happily in his direction.

'Great to see you. Good flight?'

'Yes, no delays. Although I couldn't face the food, it gets worse every time.'

'Never mind, we'll eat when we get home.'

'Have you started cooking? I thought you reckoned life was too short to cook?'

'I do, occasionally, but eating out is one of the great pleasures of life in Spain. We'll go out to Sotogrande and have dinner, but I want to go home and ditch the car and take a taxi. The Guardia Civil are a bit fussy about drinking and driving. Anyway, did you miss me?'

'Of course I did! Isn't that why I'm here, even if it's only for the weekend. Although we've been so busy lately, it was hard to get the headspace to miss anyone. But it's good to see you, it really is.'

'You ought to retire, Billy, and spend your winters here with me. Then you could go back for the fishing, spend your summers in Boyle, every day on the lake.'

'I could, but to be honest I need something to do every day. I couldn't just sit in the sun and look at the blue sky, although it's not a bad prospect either. But I get my fishing in early in the mornings, or in the evenings after work, they're the nicest times to be out on the lake.'

'To tell the honest truth, Billy, this retirement thing isn't all it's cracked up to be either. I miss the daily grind, in many ways. Although the headaches, the deadlines and the financial pressures, I don't miss that side of it at all.'

'But you don't have money worries now, surely?'

'Jesus, no! I'll never again have to worry about the price of anything, I couldn't spend all my money in my lifetime, if I tried. Although would you believe I still look at the prices when I'm buying anything in the supermarket? I'll always go for the special offers and the best value, even though it really shouldn't even concern me.'

'Habits of a lifetime?'

'Not just that, I can't get my head around the amount of money I've got, it's so far removed from my reality that I have no concept of how much I actually have. It could even be a headache, if I let it.'

'How?'

'Every time I go into the bank in Gibraltar the manager is fawning over me, trying to sell me this investment package or that life insurance policy. He can't seem to understand that I just want to live my life without any fuss, and I don't need to invest to make more money.'

'That goes with the territory though. The manager of my own bank in the Isle of Man has my head annoyed with the same shite. Invest, invest, invest. I couldn't care less about that stuff, about bonds and shares and stuff. I just have no interest in it.'

'You haven't done too badly since I left, either! You extracted a lot of money from the Russians and the Americans. I hope neither side finds out about the deal you did with the other.'

'They won't. They're too busy keeping secrets from each other. And if there's one thing I learned from the last time, it's that governments splash money around in a pandemic as if it was going out of fashion. If I'd asked them for a couple of million, they'd have asked me for a detailed breakdown, but mention a nice round figure like ten million…'

'Well played anyway. I assume you don't need the half of it to follow up on the research?'

'Of course I don't! I don't need any of it, if the truth be

known, but I'll splash some of it around with the team if they pull it off.'

'And do you think they will?'

'They may do, but who cares? To tell the truth, Miriam, I quite like the idea of a world where skin colour becomes less of an issue. Imagine all the problems it would solve if we all had skins that were the same shade of brown?'

'I don't know, I quite like being white.'

'Then why do you spend so much time lying out in the sun, trying to get black?'

'Not black. A nice tan maybe, but not black.'

She reached through the open window and waved her card at the electronic toll gate. The barrier swung up and she accelerated along the motorway towards Gibraltar. At the Casares exit she slowed and took the slip lane to cross the motorway bridge towards the coast, driving downhill towards Manilva. She drove slowly through the village and headed west along the shore. Gibraltar loomed large in the windscreen, and the lights along the North African coast twinkled in the clear night air. A couple of Kilometres further on she took a tight turn to the right to drive up the hill towards Bahia Las Roccas.

The road rose steeply and zig-zagged up the hillside, the view of the Mediterranean opening up behind them. On a quiet avenue she pulled into the driveway of the house and they stepped out of the car, pausing to enjoy the scents and the sound of the Cicadas.

Billy carried his bag inside and dropped it in the hall, wandering into the living room and out to the terrace to the rear. He sat in silence for a minute, looking at the view.

'You chose well, Miriam; that view never ceases to take my breath away.'

'Me too, I just love it, I never get tired of it. I ordered an

Uber, it will be outside in five minutes.'

'I see Gibraltar is flying the Spanish flag. Is their withdrawal from Britain complete?'

'Yes, they pulled out when Sterling started to drag their Pound down with it, their spending power was starting to decrease. It had a big impact, a lot of them own homes in Spain, and house prices were getting out of reach for them. I guess pragmatism outweighs patriotism, every time.'

'But they still have offshore banking status?'

'Yes, they did a sweet deal with Spain, kept all their money advantages. The Spanish were so anxious to capture the territory that they overlooked a lot of stuff.'

'Clever folk, the Gibraltarians.'

'Yes, they made a deal with Britain too, they're getting a billion euro a year rent for the nuclear submarine base, it equals over forty grand a year for every resident. The Spanish government keeps half, but the existing residents get the rest. It effectively means that anyone born in Gibraltar before this year will never pay tax.'

'Sounds a lot better than being part of the empire.'

'I reckon so. The car is outside, let's go.'

They spoke little on the way to Sotogrande. The table at the Hairy Lemon was quiet, away from the main body of customers enjoying the open-air dining. They ordered tapas and a bottle of wine, clinking glasses in salute.

'Well, done, Billy Robinson. You showed that you're more than a match for the smartest spies in the western world.'

'I try, Miriam. I had a good teacher, in fairness.'

'Any ideas what you'll do with the money?'

'Like I said, I'll splash some of it around the team, but I'm toying with an idea. However it will depend on the current research that Karen and Kevin are doing.'

'The half-black possibility? Stopping the blackening at a certain stage? How do you hope to monetise that?'

'What's the biggest non-essential spend by women in Ireland? You ought to know this one, you're a woman, after all.'

'Clothes?'

'Clothes are essential. Maybe not all of them, but our climate doesn't really allow for the naturist option.'

'Shoes?'

'Ditto. Barefoot isn't an option either.'

'I don't know. Tell me.'

'Fake tan. Do you know how much was spent in Ireland on fake tan products and body-spraying last year?'

'I don't know, but I'd say it was a lot.'

'We've got the second highest market for fake tan in the world, after Sweden. I suppose it's about our white skins and lack of sunlight, but we spend nearly two hundred million a year on it, between home tans and salon spraying.'

'Wow! I wouldn't have thought it was that much. So you're going into the tanning business?'

'I thought about opening a spa in Boyle, A very high-end place where a woman can come, it's mostly women, and she can get tanned to any shade she likes over a weekend.'

'Using the vaccine, or a variant of it? You're a fucking genius, Billy!'

'If we could develop an injectable product, get it approved as a vaccine against the virus, and hold all the patents and licensing within a dedicated company, we'd be sitting on a goldmine.'

'Would it have to be injectable?'

'Yes, the precise quantity would have to relate to body mass, otherwise it could push the recipient past the tan colour and on to black. There might be other variables as well, that's why it could only be done in a very controlled environment.'

'And would the tan be permanent?'

'Hopefully not. In an ideal world, customers would have to come back every year for a top-up. Once we had a customer base, we'd effectively have the keys to the mint.'

'And where would you build this place, in the town?'

'At the back of the lab, there's plenty of room there, the piece of land we rent to the sheep guy.'

'But aren't you forgetting one little detail? The lab belongs to the Russians.'

'Yes, but don't you think they'd be happy to get rid of it at a substantial discount, given all the problems?'

'For somewhere between ten and twenty million, you mean? As in the money you squeezed out of them and out of the Yanks for your imaginary extra staff and equipment?"

Billy laughed.

'I reckon if I wave ten big ones at them, once I time it right, they'll bite. Especially if there's a bit of cash on the table for the negotiators. Or under the table, to be more exact.'

'I never saw you as anything but a scientist, Billy Robinson, but you're one smart operator. All that fishing taught you something, although I'm not sure what, exactly.'

'These kinds of guys make one very common mistake, Miriam. They play on a big stage and they assume that a small-town hick is of necessity going to be stupid, not in their league. They thought you'd be a pushover, and you wiped the floor with them. In my case, I'm just mopping up the spills.'

Miriam waved to the waiter and ordered more tapas. She topped up their wine and sat forward eagerly.

'Every time I think I have you figured, Billy, you surprise me. So go back to what you were saying about permanency, does that mean the existing vaccine isn't going to last, in terms of the black colour?'

'This is between you and I, okay? I haven't shared this with the others, and I don't intend to, yet. I don't want to distract them from what they're doing, and I don't want the Russians or the Americans to figure out that it might not be permanent. I've been doing some computer modelling myself, and all my results are showing a gradual fading off over time, but I can't say what that timeframe is. It could be a month, or a hundred years.'

'You should make that public though, shouldn't you? It would give some hope to the afflicted. A lot of people in America are black now, it's causing chaos.'

'It's not, that's the thing. If anything, it is uniting black people and the newly black, what they're calling the Oreos.'

'Black outside, white centre?'

'Something like that. So no, I won't make it public. Not until I have data to back it up anyway.'

'So where will you get the data? It's going to be hard to get volunteers to have their skin colour changed, surely?'

'On the contrary. Monica, the Russian lady, she wants to try a colour change. She says she hates her pale skin because it's too Russian and she hates everything Russian now. She wants to be black, like her man.'

'And is she willing to be a guinea pig for the half-way experiment?'

'Yes, but she's not the only one now. We've found that a lot of students want to go black, in solidarity with minorities, or just to piss off their parents. It's a kind of attention-seeking stunt, but they're all willing to sign up, as long as there's some beer money involved of course.'

'But why would you want to get involved in a big business venture, Billy? You've made a lot of money, you don't need any more.'

'For the town. I want to put Boyle on the map, make it a luxury destination, create hundreds of local jobs with good salaries. I reckon the presence of a high-end spa could act as a nucleus for further development.'

'The town never worried about you.'

'That's not true. I like living in Boyle, it's a friendly place and it has everything I want. Okay, there are some miserable gits there, but most of the people are great. The day you persuaded me to move there to help start up the lab was probably the best day of my life, in hindsight. Even if it was a bit of a rocky road, it was all good. I found my Nirvana, have you found yours?'

Miriam swirled the wine slowly around in the glass.

'I thought I had, but to be honest I get bored sometimes. I love this area, and the house, and the lifestyle, and the neighbours are great. But sometimes I get a feeling that I should be at work, doing something. All this idleness can wear a bit thin.'

'I have a cure for that.'

'I know, but let's finish our dinner, the night is long.'

'Not just that, would you be interested in owning a slice of the world's most expensive Spa?'

'Maybe I would. It would be different, that's for sure. Keep me posted on any developments and I'll give it some thought, at least.'

Chapter Fifty Two

Mike Callaghan spread plates on the table and unpacked the takeaway containers while Lucy opened the bottle of Rioja.

'I don't need all that rice, Mike, just around half the portion will do. I'm putting on weight, and in my case it all goes to my Latino butt.'

'It seems to be spread around nicely, all the same.'

'Steady, guy! At least let's eat dinner before you start laying all that sweet romantic talk on me.'

'HG thinks you have a great ass.'

'Like I give a shit what HG thinks! I'm beginning to think he is missing a few circuits. I guess we should be grateful he thinks at all.'

'He reckons the Chinese have made this black virus to cut us down to size as a nation.'

'Idiot! Is that why he sent you off to Tennessee again? Talk about a waste of a day!'

'It wasn't entirely wasted.'

She poured wine and they tucked into the food hungrily, both keeping an eye on the Screen where the CNN rolling news was showing. Mike pointed his fork at the news item.

'The genie sure is out of the bottle now, the black story is everywhere. And they're blaming the vaccine too, or some of them are. Although the scientists seem to have changed their tune now, they're all calling it as a new virus.'

'Would that have anything to do with what you said, about HG threatening to take away their research funding?'

Mike added a couple of extra spoonfuls of rice to his plate and used it to mop up the sauce.

'This sure is tasty. Yeah, I reckon the funding threat has made the boffins back off from the vaccine angle.'

'Even though it means they're wrong?'

'They know which side their bread is buttered on, those guys live and die by their research grants and all the fancy award dinners that go with them. HG might be in the dark most of the time, but he knows where the light switches are at.'

'I guess. Anyway, what about the trip to Tennessee? You're getting to see a lot of that Corner Creek place these days.'

'I'm starting to like that little town, to be honest. They're real nice people, once you get past the rough exteriors and all the hillbilly stuff. Real neighbourly, just real nice.'

'You find out anything new?'

'Yes, but nothing I can share with HG. The local Klan has disbanded since the acting chief turned black a couple of days ago. He had thought he was blessed by God with being the only Klansman who had stayed white, but it got him in the end.'

'The water, or the ice?'

'The water, I guess. I was able to gather from talking to Randy Corless that the guy isn't on the water main and doesn't buy ice, but he did drink a lot of water when he was chairing the last Klan meeting.'

'That's gotta be the route.'

'Yeah, so now they've closed down operations. Same with the Klaverns in all the towns down that valley, they're all black now, every damn one of them.'

'All from the water?'

'No, not all. One town, I can't recall the name, it isn't on the Corner Creek pumping station. It gets its water from the river and treats it in its own plant. It's not part of Tennessee Water, some historical dispute where they decided to go it alone in case the Feds decided to poison them, apparently.'

'Not too far wrong, in a way.'

Mike laughed.

'You could say that. But I figured it out anyway. The Corner Creek sewage plant discharges treated water into the river, just clean water obviously, but I took a test sample from the outfall and it has a fairly high concentration of vaccine in it.'

'The gift that keeps on giving?'

'Yeah, this vaccine is out of control, in a way. It's in a lot of waterways now, which means it gets into water supplies, into the food chain. Everywhere, it's everywhere.'

'At least we won't have any more problems with the virus.'

'Yeah, the virus is pretty much wiped out. We've stopped it in its tracks faster than any vaccine in history. We probably saved us a million lives too. Although I'm not sure the result is all good.'

'Because of the black?'

'Yeah, I love it in one way, but I'm nervous of it too. We're creating a whole new world order here, a black America, but maybe black other places too.'

'Your wife was black, you're not too hung up on skin colour?'

Mike finished his meal in silence. Lucy put her hand on his arm.

'Sorry, I shouldn't have mentioned her, it must still hurt.'

'Sure does, but it's okay, don't beat yourself up about it. I loved the ground she walked on, you know that.'

'I know. But she died a hero, defending her country.'

'I'm not sure it was her country, that's the bit that still bothers me. This was very much a white man's country, even ten years back. She died fighting for a country that didn't really care about her, or any black woman. She was just cannon fodder, they would have shed more tears over the chopper she was flying than one dead black pilot. I know they did the full honours, the flag on the coffin, all that shit. But it wasn't her country, no Sir. It was all for the white man.'

'So maybe we can change that, this time?'

'Maybe we can, but are we unleashing a monster? Are we saying that a black majority will treat a white minority, even a small one, better than if it was the other way around? I ain't so sure about that, that's my problem.'

'But the amendment will do it, won't it?'

'It should help, but bullies will always find a way.'

Lucy picked up the bottle and topped up the wine glasses. She put an arm around Mike's shoulders and kissed his cheek.

'Let's give it our best shot, Mike Callaghan. Let's see what we can make of it. At least you got the vaccine pump installed in the Adams County water station.'

'Yeah, it's pumping away, it's about to give our flabby white boys on the hill a hell of a shock, that's for sure. They're cocooning themselves in their apartments, afraid they'll catch the black virus. Little do they know, it's coming out of their faucets every time they draw a glass of water.'

'You were talking about your friend, Randy Corless. What was it you were saying, when I interrupted you?'

'Oh, yeah. Randy has set himself up as a preacher, using the old Klan meeting-hall. He learned a lot of the tricks by watching a preacher in the next town, so now he gives bible readings and they sing hymns. Then once a week they have a church supper, real neighbourly it is too.'

'He must have had a talent for it, under all that yokel façade.'

'He's surprising, it's as though being black has given him confidence, he speaks real well and he has a great down-home turn of phrase.'

'A good communicator?'

'Yeah, he was talking about how the Lord likes to plough fertile ground with his word, and how sometimes it's like ploughing a good field with a new John Deere and a four-sod Bison and sometimes it's like trying to plough the interstate with a wooden plough and a three-legged mule. Goes down real well with his audience.'

'You went to his service?'

'Just briefly, we had to leave early to avoid night flying. The White House chopper isn't rated for after dark. Cutbacks, can you believe that?'

'I'm glad they are taking the church route and not rioting or killing people.'

'Yes, it's real nice, a nice feeling of friendship between neighbours. One old guy, he owns a store, he said it might be the best thing ever happened to Corner Creek. There used to be too much hatred and bitterness, he said, especially when that sheriff was in charge. He was a nasty damn racist, that guy, used to pick on black folks if they as much as drove into the town.'

'He's the guy that died?'

'Yeah, the guy my men killed, to be more exact. Sometimes the Presidential guard can be too trigger-happy; maybe they're over-trained, or something.'

'They have to protect the President, regardless of who he is.'

'Yeah, but maybe a little less force, sometimes…'

'So, when do you think they will turn black, the folks on Capitol Hill? And us, too?'

'If we use the Klan guy as a reference, it should take about another week.'

'So we can tell HG that we will have the amendment ready by Monday?'

'Yeah, that should do it. I reckon both houses need to see the draft amendment before they get the black, but they need to change colour before they get too entrenched in their positions towards it. So if they have it on Monday, and they turn black on Wednesday, we will have the perfect storm. I reckon the amendment will sail through both houses.'

'And I'll be sleeping with a black man.'

'There is that, too. So let's make the most of your last few days with your white lover.'

Chapter Fifty Three

Ivan Turgenev drove quickly down the M7 across the centre of Ireland, his diplomatic plates saving him any concerns about the speed limit. He pulled into the truck stop at Portlaoise and did a lap of the forecourt before exiting to the motorway again. He glanced in his rear-view mirror and was pleased to see that the grey BMW was no longer behind him. He cranked up the speed to a hundred and eighty and left all the traffic behind him for a while. At the Moneygall exit he braked suddenly and took the slip road leading to the Barak Obama Plaza, taking a convoluted route around the truck park and making a second lap of the pumps and the charging area before exiting again at speed and rejoining the motorway. He watched the mirror carefully and relaxed for the first time since leaving Dublin.

In Washington, Mike Callaghan stood behind the chair of the young officer in the darkened control room. They watched the map on the screen and the red car icon moving quickly west on the motorway. The younger officer was puzzled.

'What the hell is he doing?'

Mike laughed and pointed to the western edge of the map.

'Collecting somebody from Shannon Airport, I reckon. But why is he driving the car himself, and why use the staff runabout and not the official limo?'

'Hell knows! Does he not trust his own driver?'

'Could be. They might be having a problem with leaks, so they'll be getting paranoid. I guess they don't know we have trackers on all their fleet. Might be a liaison with a mistress, or it could be something more important. Keep an eye on him anyhow, and keep in contact with the camper van and with Hank, let them see this feed. They can pick up the close surveillance if and when it becomes necessary. As long as he stays in the car though, this is the safest way to follow him.'

Igor Kuznetsov emerged from the airport terminal and stepped quickly into the waiting car, throwing his weekend bag into the back seat. His colleague accelerated away from the airport and joined the M17, heading north. He turned to his visitor with a worried smile.

'We are really in the shit now, Igor Kuznetsov. Comrade President Zhadnyy is not a happy man, and he is not far away from wanting both our heads on a plate.'

'Relax, Ivan. It can't be all that bad, he just suggested to me that I come here to help you out. It wasn't what I'd call a 'level-one' command. If it was critical, he'd have done a video call, but he just called me on my mobile.'

'He is apparently very self-conscious about his appearance, he hasn't showed his face at all since he became a black man. But he now has a bigger problem, one that the Americans will turn into a circus if they find out.'

'Problem? What kind of problem?'

'It appears that the vaccine which causes the blackening of the skin is easily spread to secondary contacts through body fluids, if you understand my meaning.'

Ivan Turgenev smiled knowingly.

'One of his mistresses has turned black?'

'Not exactly, but close. Apparently a number of high-end hookers in Moscow have had to be taken away from the city and put in a facility in a closed corrective colony in Siberia.'

'What we might call a prison?'

'We might, at our peril. But they have also been joined by two junior officers from his personal guard, both of whom are also apparently showing a change of skin tone, you might say.'

'His wrestling companions?'

'Yes, apparently, or so my information suggests. Apparently all of them were snatched quickly and flown to the facility and are in a small but secure wing, where they will stay until a cure is found for the condition.'

'Then Comrade President Zhadnyy has already solved the problem, has he not?'

'For now, but there may be others who are in hiding for instance. One young officer has disappeared from his post and the rumour is that he was seen walking by the Moscow River while drunk, but that smells of bullshit, quite honestly. It is likely that some other black Russians are out there, and sooner or later somebody will connect one of them to the President.'

Igor Kuznetsov sighed and seemed to shrink into the passenger seat.

'It's a shit-storm, Comrade. I know what it feels like, being black, and I'm even getting used to it. It's not nice, but at least in America nobody seems to give a damn. I wouldn't like to be the only black man walking down a street in Moscow, for sure.'

'I didn't like to comment. How did you catch it, do you

know? You didn't accept the vaccine, I'm sure, did you?'

'Of course not. I believe it is in the water supply, that's the only explanation for it. I was very careful, no hookers, no women other than my wife, nothing. Then last week I woke up and I was slightly black, but by the time I had finished breakfast I was a fully baked Black. My wife is now black too, but she is not concerned. She says maybe she may not go back to Russia ever, if this is to be her colour. She believes that black people are more accepted in America compared to almost anywhere else.'

'Compared to the Mother Country, for sure.'

'So, Ivan, what are we supposed to do, here? I didn't like to ask too many questions of our leader.'

'It appears that some of the staff in Boyle Labs may be getting close to finding a solution to the problem, and our leader wants us to sit on the place and make sure the Americans don't get their hands on it. He doesn't trust the management there, particularly the older guy, Billy Robinson. The two nephews of General Morozov believe that Mister Robinson has little time for Russians, he appears to dismiss them as idiots and they feel insulted.'

'He's not too far wrong, about the idiots.'

'That is as may be, but the nephews reckon there's some kind of excitement around the place these days, which may indicate that they are managing to crack this puzzle. In any case, they are our only eyes and ears in the place. They're all we've got.'

'Then may God have mercy on us all, Ivan Turgenev!'

Chapter Fifty Four

President Donald Daniels stepped on to the low platform in front of the White House, flanked by his Chief of Staff and the Country's Chief Medical Officer. He moved behind the centre podium and tapped the microphone.

'Is this alive? Thank you, ladies and gentlemen, and I'm sorry for the shock you must feel, but I assure you it is nothing to the shock I got when I looked in the mirror yesterday. You better believe it!'

There was a titter of nervous laughter around the gathered group of reporters. The President paused before continuing.

'As you will see, and there is no point in denying it, my colleagues and I have caught the Chinese black virus. My Chief of Staff woke up this morning and found he had joined Doctor Brady and myself in the black community, where we have been since yesterday. I would like to point out that some false news circulating for more than two weeks had suggested that I had caught it a couple of weeks back, but that was nonsense. Your President will always let you know when something changes that you should know about.'

'Now, I want to point out that I don't have a problem

being a black man, although it sure takes some getting used to. I also want to point out that the change to the constitution, what the legal people call an amendment, was proposed by this administration several weeks ago, as the Attorney General will testify, as soon as she can get past security and into her office. She had an unfortunate incident this morning when she was turned away at the guard-post because she wasn't recognised by the facial-recognition system, but we are working on getting her a fresh ID as I speak.'

'The incident with Lucy, the Attorney General, just shows you why we had to bring in the change to the constitution. It is obvious that black folks like myself and my two colleagues are still at a disadvantage in American society, and colleagues like Lucy Martinez got twice the problem because they are women. So a few weeks ago I told the Attorney General's office to write up the words for this change, and it is being voted on today on the lower house. If it passes there, as it should, it will go to the upper House this evening and they will sit until it is dealt with. You better believe it!'

'I want to stress that this change was already on the way before this black Chinese virus struck Capitol Hill or indeed the White House. This administration is always ahead of the posse when it comes to looking after all the folks in this great nation. We don't wait around until something affects us directly, we get in there and do good stuff when folks need us to do good stuff. Or even before anybody knows that this is what has to be done.'

'I also want to tell you that our scientists are working on finding a cure for this virus, as well as figuring out ways to prevent it happening again once we fix it, which we will. But it could take a while, so in the meantime you need to tell your viewers and your readers and your listeners that nobody in this great Nation will ever suffer any kind of bad stuff because of their skin colour, or indeed because they are women, especially black women. Although white women got issues too, and we recognise that, but they won't be at any disadvantage because black women will now have equal kinds of problems. But we'll fix all that. It was always supposed to be fixed, but I guess the founding fathers didn't reckon on dealing with smartass lawyers when they wrote the original rules. It was all just a little weak in the colour section, I guess, but we're going to fix that now.'

A reporter in the front row raised his hand, catching the President's eye.

'So, Sir, if the scientists fix this skin-colour issue, will you unwind the constitutional amendment at that point?'

The President looked puzzled.

'Gee, Tony, you sure look different.'

'So do you, Sir!'

'I guess. That's a good question, Tony, I'm glad you asked me that. I guess a lot of folks want to know that, to know how they stand. Truth is, I can't say for sure, I might not be here by then, it could be somebody else who maybe looks at things different. But I guess everything is possible, I mean we're making the change now, aren't we? Are you saying you'd like it changed back?'

'No, Sir, of course not.'

'There you go! There you have it, if it's fine, it will be fine. If it ain't, it ain't. My Daddy always used to say that if it ain't broke, leave the toolbox in the damn shed. That's always been my motto.'

The President raised a hand to quell any further questions.

'I'm sorry, guys, I gotta go, I got President stuff to

do. But we'll get back together in two days' time, if the changes go through Congress okay, as they surely must. We can then talk about how this will all make life better for everybody.'

The three men left the area and went indoors. In the Oval office, Mike Callaghan closed the door and went to the side table to pour himself a coffee.

'Anybody else?'

The president nodded absently.

'Yeah, Mike, I need one.'

'Black?'

'What? Oh, the coffee, gotcha! Yeah, black it is.'

Mike pointed the coffee pot at the doctor.

'Coffee, Brad?'

'No, thanks, Mike. In fact, if you gentlemen are finished with me, I gotta be someplace.'

The President waved his CMO away.

'Carry on, Brad, I'll have somebody call you if I need you.'

Mike put the President's coffee mug on the Resolute desk, and sat down in one of the wicker-seated chairs with his own drink. He sipped slowly, waiting for the President to end his reverie. Eventually Daniels seemed to come to his senses, sitting down heavily in the big chair and lifting the hot coffee to his lips.

'Okay, Mike, I thought that went well. Do you think it went well? Are they going to hate me because I'm a Black?'

'Hate you? You mean the Press, Sir?'

'Nah, screw the Goddamn Press. Are the American people going to be mad because there's a Black in the Oval Office? That's not what they voted for, is it?'

'I guess not, Sir. But almost everybody in the country is

black now, Sir. I don't think it amounts to a hill of beans, to be honest.'

'You reckon folks don't care about skin colour, Mike? I can't agree, I reckon it's the one thing they do care about. Ain't nobody I know wants to be a Black, who the hell you gonna look down on if you're already at the bottom of the pile?'

'Like the man said, Sir, we're all in the same boat now. I reckon skin colour don't mean nothing when we're all the same. There ain't no point of difference anymore, which is a damn good thing, in my book.'

'I sure hope you're right. It don't seem to bother you none anyhow. But I guess you're used to their ways, you were married to one of them, weren't you?'

Mike took a couple of deep breaths before answering.

'"Their ways' are just the same as our ways, Sir. Just folks trying to get along, every day. The colour of my skin is immaterial to me, I'm still an American, it doesn't matter what I look like on the outside.'

'I guess we'll have to agree to differ, Mike. Although to be truthful I'm kinda getting used to being black, and it ain't so bad. Biggest problem was seeing a Black looking out of the bathroom mirror, but once you get used to that, it's no big deal. And my wife, she's gotten used to it too. In fact she kinda likes it, she says I look handsome as a black man.'

'Has she turned black too, Sir?'

'Yes, just yesterday, same as you and the Doc. I guess there was an outbreak around here, caught nearly everybody.'

'And she's okay with it?'

'Yeah, I guess. She looks damned good as a Black woman, kinda sexy. Like one of them expensive Vegas hookers. Anyhow, you wanted to talk to me, Mike?'

'Yes, Sir. Just to bring you up to date on today's stuff.

Our Russian allies are on the move, Igor Kuznetsov caught a flight to Shannon earlier today, the weekly military and logistics flight they run under a civilian airline badge. The last bulletin I got, just half an hour ago, was that his old colleague Turgenev picked him up at the airport. Something seems to be going down if Zhadnyy has put his old team back together.'

'Shannon? Is that a European country?'

'It's an airport in Ireland, Sir. They're in Ireland.'

'Damn, Geography was always my weak spot. I get mixed up between places. Like Thigh Land and Leg O'Land, I know one of them is in Europe and the other is in somewhere else.'

'Asia, Sir. And it's Thailand. All one word.'

'Yeah, Leg O'Land is the one that's in Europe.'

'Yes, Sir, but it's a theme park in Denmark. And it's Legoland, all one word as well. It's where they make the plastic bricks, the ones little kids use to make stuff.'

'So, not a country? Gotcha. So, the two Russians are in Thigh Land? Holy guacamole!'

'No, Sir, Ireland. They are heading for Boyle, where the lab is located.'

'The lab the Russians own, but we thought they didn't?'

'That's the place, Sir.'

'So, what are they doing there?'

The Major opened his tablet and tapped open a map. He zoomed in on a road in the west of Ireland and pointed to a small red car icon that was moving north. He pointed the moving car out to the President.

'They're still travelling, by the look of it. We have a tracker on the car, Sir, but it certainly looks like it's heading for Boyle. If it is, it will turn off just here, north of the town of Tuam.'

"Chew 'em?' Funny names they got for places in Europe.'

The major pointed to the icon, which had left the main highway and was moving towards Dunmore.

'Yep, they're headed for Boyle. I reckon they should be there in an hour, maybe less.'

'We got people on station?'

'Yes, Sir. We got a full team out now, once we realised that Turgenev was on the move. We got cameras looking at their embassy in Dublin, so when we spotted him driving the car himself we figured something was up. Normally these ambassadors lord it a bit with their chauffeurs and all the trimmings.'

'Who do we got in charge on the ground?'

'Hank, Sir. He's a good man.'

'But he missed the deal that broad made with the Russians, last time. Are you sure you can rely on him?'

'Yes, Sir. Of course.'

'I don't like it, Mike. I got a feeling in my gut, something is going down and we're out of the loop. Never trust a Russian, that's what my daddy always said. That's my motto, my daddy was never wrong.'

'Yes, Sir. He might have been right about that, anyhow.'

'I want you over there, Mike, to take charge of everything. Can you take a military plane straight away? Or can we do that?'

'Yes, we can, Sir. We got a deal with the Irish government, basically that we fly what we like through Shannon and they promise to turn a blind eye, once they can come here every Saint Patrick's day and give you the bowl of Shamrock.'

'Yeah, that salad thing? It tastes like shit, but I guess they're used to it. I just put it in the garbage. So, get your ass over to Shannon Ireland and rent a car, civilian clothes, no uniform. If anybody recognises you, tell 'em you had vacation time coming and you're looking for your roots. You could pass for a native anyhow, apart from that black face.'

'A tourist? Maybe, Sir. A native, probably not.'

'And bring a lawyer with you, in case there's another deal to be done. We got any good lawyers on staff?'

'We got Lucy Martinez, Sir.'

'The Attorney General? Is she a lawyer too? Holy guacamole, she's one smart broad. Okay, take her with you. And if she gets stroppy and refuses to go, tell her it's a direct order from the President. But keep your damn hands offa that ass, I saw it first.'

'I'll try to remember that, Sir.'

'You do that, Mike. In fact, you can consider that an order too.'

Chapter Fifty Five

Billy Robinson sat back in the armchair and looked at his two colleagues. He pulled the ring on his beer can and pointed to the fridge.

'Help yourselves, guys. My home is your home, and all that stuff.'

'Got any fruit juice? I'm trying to avoid the booze.'

'Should be some there, Karen. You okay with beer, Kevin?'

'No, I think I'll have some juice as well, thanks.'

They settled back with their drinks and Billy looked at the others questioningly.

'So, I can see you've got news, spit it out!'

Kevin smiled and glanced at Karen.

'We have two bits of news, both unrelated.'

Billy sat upright and looked at them with a slight smile.

'Surely you're not...?'

Karen laughed excitedly.

'We are! We're pregnant, can you believe it?'

Kevin squeezed her arm protectively.

'We only found out for sure today, can you believe it? We're so excited.'

Billy shook his head in wonderment.

'I'm delighted for you guys, I really am. I thought there might have been something going on between you two of late, but I never even knew you were an item, not to mention that you were thinking of starting a family. That's brilliant news.'

Karen held her partner's hand and gazed at him dreamily.

'We've only got together in the last month, since the whole vaccine business ramped up. We didn't even really get on, before that, but once we started working together intensely we just knew we were right for each other. We're even moving in together, in a house up the top of the hill here in Meadowvale.'

'Well, dang me, as they used to say in the movies. I never saw that coming, for sure. I assume I have to keep this to myself, for now anyway?'

'Yes, please. Kevin and I will tell the rest of the team in the next few weeks, but we don't want the work dynamic upset for now, until we finish wrapping up the skin colour project at least.'

'That's the other thing, I thought that was the news you wanted to share with me. So while I'm delighted at the prospect of the arrival of a tiny biochemist, I had rather hoped you had solved the big conundrum.'

Kevin sipped his juice slowly and smiled.

'Well, that's the thing, we have, actually. Or we think we have. Or we're close to it, very close. We've solved the science in any case, it's just a matter of refining the pathways to make it operational.'

Billy went to the fridge and opened another beer.

'I gotta hand it to you two, you're some team. So, where are we with it, exactly?'

Kevin began to pace around the room, one hand on his right temple as he concentrated on what he was saying.

'You know we managed to turn Monica a nice shade of light brown, like a really even suntan, and then when she wasn't happy with that and wanted to go further we were able to move her to a dark brown and then later on to black. We observed the changes at sub-cellular level during all of the process, and we were able to find out information that nobody had ever established before, about why people have differing degrees of brown or black pigmentation.'

'So you know how to reverse it?'

'I'll come to that in a minute, we found out lots of other stuff as well, but to be honest we were limited by our sample size. As you know, you can't always replicate an effect in a large population, even though it might have worked in an individual. So a lot of our results aren't at the stage where we could publish, for instance, because our small sample size is unreliable.'

'Yes, I get all that, but did you manage to find a way to control the effect?'

'In a way, yes. But I'd stress that it's early days.'

'That doesn't matter. The thing is, you made a new scientific discovery, one that could be life-changing for a lot of people.'

Karen sat forward excitedly.

'The thing is, Billy, we can reverse the black skin colour. We've done it.'

'Holy shit! Where, with who?'

'The guy from Kiltycreighton. He's now well-tanned, but that's as far as we want to go with him for now, in case we drift into albinism. It's all related to levels of tyrosinase, obviously, and the production of melanin in the epidermal cells, but without boring you with the details, we managed to lower his melanin production to a level where he's not a black man anymore.'

'And his friend, the LGBTQ… whatever… lady?'

'She's happy enough where she's at, but I told her I can probably fix it any time she likes. For the minute though, she seems to enjoy being a black woman. And she's got a boyfriend.'

'That's amazing. One question though, the big question….'

'Is whether it works on people who have turned black, or also on people who were born black?'

'In a nutshell, yeah.'

Kevin sat on the arm of the couch.

'It works on people who are born black. That was actually our biggest fear, and it does.'

'Jesus! We're talking about something that can change the world, here.'

'Yes, Billy, but not necessarily in a good way. Karen and I have talked this through for hours, we were awake half the night to be honest, wondering what we should do with this.'

'But as scientists, you must be excited beyond belief. This has to be published.'

'We're not so sure. In fact, we have really conflicting thoughts on it. We had a problem to solve, and we really pitched in to do it. So when we realised we had turned Lucky's skin a shade lighter, we were so excited. Until we stopped and thought about it.'

'You tried it on Lucky?'

'Yes, but we explained it really well, in great depth, and Caroline drafted a contract that covers every possible eventuality. We asked him to consider the implications if he turned white, or even just a bit lighter, but he was cool about it. He said that he was considered very black by Nigerian standards, that lots of his countrymen aren't as dark as that. So he wasn't at all bothered that he might be lightening up a bit.'

'But you didn't try another step-change, to lighten him still further?'

'No, because we know it would work. The step-changes are just a process, once we knew that they worked in one direction we knew they would work in another. What we weren't sure of was whether the changes would apply in the case of people born black, and not just in the case of people who had turned black from the vaccine. But now we know.'

'We surely do. Wow! So where do we go from here, do you reckon?'

Karen glanced at Kevin and motioned to him to talk. He began to pace the room again, gesticulating eagerly as he spoke.

'You see, what's happening in America right now, with the amendment to the Constitution, that's amazing. For once in history, black people, and indeed women of all shades and colours have the chance of being truly equal in the biggest economy in the world. And let's not kid ourselves, this has happened not because white America decided to give a fair shake to the rest. It's happened out of a sense of self-preservation by a white population that woke up one morning and found itself on the wrong side of the fence.'

'I agree with all that, right enough. But what does your discovery mean for this process? Surely if you have a cure, if I can call it that, for people who have turned black, the problem is solved.'

'No, Billy, it isn't. Don't you see, America is on the brink of solving the great black/white divide for the first time in its history? If we drop a 'cure' for black skin into the mix at this point, will we derail all that? That's our concern.'

'Yeah, I see that side of it too. But is division in society as simple as skin colour? I mean, look at Northern Ireland, where divisions are deeper than anything you'd see in a week's wandering in the USA. I'm just not sure it's all down to skin colour. Maybe if we solve, if society solves the colour divide, some other point of difference will emerge. Some people will always find a way to look down on other people, and that's the truth of it.'

Karen interrupted animatedly.

'Yes, Billy, but let's just take this one issue, the new amendment to the constitution in America. That really does seek to eliminate pretty much every form of discrimination in that country, it really goes into detail in a way that has never been done. Not just discrimination against people of colour, but also against women, other minorities. It even deals with housing, with hidden discrimination in the rental market, all that stuff. The concept of a ratio, based on the numbers of people of colour and the numbers of women in society, and the need for every decision-maker to be in line with that ratio, that's amazing. Whoever wrote it is a real reformer, you can see it in the wording. I read it about ten times last night, and it gets better each time.'

'Yes, I get all that, but if it removes discrimination, surely skin colour won't matter?'

'You have to look at context, if you'll pardon my scientific approach. This amendment is being supported only because the majority of Americans are now black. Take away from that, and it will get watered down, individual states won't wholeheartedly adopt the spirit of it, as well as the letter.'

'So you think we should sit on the discovery?'

'Yes, for now anyway.'

'You agree with Karen, Kevin?'

'Yes. As a scientist I'm obviously excited about what we've found, but I think we have a dangerous weapon here. I feel a bit like Oppenheimer and his crew when they designed the atomic bomb. I'm not so sure that I want to drop it. But you don't agree with us?'

'If you'd asked me that a month ago, I might have said I didn't, but at this stage I'm actually inclined to agree with you both. For me, skin colour is not something I'm in any way concerned about, although I recognise that black people often have a different experience. So maybe we should lock this away for now. Keep refining it by all means, but we won't announce it, or at least we won't announce it until we are all agreed that it is the best thing to do.

And by the way, be careful out there. The two elder Russians are back in town, and one of them is now black, the guy from Washington I think. They checked into Frybrook a couple of hours back and I'm sure we'll see them in the lab tomorrow. So if they're around, don't leave any data lying about where they can copy it or get an idea of what we're up to. Just be aware of them.'

'Not much happens in Boyle without somebody knowing about it.'

'True, Karen. And it looks like our American friends are here in force too. The so-called fisherman, Hank, he's back, staying in Frybrook, as are a black couple, both Yanks – they've rented an apartment for a week, one of the nice ones across from the Abbey. I'm sure I'll know more about them by tomorrow when I go for breakfast in King House. And of course the two guys in the campervan are back, circling around, trying to look like a gay couple on holidays but fooling nobody.'

'Boyle is suddenly an exciting place. Interesting times, anyway.'

'That's for sure, Kevin. That's for sure.'

Chapter Fifty Six

Mike tightened the scarf around his neck as he strolled arm-in-arm with Lucy along Main Street. Out of habit, he glanced over his shoulder occasionally to see if they were being followed. As the street bent left and quickly right again at the gates to King House, they crossed the road to walk on the other side. He squeezed Lucy's shoulder and held her close.

'It all seems a million miles from the White House, doesn't it?'

'It's so quiet, but it sure gets cold here in the evenings.'

'Yeah, it's a lot colder here than in Washington. That dinner was great, but I never expected Igor Kuznetsov to be there. I thought he would be keeping a low profile, not eating and drinking in a bar in Boyle.'

'I don't think he recognised us, at least I hope not. Don't forget he is used to seeing you in uniform, and seeing both of us as white. Anyhow I reckon they were too busy drinking toasts with the two goons they had with them. I thought the lady who owned the place was going to throw them out at the end. She had a quiet word with the other older man and the noise stopped.'

'That guy, the white one, is called Ivan Turgenev, he's the

Russian ambassador to Ireland. He and Kuznetsov are old comrades of Zhadnyy, all three served in East Germany as KGB officers, and later they worked on some clandestine stuff in Saint Petersburg. They would be considered as being close to the top of the tree. The two younger ones are the nephews of General Morozov, a ruthless and dangerous Mafia character who is close to Zhadnyy but not publicly so. He'd be involved in some shady stuff, barely legal at best, but apparently the nephews have no boundaries in that regard and the State Prosecutor had little choice but to indict them on some charges so they did a runner to London. It looks like they were recently ordered to move over here to manage Boyle Labs.'

'Are they scientists?'

'They don't even have a high-school education, so they have no knowledge about the business at all. I think they're just there as eyes and ears for the grownups, and judging by the presence of the two senior guys tonight, the grownups seem to have arrived. Why that is, we don't rightly know, but HG wants you and I to ride shotgun on it.'

'Sounds exciting, or maybe not. Either way, it's an excuse for us both to get out of the office for a few days.'

'We can probably do without any of that kind of excitement, and anyway we have three operatives under cover here at the minute if any dangerous stuff needs to be done. Our role is just to strategise, to make decisions on the ground. I guess we shouldn't have gone to dinner in Clarke's, but the lady who rents the apartments recommended it. I didn't expect to see our dear allies.'

'It was lovely and cosy, and the food was great, so it was a good call. I'd like to go back there, if we can, but I guess we should play it by ear.'

They rounded the corner at Shelling Hill, gasping in

amazement as the Abbey was flooded in moonlight. They paused to look at the ancient arches bathed in the blue glow. Mike shook his head in wonder.

'Sure looks old! I guess there was a serious level of culture and learning here long before the white man got to America.'

'Yeah, we often think of these European countries as backward, compared to the USA, but they sure have a depth to their civilisation that we don't have.'

She shivered in the night air.

'Let's go indoors and open that bottle of wine, it's cold out here.'

They opened the outer door with the latchkey and climbed the stairs to the first floor. The apartment was warm and cosy, and Mike pulled two chairs to face the window where they could admire the view of the ancient ruin. Lucy took the corkscrew from the drawer and put it on the small coffee table along with the bottle of wine.

'You wanna get that? I always break the corks.'

There was a discrete tap on the door as Mike picked up the corkscrew. Lucy motioned him to continue.

'I'll get it, it's probably the owner with the invoice; she said she'd drop it in.'

Lucy opened the door, smiling a welcome. The man rushed through the doorway and grabbed her by the arm, twisting it painfully in one swift movement so that it was pinned behind her back. Mike instinctively turned and grabbed the bottle, but the man shook his head as he waved the pistol beside Lucy's face.

'Do not try it, Major. I will have no problem killing you both if you don't co-operate. Just sit down, and take the phone from your pocket and put it on the table.'

Mike stood his ground, but the man snicked the safety catch to the off position.

'I give you ten seconds to do as you are told, Major, or I kill the woman.'

Lucy stamped suddenly on the man's foot with the heel of her shoe and Mike struck him hard on the temple with the wine bottle, causing him to slump to the floor. Mike grabbed the gun and set the safety before putting it in his pocket. Lucy sat down heavily on one of the chairs, her legs shaking.

'Goddamn, Mike, did you kill him?'

Mike turned the intruder over on his stomach, removing his own tie to bind the man's hands together behind his back. He quickly undid the man's shoelaces and removed them from his black leather shoes, knotting them together and using them to tie his ankles together. He checked the man's neck for a pulse.

'He'll live. Son of a bitch. He's one of the guys from the pub, a nephew of General Morozov; he's one of the twins who are running the lab. What the hell is he doing, going around threatening people with a gun? What did he want?'

'I guess we'll find out soon enough, when he wakes up. If he wakes up.'

'He'll survive. He might have a sore head for a couple of days, but that's all. Nice move, by the way, we make a good team.'

'I just remembered the self-defence classes I took back in the University days. Never fails, the top of the foot hurts easy.'

'Took his mind off the gun for half a second, that's all you need.'

'Never fuck with a Marine, I guess?'

'So they say. See if there's anything else to hog-tie him with. Any cord, or adhesive tape or anything. Even a roll of saran wrap will do.'

Mike checked the pockets of their captive and removed the man's phone and wallet. He flicked through the papers in the wallet and nodded confirmation.

'Yeah, he's one of the Morozov twins, Mikhail. The other one is Maxim, I think.'

Lucy returned from the kitchen with a roll of duct tape and a long cardboard box.

'Found this under the sink. The duct tape should do it, the box says 'cling film' but it looks like Saran wrap.'

'Maybe that's what they call it here?'

'Probably. Will I do the honours with the tape?'

'Yeah, wrap it around his legs, below the knees. Don't be afraid to do it tightly.'

'Should I wrap it around his mouth as well?'

'Let's see. If he shows signs of shouting when he comes around we'll do that. I don't want to smother him either, we'd have a lot of explaining to do if he croaks on us.'

Lucy finished her wrapping and sat into the chair.

'So, what now?'

'I don't know. I guess we were followed home, or maybe he was lying in wait for us. He may have slipped in before the door closed fully downstairs. I wonder if the other one is around someplace?'

'Probably. So I guess we wait until he appears. I'll call Hank and the boys and fill them in.'

The captured man's phone began to vibrate while Mike was speaking to his colleague. Lucy picked it up and tried to read the message.

'It's in Russian, it says 'ty poymal ikh?' What does that mean, my Russian is very limited.'

'It means 'have you captured them yet?' Just type 'Da' and send the reply.'

Lucy did as instructed. The phone vibrated again, and Mike picked it up, his own phone still jammed to his ear as he spoke to Hank.

'He says he's on his way. Are you guys in position yet?'

'Yeah, we're outside now, in the garden next door, behind the trees.'

'Sure you're out of sight?'

'We're good. You want us to grab him when he comes to the door?'

'Yeah, grab him, disarm him and put a gag on him. Only use force if you have to, but remember he's probably armed. This guy was carrying a nineteen millimetre Poloz, a dangerous little piece, loaded too. So be careful.'

'There's a black van coming up the road, driving slowly.'

'Could be him. Be careful.'

'Yeah, he's pulling over. Just one guy in it. Radio silence until you hear from us.'

Chapter Fifty Seven

Lucky Oyeleye placed his passport carefully on the desk and smiled at the red-haired policewoman on duty. She looked at the picture and then looked back at him, then checked the date on his entry stamp before scanning the document into the computer.

'So, Mister Oyeleye, did you enjoy your trip to Ireland?'

'Oh yes, Madam. You have a wonderful country, even if it is a little colder than I am used to.'

'So you're looking forward to getting home?'

'Home is always where the heart is, Madam. Yes, it will be nice to get back.'

'You weren't in such a hurry back that you kept within the terms of your entry visa, were you? Three days over, do you know what that means?'

'I'm sorry, Madam, what does it mean?'

'It means that you have broken the law and you will be denied entry the next time you try to come to Europe, that's what it means. You had a three month visa, and you stayed longer. There's no excuse, I'm afraid. Unless you have some very good explanation, I'll have to mark you as an undesirable alien.'

'Oh dear, Madam, that would be terrible. I love this place, and I have met some wonderful people. I would like to come back at some stage for a visit.'

'Do you think our immigration laws are a joke, Mister Oyeleye? Do you realise the seriousness of the offence you have committed? I mean, if everybody was to overstay their visit by three days, the next thing we know the place would be full of visitors and there wouldn't be room for the rest of us.'

'I'm sorry, Madam.'

'We'd be having to double up in our own beds, with the number of foreigners in the country. That's how it happens, you know. A day over here and a day over there, and suddenly there are millions of people in the country who just stayed for another day or two. As if it didn't matter, like.'

'I'm sorry, I didn't think.'

'How sorry are you? Really sorry, or really, really, really sorry?'

'The last one, Madam.'

'I want to hear you say it, Mister Oyeleye. I mean, it's not me that broke the law, that nearly got a black mark on my passport, is it?'

'No, it is not you who did wrong, Madam. And I'm really, really, really sorry.'

She handed him back the passport and laughed loudly.

'That's all right so. And how are they all in Boyle?'

'You know I was in Boyle?'

'Of course I do! Sure I'm only winding you up! I'm Caroline's sister, she works in Boyle Labs. She told me to look out for you today. Of course I won't mark you as an alien, sure you're a grand lad, she says. No, I'm only taking the piss. Off you go now and enjoy your flight.'

'Thank you, Madam. You gave me a fright there. Indeed you did.'

'Gotcha! Sure you have to have the crack with people, otherwise this ould job is fierce boring altogether. I told a Bishop last week that he wasn't allowed in unless he had a dog with him, you should have seen his face!'

'I can only imagine.'

'Sure you have to have a laugh. G'wan there with you now, and come back any time and see us. Sure you'd rather be oiled in Boyle than boiled in oil, wouldn't ya? Good luck, Lucky Oyeleye, and safe home to Nigeria! Ole, Ole, Ole! G'wan, ye ould devil ye!'

Lucky shook his head and smiled as he walked through the control point and into the departure lounge.

Chapter Fifty Eight

Shirley Kendall blinked in the sunlight that came through the opened shutter. She stretched and looked at Randy, who placed a mug of coffee on the shelf beside the bed.

'What time ya got, Honey?'

'It near eight o'clock, we musta overslept agin.'

'Might be overslept for yourn, Reveren, but this gal don't do mornin's.'

'Time y'all was up anyhow, Buddy he gone to town already wit a loada ice an' some brew. I tol' him brin' back breakfast, he be here soon.'

Shirley giggled and ran naked out the front door and across the porch to where the shower head was suspended from a tree. She turned the valve and ran the cold water, screeching as it cascaded down over her head and body. Randy sat on the porch and looked at her admiringly.

'Y'all sure is one helluva woman, Shirley. An' clean, too, y'all allus clean, I give yer that.'

Shirley turned off the water and raced to the porch, grabbing Randy in a wet bear hug and kissing him hard. She ran through the kitchen and into the bedroom, and he could hear her singing as she dried off and got dressed. He called out to her as he heard the old truck grinding slowly up the hill through the woods.

'Buddy home with the vittels, honey. Come an' git.'

Buddy got out of the truck carefully and brought the bag with the three breakfasts. He shook his head slowly as he divided up the food.

'Fifteen dollar, lotta money jest for breakfast. Coulda fixed it ourselv, we got the chickens an' the eggs an' taters.'

Shirley laughed and planted a kiss on his cheek.

'Don' matter none, Buddy. Me an' Randy, we got money now. I got Randall's pension, an' they givin' me half a million dollar for the life insurance. We rich, boys.'

'But that ain't ourn, Miss Shirley. That yourn. We ain't rich.'

'We all family now, Buddy. Me an' the preacher here, we getting' married. You goin' be ma brother-in-law. We gonna be kin.'

'But whar ya gonna live?'

'We gonna live right here, Buddy. Me an' Randy, we likes it here. We get us another chair on the porch, and I get me a rifle ter shoot them rabbits when they comes inter the front paddock. We mebbe build an inside outhouse too, an' a shower fer washin' usselves in.'

'But yer got a fine house in the town.'

'Don' like her, she too big an' too fancy. Like it fine here, sure do, iffen you okay wit' that.'

'Sure, Miss Shirley. We got us plenty room. Sure do.'

Chapter Fifty Nine

Mike closed the sliding door of the van and looked at the two captives who sat back-to-back, bound together with an entire roll of saran wrap. One of them moaned in pain.

'My head, it hurt very bad. You almost killing me. Why?'

'That's a stupid question, you were waving a gun at my colleague. You're lucky I didn't blow your goddamn head off. Now, I'd suggest you tell me who is behind this attempt to kidnap us, and what their motives are. And I'd suggest you are truthful with me, or I will be tempted to bring you out in a boat on the lake down there and blow your fucking brains out before feeding you to the fishes. Have I made myself clear? Vy ponimayete?'

The other man muttered an answer.

'Yes, Sir. My ponimayem. Yes, we understand.'

'Okay, who sent you, and what did they ask you to do to us?'

'Comrade Kuznetsov, he said to bring you to him.'

'Igor? If Igor wanted to see me, he has my Goddamn number. I don't believe your story, quite honestly, you'll have to come up with a better answer than that. Do I have to beat the freakin' truth out of you? Those guys outside are very capable of getting to the bottom of a story, believe me. Now, for the last time, who the hell sent you? And don't test my patience any further.'

Mike pushed the safety on the pistol and pointed it at the man who had spoken. The Russian looked at him pleadingly.

'Please, it is true. I swear. He told us to go after you and to bring you to where he stays. It is a place called Frybrook. He is waiting there for you, and for the woman.'

'Well, there's one way to find out the truth of this matter, we'll go to Frybrook now and speak to Igor. You two can stay in the van, and my friends will keep a watch on you. But remember, if I find that you're lying, you're dead.'

Mike got out of the van and handed the gun to Hank.

'You get in the passenger seat, keep that pointed at them and if they move, shoot them both. Lucy, you follow on in the camper with the other two, and stay well back from the building until I'm sure it's all clear for you to come in. Igor Kuznetsov has a lot of explaining to do, that's for sure.'

Mike climbed into the driver's seat and started the engine, following the one-way streets around the town until he came to the bridge across the river. He turned left along the narrow driveway on the riverbank and parked outside the door of the small hotel. He took his phone from his pocket and dialled the number of the Russian Ambassador.

'Igor? You wanted to see me, I'm told?'

'Yes, Mike. Come and have a drink, we're in the lounge at Frybrook, do you know it?'

'I'm sitting outside it now.'

'Great, I'll let you in.'

Mike stood back slightly from the bottom of the steps, the scene lit by the headlights of the campervan. The door opened and Igor Kuznetsov came out. Smiling broadly.

'Mike, so good to see you. Is Madam Martinez with you? We are having a drink with Doctor Billy Robinson and we would be honoured if you could join us.'

'And your idea of an invitation is to send a man with a gun?'

'What?'

'Your men burst into the apartment where my colleague and I are staying, and tried to bring us here at gunpoint. Why would you do that? You have my Goddamn number, Igor. We work together from time to time, for Chrissake. And we're in a neutral country, you could all be kicked out, Embassy and everything. What was all that shit about?'

'I'm sorry, Mike, I simply asked my two subordinates to find you and invite you to have a drink with us. There was no question of guns, or any kind of force. It was an invitation that was meant on good terms, no more. I cannot believe this. Where are they now, the two stupid idiots?'

'Here, in the back of the van.'

Mike slid back the side door of the van and pointed to the cowering, saran-wrapped twins.

'There they are. We had to disarm them and take their guns. What do you suggest we do with them? Call the Irish police, the Guards?'

The Ambassador shook his head in amazement as he looked at the two men.

'You halfwits! What were you thinking? I asked you to go after Mike and Miss Martinez and invite them for drinks. What on earth is all the other stuff about? Are you trying to create a diplomatic incident? Imbeciles!'

Maxim Morozov looked at the Ambassador with a shamefaced expression.

'I am sorry, Sir. When you asked me to bring them to you, I thought you meant…'

'Idiot! You're not in some Moscow crime gang now, you fool. When I asked you to invite my friends to come for a drink, that was what I meant, no more. You stupid idiot! Have you no brains, you fool? And the other cretin, what happened to you, you brainless buffoon?'

'The American knocked him out.'

'Is he able to speak for himself, or has he lost his tongue along with his brains?'

Mikhail Morozov moaned pitifully.

'My head, it hurts. Why did he do that, why?'

'Because you were threatening him, you fool. Did you not know that Major Callaghan is a United States Marine, like our own Spetsnaz? He could kill you with his hands, and indeed it is a pity he did not. I want you to take your brother and get the hell out of Ireland, and stay out, and I don't ever want to see you again, anywhere. I will have you replaced with somebody who has something between his ears other than an echo. Fool!'

The Ambassador turned to Mike and smiled apologetically.

'I am very sorry, and very embarrassed by this, Mike, this was all a mistake, a terrible mistake. I saw you with your colleague in Clarke's at dinner, but thought it impolite to interrupt your conversation. I didn't recognise you at first, the black skin becomes you, I believe…'

'Strange way to issue an invite, in fairness, Igor. You gave my colleague a hell of a fright.'

'I agree, I agree. When I realised you had gone I simply told them to catch up with you and invite you back here for a drink. Idiots! They can't get out of their criminal mind-set, they are nothing but mafia apes and I have told them to leave immediately before I lose my temper with them. So please accept my sincere apologies, and your colleague too. Is she here?'

'Yes, she's with some friends in that camper over there.'

Mike waved to Lucy to join them. She came forward carefully.

'What the hell is going on, Major?'

'A misunderstanding, Lucy. We're invited to join Igor and his colleague for a drink. It's okay, those two idiots were playing some kind of solo run.'

Lucy walked carefully into the area that was lit up by the lights of the camper van. The Ambassador rushed forward with an outstretched hand.

'Miss Martinez, what must you think of my countrymen? I am sincerely sorry, but maybe a drink would be good, let us start over?'

'I sure could use one, Mister Kuznetsov. I certainly didn't expect to meet with violence in a nice little town like this.'

The Ambassador took her arm and led her up the steps to the front door. Mike motioned to Hank to release the twins, and dismissed the agents in the campervan with a slight hand signal. He ran smartly up the steps to join the others, following them into the lobby and through to an elegantly decorated sitting room. Billy Robinson got to his feet in welcome.

'Major Callaghan, Madam Martinez, you are very welcome to Boyle. I'm Billy, and let me introduce Mister Ivan Turgenev, Russian Ambassador to Ireland.'

Mike and Lucy exchanged handshakes with the others, and Igor Kuznetsov rubbed his hands together.

'Madam, Major, can I get you a drink? It seems like the least I can do.'

Lucy sat into one of the comfortable armchairs and nodded.

'One of those nice European red wines would be great, a Spanish Rioja, maybe, or an Italian Chianti, if they have it.'

'They will have it, there is an excellent cellar here. And for you, Mike?'

'Same here, a nice European red sounds good.'

The Ambassador left the room for a moment and returned.

'The wine will be here in a few minutes. I assumed another beer for you, Billy?'

'Sounds good, Igor.'

Igor Kuznetsov sat back in his armchair and surveyed the room, pressing the tips of his fingers together as he spoke.

'Again, dear friends, I must apologise for the stupid actions of those two goons. Please do not judge Russia or its people by those standards. I understand that all countries have a percentage of criminals and idiots in their populations, but when they are seen to represent me, or indeed the Russian government, it is extremely concerning and a matter of some embarrassment, to be honest. I am also truly sorry for any trauma or stress caused to you, Miss Martinez, or to Major Callaghan.'

Lucy waved the concerns away.

'Let's forget the whole matter, Ambassador Kuznetsov. It was a bit of a shock at the time, but we handled it okay. And I had a US Marine in my corner, which is always a good position to be in. So, let's move on, as they say. And it's Lucy, by the way. We can drop the formalities, we're on vacation.'

'Thank you, Lucy, and Mike. And I would be obliged if that worked in the other direction too. I am Igor, my colleague is Ivan, and Doctor Robinson always prefers to be called 'Billy' in any case.'

'Sounds good.'

'So, welcome to our Irish home, we like it here very much; it is comfortable and the hospitality is excellent. I must confess I was surprised earlier to see the US President's Chief of Staff dining in a pub in Boyle, and accompanied by the Attorney General, so forgive me if I did not greet you at the time. I thought you might be discussing affairs of state, so I thought it polite to wait until you were leaving. However our two companions became a little boisterous, so I was dealing with the lady owner about that and when I looked around, you had gone. Anyway, you are here now.'

Mike stood to take the glasses from the waitress who entered the room. He placed them on the low table and handed the beer to Billy. When the wine was tasted and poured and the staff member had left, he continued.

'So, Igor, did you want to discuss business, or is this just a social gathering?'

'A social gathering, Mike, of course. Although now that you are here, maybe we should take the opportunity to discuss any matters of common interest. What do you think?'

'Sure, Igor. Do we have matters of common interest? Other than the fact that we're both public servants and we work in the same city.

'I think we do, Mike. First among them is the fact that you and I and Lucy now appear to have shared racial characteristics.'

'You mean skin colour?'

'Yes, there is no arguing that all three of us have now 'caught the black,' as they say in the US.'

'There are worse things to catch, Igor. Lots of worse things. In truth, I quite like being black, it hides my office-based pallor since I stopped being an outdoor man. And I think it quite becomes our legal colleague, don't you think?'

'Indeed, Lucy does look handsome in her newly acquired skin tone, but I assume she would be happier to revert to her normal colour?'

Lucy laughed as she sipped her wine.

'Quite frankly, Igor, I couldn't care less. The only downside to being a black woman in America was the potential for being on the wrong end of institutionalised racism, but we've fixed that now.'

'Ah, yes, the amendment. I must congratulate you on a fine piece of legal drafting. To be fair, it would appear to have addressed many of the issues. Although of course it could never work in my country.'

'Why not?'

'Russia, historically, was never a mixed-race country. Our identity is white and Christian, and the threat to our security and safety over many centuries was from the barbarians at the gate. Persons of dark skin in our country must always of necessity be seen as different, not as Russians.'

'It's a global society now, Igor. You need to get over all that crap.'

'I believe we were more advanced than the USA in many respects, particularly with regards to equality for women. Indeed, your recent amendment only now catches up with us in that respect.'

Mike interjected to keep the debate from heating up.

'We'll give you that one. Igor. So, what do you think we can do for you, in respect of your concerns about skin colour?'

Ivan Turgenev had been sitting back, listening to the conversation. He leaned forward to interrupt.

'We share a common problem, Mike, Lucy. Both of our Presidents are black, and they don't like it very much. You or Lucy, and indeed myself if I'm honest, we don't really care what colour we are. Yes, it's a big deal in my home country, but I have lived most of my life abroad and my views have mellowed. My colleague, Igor, despite his apparent racist streak, holds similar views in his heart. If he was to live out his life in Washington, for instance, I don't believe he would even think about his skin colour after a while. And neither would I, if I was allowed to retire here, in Ireland.'

'So is that the problem, are both of you due to retire, back to Russia? Is that your big concern?'

Igor laughed sadly.

'I think I am among friends here, so I can speak plainly. You work for a madman, Mike, and I work for a megalomaniac. That is the problem, in a nutshell. My colleague and I are concerned that we may be recalled to Russia, to serve out our lives in Ozersk, if you ever heard of it?'

'The nuclear waste town?'

'Yes. Although such a posting might be the least of our concerns, if matters escalate.'

'If Zhadnyy gets angry with you?'

'Exactly. Which is where I, we, need your help.'

Mike glanced at Lucy but her face was impassive. Billy Robinson stared at the top of the beer can as if it held some fascinating secret. He put the empty can on the table and took a deep breath before he spoke.

'You think we have a solution to the black skin issue, is that what you believe? And that the Americans have that knowledge and you don't?'

'Yes, in a nutshell. We have reason to believe that this is the situation.'

Chapter Sixty

Billy held the conference-room door open to allow Karen to enter. He followed her into the room where the rest of the team were gathered around the large oval table. Caroline and Kevin passed around the large pizza boxes and paper plates and they divided the food and began to eat. Billy wiped his hands on a paper napkin and smiled.

'Sorry for the short notice, guys, but a few things have come up. I had an interesting meeting last night, very interesting, and I think you deserve to know the facts.'

The others sat up attentively at his words. Kevin was the first to speak.

'With the two Russians? Is that why they've gone? They cleared out their office last night and disappeared, didn't leave as much as a paper clip. It looks like they're not coming back.'

'They're not, we've seen the end of those two, and no harm. The two older men are in charge, for now anyway. But that will change soon as well.'

'Is there another change of ownership?'

'Yes, I'm afraid there is.'

Karen looked downcast.

'Oh dear, just when we were getting used to them. I hope it isn't somebody worse.'

'No, you can relax on that front. There are two new owners, and one of them will be with us in half an hour. In the meantime, I'll tell you what happened last night, and what came out of our meeting.'

'You're a man of mystery, Billy.'

'Not me, Caroline, this is the face that can't tell a lie, at least not without it being obvious. Anyway, I had a few drinks with the two older Russian men, Ivan Turgenev and Igor Kuznetsov. Turgenev is the Russian Ambassador to Ireland, as you know, and the other guy is their Ambassador in Washington.'

'Heavy hitters!'

'They are, Mary, but they weren't the only big players in the room. We also had Mike Callaghan, whom you may know from the TV as President Donald Daniels' Chief of Staff, although I wouldn't have recognised him since he turned black. And, get this, he was accompanied by the US Attorney General, Professor Lucy Martinez. It was a very high-level summit, I felt a bit out of my depth, to be honest.'

'I'm sure they got nothing out of you that you didn't want them to know.'

'I'd hope so, Karen. But these guys are highly skilled diplomats, and I'm just a country boy. Anyway, I'll tell you what happened.'

'This sounds interesting.'

'It is. First of all, they seemed to know a bit more about what we have achieved than we told them. The Americans were either in the dark or were playing a good poker game, but the Russians knew we had cracked the puzzle.'

'How could they have done that?'

'I was thinking about that, Karen, and I have some

thoughts on it. Caroline, do you recall Lucky ever mentioning his skin colour change when he was calling his wife?'

Caroline reddened.

'Shit, yes, he did. To be honest I didn't really eavesdrop on their conversations, I was usually doing some work while he was on the phone and I was just there to discourage him discussing the project. But now that you mention it, the night before he left he told her his skin was a little lighter, and that she shouldn't be alarmed when she saw him. It was just a throwaway remark, but it rang a slight alarm bell with me at the time.'

'Did he say how it had happened, how his skin had changed?'

'Yes, kind of. He just said he'd taken some medicine that had lightened his skin a little, but that it was no big deal.'

'Then that's it. They have obviously been monitoring all calls from within the lab. These countries have sophisticated systems that can record telephone conversations and pick out key words, so it would have been easy for them to do that.'

'I'm really sorry, I should have been on top of that.'

'Don't blame yourself, Caroline, there was nothing you could do to stop it. And I'm sure Lucky meant no harm, it was just to forewarn his wife so she didn't get too much of a surprise when she saw him. Nothing we can do about it anyway.'

'So the cat is out of the bag?'

'It is and it isn't, Kevin. The Russians and the Americans now know we have the antidote, if that's the word, to the blackening of skin. But the strange thing is, the Americans don't seem too bothered, and neither do the two Russians.'

'They don't want the treatment?'

'The Americans certainly don't, although they reserve the right to come back to us on that. And of the Russians, Kuznetsov wants a treatment for himself, so I promised that Mary would inject him today, once she has weighed him. It's crucial that we don't overshoot, he'd become the original White Russian, whiter than the driven snow and all that. We need to just bring him back to where he was before he turned black, no more. Are you happy enough to take that on, Mary?'

'No problem, Billy. We have a very accurate weighing scales in the secure unit, we can give him a very exact dosage.'

'Great! On top of that, they want to bring President Zhadnyy back to his original colour, and they are currently speaking to his doctors to determine his exact body mass. They will then bring a precise dose that we have prepared to Russia and get the doctor to inject the great man, so he'll be happy once that is done. Apparently they are afraid of being posted to some town that has a big nuclear dump if they get it wrong, so precision is critical.'

'We can do that, Billy. We don't want to upset one of the most powerful men in the world, and the owner of this lab to boot. Or is the Russian government involved in the new ownership structure?'

'That was my next point, and the answer to that question is no. As of today, Russia doesn't want to own this place, we settled on that last night. In return for some cash for the two Ambassadors, and a not insignificant payment to the Russian government, there is a new team in place at Boyle Labs. I'm one of the new owners, and if I'm not mistaken that sounds like the majority shareholder coming down the corridor now.'

The others turned expectantly as Miriam O'Hagan pushed the door open and breezed into the room.

Chapter Sixty One

The two men stepped off the train, carrying their suitcases, with their overcoats draped over their arms. They walked slowly through the small station building and out on to the street, looking around in shock at their surroundings. Igor Kuznetsov turned to his companion in surprise.

'It is actually a very beautiful place, Ivan Turgenev, all the trees and the nature, and the lake. I had expected a wasteland.'

The other man sighed sadly.

'I imagine when we look at our radiation monitors, we will see what this nature covers up. But I agree, it is on the surface very appealing. I think my wife would have liked it here.'

'But she still would not come?'

'No, she is happy in Washington, and Major Callaghan has kindly arranged for her to get a legal residency, a green card as they call it. I'm afraid my marriage is over, thanks to Comrade Zhadnyy.'

'And mine. Svetlana will not leave Dublin, she has many friends there and has no intention of coming to this place.'

'I suppose it is better than being found on the highway under Dumbarton Bridge.'

'Yes, or run over by a stolen car, like Belyaev.'

They trudged down the tree-lined road towards the town. Ivan paused to switch his suitcase from one hand to the other.

'If only he had listened. I never expected him to do such a stupid thing.'

'I suppose in hindsight we should have foreseen it. When he asked for doses for the two boys, his wrestling companions, I did not think there was anything odd about it.'

'It did raise a small concern with me, but I said nothing. Maybe I should have. Did it cross your mind, as it briefly did mine at that time, that our leader might be somewhat inclined towards being a gomoseksualist?'

'No, not in the slightest. Whatever about anything else, he is a real Russian man, he cannot possibly be one of them.'

'That is my primary thinking on it, for sure. But when he showed concern for the two boys only, it was a thought, you know?'

'It is not possible, no Russian man would countenance such a disgusting thing. Just because he likes to engage in naked wrestling with these boys, it doesn't mean he has the English condition.'

'You are right, I suppose I never truly thought he had any ulterior motive, any personal motive. So I wondered at the time whether he might have feelings for those boys.'

'That angle did not occur to me. But if we look back at our knowledge of him over many years, we should have known the apparent concern for the boys was just a story. Comrade Zhadnyy will never have enough of anything; if one dose is good, then three are better, in his book. He must have persuaded his doctors to inject him with all three vials of the treatment.'

'It certainly worked!'

'True, Comrade Kuznetsov. But he can never be seen

in public again, ever. He looks like a ghost, if he walks outside in winter the snowploughs will run him over. I never in my life saw anybody so white, he is whiter than a political prisoner who was kept in the prison cellar for ten years.'

'Do you think they will find a cure for it?'

'It is unlikely, but it is probably our best hope. Our only hope.'

'Do they have vodka here, in Ozersk?'

'I certainly hope so, Comrade Turgenev. I certainly hope so. But thanks to Doctor Robinson, at least we have plenty of money to buy it.'

'That is true. That is true. We must bake bread with the flour we have been given, Comrade.'

'Indeed, Comrade. Otherwise we will have no bread at all.'

Chapter Sixty Two

Mike Callaghan sat back against the webbing of the seat on the transport plane. Lucy got up from the jump-seat between the two pilots and came back to join him. She was smiling broadly.

'Amazing view up there, Mike, you want to take the middle seat for a while?'

'No thanks, Lucy, I've looked out too many cockpit windows in my time, I'm happy back here.'

'What are you going to tell HG, when we get back?'

'As little as possible, as usual. Of course I'll tell him that the Russians have sold Boyle Labs back to the original owners for a fraction of the original price, and that the research team there is working away to try to find a cure for the black. And I'll tell him that I'll need to make regular visits there to check up on them.'

'Sounds good. I loved that place, it's beautiful.'

'Sure is, I'd go back there in a heartbeat. That guy Billy, he's a good man, even if he stiffed our government along with the Russians. He told me why he decided to bury their findings, him and his two best scientists. You know they could have made an awful lot of money by publishing.'

'I know, Karen filled me in on the detail. But they

promised to treat HG if you or I thought it was necessary at some point. Although she said it would have to be with good reason, she loves the idea of a black, united America. Do you know what she said about it, about the USA?'

'Something profound, I expect. She strikes me as a deep thinker.'

'She said that the USA was never anything more than the SA, that the word 'United' was a misnomer in that context. But she said we had managed to add it in. I thought that was nice to hear.'

'To be fair, Lucy, that's what you've done. Our job now is to make that stick, and if that means keeping HG in the dark, or even in the black, then that's what we gotta do.'

'Do you think we will eventually be faced with treating all the Oreos, Mike? All the people who turned black, will they clamour to become white again? After all, they will eventually find out about Zhadnyy, and even Igor Kuznetsov. That stuff gets out, eventually. There are no secrets in this world anymore.'

'That was what I said to Billy yesterday, but he had a different view. He reckons the black colour will fade, eventually. We should probably enjoy our black skin while we have it.'

'Is that based on a hunch, or on research?'

'I'd be willing to bet that even when Billy says he has a hunch about something, he probably has a fair bit of research in the bag already to back it up. But he's playing his cards close to his chest, as usual. Anyway, as long as we get to change the world first, that'll do me.'

'You're a good man, Mike Callaghan, I'm glad you're on my side.'

'I'm no better or worse than the next man, Lucy, but I accepted this job in the hope that I could make the world a little bit better. Thanks to meeting you, maybe I have succeeded, a little bit anyhow.'

'We'll have to set up a mutual admiration society, Mike. We can have our annual outings on one of your trips back to Boyle. Do you think you'll be able to take me with you, on one of those junkets?'

'Of course! I think a man should always take his wife with him, when he goes somewhere.'

'My God, Major Callaghan, is that a proposal?'

'It's about as romantic as you're gonna get from this Marine, I'm afraid.'

'Then let me just say that the party of the first part agrees that the party of the second part......'

'I'll take that as an affirmative.'

'I think you can safely say that.'

Chapter Sixty Three

Mickey Small sat up in the bed and looked at his sleeping companion with a sense of wonderment and joy. He kissed her bare, darkly-tanned arm where it lay on top of the duvet. He wondered what time it was, he felt hungry and he was beginning to have thoughts about breakfast.

He slipped out of bed quietly and went to the kitchen of the small cottage and switched on the kettle. While he waited for it to boil he hugged the dressing gown around himself against the late autumn chill and stepped out of the front door. Everything was calm in the quiet of the dawn, with a small fogbank rising along the river, and no sign of anybody to break the stillness of the morning. He could hear the faint sound of running water; the river was low, and barely trickled over the weir. He stretched his arms above his head and then out in front of himself contentedly.

He stared at his bare arms and looked away, then looked back in amazement before running excitedly back into the cottage. He jumped on the bed and shook the sleeping woman awake urgently. She rolled over and looked at him through sleepy eyes.

'Mickey, where is the fire? I was having a wonderful dream.'

'Are we still in the dream, Monika?'

'No, we're definitely not.'

'Then look, Monika! Look at my arms.'

He opened the dressing gown and pointed to his bare chest.

'And here, the same. Everywhere!'

Monika scrambled for her phone and called a number. The woman on the other end answered sleepily.

'I hope this is urgent, Monika.'

'Yes, of course it is, Caroline. You need to come over here, and quickly. You have to see this.'